The
BOLEYN WIFE

The BOLEYN WIFE

BRANDY PURDY

KENSINGTON BOOKS
www.kensingtonbooks.com

KENSINGTON BOOKS are published by

Kensington Publishing Corp.
119 West 40th Street
New York, NY 10018

All Kensington titles, imprints, and distributed lines are available at special quantity discounts for bulk purchases for sales promotion, premiums, fund-raising, educational, or institutional use.

Special book excerpts or customized printings can also be created to fit specific needs. For details, write or phone the office of the Kensington Special Sales Manager: Kensington Publishing Corp., 119 West 40th Street, New York, NY 10018. Attn. Special Sales Department. Phone: 1-800-221-2647.

Kensington and the K logo Reg. U.S. Pat. & TM Off.

ISBN-13: 978-0-7582-3844-3
ISBN-10: 0-7582-3844-4

First Kensington Trade Paperback Printing: February 2010
10 9 8 7 6 5 4 3 2 1

Printed in the United States of America

Vengeance is mine; I shall repay.
—Romans 12:19

PROLOGUE

The Madwoman in the Tower, 1542

Overhead the sleek black ravens circle and caw, while below my window the workmen chat merrily, their voices hale and hearty as they call to one another above the din of hammer and saw. They brush the sawdust from their leather jerkins and woolen hose and go blithely about the business of building the scaffold upon which I shall soon die. It does not matter whether I look down or up; the sight that meets my eyes is equally grim—carrion birds or the planks that shall soon be stained with my life's blood.

They are very bold, these birds. When the workmen pause for their noonday repast, they swoop down and perch upon the burgeoning scaffold, snatching greedily at the morsels of meat and bread and tidbits of yellow cheese proffered by the calloused hands. How many deaths have these birds witnessed? I do not know the span of life that is allotted to a raven, but surely it is possible that some of them were here seven years ago when Anne bared her slender, swanlike neck to the French executioner's sword. And two days before that swift slash of silver ended her life, George, her brother, my husband, laid his foolish and proud head upon the block and died for her as did four other equally foolish men. It was my evidence that helped speed them to their deaths. I told the truth, and for it I have been punished ever since.

Did these very ravens perch upon the Tower walls to watch,

eager as the human spectators, and did they in their bird's language debate who met death with the bravest face? What will they make of me and poor, wanton little Kat, Henry's fifth queen, when it is our turn?

Neither of us deserves this fate, to have our lives snuffed out like candles upon the cavalier whim of an old man's wounded pride. But Henry Tudor is King, and as Kat's motto, the one she chose when she became queen, so rightfully proclaims, we have "no other will but his." Our lives and deaths are in his hands.

Here in the Tower my head aches always. Countless times I press my hands against my taut, deep-furrowed brow and try to will the pain away, but it will not depart. And I have long since plucked the pins from my hair and shaken it out so that it streams down my back like a wild, white-streaked waterfall, but still the pain does not ease. Had I still a care for vanity, I think I would weep. I am but a year past forty and already my hair is more white than brown; imprisonment has streaked it with silver and snow.

Jealousy and Hate, Justice and Divine Retribution, some say, have brought me to this place. "He who sows the whirlwind must expect to reap the storm," the walls whisper all around me, incessantly, in voices I know all too well. George, Anne, Weston, Brereton, and Norris—they will not let me forget that I once thought Vengeance was my sword to wield.

And wield it I did.

Though I despise the din that torments my ears by day, I am glad of the sawing and pounding, the bluff banter of working men, and even the ravens' cackling and screeching, for when these sounds cease and night falls, that is when the ghosts come out to torment me.

He stands there now in the shadows beyond the torches' reach, a grim, unwavering silhouette. And though I cannot see them, I feel his eyes mocking me, laughing at me. Sometimes she is there with him. The rustle of velvet skirts and a heady whiff of rose perfume herald her arrival, and my hatred surges so strong that to knock me off my feet it threatens. Then, in a movement fluid with grace, he lifts off his head, tucks it beneath his arm, and bows to me, just like a gentleman at court doffing his fine feathered hat to a lady.

"Well, well, Jane . . ."

He speaks my name and my heart soars. He is smiling at me—it matters not that it is mockingly—he is smiling at me, he is speaking to me, and his words are meant for me alone.

". . . you would see justice done, and soon the headsman shall give you a personal demonstration!"

"I am sorry, George!" I extend my arms entreatingly. "Truly, I did not mean for you to die! I love you!"

"Forsooth, Madame, you have a strange way of showing it! You accused me of incest and sent me to the block! If that is how you treat those you love, I shudder to think what mischief you would work against an enemy!"

The flame of hate that has burned so long inside me flares high.

"You chose the block! You chose to die with her rather than live with me! You were guilty! Perhaps you did not sin in the flesh, but you were guilty to the bottom of your soul! You loved her more than any! Yes, I helped send her to her death, and I am glad of it! *Glad!*" I hold my head up high, stamp my feet, and clench my hands into tight, trembling fists and feel my nails bite into my palms until they leave bloody little crescents behind. "And regret it I will never! Neither God in Heaven nor the Devil in Hell can make me!"

"There is still murder in your heart, Jane," his voice dolefully reproves me.

And then he is gone, and I am alone again, for now. But I dare not sleep, for when I sleep I am granted a foretaste of Hell. That is when the flames come and the stink of sulfur chokes and burns my lungs. I start awake and leap to my feet, screaming, slapping at the flames as they engulf my skirts. I circle wildly, beating at them, burning my hands, and then my over-sleeves catch fire. My Boleyn sleeves—her sleeves—the sleeves she made famous. Anne Boleyn! Even in my wardrobe I cannot escape her! I fall sobbing to the floor, scorched and smarting, and it is then that through a shimmer of smoke I see him. But no, it is not George; it is only Master

Kingston, my jailer, with his wife, come to dose me with a bitter draft to bring me quiet rest.

But George is here. I know he is! I sense his presence still, smirking in the shadows.

Oh, George, why could you not have loved me just a little? Why could you not, just once, have looked at me the way you looked at her—at Anne? Why could I, your wife, not come before your sister?

But tonight I shall not sleep. Tonight there will be no fire and brimstone chased away with a bitter decoction of poppies. No, tonight I shall tell how I came to be "The Madwoman in the Tower," and why, as much as he loved her, I hated her more. . . .

Part One

Anne

1522–1536

❧ 1 ❧

Anne Boleyn was not beautiful, but, while women were quick to take gleeful note of this, men seldom noticed; the Spanish Ambassador who dubbed her "The Goggle-Eyed Whore" being a notable exception. Yet she cast a spell like no other, this raven-haired enchantress, that caused men to fall at her feet, sing her praises, and worship her; some even gave their lives for her.

Her bearing was innately regal, as if Mother Nature had intended all along that she should be a queen. Each gesture, each turn of her head and hands, each step, was as graceful and gliding as a dance. Her voice was velvet, her laughter music and tinkling bells, and her wit sparkled like silver and was as keen as the sharpest razor. Her eyes were prominent and dark brown, with a beguiling and viva-cious sparkle. But her complexion varied in the eyes of the be-holder; deemed creamy by some and sallow by others. Nine years spent at the French court had left her more French than English, and her voice would always retain a lyrical—and some said sen-sual—lilting accent. Instead of petite, blond, and partridge-plump like all the celebrated English beauties, including her sister Mary, Anne Boleyn was tall, dark, and slender as a reed, with a cloak of glossy black hair reaching all the way down to her knees, which for her life entire she would flout convention by letting flow gypsy-free, instead of confining it inside a coif after she became a wife.

No, she was not beautiful, but at deception she excelled, cleverly concealing her flaws by the most ingenious means, and in doing so she set fashions. A choker of velvet, precious gems, or pearls hid an unsightly strawberry wen upon her throat. And she devised a new style of sleeve, worn full, long, and flowing, over wrist-length under-sleeves to conceal an even more unbecoming blemish—the start of a sixth finger, just the tip and nail, protruding from the side of the smallest finger on her left hand. Anne set the fashions other women rushed to follow, never knowing that they were devices of illusion, like the objects the court magician employed to perform his tricks and leave his audience gasping in astonishment and delight, wondering how the trick was done but nonetheless enchanted.

In 1522 when I, Lady Jane Parker, first met her, her fate was undecided. "What to do about Anne?" was the subject of many grave parental debates from her infancy onward. If only she were blond like her sister Mary, or red-haired like the King's sister, a true English rose—but no, Anne's tresses were black. If only her eyes were blue and placid, or serene and green, instead of almond-shaped and dark. If only her skin were porcelain pale with rosy pink cheeks, instead of sultry and sallow like a woman of France or Spain. If only, if only, if only! Would she ever make a good match? Would any man of standing take a dark, six-fingered bride with a tempestuous and rebellious temperament that even the stern Sir Thomas Boleyn had been unable to quash? Perhaps a convent would be the wisest choice? Filled as they were with plain, ugly, disfigured, and otherwise unmarriageable girls, surely there was a niche there that Anne could fill, and with her brains she might even rise to the rank of abbess and thus bring a small measure of glory to her family.

Then—when marriage and the future were so much on all our minds—came the fateful day when my path first crossed hers and our destinies became irrevocably entangled. Centuries from now, if anyone remembers me, it will be because of Anne Boleyn.

And for that I damn and curse her.

* * *

My father, Lord Morley, and Sir Thomas Boleyn were keen to forge a match between myself, an only child and sole heiress to my father's sizable fortune, and George, the only Boleyn son. It was a notion, I confess, that made me swoon with delight. My heart was already his, and had been ever since the day I arrived at court, a befuddled and nervous maid, lost amidst the noisy and confusing bustle of King Henry's court. Suddenly finding myself separated from my escort, I asked a passing gentleman to help me find my way. Gallantly, he offered me his arm and saw me safely to my chamber door, and there he bowed, with a most elegant flourish of his white-plumed cap, and left me.

No sooner had he turned his back than my hand shot out to waylay a passing page boy, clutching so tight to his sleeve I felt some of the stitches at the shoulder snap.

"Tell me that gentleman's name!" I implored.

"George Boleyn," came the answer.

And ever since, it has been engraved upon my heart. Every night when I knelt beside my bed in prayer I pleaded fervently, "Please! Make him mine!" I prayed to God, and I would gladly have prayed to the Devil too, if I thought Our Heavenly Father would fail to grant my deepest, most heartfelt wish. Sans regret, I would have sold my soul to have him! As I lay alone in darkness, waiting for slumber, I whispered his name times beyond number, soft and reverent, as if it were—and for me it was!—a sacrament or prayer.

When I went home to Great Hallingbury, our sturdy redbrick manor nestled in the sleepy Essex countryside, I began, like a general, to plot my campaign. Fortunately, I was a spoiled only child and, more often than not, my father was happy to indulge me.

Father was a keen classical scholar, more at ease with the ancient Greeks and Romans, their history, culture, and myths, than the backbiting, scandal, politics, and intrigue of King Henry's court. Whenever he could, he shut himself away in his library with his beloved scrolls and books, surrounded by statues and busts of gods, goddesses, and great warriors, while he worked zealously at his Greek and Latin translations, which he had afterwards elegantly bound and presented to the King, his friends, and other like-minded scholars. Whenever I could, I haunted his library, chattering endlessly, no doubt making a great nuisance of myself, endeavoring at every opportunity to insert George Boleyn's name into the conversation, and for months it was George Boleyn this and George Boleyn that, until Father took the hint and, no doubt hoping to restore serene and blessed silence to his library, made arrangements to meet with Sir Thomas Boleyn and discuss the possibility of a betrothal.

Thus, with further negotiations in mind, my father was pleased to accept Sir Thomas Boleyn's invitation to visit the family castle of Hever, a modest, mellow-stone block nestled in the heart of the Kentish countryside, surrounded by a moat and lush greenery.

Pale and patrician in sapphire blue velvet, Lady Boleyn, the former Elizabeth Howard, welcomed us warmly.

"Let all the formality be in the marriage contracts!" she declared, embracing me as if I were her daughter-in-law already.

After I had quenched my thirst and changed my gown, she directed me to the garden where I might enjoy the company of her children—George, Mary, and the newly returned Anne.

Surely my heart must have shown upon my face when he turned a welcoming smile in my direction. It was like a whip crack, a sharp, ecstatic pang, a slap, lashing hard against my heart. Love was the master and I was the slave!

At twenty, George Boleyn was breathtakingly handsome, endowed with a lively wit and a reputation for being something of a rake. He was slender and tall, dark as a Spaniard or a Frenchman, with sleek black hair and a short, neatly trimmed beard and mustache, eyes the warmest shade of brown I had ever seen—they reminded me of a sable robe I wanted to wrap myself up in on a cold winter's day—teeth like polished ivory, lips full, pink, and sensual, and skin the warm golden hue of honey. A poet and musician, his pen and lute were always at his side, and when he strummed his lute I felt as if my heart were its strings. How could I not love him?

But I was never fool enough to think that he loved me. I hoped, I yearned, I burned with lust and jealousy, but I never cherished that illusion. Was there ever a Jane plainer than I? Me with my nose like a beak, my face and figure all sharp angles with no plump, pillow-soft bosom or curves, and my hair a lank and lifeless mousy brown, I could never stir a man's loins and make his blood race. But reality didn't stop me from wanting, hoping, and dreaming. And in our world, where titles, lands, and fortunes—not love—are the stuff of which marriages are made, the odds of winning him were not entirely stacked against me.

As I followed the garden path, the summer breeze carried the tart tang of lemon to my nose and I turned to seek its source.

Indolent and lush as a rose in full bloom, Mary Boleyn lounged in a chair situated to take best advantage of the sun. Gowned in gold-embroidered peacock blue and fiery orange satin, far too rich for such a rustic setting, Mary lolled back against her cushions like a well-contented cat. Upon her head she wore a straw hat with the crown cut out and a very wide brim upon which her long golden tresses, soaked thoroughly with lemon juice, were spread to be bleached blonder still by the sun's bright rays. And beneath her orange kirtle her stomach swelled with the promise of King Henry's child.

The most amiable of wantons was Mary. She lost her virtue early, to no less a personage than the King of France. She comported herself with such lascivious abandon that she was banished from that most licentious and hedonistic of courts for "conduct unbecoming to a maid," and sent home to England, where she at once caught King Henry VIII's eye and went merrily and obligingly into his bed. Perhaps she was too obliging, for he soon tired of her, but not before his seed took root inside her womb. Thus, for the second time in her life, Mary Boleyn, then aged but one-and-twenty, found herself banished from court, and to Hever Castle she was exiled to await her hastily procured bridegroom, Sir William Carey, a cheerful knight of modest means who was glad to undertake this service for his King.

Like many, I stood in awe of her dazzling beauty—she had been plucked so many times it was hard to believe her bloom had not wilted or faded—and her equally astounding stupidity. Mary must have been unique amongst courtesans; she had been mistress to not one but two kings and had failed to profit from either. Indeed, Sir Thomas Boleyn had railed at her and boxed her ears and pummeled her until it was feared he would dislodge the King's bastard from her womb. Now he never spoke an unnecessary word to her. He regarded her as a failure and declared it would be the most outrageous flattery to call her even a half-wit. Mary had been handed power on a plate and had refused to partake, and this Sir Thomas Boleyn could never forgive.

"Jane . . ."

George began to speak and my breath caught in my throat. My eyes were so dazzled by the sight of him I almost raised my hand to shield them, but to be deprived of the radiant sight of him would have been unbearable. A god in yellow satin, he was indeed the sun that lit up my life.

". . . I bid you welcome to Hever. Of course you already know my sister Mary"—he nodded towards the dozing wanton—"but you have yet to meet Anne."

My ears pricked at the tenderness and warmth with which his voice imbued her name. It was a tone, I would all too soon discover, that he reserved exclusively for her. It was then—the moment I first heard him speak her name—that I began to hate her.

She was seated upon a stone bench and, even as he spoke to me, George stepped behind her and gently took the ivory comb from her hand and began to draw it through the inky blackness of her damp, newly washed tresses.

Like her sister, she was too grandly gowned for Hever. She wore black damask with a tracery of silver, festooned with silver lace. A ribbon of black velvet encircled her long, swan-slender neck and from it dangled her initials, *AB,* conjoined in silver with three large pendent pearls suspended from them. She was, like me, aged nineteen. She had only just returned from the French court, well-esteemed and, unlike her sister, with her virtue and respectability firmly intact. Indeed, all sang the praises of Mistress Anne and lamented her departure back to her native shore.

"It is a pleasure to meet my brother's bride-to-be." She smiled warmly and addressed me in that beguiling French-tinged English that made her speech so unique. "You are one of Queen Catherine's ladies, I am told. I have just been appointed to her household, so we shall serve together and have the opportunity, I hope, to become friends; I do so want us to be."

I felt the most peculiar dread, like a knot pulled tight within my stomach, and I could not speak, could only nod and stare back at her like a simpleton.

She then began to inquire of my likes and dislikes, my pleasures and pastimes.

"Are you fond of music? Do you play an instrument? George and I"—she smiled up at him—"live for music. We have melodies in our blood, I think, and our minds are forever awhirl with songs!"

"I enjoy music, of course, but as a performer I am, alas, inept," I confessed. And at her brief, sympathetic nod I felt the distinct urge to strike her. How dare she, with her fancy clothes and Frenchified ways, make me feel so far beneath her!

"Well, it is no great matter," she trilled. "Do you like to dance or sing?"

I blushed hotly at the memory of the French dancing master who had nobly retired rather than continue to accept my father's money, admitting in all honesty that I was as graceful as a cow. The Italian singing master had also withdrawn his services; he could teach me nothing; I had a voice like a crow.

"I . . . I am afraid I lack your accomplishments, Lady Anne," I stammered haughtily, jerking my chin up high, as my face grew hot and red.

In truth, I had no talent to speak of.

"Oh, but I am sure you have many talents!" Anne cried, as if she had just read my mind.

"The embroidery upon your kirtle is exquisite!" She indicated my tawny underskirt, richly embroidered with golden lovers' knots to match those that edged the bodice and sleeves of my brown velvet gown. "Is it your own work? Do you like to design your own gowns?" As she spoke, her right hand smoothed her skirt and I knew this too numbered among her talents.

As for my own gown, other than selecting the materials I had done nothing but stand still for the dressmaker. I had left the style and cut entirely to her discretion; my father was rich and she was grateful for my patronage, so I could trust her not to make me look a fool or frumpish. My own skill with the needle was adequate, but nothing to boast of.

"Do you enjoy reading or composing poetry?" Anne persisted. "Are you fond of riding? Do you like to play dice or cards? Queen Catherine, despite her pious nature, I am told, is a keen card player."

"Her Majesty only plays for the most modest stakes and her winnings are always given to the poor!" I answered sharply while inwardly I seethed. How dare she play this game with me? Flaunting her accomplishments in my face and making it quite plain that as a candidate for her brother's hand she deemed me most unworthy!

And through it all George just stood there, smiling down at her, drawing the comb through her hair, even as he glanced inquisitively at me each time she posed a question, waiting expectantly for my answers and feigning an interest I knew he did not feel. As I stood before them I felt like a prisoner on trial, and most fervently wished that the ground would open beneath my feet and swallow me.

Thus began my association with the Boleyn family, though three years would pass before I officially joined their ranks; Sir Thomas and my father haggled like fishwives over my dowry. Meanwhile, I returned to court, where I was soon joined by Anne, in the household of Queen Catherine.

I remember the day she arrived at Greenwich Palace. The Queen had been closeted all day in her private chapel, fasting and kneeling before a statue of the Virgin surrounded by flickering candles, while we, her ladies, lolled about, lazily plying our needles over the shirts and shifts she bade us stitch for distribution among the poor. We gazed wistfully out at the river, sighing longingly at the thought of the cool breeze, and eyeing enviously those who already strolled along its banks. From time to time one of us would pluck desultorily at a lute, toy with the ivory keys of the virginals, or yawningly take up one of the edifying volumes about the saints' lives that Her Majesty encouraged us to take turns reading aloud.

Suddenly there were footsteps and laughter upon the stairs. Like Lazarus risen from the dead, we came to life, pinching our cheeks to give them color, hastily straightening headdresses and tucking in stray wisps of hair, daubing drops from our dainty crystal scent vials, smoothing down skirts and sleeves. Then the door swung open and in sauntered the King's gentlemen, with George Boleyn leading the pack.

They were like a flock of tropical birds, a veritable rainbow of gorgeous, gaudy colors in their feathered caps, satin doublets, and silk hose, with elaborate blackwork embroidery edging the collars and cuffs of their snowy-white shirts, and gemstones flashing and twinkling in their rings, brooches, and on the hilts of their swords. All young, handsome, debonair, and carefree, rakish and wild, they were the wits and poets of the court, happy-go-lucky and devil-may-care, the peacocks and popinjays in whose presence life was never for an instant dull.

Laughing heartily, with one arm flung around the shoulders of his best friend, Sir Francis Weston, George approached us.

"Ladies"—he doffed his cap and bowed to us—"we bring you fruit!" He indicated the big straw basket carried by Sir Henry Norris. Then, assisted by his friends, he began to distribute it among us—apples, oranges, plums, grapes, cherries, and pears. And soon joyful banter, merry laughter, and coy flirtations replaced the sleepy air of boredom and gloom that, only moments before, had pervaded the room.

Sir Thomas Wyatt, of the sable beard and smoldering eyes, renowned as the most brilliant poet of the court, plopped himself down upon a cushion at Lady Eleanor's feet and began to strum his lute and serenade us with a song about the fruits of love. As he sang, his dark eyes lingered meaningfully upon that lady's bosom, while that beloved, one-eyed, flame-haired rogue, Sir Francis Weston, and blond, blue-eyed, baby-faced Sir Henry Norris settled themselves on either side of Madge Shelton and began to playfully vie for her attentions. A tawny tendril of hair had escaped from the back of her gable hood, and each begged to be allowed to cut it and wear it forever enshrined in a golden locket over his heart. And tall, patrician Sir William Brereton smilingly commandeered

Lady Margery's fan to cool himself and settled back with his head in her lap to let that awestruck damsel feed him grapes and timidly stroke his sleek, raven-black hair.

Only George stood apart. Though a smile and a witty remark were always upon his lips, his eyes constantly strayed to the windows.

"Will you sit, my lord?" I asked, moving aside my skirts to make room for him beside me on the window seat.

Smiling his thanks, he accepted and turned at once to prop his elbows upon the sill and lean out, eyes squinting into the distance, to scrutinize the road.

"You are awaiting a messenger from your father, perhaps?" I queried.

"Anne," he answered, his voice rich with warmth and longing, "Anne arrives today." His body tensed and he leaned farther out. "Will!" He beckoned anxiously to Brereton. "Come here; your sight is sharper than mine. Look there and tell me, does the dust rise or only my hopes?"

And, sure enough, there in the distance was a cloud of dust, and in its midst we could just discern a cart and a small group of riders. Then he was gone, sprinting down the stairs, taking them two at a time.

"Is it Anne? Has Anne come?" George's friends chorused excitedly. And, forgetting all else, without even a bow or a by-your-leave, they bounded after him, jostling and tripping each other in their haste.

"Sir William, my fan!" Lady Margery called after Brereton. But it was too late; they were already gone. And we were left to our own devices, and each other's dreary and familiar company, once again.

From George's abandoned place, I leaned from the window and watched the scene below.

He called her name and waved his cap in the air.

She waved back and, spurring her horse onward, left her attendants, with their burden of pack horses, cart, and luggage, coughing in the dust.

She had scarcely reined her mount before George was there,

sweeping her down from the saddle and spinning her round and round in a joyous embrace. Their laughter blurred together and became one, and the skirt of her rich brown velvet riding habit billowed out behind her.

"Greetings, Anne, and have you a kiss for your oldest and dearest friend?" Sir Thomas Wyatt asked, elbowing past Weston and Brereton, flaunting the privilege of prior acquaintance. The Wyatts of Allington Castle were neighbors of the Boleyns in Kent, and Tom and his sister Meg had been their childhood playmates.

"Indeed I have!" she answered, and promptly turned to plant a kiss upon George's cheek. "And one for my second oldest and dearest friend as well!" she added, giving Wyatt the requested kiss.

"And what of me?" Francis Weston demanded. "Though we have never met, Mistress Anne, George has told me so much about you that I feel I have known you my whole life!"

"Indeed, Sir Francis, George has told me so much of you that I feel the same, although . . ." With a tantalizing smile she hesitated. "Methinks my reputation would soon come to grief if I were to bestow such a familiarity upon you!"

His friends burst into laughter and slapped Weston's back and nudged him playfully.

"Now, Mistress Anne, I protest!" he cried, dropping to one knee with a hand upon his heart. "I am no cad, no matter what they say of me!" he finished with a saucy wink.

"It matters not where the truth lies," she said graciously, extending her hand. "You are George's friend, and so you shall be mine as well!"

Then Henry Norris and William Brereton were pressing forward. There they were, the brightest stars of the court, clamoring for her attention, for just one word, one glance. Like starving beggars devouring the crumbs tossed to them. What fools men are!

They were all talking at once now—all but George, who merely looked at her and smiled adoringly—jostling and shoving each other aside, begging to be the one to escort her to her chamber. Then, without a word, George proffered his arm and she took it. The others groaned, long and loud, like men dying upon a field of battle. To console Brereton, Anne let him carry her riding crop; he held it as if it were some sacred relic that he would lay down his life for.

"Hold a moment!" Norris cried. He darted in front of Anne and, from the basket over his arm, began to strew crimson rose petals in her path. "I knew my lady would be arriving today, so I was up with the dawn to gather a carpet of roses for her to walk upon!"

"He means his valet was up with the dawn to gather them!" Weston chortled.

Not to be outdone, both Wyatt and Weston announced that they had written sonnets to welcome her. And before Wyatt could claim the privilege of prior acquaintance again, Weston loudly commenced reciting, only to have his words curtailed by a sharp cuff upon the ear.

"You look a pirate and it is a pirate you are!" Wyatt hotly declared, referring to the patch Weston wore over the empty socket of his left eye. "You have pirated my entire second verse!"

"It is a bold accusation you make, Sir, and for it you shall answer!" Weston's hand sought the hilt of his sword and he advanced towards Wyatt, the large pendent pearl dangling from his left earlobe swaying violently.

It was then that Anne came between them, laughing and resting a hand lightly upon each of their indignantly heaving chests.

"Verily, this is the most passionate welcome I have ever had! Please, gentlemen, do not spoil it by brawling. Let these rose petals be the only red that falls upon the ground this day, and not your life's blood!"

Then, all thoughts of violence dispelled, they followed her inside.

Anne had scarcely arrived at court—indeed her servants had not had time to unpack all her gowns—before love literally fell at her feet.

Love came in the form of Harry Percy, the Earl of Northumberland's son and heir. Tall, gangling, ginger-haired, stuttering, shy, and constantly tripping over his own tongue and feet, Harry Percy was the last man anyone would have expected to win Anne Boleyn's heart. For his clumsiness he was famous; I once saw him mount his horse on one side and fall right off the other. And it was said about the court that "anyone can fall down stairs, but Harry Percy has made an art of falling up them!" He looked like a farm boy masquerading as a prince, and only the most mercenary of maidens would have been smitten with him. And, as much as I would like to paint Anne blacker, and say that such a one was she, to do so would be a lie. The love that shone in her eyes and the tender, indulgent smile that graced her lips whenever she looked at Harry Percy told their own tale.

It was upon her first day to serve Queen Catherine, when she sat sewing beside me, that Harry Percy came in with a group of gentlemen, tripped over a footstool, and fell sprawling at Anne's feet. We rocked with laughter until tears ran down our faces. Even Queen Catherine herself could not suppress a smile, though she tried to hide it behind her hand. Only Anne was silent. Then, with a gentle smile, she bent down and softly asked, "Did you hurt yourself?"

"I . . . I . . ." Percy stammered, staring up at her with eyes big, brown, and adoring as a spaniel's. "I tr-tripped."

His words inspired a fresh burst of laughter.

"Take no notice of them," Anne advised. "Anyone is apt to trip."

"And what a nice trip it was, eh, Percy?" Francis Weston quipped, laughing harder still when Percy failed to comprehend the jest.

But Anne and Percy were oblivious to it all; they had eyes only for each other.

It all came so easily for her. She had found true love and her niche, occupying a unique place at the heart—and in the hearts—of that band of merry wits. With George, Wyatt, Weston, Brereton, and Norris she was most often to be found. Together they would sit huddled in a window embrasure or outside under the trees, laughing and setting sonnets to song or devising clever masques to entertain the court. She was the flame to which they, like moths, were drawn. Women envied her yet rushed to emulate her—the cunning sleeves, doglike collars, and the French hood (a gilt-, pearl-, or jewel-bordered crescent of velvet or satin that perched upon a lady's head, often with a veil trailing gracefully behind) which she favored over the more cumbersome gable hood with its stiff, straight wooden borders and peaked tip that framed the wearer's face like a dormer window. And now she was set to wed the heir to a rich earldom, and it was a love match to boot! Even Dame Fortune seemed to fawn on Anne Boleyn!

But then came a hint of trouble, the distant rumble of thunder, like a storm brewing just over the horizon, and I was among the first to heed it.

❧ 2 ❧

At first, it was just like any other night at court; no special cause for celebration, no privileged guest to welcome or holy day to mark. We dined in the Great Hall, and afterwards we danced. The King and Queen sat on their thrones, and hovering nearby, at the King's beck and call, were Cardinal Wolsey—the butcher's boy turned priest, who had made himself indispensable to the King and now held the reins of power as Lord Chancellor—and his perpetually black-clad, equally grim-faced henchman, the ruthless and clever lawyer, Thomas Cromwell.

Henry VIII was in one of his moods, sullen and silent, a dark scowl perched like an evil gargoyle upon his face. His beady blue eyes narrowed and his cruel little pink mouth gnawed distractedly at his knuckles above the magnificent jeweled rings that graced each finger.

He was like two souls warring for control of a single body. He was "Bluff King Hal" when it suited him, always smiling, always laughing. At such times he could speak to a person—noble or peasant—and make him feel as if he were the most important person in the world. He would look deep into their eyes and nod thoughtfully, as if his whole existence hung upon their every word. But when he was in a red-hot temper or one of his black moods, it was like the Devil claimed him body and soul, and he became a bloated, red-faced, raging monster; a tyrant, ready to shed the blood of friend or foe, anyone who dared cross him.

He was a giant of a man, massive and muscular—at the time of which I now write, an active life of dancing and sport kept the future promise of fat at bay—with broad shoulders and trim, finely shaped calves of which he was inordinately vain. He was very handsome, ruddy-cheeked, with red-gold hair and a short, neatly groomed beard. And his mode of dressing made him seem larger and more dazzling still. His velvet coats, which reached only to just above his knees lest they obscure his shapely calves, were padded at the shoulders to make them look bigger and broader still; his doublets were a frenzy of jewels, gilding, embroidery, puffing, and slashing; and his round, flat caps were garnished with gilt braid, jewels, and jaunty curling white plumes. Silk hose sheathed his legs, and the square-toed velvet slippers he favored were embroidered with golden threads and precious gems. And round his neck he wore heavy golden collars and chains with diamonds, and other magnificent gems, as big as walnuts.

From time to time he would dart swift, peevish glances at the woman by his side—Catherine of Aragon.

At the age of fifteen a golden-haired Spanish girl named Catalina had bid farewell to her parents, Their Most Christian Majesties Ferdinand and Isabella, changed her name to Catherine, and left behind her native land, to brave a savage, storm-tossed sea and marry Arthur, Prince of Wales. The moment that that frightened, weary, homesick girl, green-tinged and fluttery-bellied with mal de mer, set foot on English soil, a miracle occurred—the people of England, always wary and distrustful of foreigners, fell in love with her. It was a love that would last a lifetime and sustain her through all the travails to come. Her bridegroom was a pale and sickly boy who succumbed to death's embrace before, Catherine swore, he could become a true husband to her, and for years afterwards she languished in penury, darning her threadbare gowns and pawning her jewels and gold plate to pay her servants and keep body and soul together, while her father-in-law, the miserly King Henry VII and her equally crafty father, King Ferdinand of Aragon, haggled over the unpaid portion of her dowry.

Then the old King died and young Prince Henry, glowing with promise and golden vitality, at age seventeen was crowned the eighth Henry. His first official act as king was to make Catherine his queen. He loved her brave, tenacious spirit, her kindness, sweet smile, quiet grace, and gentle nature. At the time, it didn't matter to him that she was six years his senior; Henry was in love. And, for a time at least, everything seemed golden.

Time passed. The luster dimmed and tarnished. All the still-births and miscarriages—only Princess Mary lived and thrived—and the poor little boys who clung feebly to life for a week or a month before they lost their fragile grasp, took their toll, as did the years, upon the golden-haired Spanish girl. Her petite body, once so prettily plump, after ten pregnancies grew stout; her waist thickened; lines at first fine, but etched deeper with every passing year and fresh sorrow, appeared upon her face; the golden tresses faded and skeins of silver and white snaked through them. And more and more she turned to religion for comfort, fasting, wearing a coarse, chafing hair shirt beneath her stiff, dowdy, dark-hued Spanish gowns, and spending hours upon her knees in chapel, praying fervently before a statue of the Virgin.

King Henry grew bored and his eye started to wander. And, even worse, his mind started to wonder why he was cursed with the lack of male issue. He needed a son, a future king for England. A daughter simply would not do; no girl, no mere weak and foolish female, could ever handle the reins of government, or bear without buckling the weight of the Crown! Thus was the impasse they had reached by the night my ears first became attuned to that distant rumble, and I knew a storm was brewing.

It was the most hilarious sight! Rarely has a dance inspired so much mirth. Indeed, at the sight of Anne and Percy dancing the galliard, some of us fairly screamed with laughter. I can see them now: Anne, grace incarnate in a splendid embroidered gown done in five shades of red, with a French hood to match, and a choker of carnelian beads. And Percy, equally resplendent in lustrous plum satin, bumbling, bumping, treading upon toes, and stumbling his way through that lively measure; twice he lost a slipper and once trod upon his own hat when it fell from his head.

Suddenly the King clapped his hands and the music stopped. The dancers froze as if they had suddenly been turned to statues.

"Enough! Enough!" Henry strode across the floor, women dropping into curtsies and men falling to their knees on every side of him. He stopped before Anne and Percy.

"Mistress Anne, you will oblige me by satisfying my curiosity upon a point that has perplexed me for quite some time. You are newly come from France, where I am told the court fairly overflows with gallant, handsome men, graceful of both step and speech. And here in England we have such men as well." He gestured to a nearby cluster of gallants, all of them eloquent speakers and accomplished dancers. "And yet, you have given your heart to young Percy here, who has feet as big and ungainly as duck boats and stammers so, it appears he can scarcely speak English, let alone flattery and flowery speeches?"

"All that glitters is not gold, Your Majesty," Anne said pointedly, her eyes flitting briefly over his ornate, gold-embellished crimson velvet doublet, unimpressed, as she sank into a deep, graceful curtsy at his feet, with her red skirts swirling about her like a spreading pool of blood.

"Indeed?" Henry arched his brows, very much intrigued. Clearly this was no blushing, demure damsel, simpering and shy, who would quail meek and fearful at his feet! "Percy! Sit you down, man, and I will show you how to tread a measure without treading on everyone's toes!" He clapped his hands sharply. "Play!" he commanded the musicians. "Mistress Anne . . ." He held out his hand, and not even Anne dared refuse him.

After the dance ended he thanked her and turned away to speak briefly with Sir Henry Norris, a dear friend as well as his Groom of the Stool, his most personal body servant. Anne dismissed the King from her thoughts as if he were no more than any other boring boy she had encountered at a dance, and headed straight for where Harry Percy sat; she never looked back. But as they stole away together, Henry's eyes followed them, beady blue and crafty, and his rings flashed a rainbow in the candlelight as he thoughtfully rubbed his chin. Then he turned and crooked a finger to summon Wolsey.

The Cardinal hurried instantly to his side. Though their words were hushed, Henry's expression was adamant, and the Cardinal's most perplexed. "See to it!" the King snapped before he resumed his throne, ignoring Catherine's gentle, inquiring smile, and brusquely brushing aside the hand she laid lightly upon his sleeve.

The golden light of the torches spilled out into the garden, and there, upon a carpet of soft green grass, Anne and her darling Percy danced alone. I watched them from the terrace. When he swung her high into the air during lavolta, Anne flung back her head and laughed joyously. In that moment, I think, her happiness was complete. It was then that Percy stumbled. Anne fell. She landed, laughing still, and rolled upon her back, the grass and her full skirts cushioning her fall. Percy was all concern. But when he bent over her, Anne seized his outstretched hand and pulled him down so that he lay on top of her. She wound her arms around his neck and kissed him long and lingeringly. Only then did she let him help her up and escort her back inside.

They never noticed me as they passed, arm in arm, smiling and staring deep into each other's eyes. Never before had I seen two people so much in love. I thought of myself and George then, and nearly sank down and wept. We had danced together twice, and he was always gallant and polite, but when he looked at me there was no love in his eyes, only courtesy and . . . indifference. And, despite all my attempts, I could not kindle a flame, not even a spark.

Weeks passed and life went on as usual. My sense of foreboding faded and I even began to think I had been mistaken. But no, it was only a quiet lull during which the storm lay dormant, gathering its strength.

It was upon the night of a lavish banquet to welcome the ambassador of the Holy Roman Emperor Charles V, Queen Catherine's nephew, that the lightning first flashed in earnest.

At Wolsey's opulent palace, York Place, an elaborate masque was to be staged and Anne and I were among those privileged to take part.

After the banquet, we hurried to the chamber that had been designated our tiring room to don our costumes. Flustered and flush-faced with excitement, we all fluttered about, chattering and screeching like caged birds, nervous fingers fussing with the laces of our gowns, fidgeting with the pearl- and gold-tipped pins and shimmering golden nets that secured our hair beneath the gold-and-crystal-bordered white satin French hoods, and snapping and slapping at the maids who knelt to hastily repair a loose hem or sagging sleeve.

It was to be a battle royal between the Virtues and the Vices. Perhaps I should have taken as a portent the roles assigned to us. Anne was Perseverance, her sister Mary was Kindness, and I was cast as Constancy.

In shimmering satin gowns of angel white, with sashes becomingly draped across our breasts embroidered in golden letters with the name of the Virtue we had been chosen to represent, we took our places upon the battlements of a large castle crafted of plaster and papier-mâché, painted in the royal Tudor colors of white and green, that had been wheeled into the Great Hall. Countless candles lit the scene, and the Cardinal's boy choir and musicians provided heavenly music.

Suddenly a shrill, fiendish screech pierced the air and in rushed the Vices—Cruelty, Jealousy, Disdain, Malice, Envy, Slander, Wantonness, and Danger. Brandishing and cracking whips, they were gowned in jet-glittering black with embroidered hell-flames of orange, yellow, and scarlet lapping at their skirts and bodices upon which in flaming letters their Vices were blazoned, and red devil horns adorned their heads of dark, unruly, free-flowing hair.

As the music soared we made a great show of panic, beseeching the heavens to send us aid, while we pelted our attackers with a volley of sugarplums, oranges, dates, figs, and nuts. Then, with a fanfare of trumpets, rescue came in the form of seven Knights clad in Our Lady's Blue satin, their cloaks embroidered with flaming hearts, and blue-dyed plumes swaying gracefully upon their golden helmets, each one bearing a shield emblazoned with his title. George was Sir Loyal Heart, and Francis Weston and Harry Percy were aptly cast as Amorous Youth and Gentleness. They were led by the tall and majestic figure of King Henry VIII himself, head to toe in scarlet and hearts aflame. Ardent Desire his shield and lusty, determined gaze proclaimed.

In a mock battle the Knights danced the Vices to their defeat and the demonic temptresses crumpled at their feet and begged for mercy. The Knights pulled them up roughly and set them spinning, twirling away as, with an adamant, imperious wave—"Be Gone!"—they banished them.

The trumpets blared and the choir sang hallelujah as we showered our saviors with rose petals of red and white. With hands upon their hearts they knelt and beseeched us to come down from our lofty perches.

After a great show of maidenly modesty, we relented and let Beauty—the King's sister Mary, Duchess of Suffolk, and erstwhile Queen of France—lead us down. She had reigned for less than a year before old King Louis died, and was famous for her shining red-gold hair, lily-white skin, and determination to trade the title of Queen for that of Duchess and marry the love of her life, Charles Brandon.

Then confusion came and threatened to dissolve the intricately choreographed masque into chaos. Ardent Desire was supposed to lay claim to Beauty and lead her out to dance, and Sir Loyal Heart and Perseverance were likewise to be partnered, and so forth. Nothing was left to chance; our dancing partners had been assigned to us from the first day of rehearsals. Yet King Henry bypassed his sister and boldly seized Anne's wrist.

With a cheeky grin, Francis Weston disdained Honor and besought Madge Shelton to bestow Charity upon Amorous Youth instead. And Harry Percy slipped upon a sugarplum and skidded into the arms of Pity instead of Mercy.

An anxious moment ensued as those of us who remained, hastily sorted ourselves into pairs. I for one did not hesitate and boldly grabbed George's hand even as he reached for Mercy, Sir Thomas Wyatt's pretty blond-haired sister Meg Lee, who was rumored to have been George's childhood sweetheart.

And then, upon the sweetmeat- and petal-strewn floor, with the nuts crunching and fruits squashing beneath our satin slippers, we danced a graceful but lively measure that ended with a flourish when the Knights swept the Virtues up into their arms and carried them away. They had defeated Vice, claimed their prizes, and would live to dance and fight another day.

As George followed close on the heels of the King, I was there to see how the King tarried before setting Anne down. He seemed determined to linger there with her in his arms, despite Beauty's icy blue, disapproving stare. It was only when Devotion, his brother-in-law, auburn-bearded Charles Brandon, clapped him jovially upon the back and exclaimed "Well danced, Sire!" that he released her.

"Mistress Anne," he said as she curtsied low before him, reaching out to tilt her chin up so she would look at him, "Ardent Desire and Perseverance dance well together. Perhaps next time we shall change roles; I should like that very much." And with those words he left her.

Anne sprang up and turned anxiously to George, her lips trembling with a question she dared not ask.

"Court gallantry, darling Nan." George smiled reassuringly and squeezed her hand.

"You are sure, George? Only that and nothing more?" she asked, clutching desperately at his hand while her eyes searched his. "When he held me close against his chest and looked into my eyes I felt naked and cold as death!"

Before George could answer, a new drama ensued to divert Anne's attention. During the dance, poor Harry Percy had trod upon a walnut, and its shell had punctured the thin sole of his dancing slipper. Now he limped over, trailing a trickle of blood. Anne instantly began to fuss over him, just like a mother hen instead of the suave, Frenchified sophisticate she really was. And, supported by Nobility, Pleasure, and Liberty, otherwise known as Norris, Wyatt, and Brereton, and with George, convulsed with laughter, trailing after, they went to seek the services of a physician.

And I was left alone and forgotten once again.

That night in my father's study at our London house, with the busts of wise Athena, chaste Diana, beautiful Venus, and bountiful

Juno staring down at me from the mantel, I sat beside the hearth and rested my head against my father's knee and asked how the marriage negotiations progressed.

"Ah, Janey." He reached down to stroke my hair, now freed from its golden net. "It is a fine match to be sure, but I confess, I've had my doubts. I'm troubled about young George and the company he keeps. I've heard tales; things not fit for your ears. Perhaps it's nothing and age will curb his wildness, but . . ." He paused thoughtfully. "I want my girl, my only child, to marry well, but I also want her to be happy."

"And I will, Father!" I sat up straight. "I will! I will be the happiest woman alive—the happiest woman who ever lived—if I marry George Boleyn!"

"Ah, Janey." He reached down to caress my cheek. "Your eyes are dazzled by a pretty face, and your heart bewitched by longing, masquerading as love! But you must trust me to know what's best; though my eyes are old, my sight is truer through the wisdom that comes with experience and age. And I am quite sure that George Boleyn—handsome devil though he is—is not the man for you."

At these words I flung myself down and wept as though a storm had broken within my heart. Such a sharp, wrenching pain seared my breast, and my whole body shook with wracking sobs that seemed to tear at my lungs, as if a cat were trapped within and trying to claw its way out. And my throat sang out a long, keening wail, a dirge of deepest despair, like a mourner's lament.

"Janey, Janey!" Heedless of his gouty knees, my father knelt down beside me and stroked my back. "I know it is hard for you to believe me now, but time will prove me right; if you marry George Boleyn he'll bring you nothing but grief!"

"I would rather come to grief with him than find the greatest joy with another!" I vowed.

"Janey, I was watching you tonight, with him and his circle of friends, and you were always on the outside looking in, but never were you a part of it."

"But, Father," I protested, "that will change, after we are married. . . ."

And in my heart I firmly believed this. Once we were alone together as man and wife, away from the pleasures and wayward distractions of the court, "darling Nan," and his band of brilliant friends, George would come to know me, and he would see that I worshipped him and that to earn his love was all I craved. My arms would always be open to him, I would give him children, and to his every comfort I would personally attend. And though he might have had a more beautiful wife, never would he have found a better one. I might lack the dazzle of a diamond, but I would make up for it with devotion as perfect as a pearl. No one could ever love him as much as I did. There was a flame in my heart that burned and yearned for him that could never be eclipsed, extinguished, or dimmed.

"And if it doesn't?" my father asked gently. "If it is always like the necromancer's magic circle and you can never, like the spirits, step inside?"

"Nay, Father, he will come to love me, you will see. I will make him love me!"

Oh, how young and full of certainty I was then. I did not know then that it was impossible, no matter how much you desire and crave it, to make someone love you.

"Please, Father, do not deny me this! My heart will surely break if you do!"

With a reluctant sigh he gave in. "It is with grave misgivings that I say this, Janey, but I will leave things as they are; I will say nothing to Sir Thomas of my doubts. The negotiations shall continue and we will see what comes to pass."

"Thank you!" I whispered fervently. "Oh, Father, thank you!" I flung my arms around his neck and covered his face with kisses.

While the threat of losing my heart's desire was but narrowly averted, Anne would not be so fortunate.

Robert, a distant cousin of mine, was a gentleman of Cardinal Wolsey's household, and from him I had the whole story.

Wolsey summoned Harry Percy into his presence chamber and, before his entire household, soundly berated him, lashing poor Percy with his tongue as if it were a whip. How dare he dally with that Boleyn girl? Nearly foaming at the mouth, jowls quivering, eyes flashing, Wolsey declared himself astounded by the sheer gall, the presumptuousness and audacity Percy had displayed by allowing himself to become entangled with a common little nobody, the granddaughter of a merchant no less! Even if the man had risen to the rank of Lord Mayor of London and had prospered to such an extent that he was able to leave £1,000 to the poor upon his death, that dark-eyed minx with her long legs and swinging gypsy-black hair was no match for the Earl of Northumberland's heir. Furthermore, Percy's thoughtless behavior had grievously offended the King, and his father would arrive forthwith to deal with him personally.

Never a very brave man under the best of circumstances, Percy stammered that he had not meant to offend anyone, but he was a grown man and thought himself capable of choosing his own wife.

"I . . . I l-l-love Anne!" He fell to his knees at Wolsey's feet, blubbering and shuddering, like a man made of jelly.

"Love? Bah!" scoffed Wolsey. "Do you think that the King and I do not know our business? Do you think your father is a mutton-headed dolt like you are? Whom you marry is no concern of yours; it is for us—the King, myself, and your father—to tell you who to marry and when to marry, and it is for you to obey without quarrel or question!"

Clutching like a drowning man at the Cardinal's scarlet robes, Percy begged him to intercede, to plead his case before the King, asserting again that he loved Anne wholeheartedly.

But Wolsey would have none of it. He ordered Percy from his sight, to be locked in his room until his father arrived.

And oh, what a sight that was! His long red beard swinging, green eyes blazing, he swept down from the North, where it was his duty to safeguard the border from marauding Scots. Without waiting for Percy's door to be unlocked, the Earl kicked it down, seized his son by the hair, and slapped him until his nose poured blood and two teeth wobbled in their sockets; then he dragged Percy out to the barge by his collar, flung him in, and bore him away, bawling like a baby, to marry Mary Talbot, the Earl of Shrewsbury's only daughter, and a loathsome shrew if ever there was one.

It was Anne's turn next, and I was there to witness it, having chosen that moment as just the right time to bring my future mother-in-law a gift of embroidered gloves.

Anne stood straight and defiant while her father paced before the hearth, raging and roaring at her. And I, seated out of the way on a window seat, my presence quite forgotten, could not help but tremble.

I was glad that Thomas Boleyn was not my father. I swear ice water instead of blood coursed within his veins, and his heart was harder than marble. Gaunt and unsmiling, his dark hair speckled with gray, he spoke in crisp, curt syllables and was liberal with his blows, which he dealt swiftly and without remorse.

"Did you not know that we had other plans for you? The Earl of Ormonde . . ."

There had been some talk of marrying Anne to her cousin in Ireland to resolve a longstanding family dispute about the rights to an earldom.

"James Butler," Anne announced, "is a drunken fool with a voice like bagpipes, he stinks like a stable, and I will not have him!"

"You will not?" Thomas Boleyn repeated incredulously.

"I will not." Anne repeated each word slowly, enunciating clearly as if she were addressing a deaf man. "It is Harry Percy I love and I mean to marry him!"

Thomas Boleyn raised his right hand and dealt Anne the first of three ringing slaps.

"That is for your impertinence!" he explained after the first. "That is for risking this family's standing with the King. We would be nothing without his favor!" he said after the second. His hand rose again and delivered the hardest and most stinging slap of all. "And that is because you failed! You have sullied your good name; your reputation has been compromised. Go now; you are banished to Hever until it is the King's pleasure to recall you. Go! I cannot stand the sight of you; I never could suffer a fool!"

With her head held high, showing the red print of her father's hand blossoming against the pallor of her cheek, Anne left the room.

I followed her, but she ignored me. The sight of her thus drew many alarmed and inquiring glances, and as she passed many fell to whispering, but Anne was oblivious to all.

George, in his dust-covered riding clothes, his white shirt open at the throat and sweat-sodden, caught up with her in the garden.

"Nan, oh, Nan, I came as soon as I heard. . . ."

Gently, he led her along the graveled path, to a quiet, leafy bower. Not once did he glance at me. I might as well have been a ghost; to him I was already invisible. His gloves fell unnoticed to the ground. I picked them up, pressed them to my nose, and inhaled their scent of spice, sweat, and leather.

"Nan!" he breathed as his fingers lightly traced the bruise flourishing on her cheek. His other hand tightened around his riding crop. "By Heaven, I should like to give him a taste of what he metes out so freely!"

"It is all Wolsey's doing," Anne said numbly. "Wolsey!" she hissed, with all the venom of a serpent. "Heaven upon earth was within my grasp and he snatched it away, because he—that butcher's boy!—deemed me unworthy. George, before you and God, I swear that if ever it is within my power I shall work the Cardinal as much displeasure as he has done me!" And with these words she fell weeping into his arms, burrowing her face into his strong shoulder as I so longed to do.

Neither of them seemed to realize what I knew from the start—Wolsey was only following orders.

The next morning, Anne, dressed for travel, knelt at Queen Catherine's feet to formally take leave of her.

"I trust Your Majesty will know the cause," she said softly, her bitterness and anger ill-concealed.

Queen Catherine leaned forward in her chair and gently took Anne's bruised and tearstained face between her hands.

"I am sorry, Mistress Anne. He is a sweet boy and I know your love for one another was sincere. Go with God"—she pressed a dainty gold filigree cross set with seed pearls into Anne's hand—"and know that you are in my prayers."

"Thank you, Your Majesty," Anne whispered, her voice shaking with the tears she was struggling not to shed.

Impulsively, Queen Catherine gathered her close in a motherly embrace.

"Do not be afraid to weep when you are alone," she counseled. "Tears cleanse the soul and will give your heart blessed release."

❧ 3 ❧

And so back to Hever Anne went, to mourn her lost love, dream of revenge, and nurse her wounded pride.

A year passed, followed by a second, and a third, with Anne stubbornly refusing to return to court. Whenever her father broached the subject, she spoke so wildly that he dared not force her lest she behave in such a manner that the King's goodwill and the Boleyns' fortunes would be lost forever. So he let her be. Bleating sheep, taking inventory of the larder, and supervising the cheese and candle making, he reasoned, must soon pale beside the remembered pleasures of the court. But Anne was nothing if not stubborn.

She changed dramatically during those three years. Gone were the elegant French gowns, packed away with sachets of lavender, and with them her jewels, locked in their velvet-lined casket. And the volatile, vivacious nature that had captivated an entire court seemed also to have been snuffed out. Like a ghost, she drifted about Hever, in somber-hued gowns of gray, black, white, and brown. And her hair too had become a prisoner of her pain, denied its freedom, confined and pinned beneath a modest coif, white and nunlike.

She went for long, solitary walks and would sit for hours immersed in a book of scripture. She wore her Book of Hours, beautifully illuminated, bejeweled, and gilded, dangling at the end of a golden chain around her waist. Except for Queen Catherine's cross, it was the only adornment she allowed herself.

She was fascinated by the "New Learning" that was sweeping Europe, heralded by Martin Luther's heated demands for Church reform—to curb the avaricious excesses of the Catholic Church, for the lucrative trade in Indulgences to cease, for people to accept that prayer alone was no guarantee of salvation, and that God and man could commune freely without priestly intervention, and everyone should be allowed to read and hear the word of God preached in their own language instead of Latin only. And though it was dangerous, and by the law deemed heresy, to possess such texts, Anne owned several, prizing greatly a book of scriptures written in French and William Tyndale's English translation of the New Testament. It was a passion George also shared, and they made use of merchants importing goods from France and like-minded friends in the diplomatic service to procure these banned volumes, which they discussed fervently, albeit in hushed tones, and kept carefully hidden. Both hoped someday to see the Bible fully translated into English and legally sanctioned. For how else could the word of God reach the people, most of whom understood not one word of Latin, it being the tongue of priests, lawyers, and scholars and not the common man?

It was a lonely life Anne led at Hever. Her parents and Mary were almost always at court. But George did not forsake her. Whenever he could obtain leave from his duties at court, straight to Hever he would ride. If she wanted to talk they would talk; if she wished to sit in silence he would speak not a word and instead give her the comfort of his presence. He was the only one who could draw her out of her cloistered shell and make her smile. As they debated the tenets of Lutheranism, the new ideas espoused in their forbidden books, or made music together, the shell would crack to reveal a glimmer of the old Anne. Her spirit was not dead, only sleeping.

Another frequent visitor was Sir Thomas Wyatt. Most unhappily wed to a wife who shamelessly cuckolded him, he would tarry long with Anne at Hever.

He laid siege to her, bombarding her with sonnets.

"Persistence is my only virtue," I heard him once declare as he lay sprawled upon the grass at her feet, "and with my heart entire I hope that it may be rewarded."

"Oh?" Anne arched her brows. "Are loyalty, friendship, and kindness masks you don only to woo me?"

"Nay, dear Anne, but I do not want to claim too many; it would ruin my reputation if I were to appear overly virtuous. It is more exciting to be a sinner than a saint!"

I sometimes visited her too. I thought it would please George if I affected a sisterly interest in Anne. And—honesty compels me to admit—I was curious and fascinated. Thus, I was in a position to observe her, and though Anne adopted drab and modest garb like a nun, I discovered she was a far cry from being one.

One dreary autumn afternoon I claimed a headache and excused myself, but instead of retiring to my room I stealthily followed Anne out into the forest.

The lilting strains of Wyatt's lute provided a trail for us to follow. Anne stepped into a clearing, while I hung back, hiding behind the trunk of a large tree, congratulating myself on my fortuitous choice of attire, a brown gown, which allowed me to blend in with the scenery.

Smiling and still strumming his lute, Wyatt came to greet her. He gestured downward and I saw that he had fashioned a bed of leaves, a dry and crackling festive array of brown, orange, yellow, and red. From a basket he offered her wine and dainty cakes. Then he reached for her.

Gently, he lifted the plain white coif from her head and plucked the pins from her hair until it fell like an ebony cloak about her shoulders, and he drew her close for a lingering kiss. When their lips parted their eyes met in a long and silent stare. Anne was the first to look away. Eyes downcast, she nodded in a manner that seemed more resigned than anything else.

Slowly, she lay back against the bed of leaves.

His lips were upon hers, then trailing slowly down to her throat and breasts, while his hand gathered up her full gray skirt and petticoats.

All the time Anne lay passive, her arms draped loosely about his back. While he moaned and sighed, she stayed still and silent. Only once did she cry out, when he lay full upon her and with his fleshly lance shattered the shield of her hymen.

Suddenly he drew back, bolting up onto his knees, to let his seed spew onto the leaves.

Anne just lay there, rigid, staring up at the sky through the lattice of naked branches and dead leaves while he put right his garments.

With a tender smile, Wyatt extended his hand and drew her up for another kiss. Softly, they spoke, too low for me to hear, and then he left her and rode home to Allington Castle, and his wife.

Anne sat for a long time, hugging her knees, upon that bed of leaves. Then from out of her bodice she drew a slim gold chain—a locket. She parted the gleaming halves of the golden oval and gazed down with such sorrow that I felt the tightness that portends tears well up within my own throat.

"I wanted it to be you!" she cried, and I knew that it was upon Harry Percy's likeness that she was gazing.

With a wrenching sob, she flung herself facedown into the leaves and wept until the sun set.

Witnessing her despair, I almost felt ashamed for telling her what had befallen poor Percy since his ill-fated marriage.

Between Harry Percy and Mary Talbot it was hate as black and thick as treacle at first sight. Their marriage was never even consummated, and after the wedding his wife went home to her doting father. Percy was left alone in his drafty, cavernous castle. There he tried to drown his sorrows, scrutinizing the bottom of each tankard and goblet he drained, hoping to find consolation written there. Stomach pains became the bane of his existence. And though still a young man in the midst of his twenties, he looked twice that; already sorrow was steadily bleaching his ginger hair white. He often gave way to tears of self-pity, berating himself for his cowardice, denouncing himself as "a jelly, a spineless jelly!" And every night, when he slumped facedown across the table in a drunken stupor, he would cry her name—"Anne!"

* * *

In the third year of Anne's exile, George and I were married in the royal chapel at Greenwich. I wore white damask and deep green velvet with my late mother's pearls and a special brooch Father had given me pinned to my bodice. A curious, ornate piece of exquisite craftsmanship, it was heavy burnished gold set with a large green agate topped by a head in the antique style depicting some ancient goddess, Persephone perhaps, with long, flowing hair strewn with enameled flowers. A wreath of gilded rosemary with trailing green and white silk ribbons crowned my unbound hair. It was the last time I would ever appear in public with my hair unbound; henceforth, my tresses would be covered with a coif and headdress and reserved as a sight for my husband's eyes alone in the privacy of our bedchamber. As I knelt at the altar beside him, I remembered George combing Anne's hair and smiled at the thought of him soon doing the same for me. Perhaps it would even become a nightly ritual, something we did before retiring to bed.

I was radiant with delight and my face ached from smiling. As I held George's hand tightly in mine, I swore I would never let go. He was mine now, all mine, bound to me with Church rites and golden rings!

I was restless throughout the banquet that followed, aching for the moment when I would be left alone with him behind the velvet curtains of our marriage bed. And then that moment came, and I learned a valuable lesson—anticipation only makes the disappointment keener.

He was kind, very kind, but maddeningly aloof. Indifference stared back at me from behind his luminous, wine-glazed brown eyes. How could he be so close to me and yet so far away? We were like two people facing each other across a great chasm where the bridge had collapsed. But only I wanted to cross over; George was content to stay on his side.

He kissed me. I clung to him, fiercely, like a drowning woman wild to survive. I giggled, squirmed, and sighed at the delicious new sensations of his fingers gliding over my breasts and down to my cunny. I cried out my love as he entered me, heedless of the pain, and clawed at his back until his blood was caked beneath my nails. For a moment I thought I spied something akin to irritation in his eyes, but otherwise he was unmoved by my passion. His seed spewed into me, then it was over. He rolled off me, bid me good night, and turned his face to the wall. I wrapped my arms around his waist, nestled against his back, and cooed over the scratches my nails had made, kissing them and lapping at them kittenishly with my tongue, but he just lay there, silent and still as a marble tomb effigy.

How many ways can a husband tell his wife that she means nothing to him without actually saying the words?

We divided our time between court and Grimston Manor in Norfolk, which the King had given us as a wedding present. And yes, it was grim and made of gray stone as cold and hard as George's heart was to me.

After our wedding night, he never passed an entire night with me. On the rare occasions when he came to my bed at all, after he had spent his seed he would shake off my clinging hands and curtly dismiss my pleas. "Leave off, Madame; my duty is done for tonight at least!" he would snap peevishly as he headed for the door, even as I clung to him and begged him to stay and sleep the night with me. He would flee into his own bedchamber, which adjoined mine, pressing his shoulder firmly against the door and bolting it even as I flung myself against it. And I would slump there against the door, in tears and agony, while his seed snaked down my bare legs. And at each sound that filtered through the thick wood to my ears I wept all the more. The splash of water into a basin told me that he was washing himself, washing away all traces of me, the evidence of our coupling. This was invariably followed by wine sloshing into a goblet, twice or thrice at least, but sometimes more. Sometimes then would come the scratching of a pen upon parchment or the poignant pluck of lute strings, but, more often than not, I would hear the rustle of clothing, the clothespress banging open and shut as he dressed himself. Then the outer door would open and I would hear his footsteps heading for the stairs.

I knew where he was going. Sometimes I even followed. I listened, I saw—the carousing, the drinking, the gambling, the whoring, all the obliging court ladies and harlots in taverns who raised their skirts and opened their arms and legs to him. There were rumors that he sometimes dallied with men, reveling in the forbidden sin of Sodom and, if caught, risking a fiery death at the stake. I suppose it was, for him, the ultimate gamble.

Francis Weston's was the name linked most often with his—a hot-tempered rascal, with a wild, unruly head of hair of the brightest red I had ever seen. His right eye was a shade of gold-flecked brown that reminded me of amber. He had a hundred tales to explain how he had lost his left eye, each more amusing than the last. A generous offer to let a friend shoot an apple off the top of his head during archery practice had gone tragically awry. A quarrel in a tavern over the last sausage on a platter. "The lesson here is not to quarrel at meals and to be wary of forks; in the wrong hands they can be a dangerous weapon!" Other times he cautioned his audience not to pick their teeth while riding in a litter, or to try to pin a brooch onto their hat brim while on horseback, or to tease their ladylove's pet monkey or parrot. "And never, never tell a temperamental tailor that you will be delinquent in settling your account while he has a pair of newly sharpened shears in his hand!" But whatever the truth, by his loss he seemed undaunted.

The storm that had flashed, then fallen dormant, finally began to show its strength in the summer of 1526.

I was at Hever, sitting in Anne's chamber, embroidering and talking idly with Anne and her mother, when we heard the distant trill of hunting horns.

Hoofbeats came clattering urgently across the wooden draw-bridge, and Sir Thomas Boleyn flung himself from the saddle and rushed inside as if the hounds of Hell were nipping at his heels. Within moments he stood before us, panting and dripping with sweat. Ignoring us, he went straight to the clothespress and com-menced flinging dresses and kirtles, bodices and sleeves about until the floor was lost beneath a welter of satin, silk, velvet, damask, and brocade. Suddenly he stopped, a spring green silk gown exquisitely embroidered with white roses, with just a shim-mer of silver glimmering amidst the pearly threads, clasped be-tween his hands.

"Tudor colors . . . green and white . . . roses . . . the royal emblem . . ." I heard him murmur intently as he scrutinized the gown. "It's perfect! Here! Wear this!" He tossed it onto Anne's lap.

I recognized the material at once. George had brought it back with him from a brief pleasure jaunt to France. I had coveted it for myself at first glance, but no matter how I oohed and ahhed over its beauty, and hinted at the nearness of my birthday, George had ignored me and given it to Anne instead.

"No more of these drab, colorless dresses!" he continued. "If you want to dress like a nun I will send you to a convent! That is the traditional fate of spinsters who fail to make a proper marriage. Need I remind you, Anne, that you are now three years past twenty and woman's youth is fleeting?"

He reached out and yanked the plain coif of pleated white linen from her head. "Take down your hair! You've half an hour to prepare yourself; when you are ready, wait in the rose garden. Take your lute and play, or stroll about and admire the flowers, whatever you will, as long as you appear pleasing to a man's eye!"

And then he was gone, slamming the door behind him.

I knew something important was about to happen. While Anne, clutching her lute and arrayed in the spring green gown, sullenly descended the three stone steps into the sunken rose garden, I rushed to hide behind the tall, dense green shrubberies surrounding it.

She left her lute lying upon a bench and idly roamed the pebbled path, lost in thought, crushing the fallen petals of red, pink, yellow, and white beneath her satin slippers, while all around her roses in full, heady bloom swayed gently upon their thorny stems.

Then there he was—King Henry VIII himself in all his might and majestic glory. In his eagerness he had ridden ahead of the hunting party, thus no cavalcade of clattering hooves and blaring horns heralded his arrival. He stood there, a ruddy giant of a man, hands on hips, sweaty and flush-faced from heat and exertion, legs parted as if he meant to straddle the world and declare himself its master.

The crunch of his boots upon the gravel startled her, and Anne spun around and sank quickly into a curtsy. Any woman less graceful and nimble would have lost her balance and fallen flat.

"Up! Up!" he gestured brusquely. "No ceremony, Mistress Anne. You see I come before you not as Henry of England . . ." At this, her brows arched skeptically. "Ardent Desire has come to call upon Perseverance. You persevere in staying away from court while I ardently desire your presence!"

"Alas, Sire, I am done with all that!" she answered. "The pleasures of the court have lost their allure, and my heart is yet too sore to contemplate . . ."

"Three years is time aplenty for a broken heart to mend! You have been overlong at nursing your grief, Mistress Anne, and I command you now to cease!"

"With all due respect, Sire," Anne retorted, "my heart is not yours to command."

Undaunted, he answered, "It will be."

"I daresay anything is possible." Anne shrugged.

"Aye, it is, Anne, it is!" he vowed, nodding eagerly. "With us, anything is possible!"

"As you say." She shrugged disinterestedly.

"Come, take my arm, show me the garden."

"As you wish."

"Nay, dearest Anne"—Henry turned and lightly caressed her cheek—"I've yet to be granted my wish."

"Then if Your Majesty will follow me along this path, I will be glad to show you the garden," Anne said coldly, turning away from his touch.

"For you, Mistress Anne, I would follow the path to damnation itself!" he declared as they proceeded along the petal-strewn path.

"Ah! What fine roses flourish here at Hever!" His meaty fingers caressed a lush crimson bloom while his eyes devoured Anne.

"Thank you, Your Majesty. I shall give the gardener your compliments," said Anne, her voice crisp and cool as winter.

"You are not your sister," he observed.

"No, Your Majesty, I am not."

"What a rare blossom you are, Mistress Anne! An English rose who weathered the lusty storms of the French court and came home to us fresh and unplucked! The King of France, I am told, is an ardent gardener who likes nothing better than to gather a beautiful bouquet for his bedchamber. However did this English rose escape his attention?"

"One can attract attention without bestowing one's attentions, Sire. And, as you say, I am not my sister. I would never sell myself so cheaply."

"Cheaply?" he repeated incredulously. "Many would account it a great honor to be the mistress of a king!"

"As Your Majesty rightfully observed, I am a rarity, the exception rather than the rule. Never would I sacrifice my honor for the brief, fleeting favor that can be found between the sheets of a royal bed."

"You are proud, Mistress Anne."

"Too proud to be plucked by a King and then discarded. A rose does not survive long once it has been plucked, and I will not, like some dried and wizened petals made into a potpourri, be parceled out as a gift to some obliging courtier, as my sister was to William Carey!"

King Henry just stared at her, pulses throbbing. There was a sharp snap as his fingers tightened round the stem of the crimson rose.

"Roses are meant to be plucked, not to wither upon their stems, their petals by the winds and rains dispersed and trodden underfoot!"

"That would depend, Sire, upon who does the plucking. I think it is not meet for someone to steal into a garden and take whatsoever he desires, like a thief in the night. Better that it be done lawfully, by one who has the right!"

"It is not for roses to decide who plucks them! I look forward to seeing you at court, Mistress Anne."

"I thank Your Majesty for your kind invitation. . . ."

"It is not an invitation."

"It is a command?"

"We understand each other perfectly. Good day, Mistress Anne." He extended the rose to her and, with a curt nod, left her.

With her left hand Anne tore the petals from the rose and flung them fiercely aside as her right hand did likewise with the stem; then, with a swirl of spring green skirts she turned and ran from the garden to lose herself in the maze where I dared not follow.

* * *

That night Anne kept to her chamber, ignoring her father's repeated summons to come down to dine.

"The King requests your presence," the first message said. Another followed shortly afterwards, saying, "Bring your lute; the King desires you to play for him."

Anne sent her lute downstairs with her answer. "Play it for him yourself. My head aches and I am going to bed."

Sir Thomas Boleyn did not dare send for her again and made her excuses instead to the much annoyed monarch.

The next morning we assembled in the courtyard to bid the King farewell. Only Anne, to her father's supreme annoyance, was absent.

King Henry pursed his lips and a cloud of anger seemed to hover above the swaying white ostrich plumes on his round velvet cap.

"We hope Mistress Anne will soon regain her health and grace our court again," he mumbled gruffly.

"Indeed she will, Your Grace, I am certain of it!" Sir Thomas assured him. "I am certain of it!" he repeated as he knelt upon the dusty, sunbaked flagstones to hold the gilded stirrup for the royal foot.

It was then, as he started to swing himself up into the saddle, that King Henry looked up.

Framed like a painting by a master artist, Anne stood at her ivy-bordered window, still in her thin, clinging white nightshift, idly running an ivory comb through her long black hair. Her eyes were staring straight ahead, out into the distance, pointedly ignoring what was happening in the courtyard below. Then, abruptly, she turned away and disappeared from sight, even as King Henry breathed a long sigh and shuddered with desire.

"Tell your daughter that Love is the physician who cures all ails," he commanded. Then he leapt into the saddle and spurred his horse onward and, with his retinue following, took to the road again.

❧ 5 ❧

And so it began, the chase, the hunt, that would consume the better part of seven years, shattering and destroying lives, and shaking and tearing the world like a rat in a terrier's mouth. Nothing would ever be the same again, all because of Ardent Desire and Perseverance.

At Sir Thomas Boleyn's command, an army of dressmakers descended upon Hever, and the rustle of costly fabrics, the snip of scissors, the snap of thread, and the chatter of women soon filled the sewing room. Lace makers, furriers, clothiers, perfumers, jewelers, shoemakers, stay makers, all rode forth from London as reinforcements summoned by her anxious father, to outfit Anne for battle even though she herself stood haughty and recalcitrant in their midst, with no intention of fighting.

"When Henry of England desires a woman there is never any other answer but 'Yes,'" Sir Thomas counseled, circling Anne appraisingly as she stood upon a stool while a seamstress knelt to adjust the hem of her new, sunset orange gown.

"Then I shall teach him a new word—No!" Anne announced, prompting George, lounging in a chair draped with swags of silk and lace, to burst into great, rollicking peals of laughter, thus earning himself a sharp cuff upon the ear courtesy of his father.

"But he is the King!" Elizabeth Boleyn protested, wringing her hands despairingly. "Please, Anne, do not provoke his anger! By refusing him you risk all that we possess, all that your father has worked so hard for, all these years!"

"Ah, the life of a court toady!" Anne sneered. "Such backbreaking labor almost makes one envy a bricklayer!"

In his chair George sniggered helplessly, despite his father's warning stare.

"Enough!" shouted Sir Thomas Boleyn. "You are a clever girl, Anne, so I know that you will understand what I am about to say to you. Your matrimonial prospects are nil; men may flirt with you, but there are no suitors banging at the door begging for your hand. So now you must choose: a life of gaiety at court, where you will do everything that you can to make yourself pleasing to His Majesty, or a bleak life of silence, contemplation, and prayer, locked inside a nunnery. The choice is yours. You should account yourself fortunate that the King casts even a glance at you! Mark me, you are no beauty. A tall, skinny stick topped with long black hair is what you are; your skin is sallow, your bosom small, your eyes too large, and your neck too long. Then there is that ugly wen upon your throat, and that nub of a sixth finger you hide so well with your oh-so-cunning sleeves. And yet . . . for some unaccountable reason, the King has noticed you; he wants you, and what Henry wants he shall have! I as your father command you, Anne, to make the most of this opportunity. Take it and make it turn to gold!"

"You would serve me to him upon a platter if it would enrich your coffers and elevate your station," Anne said bitterly.

"Indeed I would! You are a gambler, Anne, so play him, Anne, play him; and take Henry Tudor for all that he is worth! Just don't lose like you did with Percy. I think it is safe to say that you will not have another chance. Now I will leave you to your thoughts, though I trust that you have already decided."

And with those words he left her, with his wife trailing after him, admonishing Anne to listen to her father, for he was a wise man and surely knew best.

"Sacrificed upon the altar of parental ambition!" Anne sighed. "It is either the King's bed or a convent cot!"

"Nan, listen to me." George went to her and lifted her down from the dressmaker's stool. His hands lingered on her waist as hers did upon his shoulders as they stood close together, leaning into each other's embrace. "I have been at court long enough to know that it is the chase that delights him most, so lead him, Nan, and lead him long; resist and run until he wearies. His interest will wane, and he will turn his eyes towards a different, and easier quarry. He is not the most patient of men, and there are women aplenty who line his path ready to throw themselves at his feet."

"Aye, my sweet brother, have no fear." She reached up to kiss his cheek. "Perseverance will outpace Ardent Desire. I will give Henry Tudor the run of his life!"

"I know you will, Nan." He smiled. "There's none who can match you, Nan, none!"

Seeing them standing there, so close, so lost in one another, made my blood boil. By now I was well accustomed to these displays of tenderness and intimacy. I used to watch them, as vigilant as a hawk. The way they walked together, talked together, danced, sat with their heads together whispering confidences, composing songs and sonnets with their pens scratching over parchment, or bent over their lutes; the way they touched hands, embraced, and kissed; the way George's hands would linger at her waist when he lifted Anne down from her horse; and the way sometimes of an evening or a rainy day by the hearthside he would lay his head in her lap and she would lean down with her hair forming an ebony curtain around him . . . they looked like lovers. It was as if they were made to be together and, as blasphemous as it sounds, God had made a mistake when He made them brother and sister so that full passionate love between them was forbidden. I never saw, either before or since, such a strong devotion between two people. It was as if they were bonded together, fused, with a chain of unbendable, unbreakable links; nothing could divide them. Together they were whole and complete, but apart something vital was lacking. Was everyone else blind? Why was I the only one who could see it?

"If I did not know better, I would swear you two were lovers!" I shouted at them. But even as the words were upon my lips I wondered, did I really know better? Did I? Then I ran out of the room, slamming the door behind me just as hard as I could.

George followed me and caught hold of my wrist. "What are you about?" he demanded angrily.

"You seem overeager to defy your father's wishes, George. You dislike the thought of Anne in the King's bed!" I charged with eyes blazing.

"She will find little happiness there," he answered.

"And her happiness is very important to you." I nodded knowingly. "Or should I say that it is everything to you? Tell me, George, would that not be more apt?"

He frowned at me. "Do not quibble words with me, Jane. You know well that Anne's happiness is of the utmost importance to me. We are alone against the world, I often think, and though I lost my battle, I will do everything I can to help Anne win hers. I have been a pawn to my father's ambition, and you see what it has wrought me—and you with me. Together in this bitter parody of a marriage we are bound."

I reeled back as if he had slapped me. My voice failed me, and I could do nothing but gape at him as hot, angry tears poured down my face.

"I know, Jane," he said softly as he took my hand in his and held it oh, so tenderly. "You yearn for what I can never give. For reasons I will never understand, you claim to love me, though you find fault with nearly all of me and heap scorn and jealousy upon everyone and everything that pleases me. You harp and badger, weep and shriek, jeer and cling, until it is all I can do not to strike you. And that displeases me; that I should be roused to the brink of such an ugly thing!"

"Would that I could be the only one who pleases you!" I sobbed, snatching my hand away. "Would that I came first before your sister, your dissolute, foppish friends, and all your foolish and unsavory pursuits—the gambling, wine, and whores, and the music and poetry upon which you squander so much of your time! Your will is weak, George, and I would be the one to make you strong. Banish them all, George. You need none of them—only me!"

"Oh, but I do," he insisted. "I need them all. And I do not want to be your everything, Jane. Verily, I find your love as stifling and oppressive as a tomb. When I am with you I feel as if I am boxed inside a coffin. It is a sad truth that we are mismatched, and not one common interest do we share. You married for love—or, if you want to quibble words, you married your ideal of love—while I married as my father dictated. Let us be friendly, Jane, but let us abandon all pretense and go our separate ways, and perhaps we will both find happiness after a fashion. I wish you well, Jane, and would you did the same for me."

"I've no doubt that you will go your own way, as you have always done!" I cried, and I would have slapped his face had he not divined my intentions and caught hold of my wrist. "Would that I could be like Anne; perhaps then you would love me!" Stumbling, blind with tears, I fled back to my chamber and threw myself weeping upon the bed. If only, if only, if only I could be like Anne! How very different my life would be, and George would love me!

With her sumptuous new finery, Anne returned to court and resumed her duties in Queen Catherine's household, though it was the King who most often availed himself of her services.

He summoned her to his chamber to play her lute and sing for him, or read aloud when his eyes were wearied, or to walk with him by the river or in the pleasure gardens. Dutifully, she hunted and hawked and danced with him. She diced and risked fortunes at cards with him, and applauded his performance at the tennis court, bowling green, tiltyard, and archery butts. Yet through it all she remained aloof, toying with him like a cat plays with dead things. At Henry's side she seemed more a wax figure than a flesh-and-blood woman.

It was only with George and their merry band of friends that she truly came alive. With them her spirits soared and her laughter rang like a bell. Henry noticed this too, and I think it was then that his heart first began to harden against these men who had long been his most loyal servants and friends, the gentlemen of his privy chamber who attended him at all his most private functions—his baths and bowel movements, robings and disrobings—

and who each took turns sleeping on a pallet at the foot of his great bed whenever he retired alone. Herein, I believe, is the answer to why, years later, it was so easy for him to condemn George, Weston, Brereton, and Norris—they had Anne in a way that he never could.

But Anne continued to turn her lips away from his and to shun and evade his embrace. She steadfastly refused to become his mistress, though Henry avowed, "It is not just your body I covet, Anne, but you, Anne, you! Your vivacity and bold, daring, untamed spirit! I can talk to you of books and ideas, for you are no docile, simpering sycophant; you have a mind of your own and are not afraid to speak it, and I want to possess and know all of you. I want to stir your soul as well as your body and heart!"

"Your wife I cannot be; your mistress I will not be." Those were her words, cold and to the point, like a dagger in the heart.

"But if I were free of Catherine . . ." he persisted.

"But you are not." Anne shrugged and continued along the rose-bordered path, pausing to inhale the perfume of a lush pink rose.

They were in the rose garden at Hever once again, and I was secreted behind the shrubbery, just like before.

Anne had all of a sudden quit the court without the King's consent and, summoning George to be her escort, returned to Hever, leaving Henry to come scurrying after, the moment that he missed her.

"But if I were . . ."

"But you are not and cannot be," Anne said crisply, snapping the rose's stem and holding it against the skirt of her pink satin gown. "Her Majesty strikes me as being a woman in excellent health, nor have I heard her express the desire to renounce the world and retire to a convent."

"For the third and last time"—Henry seized her arm and spun her round to face him—"if I were free of Catherine, would you marry me and give me sons?"

"Verily, Sire, I do not know," said Anne, idly twirling the rose by its stem. "I should have to think on it."

She pulled her arm free of his grasp and strolled onward, humming to herself and twirling the pink rose.

This was the spark that lit the fuse of what would at first be called "The King's Secret Matter," then "The King's Great Matter" when it became common knowledge.

Henry confided to Anne that for some time his conscience had been troubling him. He feared that his marriage was accursed by God, and for this reason he had been denied a living son, the male heir that was vital to safeguard the succession.

It all began with a verse from Leviticus that Henry interpreted to suit his desires. "If a man shall take his brother's wife, it is an unclean thing: he hath uncovered his brother's nakedness; they shall be childless." These words hammered at his mind, while lust for Anne hammered at his loins. To Henry's mind, being childless and sonless amounted to the same thing.

Catherine had been first and briefly wed to his elder brother Arthur, and by marrying her, Henry had convinced himself, he had unknowingly committed a sinful and incestuous act. God had shown his displeasure by denying him living male issue; all the baby boys had been born dead or died shortly after as divine punishment. The Pope who had issued the dispensation that allowed them to marry had committed a grave error, he insisted, and it was one that must be rectified as soon as possible. The Pope must grant him a divorce from Catherine so that he might lawfully remarry and beget sons while there was still time. And Anne, he had already decided, would be the mother of those sons. Already he could see them in his mind's eye, a brood of hale and hearty red- and black-haired boys, replicas of himself, lusty, broad shouldered, and strong-minded. To Henry it all seemed such a simple matter.

❧ 6 ❧

Like a shuttlecock hurtling to and fro, Anne would, upon a moment's whim, leave court and return to Hever. Then the King would come, hot on her heels, or else his messenger would follow, bearing lavish gifts and ardent love letters.

But every time, Anne would just laugh and dismiss the messenger with a haughty wave of her hand and the words, "No answer."

Often she allotted these outpourings of the King's anguished heart no more than a cursory glance, and she was very careless with them, leaving them lying about where anyone could find them.

I remember a day when she sat idly by the hearth in the Great Hall, with Henry's latest letter in her hand and the accompanying gift lying at her feet.

" 'Because I cannot always be in your presence,' " Anne read aloud, aping Henry's voice—she really was an excellent mimic— " 'I send you the thing that comes nearest—my portrait set in bracelets, wishing myself in their place. Signed, Your Servant and Friend, Henry Rex.' "

With a bored and indifferent sniff and a shrug of her shoulders, Anne let the letter fall to the floor, ignoring her father's pursed lips, her mother's worried frown, and Mary's quizzical stare as she again grandly intoned the words, "No answer," and sent the messenger on his way.

"Anne!" Elizabeth Boleyn wrung her hands and looked near to tears. "It is cruel of you to keep the poor King dangling with no reply!"

"Indeed, Mother, I never said it was not."

"Anne." Sir Thomas Boleyn approached her, rubbing his palms, with a crafty gleam in his eyes. "Your mother is correct. It is most unkind. . . ."

"Verily, you should know, Father. Upon unkindness you are expert!" Anne answered flippantly, while toying with her sapphire velvet sleeves.

"Anne"—he paused, biting his lip and making a great effort to control his temper—"would you like me to compose a reply to His Majesty? Then all you need do is copy it in your own elegant hand and sign your name."

At this offer Anne threw back her head and fairly screamed with laughter.

"It is no jesting matter, girl!" he snarled. "Look at those diamonds!" He snatched up Henry's neglected gift and shook the bracelets in her face. "Just look at their clarity, their sparkle; clearly these are diamonds of the first water!"

Mary, her mother, and I obligingly clustered round and oohed and ahhed in admiration at the King's florid and heavy-jowled countenance ringed in twinkling diamonds.

"Oh, Father." Anne sighed as, stretching languorously, she got to her feet. "It is a pity our good King Henry hasn't the Second Edward's tastes, since you are so much more appreciative of his favors than I am!" And with those words she swept grandly from the room, leaving her father speechless and boiling with rage, and her mother wringing her hands and repeating endlessly, "Oh dear!" I myself maintained an air of dignified silence, while my husband, it grieves me much to say, rolled on the floor in gleeful laughter, and a blank-faced and bewildered Mary besought an explanation regarding Anne's reference to the tastes of King Edward the Second.

But the Boleyns needn't have worried. Anne knew how and when to play her cards. Upon New Year's Day 1527 she decided the time had come to answer all the King's letters.

But she did not take up her pen to write to Henry, but to the goldsmith instead, for it was he who would fashion her answer. A brooch, but not just any brooch. Exquisitely wrought of gleaming gold, a little lady with long black enameled hair, dressed in a gown of scarlet enamel spangled with seed pearls and diamond chips, sat in a boat christened *Love*, being rocked upon a tempest-tossed sapphire sea, with her hands clasped and upraised as if to implore "Have mercy upon me!"

So there could be no doubt as to her meaning, when she knelt at the King's feet to present her gift, at a private audience where no one but her family were present, Anne wore a pearl- and diamond-spangled scarlet gown with her long black hair unbound.

A smile of pure delight spread across King Henry's face as he gazed first at Anne, then down at the brooch upon its bed of tufted black velvet, then back at Anne again. But when he reached for her, Anne swiftly stepped back.

"If you make me Queen of England I shall brave the storm that is your love and give you sons!" she announced; then, after bobbing the briefest of curtsies, she turned her back, in direct violation of royal etiquette, and walked out of the presence chamber.

❧ 7 ❧

Anne immediately resumed her old ways, going back and forth to Hever, ignoring the enamored King's increasingly ardent love letters, and dismissing the messenger with "No answer."

Anne had played her card. Now it was time for Henry to make his move.

A secret court was convened, presided over by Cardinal Wolsey, with a panel of bishops to weigh the evidence and render a verdict.

Henry presented himself, slump-shouldered and morose, as a man whose conscience was sorely troubled by the nagging thought that he, by taking his dead brother's wife, had unwittingly sinned against God. Queen Catherine, he solemnly avowed, was a fine woman and he would like nothing better than to hear that all was well and that she could remain at his side as his wife always, but the qualms that assailed his conscience were just too great to be ignored. Thus, he looked to them, the cardinals and bishops of England, to free him from this torment. It was a grand performance. Only those in Anne's inner circle knew that she was the cause of it all, this intricate, tangled web of theological and legal quibbling that would soon rise from a whisper to a scream. Even Wolsey never suspected that it was Anne Boleyn Henry aimed to wed; he was led to believe it was a French princess Henry coveted so that he might have legitimate male heirs and a dynastic alliance all in one stroke. Queen Catherine was also kept unawares until the wily Spanish Ambassador whispered the truth in her ear. But by then Henry had lost his round.

After three days of heated debate, the court concluded that the marriage was sound, since a papal dispensation had been issued beforehand. Henry was assured that his conscience could rest in peace.

But Henry refused to accept the verdict, and Wolsey bore the brunt of his displeasure. Wolsey, that upstart son of an Ipswich butcher, who used the Church as a stepping stone to power and cared more for worldly goods than the word of God, had promised Henry the verdict he desired.

But then failed to deliver.

To make matters worse, now Queen Catherine had been dealt into the game, and she had a very powerful card to play. Her nephew Charles V, the Holy Roman Emperor, would never sit passively by and let his aunt be humiliated and cast aside.

Never for a moment would Catherine's convictions waver. She was Henry's lawful wife and Queen of this realm, and such she would remain until her dying day. Nor would she oblige the King by slinking away to a nunnery. Though her faith was strong, and she was without a doubt devout, she had no vocation; she would not, like some she could name, use the Church as a means to achieve an end. She loved her husband dearly and was sorry to court his displeasure by disobeying him, but God and her conscience must come first.

At that time the situation in Rome was dire. The Holy City had been sacked; mercenary soldiers in the Emperor's service ran amok, raping and pillaging; the streets ran red with the blood of the slain; and the air was filled with smoke, flies, and the cries of the dying. Pope Clement himself was a prisoner, and he was not about to risk the Emperor's further wrath by siding with Henry.

It should all have ended there, but Henry was not about to let his desires be thwarted. Come what may, he would have Anne Boleyn.

*   *   *

Around this time Tom Wyatt, dallying with Anne and their friends in the palace gardens, playfully snatched a little bejeweled tablet that dangled from a delicate gold chain Anne wore about her waist, claiming it was high time she gave him a love token. He pressed it to his lips, then, laughing, held it high, beyond her reach, as she leapt and grasped for it, once even daring to duck his head and swiftly steal a kiss.

"Keep it if you like." Anne shrugged. "It is but a little thing, and of no great consequence. And while that bauble may be beyond my reach, greater jewels than that are within my grasp." And upon her right hand she proudly displayed an enormous emerald. "The stone of constancy, His Majesty says, and thereby a most fitting symbol of his love for me."

She did not confide that in exchange for this great, gaudy, glittering green ring, King Henry had snatched from her finger a dainty ruby heart set in lacy gold filigree. "I shall take this heart until you vouchsafe me your own," he said as he forced it onto his little finger, the only one it would fit upon.

A few days later the King and his gentlemen gathered for a match upon the bowling green while Anne and a bevy of ladies assembled to watch and cheer them on.

The King and Tom Wyatt were both expert players, and a moment arose when it was uncertain whose bowl had rolled nearest the jack; it was so close, sight alone could not settle the matter.

"Wyatt, I tell you it is mine!" Henry's voice boomed as he pointed to the smooth, round wooden bowl lying in the grass, seemingly just a hand's span from the upright white jack. As he pointed he waggled his little finger, making sure Anne's ruby heart caught Wyatt's eye.

With a cocky smile, Wyatt withdrew Anne's jeweled tablet from inside his doublet.

"If Your Majesty will give me leave," he said, extending the golden chain, "I shall measure it with this, and hope that it shall be mine." And boldly he kissed the jeweled tablet.

Already flushed from the heat of his heavy brocade and silken garments and a vigorous game on a warm day, Henry's face flamed scarlet. His eyes narrowed and that cruel little mouth became crueler still.

"It may be, it may well be that I have been deceived!" And with that he turned his back on Wyatt and stormed from the bowling green. Abruptly he stopped and spun round and went to confront Anne.

"Mistress, you will explain! How haps it that trinket is in Wyatt's possession and that he wears it upon his heart?"

"Thievery," Anne answered smoothly. "The same manner in which Your Majesty acquired my ring."

For a long moment no one dared move or breathe. Anne had just called the King of England a thief!

"As for why he wears it above his heart," Anne continued, "I can only suppose that were he to wear it around his waist, as intended, people would laugh; the effect is not quite so becoming without skirts."

Henry threw back his head and roared with laughter.

"By my soul, Anne, what a woman you are!" He offered her his arm and together they strolled back into the palace, all smiles and merry spirits.

Watching them, George shook his head and smiled.

"There is no one like Anne!" he declared with pride.

It was all I could do not to snatch up one of the wooden jacks and beat him over the head with it. I had a vision of myself doing so, so vividly real it was ghastly and made me feel sick with shame. In my mind's eye I saw myself raising the jack, and bringing it down with all the force I could muster, and hearing his skull crack, and his voice cry out, pleading with pain, as blood gushed out, and I raised the jack and brought it down again and again and again, hoping and wishing with all my might that I could bash all thoughts of Anne out of his brain.

By now the whole court knew that the King wanted Anne, and bets were being laid about how long she would resist before she became his mistress. But Anne herself only hinted at her true intentions, saying once to her sister, "You went first, but I aim to go further."

Even Queen Catherine knew. Always before she had stoically

endured her husband's infidelities, pretending that she did not hear or see. But this was different; Anne was different.

One afternoon Her Majesty bade us join her for a game of cards. Obediently we sat down around the table. At her request, I dealt the cards. All continued amicably until Anne triumphantly slapped down a card.

"Mistress Anne." Queen Catherine regarded her sadly. "You have the good fortune to stop at a King, but you are not like the others, I think. You will have all . . ."

". . . or nothing," they finished as one.

Their eyes locked, Catherine's intent and searching, Anne's scorching with ambition.

At last, Catherine sighed and shook her head, her gray eyes misty with sorrow and what, for just a moment, looked like pity, but it passed so quickly I could not be sure.

"That will be all," she said quietly. "Leave me now. I am weary," she murmured, pressing a hand against her brow, her fingers rubbing as if they could erase the lines that time and worry had etched there, while her other hand reached for the rosary beads ever present at her waist.

As we walked away Anne said, "She is as stubborn as one of her Spanish mules! Even a blind fool could see the King no longer loves her. Why doesn't she just accept it and get the best terms while she can? Henry is prepared to be generous; he will allow her the title of Princess Dowager and love her like a sister—which is what she is—his sister by marriage. Why does she not give in? I do not understand her at all!"

And she would not understand until she herself stood where Queen Catherine stood now.

Henry's next move was to dispatch Wolsey to France to barter for a French bride; while at the same time another messenger was, unbeknowst to the great and powerful Cardinal Wolsey, sent secretly to petition the Pope in Rome.

Henry chose to keep Wolsey in the dark simply because he feared the Cardinal would not work as hard to bring about the divorce if he knew Henry's intended bride was Anne Boleyn.

When Anne learned of this she scoffed, "You all but bend your knee to Wolsey! Are you King of England or does the butcher's boy wear the Crown? I thought it was the Chancellor's task to do the King's bidding, not the other way around!"

Thus she brought the King around to her way of thinking, and Wolsey's star began its slow descent.

❧ 8 ❧

While Anne played for a King, her heart would suffer another blow when Tom Wyatt chose to graciously withdraw from the field where he had battled Henry for Anne's
love.

Ever the poet, he renounced her in a poem:

> *Whoso list to hunt? I know where is a hind!*
> *But as for me, alas! I may no more;*
> *The vain travail hath wearied me so sore;*
> *I am of them that farthest cometh behind.*
> *Yet may I by no means my wearied mind*
> *Draw from the deer; but as she fleeth afore*
> *Fainting I follow; I leave off therefore,*
> *Since in a net I seek to hold the wind.*
> *Who list to hunt, I put him out of doubt,*
> *As well as I, may spend his time in vain!*
> *And graven in diamonds in letters plain,*
> *There is written her fair neck round about:*
> *'Noli Me Tangere; for Caesar's I am,*
> *And wild for to hold, though I seem tame.'*

I was there the night he stood up and recited it to the court. And I saw sorrow, true and deep, in his brown eyes.

Their eyes met across the banquet table where Anne sat beside the King, who possessively rested one meaty, jewel-laden pink paw upon her knee. They shared a long glance of regret, mourning for what could never be.

Though Wyatt had never replaced Percy in her heart, Anne truly did love him in her way. And, had he been free, I am certain they would have wed.

When he spoke the last four lines, Anne's hand reached up to touch the choker of diamonds encircling her neck, and a pained expression flashed across her face. Then it was gone and she cast her eyes sideways at Henry, who was nodding in approval at the words "Noli Me Tangere (Touch Me Not), for Caesar's I am."

When he finished Wyatt bowed low to the sovereign, and Henry leapt to his feet, applauding loudly. The court, ever quick to follow the King's lead, did the same.

Only Anne remained seated and silent, then slowly she stood. I was seated only two places down and I heard her softly plead a headache and that she must go at once to bed.

As she passed him, Henry seized her wrist and said in a voice that made me shiver, "Rarely when I hunt does the quarry escape me, no matter how fleet of foot or cunningly it hides. Make no mistake, Mistress Anne, I will catch you, and you will be mine!"

Anne curtsied quickly and fled.

Tom Wyatt's eyes followed her as his body dared not do. He pressed a hand briefly to his heart as if it pained him, then he forced himself to smile and gave himself over to the congratulations of his friends.

The clock had just struck midnight when Anne appeared at George's door, huddled in her satin dressing gown and trembling violently.

Wordlessly, he gathered her in his arms.

Her words came out in a rush. A nightmare. Anne in a fawn satin gown running frantically through the forest, pursued by baying hounds, hoofbeats, and hunting horns. Then she was cornered, her

THE BOLEYN WIFE   69

back against a tree, and the King was there before her, steadily advancing, willful and determined, pressing into her, holding her fast, and lifting her skirts. It was then that she awoke, screaming.

Murmuring soothing words, George led her to sit beside the fire. There was wine warming in a small cauldron and he ladled some into a goblet and pressed it into her hands.

Both of them ignored me standing in the doorway.

"I want to stop, George," she sobbed.

"Then stop," he said as he sank to his knees before her and, taking the goblet and setting it aside, took both her hands in his.

"I cannot! It has gone too far! I thought when the court failed to deliver the desired verdict that would be the end of it, and I could wave farewell and dance away from him, but he will stop at nothing to have me! I have become trapped in my own net! And Father and Uncle Norfolk never stop pressing me. Winning is all that matters, they keep telling me—it doesn't matter how I play the game, only that I win! 'Do not fail, Anne!' they caution with such hardness in their eyes it takes all the will I have not to let them see me give way to tears. They come at me from all sides, urging me to 'Give in, Anne, give in! It is a great honor to be the mistress of a King!' until it is all I can do not to stamp my feet and scream and tear the hair from my head! Were he not King I would tell him what I truly think of him! Every time I see him I must bite my tongue to keep the words from spewing forth else he send me to the Tower and have them chop off my head, and yet I cannot help but think that at least then I would die with the truth upon my lips; that would be better than living a lie!"

"You mean you no longer want to be Queen?" I asked.

Sobs shook her and Anne buried her face in her hands.

"If the prize is within my grasp I shall take it; it would be folly to reject it, and there would be no forgetting or forgiving if I did, but do not ask me whether it is worth it because I no longer know! I am so tired, George, so very tired, yet the battle rages on and I must keep fighting!"

"Then you must rest, darling Nan." He stood up and gathered her tenderly in his arms and carried her to his bed. "Sleep now," he said as he laid her down and drew the covers up over her. "And I shall sit here"—he brought a chair close to the bedside—"and see that no one disturbs you."

And there he sat, stroking her hair, until sleep claimed her.

"Damn them all for doing this to you, my sweet sister," I, still lurking in the doorway, heard him whisper.

"Now you have what you have always wanted," I jibed. "Your sister is in your bed! Do not let my presence keep you from joining her!"

"Bite your viper's tongue!" George hissed, and flung his slippers at my head.

I turned my back and started back to my own bed, but my feet had scarcely crossed the threshold when I felt his fingers biting into the soft flesh of my arm.

He pushed the door shut so our conversation would not disturb his dear, precious Anne.

"Why do you always do this?" he demanded. "Why do you say these awful things? What has Anne ever done to you to make you despise her so?"

"She has stolen what is rightfully mine!" I rounded on him furiously. "She has stolen my husband!"

George laughed wryly and threw up his hands.

When I heard him laugh at me, mocking me, I wanted to throw myself at him and claw at his face, raking long, bloody furrows into that handsome visage with my nails. In my mind's eye, I saw myself doing so, and I hated myself for it. How could I have such violent, bloody thoughts about hurting the person I loved most? It was Anne who deserved pain and punishment, not my beloved George.

"You are a madwoman!" he declared. "You talk naught but nonsense. Anne is my sister. You talk of her as if she were my mistress!"

"She is!" I shouted. "She is your mistress! Mistress of your heart! No brother loves his sister as you do her—it is unnatural, George, unnatural! I should not have to compete with my sister-in-law for my husband's attention, or his affection, but I do. Every day of my life, Anne is always between us. I know you bed other women, but I never worry about them because I know that for you there is only Anne, and that with her no other woman can compare! You don't want a wife or a mistress, George; the only woman you want is Anne! And I hate her for it!"

George just stood there staring at me, then he shook his head and laughed at me. "You are deranged," he said, and then he left me. He went back to Anne, and I fell weeping onto my bed to cry myself to sleep.

But there would be no true rest for Anne. Henry continued to press her to grant him the ultimate favor, and all of her family, except George, took his side.

I spied on them one moonlit night in the gardens of Greenwich.

Anne stood steadfast in a gleaming gown of silver tissue, with diamond stars sparkling in her hair, while the King groveled at her feet like a lovesick swain.

Suddenly Anne seemed to wilt and pressed a hand to her brow. In the moonlight she seemed very pale.

Henry saw his chance and seized it. He clutched her close, pressing and grinding his loins, forcing her to feel his hardness through her skirts. His lips found hers, then traveled down her neck to her breasts, trussed high above the low, square-cut diamond-bordered bodice. He peeled her gown down from her shoulders until her breasts were fully exposed, with the cool evening air stiffening her nipples. She tried to pull away but he held her fast, his cruel little mouth closing round each rosy pebble of flesh and leaving it glistening with drool. But when his hands began to fumble with her skirts she somehow found the strength to shove him away.

"Anne, have mercy upon me! For three years I have lived like a monk, all for love of you! Do not be so cruel to one who has been nothing but kind to you. Give yourself to me, tonight, Anne!"

Anne drew up her gown, tucking her breasts back inside and folding her arms protectively across them.

"And tomorrow have you show me what a nimble dancer you are as you dance out of your promise to make me queen?"

"You are queen of my heart already!" he protested.

"But not of England! If you make me Queen of England I shall share your bed and give you sons; it was that we agreed upon, and I will keep my end of the bargain only if you keep yours!"

"In time, Anne, all shall be yours in time! But for now . . ." He reached for her again, but Anne slapped his hand away. "Is it not enough that I promise you my undying love?"

"Would you chance your son being born a bastard?" Anne asked icily.

"No, no." Henry sighed, his great padded shoulders sagging in defeat. "That I cannot risk. For the sake of my unborn son I must damp my carnal lust, though I am in the sight of God a free man. . . ."

"But not in the eyes of men," Anne reminded him. "And until that day comes, I shall go alone to my bed." And with only the briefest of curtsies she left him.

Gleefully, I gathered up my skirts and raced back inside, eager to taunt George with what I had just seen. But George was not there and his valet could not—or would not—say where he had gone.

The valet was putting away some freshly laundered linens when I came in, and every time I asked his master's whereabouts he studiously lowered his eyes and murmured, "I do not know, my lady." As he bent over the chest, I drew back my foot and kicked his plump posterior as hard as I could; then, seething with annoyance, I stormed into my own chamber and slammed the door.

I was very curt with my maid as she undressed me.

Joan was a timid country girl I had brought from Great Hallingbury to serve me; she had previously been a dairy maid and was not accustomed to waiting on great ladies. Her nervous fingers often fumbled and she was ever prone to dropping things. Father had always taught me that we must be patient with our inferiors, but tonight I was in no mood to remember the teachings of childhood, and when she pricked her finger on my ruby, pearl, and emerald flower brooch and dropped it, and one of the stones popped out of its setting, I swung round and struck her soundly across the face.

As she cringed and cowered before me, a trickle of blood snaking slowly from one nostril, I should have deplored my anger and tried to comfort her, but tonight I was so incensed by George's absence that I just could not control myself, and instead I called her "a fumble-fingers" and said she was "as stupid as the cows she used to milk." I seized my heavy silver-backed hairbrush from my dressing table and flung it at her head as I ordered her from my sight. "Go back to your cows until you learn how to properly attend a lady!" I shouted as she ran out, whimpering, with tears streaming down her face.

I finished undressing myself, and in my temper and haste I tangled the laces that fastened my ornate over-sleeves to my bodice and ended by tearing them badly. Furiously, I flung them down on the floor and kicked them into a corner in disgust. They were my best and most expensive sleeves—red velvet trimmed with golden tinsel and intricate gold embroidery—but at that moment all I cared about was the fact that George was elsewhere, making merry with his dissolute friends, no doubt.

Then, in my nightshift and dressing gown, I went into my husband's room, ordered his valet to bank up the fire and be gone, and settled down in a chair to wait.

Hours passed and I fell into a doze. The dawn was already breaking when I finally heard voices outside the door. I sat up, wincing at the crick in my neck, and watched with mounting fury as the door swung open to reveal Francis Weston and Will Brereton supporting a very drunken George. He sagged there between them, his arms slung across their shoulders, head drooping, feet dragging, too drunk to walk unassisted.

Brereton was bemoaning the loss of a pair of fine Spanish leather boots that he had wagered when his coins were gone.

"Be of good cheer, Will," Weston advised him. "All things Spanish are on their way out—or will be if the King has his way. You have merely anticipated the fashion!"

"Aye." Brereton nodded. "He seeks to discard Queen Catherine like an old boot!"

It was then that they noticed me.

"Ah, my Lady Rochford!" Sir Francis exclaimed, using my new title. The King had given George the title of Viscount Rochford to please Anne. "I bid you good morning!"

I was in no mood to bandy words. "Put my husband down upon the bed and get out!" I ordered sharply.

They smirked and exchanged a knowing glance as if to say "Is she not a bitch?"

Well, let them think what they would of me! Harpy, shrew, termagant, scold, bitch; I knew they called me all these things and more, lamenting that George was bound to me. How dare they keep my husband out, carousing the whole night through, then bring him home as insensate as a corpse with drink? What wife would not be upset? What right had they to smirk and roll their eyes at me when it was clearly their fault that George was in such a state? Did they honestly expect me to make them welcome, invite them to sit down by the fire, while I sent a servant running to fetch wine and cakes?

"As you will, Lady Rochford!" Weston shrugged. "Come, Will, let us not be remiss in giving satisfaction to the lady."

"Aye, never let it be said that we failed to give satisfaction to a lady!" Brereton chortled as they deposited George upon the bed.

"Or gentleman either!" Weston added cheekily.

"Speak for yourself, Francis." Brereton patted him upon the back as he headed for the door. "You and I do not enjoy all the same games."

Impatiently, I held the door open wide.

"Upon my soul, Lady Rochford, never have I seen a more vicious vicountess with such a viperous tongue and so much venom in her eyes!" Then, chuckling at his own wit, Brereton tipped his cap and sauntered away, whistling a merry tune.

I turned back to the bed impatiently, wondering why Weston lingered. And then I saw—George had begun to stir and had clapped a hand round Weston's wrist and was trying to pull him down on top of him.

"Nay, George," he said lightly, pulling back, "you are drunk, and I would not take advantage of you in such a state."

"Why ever not?" George murmured, still holding fast to Weston's wrist. "I want you to."

"Well, that makes all the difference in the world! But, nay, George, tempt me not! I would not have you for my lover, I would

rather keep you as a friend; friends last longer. Now release me."
He gently extricated his wrist. "Your wife is impatient to have me
depart."

"As I am impatient to have her go!" George cried with surpris-
ing savagery.

"And where would you have me go, George?" I inquired, coming to stand at the foot of the bed and tug off his muddy boots.

"To the Devil!" he shouted, wrenching his foot free and kicking out at me.

I jumped back, my left hand smarting from a well-aimed boot
heel. "Go now, Sir Francis!" I commanded, pointing adamantly at
the door.

"Your wish is my command!" he said, gallantly doffing his cap.
"Such scenes of domestic bliss are not for my eye."

"No doubt you are well accustomed to such scenes on the rare
occasions when you deign to visit your wife!" I cried.

"Nay, Madame." He shook his head impishly. "When I am with
my wife I am as good as gold. Verily, she thinks me a saint and wor-
ships the ground I walk upon. It would break my heart to disillu-
sion her, so it is best she keep to the country while I tarry here at
court."

"Well, you shall not tarry here!" I shouted, flinging George's
boot at him. It thudded against the door just as Weston shut it.

"George . . ." I turned back to him and shook his shoulder, but
he only slapped my hand away and snarled at me to "Leave off!"
Undaunted, I slipped off my robe and climbed into bed beside
him and wrapped my arms around him.

With great effort, he pulled himself up, shouting in a voice loud
and slurred that he was going to find another bed, but as he took a
step forward, he staggered, fell to the floor, and vomited.

"Oh, George! George!" I railed at him, pounding the bed with
my fists. "Why do you let them do this to you? The loathsome
creatures!"

At the sight of my husband lying huddled upon the floor, retch-
ing and heaving up the wine and rich food Weston and his friends
had urged upon him, my heart surged with tenderness. I felt a
great need to comfort and protect him even as I clucked over his

misdeeds like a mother hen, nurturing and at the same time chiding her chick. I knelt beside him on the floor, stroking his hair, shoulders, and back, until the spasms ceased; then I struggled to help him up and back onto the bed. He lay there, moaning and groaning in misery, grudgingly tolerating my soothing hands and the kisses I showered upon his brow.

"Lie still, my love, and let me take care of you!"

He lay still and let me bathe his face. At my tender coaxing, he sat up so I could ease the doublet from his shoulders and draw the stained and stinking white shirt over his head. Then, with a groan, he fell back against the pillows and was still once again, offering no resistance as I peeled away his breeches and hose, pausing to kiss and glide my hands over his flesh. I could not help myself. I kissed and caressed every part of him, and he did not resist me. His manhood sprang to life between my hands and, with an exclamation of triumph and delight, I lifted my nightshift over my head, casting it aside with carefree abandon as I straddled him.

"Give me a child, George!" I pleaded. "If you cannot love me, give me a child who will!"

I so longed to have a baby, a son, a little living, breathing replica of the man I loved, with one crucial difference—my son would actually want and need my love, and not push me away. He would fill the void in my heart and the empty, endless, dragging hours when I yearned for George, but he was elsewhere because his court duties and the more pleasing company of others took him away from me; and, if the truth be set down stark and plain, he did not want to be with me; he did not love, or even like me.

I took his hands and placed them upon my breasts, forcing him to knead them with his strong fingers, then guiding them down to probe and play with my cunny. Then, I do not know whether it was lust or instinct that took over, but with a sudden lunge he rolled me over onto my back and thrust inside me. I screamed with joy as I wrapped my arms and legs tight around him, determined never to let go, and thrust my hips up to meet his.

Afterwards he fell asleep, his head upon my breast, and I, glorying in his weight and warmth, and with tears of happiness still wet upon my face, met slumber with the most radiant of smiles, and a prayer that God would see fit to allow George's seed to take root inside my womb and blossom into a child who would be the savior of my heart and life. I so desperately needed someone to love who would love me in return!

But the harsh sunlight of full morning brought unwelcome truths. I awoke to find George splashing cold water on his face and cursing his "wretched head."

"Come back to bed, my love," I urged, letting the sheet fall to reveal my nakedness as I patted the bed.

Wincing, George bent and picked up my robe and threw it at me. "I must ready myself to attend the King. Either cover yourself or leave, Jane; my valet will be here soon."

"Send word that you are ill! It would not be an untruth. Stay with me. I want you here!" I pouted and purred, trying hard to tempt him. I left the bed then, heedless of my nakedness, and went to stand behind him and let my hands knead his shoulders. "Sleep again with me and then take me again! Fill me, George, fill me!"

"Again?" He frowned, rubbing his bloodshot eyes and moaning miserably. "Good God, Jane, was that you?"

I flinched as if he had struck me.

The pain must have shown upon my face, for he turned to me and tried patiently to explain.

"Jane, I was drunk and, in truth, I remember but vaguely what I did or who I did it with. It is all a golden blur interspersed with intervals of darkness. There was a bearbaiting. I found it cruel and distasteful, so I began to drink until a nimbus of glowing gold came to surround me. Then I could laugh, place bets, and make merry with the others. Then there was a pleasure house filled with charming women, and after that a tavern, or two or twenty. I only know that hours passed and I drained many cups. There was music, laughter, singing, and foods spicy and rich, a brawl over a dice game, a charge of cheating, tables and chairs smashed, and another warm body, and after that . . . darkness."

I thought again of myself, mothering him, loving him, and then . . . that beautiful moment when he turned to me. I knew he was drunk, but still I had hoped . . . And now I knew . . . I could have been anyone, any whore or lightskirt; any body, male or female, could have roused him.

Blinded by my tears, I snatched up my robe and ran back to my room. And all the time I was haunted by this thought: he did not even bother to apologize. He was so blunt about his misdeeds; he didn't try to sugarcoat or disguise the truth at all. And yet I knew in my heart he was not to blame. Were it not for men like Weston and Brereton, who shamelessly neglected their wives and thought only of their own pleasure, George would be a better husband to me. He only aped their antics like a trained monkey because he knew no better. I wished with all my heart then that a plague would come and wipe these men, and the maddening distraction that was Anne, from the face of the earth. Then George would be mine entirely.

❧ 9 ❧

Perhaps there is great power in wishing when it is inspired by hate. That summer of 1528 a plague did come, the dreaded Sweating Sickness that took only the young and healthy and spared the old and weak. It began with a headache and a feeling of weakness in the limbs, then the fever came, bringing with it a feeling of oppressive heat and unquenchable thirst, and the whole body began to shake, jerking and quaking violently, while a foul, stinking sweat poured from the groin and armpits.

The King was a great coward when it came to sickness, and in the face of "The Sweat" he fled, racing from place to place, a country manor one night, a hunting lodge the next, hoping to outpace it.

Anne was then at Hever and he sent her a detailed letter of instructions: Eat and drink but sparingly, keep coal braziers burning constantly in every chamber, have the servants wash the walls and floors with vinegar, and above all avoid crowds. But it was already too late, for by the time she received his letter Anne was fighting for her life, and so were her father and George.

The moment I heard George was ill, I rushed instantly to his side. But he did not want me. Even in his delirium, it was as if he could sense it was me; my every touch he pushed away. He would not let me bathe him, nor would he let me feed him. Every time I tried I ended up being scalded when the hot soup sloshed out of the bowl and over my fingers and onto my lap to seep through my skirts. I wished just once, as he tossed and turned upon the stinking sweat-soaked sheets, that he would say my name and call for me, but the only name that ever passed his lips was "Anne!"

Every day and every night I prayed fervently upon my knees, "Please let Anne die and make the world right again! Spare George, but take Anne!" But if God heard my prayers He chose not to heed them.

All the Boleyns soon recovered, but others were not so fortunate.

Mary's husband, William Carey, died within three hours of being stricken and left her destitute, with two little children to care for. And soon she came begging to Hever, careworn and threadbare, no longer "Mary of the Sunshine Hair," as Henry used to call her. With two little children to tend, and a lazy, drunken slattern for a nursemaid, who was more trouble than she was worth, Mary no longer had time to sit in the sun with her hair soaked in lemon juice, and her tresses had darkened to a dull, dark golden brown. If she thought to find mercy at Hever, she was greatly mistaken. Sir Thomas Boleyn dismissed her without a coin or a care to make her own way in the world, telling her plainly he did not care what became of her, reminding her that she had had not one but two chances to be freed from financial woes for life, and had disdained both. "The whores in the streets of London have more sense!" he thundered. And in the end it was Anne, knowing Henry could deny her nothing, who took up her pen and procured a small pension for her sister.

Mary and I passed many hours sitting in the shade of her beloved lemon tree, watching her children play.

"One would think the King would have done more for you considering . . ." I once ventured, glancing pointedly at little russet-haired Catherine and her brother Henry, a robust, rosy-cheeked cherub with a mop of burnished copper curls.

Mary merely smiled at me. "Love was all I ever asked of him, and when he could no longer give me that I would not presume to ask for money."

"But you have borne him two children!" I protested.

"Catherine is his, yes, but who is Harry's sire I do not know. I loved my husband." As she spoke she twisted the plain gold band round her finger. I noticed then that her beautiful white hands had grown red and rough now that she could no longer afford the services of a laundress. "Even though we did not marry for love, to our everlasting joy, we found it after we made our vows. Will was such a sweet, kind man, always smiling and never cross. I think that is why he failed to prosper at court; he lacked the necessary ruthlessness. His only ambition was to be happy, and he was. Many a time he would say to me, 'Mary, I would rather live in poverty with you than be the richest in the land!' I like to think that Harry is his, that something besides my memories is left to me of Will."

Tears filled my eyes, and my heart felt like a great lump of lead inside my breast. There was nothing I would not give; no sacrifice—not even my immortal soul—would be too great, if George and I could have a marriage like Mary and her dear Will.

But my thoughts were not entirely selfish as I sat with Mary. Her gown, I saw, had been hastily and most ineptly dyed black, so that the color was streaked and uneven and I could glimpse traces of the underlying crimson. And, sitting so close to her, I could see that around the low, square-cut bodice the stitches that once held a decorative border had been unpicked, most likely because it had been jeweled and had, like the rest of Mary's valuables, been laid before the pawnbroker.

"Do not be sad for me, Jane." She forced a smile and reached over to pat my hand. "I shall get by. Anne has promised me a place among her ladies when she becomes queen, and she will see that my children are properly educated. Meanwhile, I shall take cheap lodgings in London and hope that good luck will find me."

I had to ask her then, "Do you not mind that Anne has supplanted you in the King's affections?"

"No! Oh no!" Mary laughed and shook her head. "My dear

Jane, I have had my moment of glory; now it is Anne's turn, and that is how it should be. He is a great man, but none can hope to hold his heart for long; it is like a wild stallion that cannot be broken to bridle or saddle, so it is best to enjoy the ride for the little time it lasts. Anne has lived long in my shadow. I was always the beautiful sister, but her future was always despaired of. Our parents thought no one would ever want her, while for me they prophesied that the future would be golden. It is strange, is it not, how the opposite has come to pass? And yet, in my heart, I am afraid. Anne thinks she has tamed him because she has taught him to eat out of her hand, and the sense of triumph and power she feels has gone to her head like strong wine. It will not last—this I know."

And Mary was right. The Boleyn girl everyone dismissed as a fool turned out to be the wisest.

In October, Cardinal Campeggio, the Papal Legate, arrived in London to hear the case. Travel-worn and suffering the agonies of the damned from gout, he went straight to bed and did not rise again for a fortnight, leaving the King festering with impatience.

Wolsey tried to soothe the royal temper, reminding Henry that he, Wolsey, was to share equal power with Campeggio when the court convened. Campeggio was old and sickly, so any opposition he presented would surely be feeble at best. It would all be over in a matter of weeks, Wolsey promised, and then Henry would be free.

"Have patience, Sire. The verdict you desire shall be yours. I am Your Majesty's most devoted servant!"

"So you say," Henry growled darkly. "Now prove it!"

Wolsey now knew that his life depended on this verdict. But what Wolsey did not know was that before Campeggio departed Rome, Pope Clement had commanded him to decide nothing. This trial was to be nothing more than a grand display of the fine art of shilly-shallying. Delay was the name of the game. The longer the verdict was withheld, the greater the chance that Henry would tire of Anne and forget the whole thing.

Cardinal Campeggio grasped all the intricacies of the situation, and a full eight months would pass before the trial even began. During that time he talked long and patiently with Henry, complimenting his knowledge of theology and ecclesiastical law, and even offered a balm to ease his troubled conscience—Pope Clement would gladly issue a new dispensation declaring his union with Catherine entirely valid before the eyes of both God and man. This was the last thing Henry wanted, though he must feign gratitude. No, the uncertainty and fear weighed too heavily upon his mind. He could not rest until the court had fully delved into and debated all the evidence; only then, Henry hoped, could his conscience be appeased.

I was lurking in the corridor when Campeggio hobbled out, leaning heavily upon his cane, and to his secretary I heard him say, "His Majesty has studied his case so diligently that I believe he knows more about it than any theologian or lawyer. He told me he wishes only for a declaration whether his marriage is valid or not, himself always assuming that it is not. And I think that an angel descending from Heaven could not persuade him otherwise."

Campeggio fared no better with Queen Catherine. Like others before him, he stressed the dignity and glory of taking the veil and giving oneself to God. But Catherine merely repeated her feelings about those who entered the religious life knowing they lacked a true vocation. And when the delicate question about whether she was still a virgin when she first came to Henry's bed was raised, she stood, placed one hand upon the Bible and the other upon her heart, and declared, "Were I to be torn limb from limb for declaring myself to be the King's true wife, still I would say it, because it is the truth!"

Then Catherine proved that she also knew how to play the delaying game, and revealed that her clever father, King Ferdinand, had foreseen that this might someday become a sticking point and had expressed his concerns to Pope Julius; thus a second dispensation had been issued alongside the first, stating that the marriage could proceed regardless of whether the previous union had been consummated.

At this revelation a mighty storm broke. Henry raged, doubted the dispensation's existence, and demanded to see it with his

own eyes. It was archived in Spain, the Spanish Ambassador informed him.

"Have it sent at once upon the fastest ship!" Henry ordered.

But the Emperor Charles refused to let the original document
out of his hands, though he would gladly send a notarized copy.
And so the delays continued.

❧ 10 ❧

Christmas came, and this year there were two queens, one in name and one in deed, presiding over two courts. While Catherine, regally enthroned at Henry's side, presided over the court's Yuletide celebrations, greeted foreign ambassadors and guests, and warmly dispensed alms to the poor, Anne was grandly ensconced at York Place.

She lived like a queen in all but name, with ladies-in-waiting to attend her every need—I was one of them—and she even had her own food taster, a cupbearer, a little page boy to carry her train, and even a female fool, a jolly little dwarf woman who capered about in parti-colored petticoats trimmed with tinkling gold bells, a mock scepter adorned with a cluster of tiny bells, and a gilded tin crown on her bald, shaven head. But every night the Great Hall was almost empty, though minstrels played merrily in the gallery and the table was laden with sumptuous fare. Only Anne's closest friends and staunchest supporters rallied round her.

Always men to stay on the winning side, Sir Thomas Boleyn and his equally cold and ambitious brother-in-law, the Duke of Norfolk, were careful to dutifully appear at court and bow to Catherine, just in case she came out the winner.

Anne fumed at this perceived insult, insisting that she belonged at the King's side, not Catherine. She spoke wildly, saying that she hated the Queen and would rather see her hanged than acknowledge her as her superior.

On Christmas Day, Henry sent her a weighty purse of gold. Anne threw it at the wall, then thought better of it and laughed at the sight of Weston, Norris, and Brereton crawling on their hands and knees, gathering up the coins, grinning mischievously as they pocketed a few.

That evening Henry stole away from the official court celebrations to visit her. He found her making merry with her friends and drinking steaming cups of spicy wassail.

Only I sat apart. George was, as always, at Anne's side, and I felt my hatred for her growing like a cancer inside me. I had watched earlier as he lovingly fastened a rope of creamy, lustrous pearls around her neck, with a large gleaming gold *B* pendant from which three goodly sized teardrop pearls dangled, while I, his wife, must make do with a plain bracelet of carnelian that doubtlessly he had gotten at a discount on account of an unsightly flaw in the stone and the ugly unevenness of its color.

Before us all, King Henry knelt at her feet and said, "I promise this is the last Christmas you shall ever spend apart from me. Henceforth, that shall be Catherine's fate!"

While he was instructing the musicians, Anne rolled her eyes and said, sotto voce, "To spend a Christmas apart from Henry; that is a fate worse than death!"

George and Brereton were hard put to stifle their laughter, Norris choked on his wine, and Weston rolled on the floor howling with glee, thus sparking the King's curiosity.

"He is laughing at me, Your Grace, for being a softhearted, sentimental female," Anne deftly explained.

"Really, darling?" Henry gathered her in his arms, his plump, pink fingers roving over the back of her sable-trimmed scarlet satin gown, its color red as holly berries, as if they longed to undo the laces. "What did you say?"

"That I almost pity Catherine, for to be exiled from your affection, especially at Christmas, is a fate worse than death."

"Aye, sweetheart, but it is a fate you will never suffer!" Henry promised. "Eternal and evergreen shall ever be my love for you. And to prove it, I have written this song for you."

He bade us all be seated. Then, standing at the center of the room, the emeralds and diamonds upon his cloth-of-silver and green velvet doublet flashing in the candlelight, he signaled the musicians, and, in a fine tenor voice, began to sing:

> *"Green groweth the holly, so doth the ivy.*
> *Though winter blasts blow never so high,*
> *Green groweth the holly.*
>
> *As the holly groweth green*
> *And never changes hue,*
> *So I am, and ever hath been,*
> *Unto my lady true.*
>
> *As the holly groweth green,*
> *With ivy all alone*
> *When flowers cannot be seen*
> *And greenwood leaves be gone.*
>
> *Now unto my lady*
> *Promise to her I make:*
> *From all others only*
> *To her I me betake.*
>
> *Green groweth the holly, so doth the ivy.*
> *Though winter blasts blow never so high,*
> *Green groweth the holly."*

As he sang his eyes never once left Anne's face.

Anne sat very still, seemingly lost in thought; she was by this time well accustomed to inspiring poetry and songs. Thomas Wyatt had already made her famous. "Noli Me Tangere (Touch

Me Not) for Caesar's I am." There was nary a soul who did not know that oft-quoted line from Wyatt's famous poem. George sat beside her, intently watching her face, his hand stroking the wide sable cuff of her sleeve.

When the King's song was done and all dutifully applauded, Francis Weston sniffed and pantomimed wiping a tear away from his one eye.

"It almost makes one believe in undying love!" he quipped.

"Everything dies, Francis," Anne answered. Then she rose and went to Henry. Taking both his hands in hers, she said she would never forget this night when he gave his song to her; it would live forever in her memory and heart.

"As it will in mine, sweetheart," Henry vowed as he again embraced her. Then he called for wine, to drink a toast "to undying love."

❧ 11 ❧

The trial finally commenced in June, a full eight months after Campeggio set his gouty feet on English soil. The case was to be heard in London, at Blackfriars Hall in the Dominican friars' Charter House.

Courtiers, commoners, churchmen, students, scholars, and interested foreigners all crowded into the vast hall; satin, sackcloth, silk, and homespun rubbing shoulders as all sought a seat or a place to stand.

The King arrived first, but Catherine was so late bets were being laid that she would not appear at all. Then, from outside, in the city streets, a deafening cheer arose. The doors swung wide and there she stood, with the people of England behind her shouting their good tidings. She wore a stiff, austere, high-necked Spanish gown of black velvet with a long, royal purple satin robe over it. A large silver crucifix studded with amethysts adorned her breast. Her pale, gaunt face was framed by a black gable hood edged with pearls. And a rosary of pearls was twined around her clasped hands.

Head held high, back straight and proud, she began to move forward. A hush fell as she approached the dais where the King sat, and the only sound to be heard then was the rustling of her gown.

Disdaining the throne that had been provided for her beside the King's, Catherine sank to her knees at Henry's feet. Then, in a voice heavy with emotion and the lingering accent of Spain, she began to speak.

"I take God and all the world as my witness that I have always been a true and obedient wife to you. I have been pleased and contented with everything that delighted you. I loved all those whom you loved, for your sake, whether they were my friends or enemies. These twenty years and more I have been your true wife, and by me you have had many children, though it has pleased God to call them from this world. And when you had me at the first, I take God to be my judge, I was a true maid, who had never known the touch of man; and whether it be true or not, I put it to your conscience. And to God I commit my cause!"

Silence reigned, tense and taut as a bowstring, as Catherine remained kneeling, like a supplicant, at Henry's feet. But Henry said nothing, not one word. His eyes narrowed, as cold and flinty as chips of blue ice, and the telltale red blotches of rage mottled his face as he leaned forward, his hands shaking as they gripped the arms of his throne in a supreme effort to restrain himself from reaching for her neck.

At last Catherine stood and, with a deep curtsy, turned and left the courtroom.

Thrice the court crier called her back. "Catherine, Queen of England, come in to court!" But she ignored him. She had had her say, so why linger in this court where the Pope's man was of uncertain mind and all the English judges were Henry's creatures? When the wide double doors opened and the people saw her they raised their voices in deafening cheers. "God bless Queen Catherine!" they cried again and again. Only when the doors had closed and the cheers had ceased did Henry rise to speak.

With his hat held humbly in his hands, he declared that Fortune had indeed blessed him by giving him such a wife as Catherine. He praised her loyal and obedient nature and swore with his hand upon his heart that no fault with her person or age, nor carnal lust for any other, had prompted him to undertake these proceedings. And were it not for the grave doubts and fears for the succession that assailed his conscience without rest night and day, he would be content to dwell in a state of matrimony with her to his dying day.

But not a soul believed him; his words did not ring true. Everyone knew by now that Anne Boleyn, "The Night Crow" as some called her, was always at his side and often perched upon his lap. And though they loved their King, their "Bluff King Hal," the people of England believed in justice and Queen Catherine. "We'll have none of Nan Bullen!" they roared, spitting and shaking their fists whenever they saw Anne. Had she shown her face at Blackfriars that day—and what a pity she did not!—I am certain she would have been torn to bloody bits.

But Henry did not get the verdict he desired—he did not get any verdict at all. Instead, after almost two months of argument, Campeggio decided that they should recess for the summer, then reconvene in Rome before the Pope. So, once again, it had all been for nothing.

It was Wolsey who bore the brunt of the King's displeasure. Wolsey had promised him the verdict and failed to deliver. Craftily, the Cardinal played for time by renouncing all his worldly assets, including Hampton Court and York Place, both more lavish than any royal palace, and giving them to Henry, replete with all their furnishings, a treasure trove of gold and silver plate, tapestries, and art. But he knew it was only a matter of time before he would pay the ultimate penalty unless he could defeat Anne.

I tried to help him, not out of any love for Wolsey—only the burning, soul-consuming desire to destroy Anne Boleyn.

One afternoon I spied the Cardinal's secretary, Thomas Cromwell, a loathsome, squat, oily-skinned toad of a man who always dressed in black. He was strolling in the palace gardens, his dark reptilian eyes perusing a sheaf of documents.

"The Cardinal would do well to look to Mistress Anne's reading matter," I said, low but clear, as I passed him.

And, before the week was out, the hint—and a certain forbidden book—was taken.

A diversion caused Anne's attention to wander, and she most

unwisely left her book—William Tyndale's *Obedience of a Christian Man*—lying on the window seat. Swiftly, as if it had sprouted wings and flown, it found its way to Wolsey. It was just the weapon he required; for Henry, despite his present difficulties with the Church, was a man who took his faith very seriously. Indeed, he had even penned a volume defending the sacraments against Martin Luther's virulent Protestantism, for which the Pope had dubbed him "Defender of the Faith." Surely this was dangerous terrain where not even Anne dared to tread!

But Henry Norris—damn and curse him!—had seen, and rushed to warn Anne. I saw him take her arm, draw her aside, and whisper urgently in her ear.

With a swish of skirts she was off and running. She met the King in the gallery, heading for the stairs, while down below, at the foot of the stairs, stood Wolsey with the heretical volume clutched in his hand.

In a fit of weeping frenzy, Anne flung herself at Henry's feet.

"Sire, I have done something foolish, and I am afraid! Please be merciful and help me!"

Tenderly, Henry stooped and raised her to her feet. "Come, come, sweeting, it cannot be as bad as all that!"

In halting sobs, Anne explained how curiosity had prompted her to read Master Tyndale's book in the hope that she might find something to aid their cause. But now the book had disappeared and she was afraid it would fall into the hands of some impressionable young person and be read for all the wrong reasons.

Then, before Henry could answer, she spun around to face the steadily advancing Wolsey. "The book! It has been found! Oh, thank you, my lord Cardinal! Thank you! Now my mind can rest easy; no harm has been done!" She rushed over and snatched it from his hand while he just stood there, struck dumb by her audacity.

Meekly, she returned to the King and knelt before him and humbly surrendered the book. "It would be safer in Your Majesty's keeping. I relinquish it now into your hands and most humbly beseech your pardon."

"Darling"—he leaned down to caress her face—"stand, do not

grovel; there is nothing to forgive!" He kissed her tear-damp cheek and trembling lips. "Come, take my arm, and walk with me."

As they walked away Henry began to idly peruse the book, flipping through its pages until he came upon a scrap of scarlet ribbon tucked inside.

"I did encounter a passage of particular interest," Anne explained. "Master Tyndale believes that a king is the highest power in his dominion and responsible for all matters that touch upon the welfare of his subjects, both temporal and spiritual."

"An interesting concept, most interesting," Henry said thoughtfully, pursing his lips. "This volume might prove promising after all." He tucked it beneath his arm. "I shall keep it safe and peruse it at my leisure. Thank you, Anne, for bringing it to my attention."

Standing behind me, I heard Henry Norris breathe a sigh of relief. "Thanks be to God that Anne has a quick mind!"

With a cry of outrage, I swung round and slapped him as hard as I could across the face.

Why did fortune always favor Anne? Had I been caught with such a book I would most certainly have been fined and jailed, maybe even burned at the stake! But Anne . . . Anne could do no wrong!

That night George was very curt with me, taking me to task for wishing ill upon his sister and inflicting violence upon his friend.

"It is being bruited about that you are touched by madness, Jane. If you continue in this vein, you must not look to me to contradict them."

"Indeed, husband, I would not expect you to defend me! I am not your sister!"

"What a pity you are not," he sighed as he headed for the door, leaving me as always. "It would be easier to ignore you if you were. But alas, a wife's claim upon a man's attention is greater than a sister's."

"Tell that to Anne!" I screamed, snatching up a candlestick and hurling it after him. "Methinks you confuse our roles and take her for your wife!"

Eyeing me coolly, George calmly stamped out the little tongue of orange flame and beneath his boot the candle snapped.

"Be careful that your rage does not burn down the King's palace, Jane."

Without another word he closed the door behind him. Why must he always be so cold, so cold as ice? And why must I always let my temper gain the upper hand and have full sway, and make me say things that I knew would only make things worse and make him even more eager to quit my company? Why did I provoke him? Why did I let my own tongue betray me? I knew that sugar and honey catch more flies than vinegar and pepper; even the simplest simpleton knew that, and yet I could not fix that simple truth firm in my head when the rage overwhelmed me. At such times I felt as if my soul left my body and hovered way up high and looked down upon my screaming, vengeful, hateful self, watching me helplessly as I spoke words that would only serve to push my husband even farther away, when all I wanted was to draw him close to me, to feel his arms about me, his lips on mine, and to hear his sweet, tender words assuring me that he loved me and would never leave me. That was all I really wanted, yet I fought against myself, and made that ever more impossible with every word I uttered.

I was not the only one whose temper threatened to ignite. Time rolled on as Henry and his advisers pondered what to do. At that time, one Thomas Cranmer, a churchman with strong Protestant leanings, but a most timid, soft-spoken man, was brought to the King's attention when he opined that it would be wisest for the King to canvass the universities regarding the legality of his marriage.

Meanwhile, Anne was growing impatient; she was sick and weary of debate and delay, and the strain was beginning to show.

I was with her the day when Anne, on her way to the stables in a splendid new riding habit of tawny and river green velvet, encountered a maidservant carrying a stack of Henry's shirts. Recognizing them at once, for no other man possessed such fine shirts of snowy white linen with exquisite blackwork embroidery on the collars and cuffs, Anne halted her, using her riding crop to bar the girl's path, and demanded to know where she was taking the King's shirts.

"Why, to the Queen, my lady!" the girl replied. "Her Majesty always mends the King's shirts!"

Anne's face clouded with rage and I knew she was about to explode in a magnificent tantrum. She cast her riding crop aside and it clattered loudly against the wall.

"Give them to me!" she ordered and, with myself and Meg Lee trailing after her, she strode straight into the King's privy chamber where he sat in conference with Sir Thomas Boleyn, the Dukes of Norfolk and Suffolk, Cromwell, and Thomas Cranmer, and flung the stack of shirts straight into Henry's startled and bewildered face.

"I have been waiting long, and might in the meantime have married and borne children, which is the greatest consolation in the world; but alas"—she threw up her hands—"farewell to my time and youth, wasted to no purpose at all!"

As she turned to go, Henry leapt up and caught at her arm.

"Nan, Nan, what is the meaning of this?" he implored. "Whatever has upset you?"

Anne wrenched away from him. "Would you not say that the mending of a man's shirts is a wifely duty?"

"Aye, Nan, it is," Henry affirmed.

"Well, then"—Anne nodded gravely—"it is plain that you do but trifle with me! If Catherine is still entrusted with the mending of your shirts, then in your eyes she must still be your wife. Therefore, I shall bid you adieu and take my leave."

"Anne! Anne!" Henry ran after her. "Do not walk away from me, Anne! By the Cross, I swear all shall be yours in time. You need only wait a little longer!"

"It is always a little longer," Anne said without stopping or turning back.

"She shall be sent from the court!" Henry shouted, and this time Anne stopped. "When we return from the summer progress, I promise you, she shall be gone!"

Instantly mollified, and with a small smile of triumph playing across her lips, Anne let the King embrace her.

* * *

A few days later, Anne encountered Queen Catherine for what was to be the last time.

Again with Meg Lee, I was following Anne's crimson velvet–clad figure down the stairs as the sad, somber, black-gowned Queen was slowly ascending them, a string of black rosary beads wound round her hand and a mantilla of black lace veiling her silver-streaked hair.

They paused on the landing to regard one another face-to-face.

With sorrowful gray eyes, the skin around them puffed and red from tears and lack of sleep, Catherine of Aragon searched Anne Boleyn's face intently.

Anne's back stiffened, yet she held the Queen's gaze.

Then Queen Catherine said something that surprised me. Of all the things this much wronged woman could have said, this I never expected.

"I pity you. With your forbidden books you have given him the key that will free him from the shackles of any union that bores, wearies, or in any way displeases him. No one, no thing, not even Holy Mother Church, can hold him now. And someday he will seek to free himself from you. Be forewarned, Mistress Anne, your victory also holds the seeds of your destruction."

Anne flinched as if the Queen had just flung ice water in her face. "The son I bear him shall keep me safe."

"I pray that shall be so, Mistress Anne. I will remember you in my prayers," she said as she gathered up her skirts and continued up the stairs. "One day you may have need of them."

Anne did not tarry; she gathered up the full, trailing skirt of her riding habit and ran the rest of the way downstairs and out into the sunny courtyard where Henry awaited her, tall and proud in the saddle, the rainbow of jewels upon his hat and doublet sparkling in the summer sun. A groom in the green and white Tudor livery knelt to cup Anne's dainty red leather–booted foot in his hands and help her up into the crimson-fringed and gilded saddle.

Smiling broadly, Henry held out his hand to clasp hers. "Let us be off, sweetheart. I want all of England to see what a lucky man I am to have you by my side!"

As I nudged my horse forward, I looked back and saw Queen Catherine standing at the window overlooking the courtyard, gazing wistfully after the departing figure of her husband, the King. She raised a hand to her lips and blew him a farewell kiss.

But Henry, at the head of that magnificent cavalcade thousands strong, which would accompany him on the summer progress, never once looked back. Catherine was a part of his life he was determined to put behind him; she was the past, and Anne Boleyn was the future.

When we returned Catherine would be gone. She would spend the rest of her life being shunted from one dilapidated, crumbling castle to another, freezing in winter, surrounded by noxious, reeking marshlands in summer, her health steadily deteriorating. Henry would show her no mercy; his envoys would hound, bully, and beseech her tirelessly, in a vain attempt to make her repudiate her marriage vows. They even kept her apart from her beloved daughter, Princess Mary, as punishment, hoping to weaken her resolve, and even denied mother and child the consolation of letters. They promised her a life of quiet comfort and rest, and restoration to the King's good graces. She could style herself the Dowager Princess of Wales and Henry would always think of her fondly as the widow of his dead brother.

But Catherine would not be swayed; she would answer to no other title but Queen of England until the last breath left her body, and if she must wear rags and sit in the midst of a stinking swamp, then so be it; come what may, to God and her conscience, she would be true.

Wolsey would soon join Catherine in banishment and disgrace, to live out the rest of his life deprived of the shining sun of Henry's favor.

When he came to join the court at Grafton, he found that there was no place, no room, no bed, for the man who for twenty years and more had been the King's right hand.

In the courtyard he stood alone, wounded and bewildered, pacing the cobblestones, sweating in his voluminous scarlet robes, while the courtiers kept their distance, whispering and smirking. Only one person deigned to show pity. Kind Henry Norris detached himself from his friends and crossed the cobbles to offer Wolsey his room. And so at the end of his glorious career the great Cardinal Wolsey was forced to humbly bow his head and accept charity from one of Anne Boleyn's most ardent supporters.

The gentle scholar Thomas More took Wolsey's place as Chancellor, and Wolsey retreated to his long-neglected bishopric of York to hide from the King's anger and mourn all that he had lost.

⤙ 12 ⤙

During that dull and listless summer when all were, like Anne, weary of waiting and wondering, Anne impulsively decided to visit her grandmother, the Dowager Duchess of Norfolk. Thus we piled into a barge and journeyed forth to Lambeth, where Agnes Tilney, that wizened old coquette, spent her days primping and painting her face, dreaming of past and future glories, planning the gowns she would wear to Anne's coronation and the christening of the prince Anne would most assuredly bear, and turning a blind eye to the fact that her servants' quarters were rife with debauchery. The Maids' Chamber, the long room at the top of the house where her ladies-in-waiting slept, was practically a brothel, except its denizens gave their favors away for free or for paltry gifts of fruit, flowers, and hair ribbons.

The Dowager Duchess arranged an impromptu picnic upon the sprawling green lawn, and while we lolled back on plump silk cushions and feasted on strawberries and cream, honey cakes, and wine, she regaled us with gossip. Though she was now well into her sixth decade, she flirted like a girl—a very wanton girl—goading Norris that he had been a widower far too long and if he did not find himself another wife soon she would lead him to the altar herself.

"Flaxen, raven, and scarlet," she sighed wistfully, ruffling the hair of Norris, Brereton, and Weston, seated in a cluster round her feet. "I don't know which of you boys I like best! Were I but ten years younger, I would give in to temptation and find out!"

"Methinks someone is not so indecisive," Anne said slyly, indicating the tiny girl staring in wide-eyed fascination at the dazzling figure of Francis Weston. Like one entranced, the auburn-haired tot was creeping forward and reaching out a tentative hand to touch one of the fine, shapely legs encased in lime green hose with ruby-encrusted garters twinkling above his knees.

"Katherine Howard!"

Upon hearing her name screeched so shrilly, the child started and snatched her hand away. In her guilty confusion, she tripped over her skirts and fell sprawling flat on her back at Weston's feet.

"Oh!" The Dowager threw up her hands. "Get up, you clumsy chit, get up! You're five years old, and it's high time you were learning some grace! Go and make your curtsy; greet your cousin Anne!"

"Is this my little cousin Katherine, then?" Anne asked.

"Aye, one of that hapless wastrel Edmund's passel of brats," the Dowager affirmed glumly. "Couldn't feed 'em all or keep 'em in shoes, so he sent this one to me! Out of the goodness of my heart I'm to rear her up to be a lady and see her properly wed. She's a Howard, even if she springs from a poor branch, and the Howards breed fine women, like your mother, Anne. Elizabeth Howard, now she was a rare beauty; it was fortunate your father was to snare her!"

But Anne was not listening to the tale of her parents' courtship. Lying back against a heap of cushions in her white silk gown and black damask kirtle, lazily plying her fan of white ostrich plumes and letting George feed her strawberries, she was studying the shy little figure in the patched and faded moss green frock bobbing a hasty curtsy before her.

She was so tiny it was hard to credit that she was five; I myself had judged her to be no more than three.

"Come here, Little Kat," Anne beckoned, drawing Katherine down to sit beside her. "Do not mind Grandmother overmuch; her bark is worse than her bite." Her fingers played gently with the long auburn curls, twisting them into smooth ringlets. "Attend well to your lessons, Little Kat, and learn the proper graces, and when you are older I shall send for you to be one of my ladies."

"R-Really?" The child's face lit up with the most radiant and hopeful of smiles.

Anne nodded and smiled as Katherine impulsively threw her arms around her neck, ignoring the Dowager's appalled exclamations that this was no way to behave, that a well-brought-up girl mustn't be so free with her embraces.

"You are going to be a great beauty someday, Katherine Howard," Anne prophesied. "It is fortunate that I shall be an old woman by the time you come to court, else I should fear you as a rival. See now"—she tilted her head towards the bevy of men teasing Francis Weston about his latest conquest—"already you have set the men's tongues wagging; they can talk of nothing else but you, and I"—she sighed in mock melancholy—"am all forgotten!"

"Never!" the men shouted as they rushed to surround Anne and reassure her of devotion deep as the ocean and high as the sky.

"Aye, the sly little minx already has quite an eye for the men," the Dowager acknowledged sourly, her rouged lips taut with disapproval.

"Do not fault her for being drawn to Francis," Anne coaxed smilingly. "He is quite the peacock, and when he struts about in his finery few are the eyes that are not dazzled."

"It is true." George nodded. "When he wanders into the palace gardens the peacocks sulk and hide their heads beneath their wings because they cannot compete with his glory."

"Hush, now!" Weston cried, making a great show of tweaking and puffing the scarlet satin peeping through the slashed, lime green sleeves of his doublet. "You will give the child the impression that I am vain!"

"Oh surely not!" George scoffed as they all burst into laughter.

Only I sat silent and apart. I was never included in their jests unless I was the butt. In their eyes I was like the grass beneath their feet, born to be stepped upon. I knew full well that I had only been invited to accompany them because it was not seemly for Anne to gad about in exclusively male company.

"Come, Jane!" My husband called me like a dog. They were ready to depart. "Come, Jane!" he repeated as he gave his arm to Anne. And I was left to shift for myself, to rise to my feet unaided and make my own way back to the barge.

"Poor George!" I heard that wrinkled white prune, with her gaudy rouged cheeks and garish red gown, sigh dolefully. "What a sour countenance your wife has; one would think she was sucking upon a lemon!"

And once again I became their joke—"Sourpuss Jane!"

Flustered and furious, I dropped my fan.

With a timid smile, little Kat Howard retrieved it. And when she looked up at me, there was such open, earnest kindness in her little face, and in those beautiful amber-flecked green eyes, that my heart felt as if it had been plunged into a warm bath.

There was no mockery in her gaze; no pity, condescension, or scorn in that angel face.

Separated from her father and nine siblings, her mother dead of too many children and woes, lodged with her sharp-tongued grand-mother and wanton, lust-mad maids, Katherine Howard just wanted someone to love her.

"Thank you, Katherine," I whispered fervently; then, as tears welled in my eyes, I turned and ran back to the barge; George and the others were getting impatient.

"Don't dawdle, Jane! Do hurry up, Jane!"

Ten years would pass before I would see Katherine Howard again and learn what an angel will do for love.

❧ 13 ❧

The decisions of the universities began to slowly trickle in as the year neared its end.

The English colleges, Oxford and Cambridge, were, as was to be expected, in support of the King, Spain was vehemently opposed, and Italy undecided. The German Lutherans were eager to strike a blow against Catholicism and lent their support, though most personally disapproved. And the French gave their support only because their king emphasized the need to have England as an ally.

A petition was drawn up, signed by all who supported the divorce, and sent to the Pope. But still Pope Clement dithered, unwilling to commit to a decision.

And soon a new treachery was revealed. Wolsey had been in secret communication with the Pope, urging him to issue an ultimatum threatening the King with excommunication if he did not abandon Anne Boleyn. Thus Wolsey sealed his doom and signed his own death warrant.

Upon a frigid November day at Cawood Castle, near his diocese of York, Wolsey was just sitting down to dine when his chamberlain announced a most unexpected guest. Harry Percy, now the Earl of Northumberland in his own right, had come to arrest the Cardinal.

Poor Percy, I heard, trembled and spoke so faintly that Wolsey had to lean forward with a hand cupped round his ear and ask thrice for him to repeat the stumbling, stammering words: "In th-the n-n-name of th-the K-K-King, I . . . I . . . I a-r-r-rest y-you f-for h-high tr-tr-treason."

Percy was so overcome by the enormity of his task that he nearly fainted and had to snatch Wolsey's wine goblet off the table and gulp down its contents.

They took to the road early the next morning, the horses' hooves slipping precariously upon the ice and slush, shivering in the freezing drizzle and blasts of icy wind. And through it all, Wolsey was forced to endure the supreme indignity of having his legs bound beneath his horse like a common felon's.

They stopped to dine at Sheffield Park, the home of Percy's father-in-law. And there, after partaking of a dish of baked pears, Wolsey was overcome by a violent attack of colic and diarrhea. An apothecary was summoned and by the next morning Wolsey had recovered enough to resume the journey. He made it as far as Leicester Abbey, where he collapsed in the arms of the Abbot and died proclaiming, "If I had served God half as well as I served the King, He would not have forsaken me in my gray hairs!"

The nature of his death occasioned much speculation. Many believed a dose of poison had killed him. But Percy had taken great care to have all the Cardinal's meals tasted. Even the apothecary was forced to wait while his remedy was tested before a drop was allowed to pass Wolsey's lips. Some thought that Wolsey himself, determined to outwit Anne and cheat the headsman's axe, had carried a few grains of a most potent poison secreted inside the hollow of a ring or hidden in the hem of his scarlet robes. I suppose we will never really know.

At court, Anne and her coterie celebrated his demise with a special masque called "Cardinal Wolsey Goes To Hell," wherein they donned garish costumes equipped with red devil horns and tails, painted their skins red, and danced the Cardinal off to the fiery pit of Hell, even as he cowered fearfully and begged and pleaded for God's mercy. Francis Weston had a grand time playing Wolsey, swirling his voluminous scarlet robes about at every opportunity to display his handsome legs sheathed in scarlet hose and the rubies winking on his garters. Myself—though I had no great liking for the late Cardinal—I found the whole spectacle in very poor taste.

Anne now occupied the Queen's rooms and lived as if she were Queen already. She was given precedence over every other lady at court, including the King's sister.

The Duchess of Suffolk quit the court in protest, and her husband loudly proclaimed within the King's hearing that, though Anne could be called many things, "The Night Crow," "The Goggle-Eyed Whore," and "The Concubine," to name but a few, "Virgo Intacta" was not one of them; it was common knowledge that she had carnally known both the poet Wyatt and Harry Percy.

The King was outraged; he had long been convinced that Anne was a true maid, bound and determined to preserve her precious chastity until their wedding night.

And oh, I was jubilant! My face was wreathed in smiles, and I wanted to sing and jig round the room. Now George's "darling Nan" would surely get her comeuppance! It was not meet to deceive the King about one's maidenhead! I knew full well that virgin she was not; with my own eyes I had witnessed the surrender.

This time it was Weston who rushed to warn her. Perhaps he was not just playing the court gallant when he said to her, "Lady, I would swim through seas of fire to save you!"

Again, Anne did not hesitate. She stormed through the crowded antechamber, head held high, insolent and proud, and came to a halt before Henry.

"You may summon a midwife to examine me and prove that I am as true a maid as any woman who graces this court," she announced, "but—if you do—then know that I shall lose all the respect I have for you. I could never love a man who doubts me!"

Then she was gone in the same manner she had come.

It was a bold gamble and a brazen lie, though genuine virtue was a rare commodity in any royal court, despite maidenly protestations to the contrary. Anne staked all on the hope that Henry would not send for a midwife and prove her false, and once again she triumphed.

With all my heart, I wanted to rush at Francis Weston like a screaming harpy and claw out his remaining eye, I hated him so much. Even more than that I wanted to hurt Anne; I wanted to see her brought low and suffer as much as she had made me. She had stolen what was rightfully mine—George's love—and somehow, someday, I swore to God and all his saints, and Satan and all his imps, I would make her pay for it.

The crisp morning of September 1, 1532, found me wearing a new red damask gown and standing behind Anne, brushing her hair into a lustrous black gloss, while the peers of the realm assembled downstairs in the Great Hall at Windsor Castle to witness an unprecedented ceremony.

Anne was to be created the Marquess of Pembroke in her own right, independent of any man; she was to bear a man's title and take precedence over all the peers of the realm. And, most significantly, the title would pass to any male child born of her body, lawfully begotten or not.

This last sparked rumors that Anne was with child, while others speculated that this honor was a parting gift to recompense Anne for all her wasted years.

"Nay, Jane," Anne explained as I drew the brush through her hair, "I mean to safeguard my future. I am sure you have noticed that the King is a large and determined man, endowed with an ardent nature and powerful physique; should he force his will upon me, his kingship bars me from defending myself as I would against any other man who dared the same. By tempting him I play with fire, and one cannot play with fire without risking burns, so, come what may, I mean to be prepared; I must protect myself."

Regally gowned in crimson velvet trimmed with ermine, Anne knelt before the King as a private gentlewoman and stood up a marquess.

But things were changing. Though Henry continued to profess his undying love and shower her with gifts, there hung about him the brooding air of a man who has grown tired of waiting and is beginning to wonder whether it is really worthwhile. . . .

❧ 14 ❧

Anne's sweetness towards the King was souring fast. Her temper grew increasingly tart and shrill as she began to nag, berate, and rage at him until they quarreled more than they kissed. And odds were being laid that the end was near.

A visit to Calais to meet the King of France was being planned. Anne was to accompany the King and it was being wagered that though she might travel across the Channel in queenly fashion, she would return as a discarded mistress.

As Anne reclined upon a couch, blatantly reading one of her forbidden books, her father came in.

Thomas Boleyn was not a man to mince words.

"Your hold on him is slipping."

"Is it?" Anne arched her brows, stretched her arms above her head, and yawned in feigned disinterest.

"As much as you despise that Spanish cow, there are lessons she can teach you, if you have the wit to learn from your enemies. Catherine mothered him, she coddled and cosseted him as if he were a little boy, but you—you lash at him with your tongue as if it were a whip, and shriek and scream at him like some shrill, black-haired banshee! You no longer smile at him, you sneer! How many nights of late has he forsaken your company? Henry Tudor is not a man renowned for his patience, and you have kept him waiting longer than he has ever waited for anyone, but he will not wait forever. Acquire some sweetness before it is too late; put some honey in your voice and smile, or you are doomed! Mother him a little if you can, though I daresay a barn cat is a better mother than you'll ever be."

"You are wrong!" Anne cried, tossing her head proudly.

"Only when I see it shall I believe it," Thomas Boleyn answered. "In my mind, the pen is poised to write you off as another lost cause, just like your sister Mary!" Upon these words he slammed the door.

Like a caged and restless animal, Anne began to pace. Her ladies kept their distance, watching warily, none daring to approach or address her. In that quiet chamber the rustling of her skirts seemed loud as thunder. She bit her trembling knuckles, and her hair swung out as she reached one end of the room and turned round to stalk back across the floor. An hour passed, and then another. And then she stopped.

"Summon my dressmaker! And bring me paper, ink, and quills! Now!"

By the time the dressmaker arrived, Anne had designed the most alluring of nightgowns, breathtaking black satin with yards of trailing skirts. The bodice would be stiffened with buckram and cunningly fastened with a row of black velvet bows down the front. It was far too uncomfortable and ornate to sleep in, but that was never Anne's intention. She had also written out an order for a complete set of black satin bedclothes—sheets, coverlet, pillowslips, curtains, and canopy—everything to garb her bed entirely in black. And all of it must be ready in time for her to take to Calais.

And so to Calais we went, with Anne striving to subdue her temper. It seemed no respectable French ladies could be found to receive her. Both the Queen and the King's sister made their excuses. To temper the slight, and save face, Henry announced he would rather they met as brother-kings, en famille, without the encumbrance of large retinues and lavish ceremony. Thus, apart from the necessary maids, her sister Mary, Meg Lee, Madge Shelton, and I would be the only ladies included in the English party, since Anne must be properly chaperoned.

It was a dreary place, Calais, England's last tenacious foothold across the Channel. The weather was abysmal. We were lodged in a bleak, windswept fortress that might have been made of blocks of ice for all the warmth it afforded us. But Anne was determined to make a good show. The sole purpose of this visit was to win King Francis's support. It was crucial. Should the Emperor invade to avenge his aunt Catherine, England would need a strong ally.

What a sight they were to behold! The two greatest kings in Christendom, both tall, broad shouldered, and bearded, sporting rings on every finger and heavy gold chains about their necks, their lavish doublets sparkling with a myriad of costly gems. There they sat, Francis, dark-haired, sensuous, and jaded, and Henry, red-gold and ruddy, all smiles and bluff manner, both of them laughing and clapping each other upon the back as they dined off golden plates, pretending to be the best of friends instead of the shrewd, calculating diplomats they really were, each trying to gauge how they could use each other to best advantage.

When their repast was finished and they sat back in their chairs, smiling and patting their stomachs, Anne gave the signal. And in we came, led by Anne, all of us masked and gorgeously appareled in gowns of cloth of gold and crimson velvet, with our hair hidden inside golden nets crowned by pearl- and ruby-trimmed crimson velvet French hoods, with gold-edged red velvet chokers about our throats. One by one, we boldly approached the gentlemen and chose our dancing partners, with Anne going straight for King Francis.

The French King was enraptured; he refused to dance with anyone else that night. With a broad, wolfish smile, he slapped Henry upon the back and urged him to tarry not an hour longer waiting for the Pope's consent, and marry this beguiling creature while he still had the chance. As he spoke, Francis reached out to stroke Anne's throat. It was the appraising, practiced touch of a born sensualist, a connoisseur's caress, and Anne closed her eyes, arched her neck, and shivered appreciatively.

Henry said nothing; he just stared. It only lasted a moment—one tense, black, strained moment—then he smiled, but, to my eyes, that smile seemed forced.

And Anne, looking at him, saw for the first time that her father was correct; her hold on him really was slipping. How had this come to pass? All had seemed well and then, without warning, boredom had set in. Panic flashed inside her eyes, then was hastily shoved aside by the calculating look of a seasoned gambler, weighing how much she dared wager.

An hour later, back in her bedchamber, Anne tossed her long black hair rebelliously and declared: "The game is not over until I say it is over!"

From the bathtub positioned beside a roaring fire, with steam rising and curling round her wet, towel-swathed head, Anne watched as the maids stripped the bed and replaced the white linen with black satin, teetering precariously on stools as they arranged the new canopy and curtains. Crafty Nan was much too clever to let King Henry take her on white sheets that would afterwards show the conspicuous lack of a virgin's bloodstain.

When she stepped from the tub, flushed and pink, she rubbed oil of roses into her skin.

I marveled at her willpower; even with my furs, velvet gown, woolen stockings, and layers of petticoats, I was freezing, yet there she was, stark naked, seemingly impervious to the cold.

When she was satisfied that all of her was rose-scented and soft, she went to stand before the full-length mirror and for a very long time she stood there, silently, staring intently at her naked body. Then, without taking her eyes from her reflection, she said in a voice calm and steady, "Bring me the black nightgown, Jane."

She dismissed her other ladies. I do not know why she wanted me to attend her. Perhaps because she knew I was, unlike the others, never prone to idle chatter. I lifted the exquisite garment over her head, and while she stood silent and still before me, lost in her own thoughts, I did up the fastenings, then combed out her hair, all the time fighting the urge to wrap it round her swan-slender neck and strangle her with it. How much happier and simpler all our lives would be, and in England all would be restored to peace, if Anne Boleyn were dead.

She went to her dainty mother-of-pearl and ebony inlaid writing table and took parchment and a quill.

"Send for spiced wine and sweet wafers, Jane," she said, without even bothering to look up from what she was writing.

When I returned she handed me a note and bade me take it at once to His Majesty, and then dismissed me for the night.

I did not dare break the seal, yet I had no need to—I knew exactly what she aimed to do. Tonight, she would play her final card and surrender herself to the King. What I would not have given to be a fly on the bedchamber wall! Tonight it would be winner take all. Would she be able to give a convincing pretense of passion? I knew she did not love him. Would Henry divine the truth when he took her? I yearned to bear witness to the scene to come, but I knew that I could not; it would not be practicable here in Calais to crouch outside in the corridor with my eye pressed to the keyhole, and there was no way I could conceal myself in Anne's chamber without her knowing it. So I did the only thing I could—I delivered her note to the King and then retired to my own solitary and lonely bed.

I could not sleep. Curiosity, mad and insatiable, kept me awake, tossing like a ship on troubled waters. I think that night I would have given my right eye for a place to hide in Anne's bedchamber.

Hours passed. I heard a noise, a knock on George's door. I bolted up and, quiet as a cat, I crept from my bed, crossed the little sitting room that separated our bedchambers, and pressed my ear against his door. Daringly, I turned the handle, opening the door just a crack, just enough for me to peek through. If I were caught, so be it; this was a risk worth taking.

George groggily fumbled for his robe. "Come!" he called as he rubbed the sleep from his eyes and swung his feet over the side of the bed and sought his slippers, wincing as his bare toes touched the icy floor.

Then there she was in her black nightgown, candle in hand, tears glistening on her cheeks like liquid diamonds.

"It is done," she announced, her hand rising to lightly touch the bruises, the scorchmarks of passion that the King's kisses had left upon her throat and neck.

"Nan! Oh, Nan!" He hugged her close to him.

"He will never say it, George. To admit it would hurt his pride, but I saw it in his eyes tonight, the question: Is that all there is? For this I have risked so much and waited all these years? Afterwards, he said not a word to me—not one word, George!—he only reached for the wine. Oh, George! All these years he has been consumed with desire for me, dreamed of possessing me, but no mortal woman could ever hope to measure up to such dreams, such fantasies! Pray that my womb quickens soon"—she pressed a hand against the firm flatness of her stomach—"or it shall all have been for nothing, and he will dance out of his promise, and I will go the way of our sister. The only difference is, I shall go as a marquess of independent means with £1,000 per annum."

She was cleverer than I thought. I thought she was blind to the truth, arrogant in her confidence, vanity, and pride, but she knew what I knew—it was the beginning of the end. Henry had started to fall out of love with her. Now that he had had what he wanted, he no longer wanted it. The hunter had triumphed; yet another doe had been felled. Only the fear of humiliation and his desperation for a legitimate male heir would keep them together, now that the fire of lust had burned itself out. Now only a pregnancy could save her. Henry would never risk England's heir being born a bastard.

❧ 15 ❧

Back in England, Anne and Henry continued the charade; both too proud to admit the truth, they pretended that nothing was wrong. They were constantly together, kissing and holding hands, and making public avowals of their affection, as if by convincing us they could also convince themselves. And every night they came together in Anne's bed. Then things began to change. Their nights together dwindled to a mere twice or thrice a week. King Henry seemed restless and bored, and he began to eat and drink more.

Anne's supporters, led by her father and uncle Norfolk, began to slowly slip away, distancing themselves, not quite daring to withdraw entirely, but adopting a wait-and-watch policy. Only a few remained true. George, Weston, Brereton, Norris, Wyatt—I could count them all on one hand. And I saw the change this wrought in Anne. During moments of quiet, when she thought no one was watching, her proud shoulders would sag, only to jerk back up arrogantly an instant later as her eyes whipped round, hoping that no one had seen. A certain shrill hysteria crept into her laughter and speech. She would lash out at those around her, saying things that she would regret a moment later. She was no longer the unobtainable object of desire. Sex had robbed her of her mystique; now she was just another woman, like all the rest. Anne Boleyn was no longer special. I watched it all, and gloated like a Roman matron watching Christians being thrown to the lions.

Nothing more was said about the divorce. An impasse had been reached and all stood still, locked and frozen, until New Year's Day 1533 when a laughing, giddy Anne danced into the Great Hall, spinning gaily, cherry red and silver skirts swirling.

"Tom!" she called breathlessly to Wyatt. "Have you an apple? I have the most extraordinary desire to eat apples! His Majesty says it is a sign that I am with child, but I tell him no, no, it cannot be!" She shook her head and laughed mischievously. And with the sly, coy look of a woman hugging a secret close to her heart, she danced out again, leaving us all whispering and wondering.

I touched my own belly, still flat and barren after all these years of marriage, and wondered, why her and not me?

I had gone cloaked and masked to discreetly consult a learned physician and, blushing hotly with humiliation, bared my body to his scrutiny. He told me that the fault was mine, that my womb was too moist to retain my husband's seed, and that like as not I must resign myself to my barren state. Afterwards, I had lain on my bed and wept for hours. Yet every time George came to me as a husband, though those occasions grew ever fewer and far between, I could not help but hope and pray that God would show His mercy to me. Now when George left my bed I didn't run after him and plead; instead I drew my knees up tight, hugging them close, and clenched tight, as I tried to hold in every drop of his precious seed and prayed it would find its way to the heart of my womb.

Why? I wondered. Why did everything always come so easily to Anne? Why did Anne always triumph in the end? Even when all seemed lost and poised to crumble into ashes, like a phoenix she always rose again.

On the 25th of January I was awakened just before dawn by a stirring in my husband's chamber. A furtive rustling and a muffled oath; noises a man trying to dress swiftly and silently might make. When I heard his door open I did not tarry. I flung a cloak over my nightshift and, ignoring the biting chill of the stone floor against my bare feet, I followed him through the slumbering corridors, taking great care to keep to the shadows and maintain a discreet distance behind him. He was going to Anne.

Before he could even knock upon her door, she stepped out, cloaked and veiled, and together they continued onward until they reached the foot of a steep and winding staircase leading up into a turret. He took her hand to guide her up the stairs, and as she gathered up her skirts to keep from stumbling over the hems, I saw that underneath her heavy gray velvet cloak and diaphanous white veil she wore a gown of garish blood red satin.

I dared not follow, so I waited, shivering in the shadows and wishing I had not left behind my slippers.

Half an hour passed before I again heard footsteps on the stairs. Hand in hand they descended.

"Adieu, my sweet sister," George said tenderly as they embraced.

My blood boiled at the sight of their shadows upon the wall, larger than life, merging as they kissed. George had never kissed me so tenderly or lingeringly. Had I seen their shadows on the wall and not known who they belonged to, I would have sworn that they were lovers parting after a secret rendezvous.

"Farewell, my sweet brother, and Godspeed!" Anne said, her hand tightly, lingeringly grasping his before they parted.

I did not wait. I broke into a run, racing back to my room by another route.

Panting, I burst into George's chamber. I had only just dropped into the hearthside chair when he walked in.

"Jane." He nodded curtly, going straight to the leather satchel sitting on his bed. "Whatever it is you want, be quick. I sail for France within the hour."

"Why?" I asked tauntingly. "Are there not harlots and rogues enough in England to sate you?"

"Upon the King's business," he answered, ignoring my jibe.

"And what does that mean?" I demanded.

"It means that it is the King's business and none of yours," he answered.

"I daresay you will manage to combine a little personal pleasure with the King's business; I cannot imagine you resisting the siren's call of the French whores or the rattle of the dice for long!"

"Do not forget the heady bouquet of the French wines, Jane. They go straight to a man's head and drunkenness comes very quickly!"

"So where have you been?" I demanded, abruptly changing the subject. "I daresay you were with someone whose company you find more pleasing than my own!"

George stood up straight and shouldered his satchel. "Few indeed are those whose company I do not find more pleasing than yours, Jane."

"Ah, you must mean Francis Weston! Or Meg Lee perhaps? I've heard that she was your childhood sweetheart, your first love. Or should I say your second love, since I doubt anyone has ever come before Anne. They say you kissed Meg and carved both your names upon the trunk of a tree and swore your undying love before you were sent away to school; then you forgot all about her the moment you reached Oxford. Or were you with Anne tonight? But of course you were! You are always with Anne! Nothing and no one is as important to you as Anne. I daresay to your nose her pisswater is perfume."

"Say one word more about Anne and I shall strike you," George warned.

And I realized then that part of me actually wanted him to strike me. At least then he would be touching me, and I could feel the sting of the blow, and afterwards watch the mark it left behind change colors as it slowly faded away, like a blossom pressed between the pages of a heavy book, to dry and treasure until the petals eventually turned brown and crumbled into dust. I just wanted to feel his hands on me, even if it was in anger. I just wanted him to touch me. I wanted him to love me!

"As for Meg," he continued, "that was long ago, Jane. It seems almost a lifetime away, and she is far better off married to Anthony Lee than to a jaded rake like me."

"Certainly it would never occur to you to stay home and seek contentment with me!" I cried.

"Contentment with you, Jane?" He arched his brows in a marked show of disbelief. "You would only speed me to my coffin with your nagging. I would have to put you in a scold's bridle to preserve my sanity!"

"Stay!" I pleaded. "Do not go to France, George. Stay here with me instead, and let us try to make a child . . ."

"Not now, Jane!" He sighed peevishly, rolling his eyes. "I cannot, I do not have the time. . . ."

"Or the inclination!" I challenged.

"I am not averse to our having a child, Jane. Every man needs an heir, and if it would get you to leave me in peace . . ."

I stepped boldly into his path as he started for the door. "Will you not kiss me good-bye, George?"

A chuckle escaped him and I saw the mockery in his eyes, but I didn't care. At least he was looking at me.

"Was ever a marriage more lacking in dignity than ours?" he said as he shook his head in wonderment. "Very well, Madame, if it will speed me on my way to the harlots and knaves of Paris, then I shall be glad to kiss you." He put his hands on my shoulders, placed a perfunctory peck upon my cheek, then gently pushed me aside. "Good-bye, Jane," he said without a backward glance.

I sagged against the doorjamb, watching him go, and thought again of the tender parting I had secretly witnessed. I closed my eyes and saw again how Anne had cupped his face between her hands when she kissed him. What had they been doing in that turret? My mind was filled with lurid imaginings, visions of them coupling atop Anne's cloak spread upon the dusty attic floor, with the pale yellow light of dawn seeping in through the grimy mullioned windowpanes to kiss their cold flesh. I bit my fist as the tears poured down my face, and vainly tried to draw a black curtain over the maddening, repulsive images that tormented my mind.

Only later would I learn that had I lingered I would have seen Sir Thomas and Lady Elizabeth Boleyn creep down that narrow staircase, followed shortly by Francis Weston, Henry Norris, Will Brereton, and Dr. Rowland Lee, the King's chaplain, and lastly by the King himself.

On that bitterly cold January morning, King Henry VIII and

Anne Boleyn had been secretly and bigamously wed. I did not know then that a plot was brewing. Thomas Cranmer stood poised to become the next Archbishop of Canterbury; he was waiting only for the Pope to ratify his appointment. Once this was done, he would declare Henry's marriage to Catherine null and void. And that was exactly what happened. On Easter Sunday, Anne was formally proclaimed Queen, and all over England congregations walked out en masse when they were asked to pray for "Queen Anne."

❧ 16 ❧

To atone for the hole-and-corner affair that had been their wedding, Henry rewarded Anne with a coronation of magnificence unsurpassed.

On the 29th of May, the great, grand, gaudy spectacle began when Anne, six months gone with child and clad head-to-toe in cloth of gold, journeyed upriver from Greenwich to the Tower of London, where she would lodge in the newly refurbished royal apartments until her coronation at Westminster Abbey.

Newly gilded so that it shone bright as the sun, her barge formed the centerpiece of a huge flotilla, led by a wherry upon which was mounted a red, gold, and green mechanical dragon belching great blasts of orange flames. And towed behind Anne, in a barge all its own, was a huge effigy of her emblem, a white falcon with insolent black glass eyes, with a golden crown upon its haughty head and a scepter clutched possessively in its talons. It was perched upon a branch amidst a cluster of red and white roses. Upon a large white banner, written in bold black letters, was the motto Anne had chosen for herself—"The Most Happy." But was she? Was she really the most happy? I hoped not.

To both sides and behind were at least a hundred barges. There was the Lord Mayor of London in his heavy gold chain of office and crimson velvet robes, and all the guilds were represented by a barge of their own. Next came the aldermen and nobles, and a multitude of musicians. In one barge a group of men cavorted, costumed as dancing savages, and in another was a passel of white-gowned, flowing-haired virgins singing sweetly. Red and white petals bobbed upon the stinking, muddy-hued waters of the Thames, and silk banners and streamers snapped and fluttered in the breeze.

In the midst of it all sat Anne, smiling triumphantly upon her golden throne, one hand resting lightly upon her pregnant belly, while a dozen silver-clad ladies, myself included, sat round her feet.

The people of London watched it all, grim and unsmiling. There was not a cheer to be heard, and not a single man was seen to doff his cap. They hated her beyond measure, this usurper of the rightful queen, this "Goggle-Eyed Whore" who flaunted her belly, bulging with the King's bastard. This "Concubine," this "Night Crow" who had used her witchery and wiles to enslave their beloved "Bluff King Hal," and turn him away from Holy Mother Church and good Queen Catherine. Words cannot sufficiently convey how much they hated her. Had they been able to reach her, there would not have been enough of her corpse left to bury; they would have ripped her into bloody ribbons and ground her bones into powder.

When Anne's barge docked at the Tower's Watergate, a hundred cannons boomed a deafening salute to welcome her, and King Henry, robed in purple velvet and gold, came to help her disembark and then embraced her. But it was not really her that he embraced, I noticed—not Anne the woman, his new, soon-to-be-crowned Queen—but her belly and the child within that his hands cradled.

Two days later, en route to Westminster Abbey, she made the slow and stately progress through the narrow London streets to show herself to the people in all her pomp and glory. She traveled upon a gilded throne mounted upon a litter borne by four white palfreys caparisoned in cloth of gold and white velvet, and her four favorite gentlemen—George, Weston, Norris, and Brereton—all sumptuously arrayed and smiling broadly, basking in her triumph, walked alongside and held a golden canopy above her head.

Upon this day she wore a magnificent iridescent gown of white-gold tissue that fascinated and beguiled the eye with shifting rainbows that danced whenever the sunlight struck it. Like a virgin, she wore her hair unbound, sitting in it, flouting convention and flaunting it. She cared not a whit that it was unseemly for a married woman to appear in public with her hair unbound; it was a sight that should be reserved for her husband's eyes alone.

Undaunted by the silent, hostile, frosty-faced folk who lined the streets and leaned from every window and crowded every balcony, doorway, and rooftop, her smile always stayed in place, never wavering or betraying that the swaying motion of the litter made her sick. This was the day Anne had waited years for, the culmination of all her dreams and schemes, and she refused to be cowed by queasiness or the sullen, sulking, funereal faces of the crowd.

In golden chariots, her ladies-in-waiting, and certain others Anne deemed worthy of the honor, rode divided into pairs, each one gowned in crimson velvet and ermine. I was paired with Anne's grandmother, the Dowager Duchess of Norfolk. Giddy as a young girl over being chosen to be Anne's trainbearer in the ceremony ahead, Agnes Tilney cackled and crowed until it was all I could do not to scream at or strike her. And behind us, either on horseback or on foot according to rank and favor, the courtiers, clergy, and diplomats followed. Of course there were heralds to make a din with their blaring trumpets that would resound for hours afterwards in our ears, and a veritable legion of guards to protect Queen Anne from being mauled and murdered by the crowd.

But for me the shining moment came when some yokel in the crowd pointed to the entwined initials of Henry and Anne, *H&A*, emblazoned upon all the banners and read it as "HA! HA!" The crowd was quick to take up this derisive cry, pointing at Anne and jeering, "HA! HA!" as she rode past, staring straight ahead with her nose in the air.

At Westminster Abbey we unlaced that lovely iridescent gown and replaced it with one of heavy royal purple velvet edged with ermine. Then after a brief respite, during which she rested and gratefully availed herself of a cup of spiced wine and the chamber pot, Anne walked in slow and stately progress down the aisle, with her doting grandmother bearing her train and the sour-faced Duke of Suffolk preceding her, carrying the heavy jewel-encrusted crown upon a purple velvet cushion dripping with golden tassels.

In full ecclesiastical regalia, Thomas Cranmer, the new Archbishop of Canterbury, awaited her, beaming with pride and no doubt congratulating himself for helping bring this happy day to pass.

In the gallery high overhead, King Henry watched it all from behind a latticed screen; this was Anne's special day, and upon it he would not intrude.

She must have been sweltering in that velvet, sweating like a mule, and I am sure it must have been a chore not to let that weighty train pull her off balance, but she never let the strain show, and with regal grace she knelt at Cranmer's feet to be anointed with the holy oil and receive the crown. After a solemn pause, he raised her and led her to the throne, and even as the Dowager Duchess fussed with her cumbersome train, he placed the scepter and orb in Anne's hands and she sat down as the crowned and anointed Queen of England.

The applause was lackluster at best. Anne had made too many enemies, and legion were those who would have happily pulled her from the throne and danced upon her grave. Indeed, George and his friends made quite a spectacle of themselves with their hearty applause; they even tossed their caps in the air. The weight of the diamond brooch pinned to Francis Weston's velvet cap nearly broke a man's nose when it came crashing down. I shot them my most withering glare, but Weston merely stuck his tongue out at me. George and the others just ignored me. George, of course, only had eyes for Anne. Tears of pride trickled down his face, and his mouth must have ached from smiling. I daresay I could have pulled my skirts up over my head and danced a jig right there in front of everyone in Westminster Abbey and he would never even have noticed me.

ও 17 ও

Now there was nothing to do but wait. Henry had kept his end of the bargain; now it was up to Anne to keep hers and deliver the son she had promised him.

Her belly became the center of Henry's world. His eyes never strayed long from it, and his hands were forever patting and petting it, and he often spoke, loving and soft, to the child within. Anne the woman, the temptress who had threatened to lead him to perdition, may have lost her allure, but now by her pregnancy she was transformed into a holy vessel, the sacred receptacle that held Henry's heir.

As that great belly of hers seemed to swell with its own importance, it sapped away all of Anne's vibrancy and vitality, leaving her weary and listless. While it thrived, the rest of her body seemed to weaken and wither, except for her milk-swollen breasts and painful ankles. Her arms, legs, and neck grew skinny as sticks, while dark-shadowed hollows appeared beneath her eyes, which seemed even larger as they peered out dully from her gaunt and sallow face. And her hair, that sleek ebony emblem of her vanity, hung lifeless and lackluster. Her bladder required such frequent release that she dared not stray too far from a chamber pot. Indeed, so urgent was this need that the great chair she sat in at her coronation banquet was specially equipped with a concealed chamber pot, so that she might relieve herself discreetly without absenting herself from the table.

Soothsayers and astrologers surrounded the King, all talking at once, jostling each other to show him their charts and calculations, all of which foretold the imminent birth of "a Tudor sun that will shine over England in Your Majesty's image."

Henry was jubilant and showered them with gold.

"At last the curse is ended!" he enthused. "Praise God, now I shall have no more dead boys and useless girls!"

He even refrained from going on his usual summer progress, since Anne must not travel and he dared not leave her side. Instead he contented himself with hunting in the forests and deer parks nearby.

It was a precarious time for Anne, Dr. Butts said. She must avoid anything that might anger, upset, frighten, or excite her, and she was forbidden to dance, ride, or indulge in strenuous activity of any kind. Her temper, he informed her bluntly, was her worst enemy.

Then, like a godsend, came young Master Smeaton. His music was like a gift from Heaven to give Anne solace and soothe her savage temper. He was but seventeen, pale, soft-spoken, and shy, with elfin features, a tad effete, with thick, wavy locks of soft brown hair, and large, celestial blue eyes; fey, unworldly eyes like drowning pools that cried "Come hither!" If I were the fanciful or superstitious sort, I might imagine he stepped straight out of the realm of Faerie. He had the voice of an angel, and upon the lute he played and composed such music that even I was in awe of his talent. The women of the court adored him; they petted him as if he were a spaniel, lavishing him with praise, little gifts, coins, and trinkets. They bought him clothes and fed him sweetmeats. And in window embrasures, corners, and alcoves they would huddle, whispering and weeping over his unhappy past, condemning the hard-hearted carpenter father who had repudiated his only son when he chose the musician's life over manual labor. But for all their wits and wiles, none of them could snare Mark Smeaton's heart—that belonged to Anne.

Day after day, no matter how vile-tempered and bloated she became, he would sit at her feet, playing his lute and staring up at her with all the devotion and worshipful adoration that Queen Catherine had displayed when she knelt before a statue of the Virgin. He composed heartrending ballads about unrequited love that, for the duration of a song, made us all despise the barriers between noble and humble birth that kept the lowborn lad and the great lady he loved forever apart. George, Weston, Norris, and Brereton used to tease her, prostrating themselves at Anne's feet, hands clutched to their hearts and writhing about like men on a battle-field perishing in great agony of chest wounds as, gasping and groaning, they recited Smeaton's love lyrics until Anne rocked and screamed with laughter.

Anne liked Smeaton well enough, for his talent and slavish de-votion, but he was never more than a servant, a hired musician, to her. Like me, he was forever fated to remain outside the magic cir-cle. Anne was to Mark Smeaton as George was to me: the star be-yond reach.

In the sweltering month of August, when all drooped and lan-guished with the heat, Anne formally withdrew from the world of men. Per royal custom, she must spend the last month of her preg-nancy sequestered, attended only by her ladies, seeing no man but the doctor, until after her child was born.

It was hot as Hell in the Chamber of Virgins, as the room chosen for Anne's confinement was called because the walls were hung with tapestries illustrating the parable of the five wise and foolish virgins. Even though it was August, all the windows were locked and covered to keep out every vestige of sunlight. And though we had candles aplenty, against the somber hues and dark woodwork they were a poor match. Braziers burned the clock around, filling the room with strong, heady incense that induced watery eyes, coughing, and sometimes dizziness, but the doctor and midwives deemed it necessary to kill any pestilence that might be lurking in the air.

We all felt like prisoners in that stifling, suffocating chamber, but mercifully Anne was the only one who was truly trapped. Her ladies took turns attending her and were free to come and go, but

Anne must remain always, sitting listless at her embroidery frame or lying in her immense crimson velvet and cloth-of-gold bed, hands folded across her great belly, a scowl upon her face, with nothing to do but wait, her eyes darting nervously towards the table against the far wall, upon which a collection of basins, stacks of linen, and the midwife's tools lay arranged like implements of torture.

"Will the pain be very great?" I heard her tremulously ask her sister.

"Yes, darling Nan," Mary gently admitted, "it will, but the moment you hold your child in your arms, I promise you, it will all be forgotten!"

Sometimes as she lay there her eyes would stray towards the silver cradle, with its ermine blankets already turned back in readiness, and a smile would spread across her lips, so confident was she of success.

It was my misfortune to attend her during this time, along with her sister and mother, her old nursemaid Mistress Orchard, her aunts Lady Shelton and the Duchess of Norfolk, her dear childhood friend Meg Lee, and the oldest lady-in-waiting at court, the deaf and doddering Lady Bridget Wingfield, who was five years past seventy. But most unfortunate of all was the Lady Mary, the erstwhile Princess, the daughter who had once been King Henry's darling and sole heiress to the English Crown.

At seventeen Mary Tudor was a pallid, pinch-faced, mule-stubborn girl, with a will of iron like her mother, and a voice deep and gruff as a man's. Toothaches, migraines, and stomach pains were the bane of her existence. She was careworn and aged beyond her years; already her auburn hair had begun to fade and thin. Anne hated her with a vengeance. And, in all honesty I must admit, Mary's own stubbornness did not serve her well. Like Anne, she had forgotten, or never truly learned, that a little honey in one's manner can go a long way to furthering one's ambitions.

Anne summoned the King's daughter from her manor of Beaulieu and commanded that she wait on her like a servant. A litter, small and cramped, with curtains of stiff, musty, age-cracked leather, was sent to fetch her, and in it Mary was forced to travel, stifled and boxed in, with the curtains drawn tight lest the people see good Queen Catherine's girl and cheer.

Orders were given for the Lady Mary to present herself to Anne the instant she arrived.

Insolent and regal, gowned in gold brocade with sable-trimmed sleeves despite the heat, with one hand resting triumphantly upon her grossly swollen belly, and the other braced against a gilded table to help support her, Anne welcomed her stepdaughter.

"On your knees! I am Queen and before me you shall kneel! Place your hand here." Anne's hand curled tightly around Mary's wrist, forcing her palm closer, to feel the life quickening beneath the gold brocade. "When your mother bore you, Lady Mary," she sneered, pointedly reminding Mary that she was no longer entitled to be called Princess, "she made a mistake, but here inside me is the remedy. When my son is born you shall be his servant. You shall wait upon him and whenever he pukes, shits, or pisses you will be there to clean up the mess!"

Mary never flinched or faltered. "And if you bear a daughter, Madame?"

Anne thrust Mary's hand away and shrieked, "A son! I will have a son, I tell you!"

She snatched up the object nearest her, a book bound in red leather with gold-capped corners, and hurled it straight and hard at Mary. One of the sharp corners gouged her forehead and drew blood.

"Go! Now! I am Queen and I command you to leave my presence!" she screamed, shaking off her sister and Meg Lee as they tried to calm and quiet her, murmuring soothing shushing sounds, and imploring her to "Think of the child!"

Trembling and pale, with blood snaking down her face, Mary staggered towards the door.

"Halt!" Anne screamed. "Do not turn your back upon the Queen! You will not depart this chamber else you do it properly!" And Mary, blood now seeping into her collar, turned, bobbed a quick curtsy, and stumbled out the door.

Upstairs, she would find that her chamber was among the worst in the palace, a servant's attic room so tiny she could scarcely take three steps in any direction; and the ceiling was so low she risked concussion every time she stood fully upright. The frame of her narrow bed bit through the wafer-thin mattress, and the bed linens bore ancient stains and were frayed at the seams and threadbare. Candles of tallow, not fine beeswax, proffered a paltry, smoky light. And there was no hearth or brazier to keep her warm, so Mary must sleep huddled in the folds of her own cloak, trembling with cold and misery as rats and black beetles scuttled behind the walls.

Anne showed her no mercy. She was assigned the most demeaning chores. Whenever Anne needed to avail herself of the chamber pot, it was the Lady Mary who must attend her, wiping her privy parts with a linen napkin, then afterwards empty the slops, and all the time Anne mocked and derided her: "the mistake," "Catherine's failure," a royal princess no more unless she would be dubbed "princess of the piss pot." How Mary endured it I shall never know.

At last on the seventh morning of September 1533, before the sun had yet to stretch its yellow fingers across the sky to push the darkness away, Anne went into a labor that can only be described as hellish. Lathered with sweat, she kicked the covers from the bed and ripped away her shift. Her naked body bucked and writhed upon the mattress as she screamed and moaned in unrelenting agony.

I stood there transfixed, riveted, as I watched Anne's blood gush out in a red river from between her thighs, and I wished it would keep on flowing until she was bled dry. Every day women faced Death on the battlefield that was childbirth, fighting to bring a new life into the world and preserve their own, and many lost— hundreds, maybe even thousands, lost—so why not Anne?

The midwife shook her head and clucked her tongue over Anne's narrow hips. And Dr. Butts, pausing to wipe the sweat from his brow, had to agree.

"She's really not built for bearing," the midwife said.

But even through the hot red haze of pain, Anne was relentless in her torment of the Princess Mary. She ordered her to stand at the foot of the bed and watch; she must not move or hide her eyes.

"I want you to see my son enter the world!" she cried as her body bucked upon the crest of another giant wave of pain.

Mary watched, silent and pallid, as the slimy, bloody babe slithered from between Anne's thighs. Slowly her lips spread in a wide smile as all about her silence reigned. No one dared move or speak, or meet Anne's eyes.

"What is it?" Anne levered herself up onto her elbows. "Why are you all so still and silent? And you"—she thrust her chin at the Princess Mary—"why do you smile so, you insolent bitch? Well? What is it? Will someone please tell me what's wrong? My son?" She gasped and panic filled her eyes. "Is he . . ."

The midwife and the doctor exchanged wary glances, then turned to the Queen's mother and sister. Clearly no one wanted to be the one to tell her.

Elizabeth Boleyn turned her pale, patrician face away, suddenly absorbed in admiration of the tapestries.

At last, it was Mary Boleyn who took the infant, now swaddled loosely in a blanket, and approached the bed.

"You have borne a daughter, Nan," she said gently as she bent to show her the baby, "a beautiful daughter!"

"God help me! I have failed!" Anne cried. And she rolled over onto her side, turning away from her newborn child.

From opposite sides of the bed the Princess Mary and I shared a smile. All Anne's boasting and arrogance had come to nothing. She had failed in a manner more spectacular than all her gaudy triumphs combined!

But Mary Boleyn was the soul of compassion. Seating herself upon the bed, the mewling babe cradled against her breast, she leaned over and laid a hand upon Anne's shoulder. "Nan, darling, sit up and look at her; look at your daughter, Nan! Take her in your arms, and I promise, you shall know such bliss as you have never known before!"

After a moment, she did. She sat up slowly, shook back her tangled, sweat-sodden hair, and held out her arms to receive her child.

The newborn princess reached up a blood-streaked fist to grip a hank of black hair. Anne raised a hand to gently free it, and the tiny infant fingers grasped hers. Her face, usually so guarded as befit the master card player that she was, was like an open book then, and I could see how she marveled at those tiny, exquisite fingers and the red fuzz that covered the tiny scalp.

"Henry's hair," she murmured. "She has Henry's hair! My Elizabeth!" She smiled proudly as, for the first time, she spoke her daughter's name. "You are a true Tudor rose!" She pressed a kiss onto the tiny, red-crinkled brow.

When the King was at last admitted, wading through a sea of courtiers and ladies, nervously nibbling sugar wafers and sipping spiced wine, the bed had been made anew with fresh linens, and the elaborate red-and-gold coverlet and curtains, removed for the birthing, had been replaced. Bathed and perfumed, and clad in a fresh shift with her hair combed sleek, Anne received her husband with all the majesty of a born and bred queen, propped up against a bank of plump pillows, with her newborn daughter in her arms.

But Henry did not wait for explanations and no one had the courage to tell him the truth before he entered the room. His ruddy face wreathed in smiles, he swooped down and plucked the startled infant from Anne's arms.

"Ah, hear him bellow!" he enthused at the babe's shrill, protesting shrieks. "That, my lords and ladies, is the voice of a King! Oh, Edward, Edward, my precious, precious boy! At last, at long last, I have a son!" He cradled the ermine and purple velvet–wrapped bundle against his heart.

"Your Majesty." Anne's voice rose like a sword to deliver the killing blow. "I have borne you a daughter."

Shrugging off my restraining hand, George crossed the room and went to stand beside Anne's bed. And, one by one, Weston, Brereton, and Norris joined him, clustering around Anne's bed in a show of solidarity.

For a moment it seemed as if the King would drop the baby, and both Mary Boleyn and the midwife took a step forward with arms outstretched, poised to dive to catch her if she fell. He stood there, teetering and pale, his jaw clenching and unclenching. Then, as if he could not quite believe his ears, he laid the infant down upon the nearest table and unwound the layers of ermine, velvet, and lace-edged linen, until she lay completely bare before him, naked and pink, thrashing her limbs and screaming in outrage.

"I have named her Elizabeth," Anne announced, "after your mother and mine."

Behind the King, Elizabeth Boleyn shrunk back to distance herself from this unwished-for honor and Thomas Boleyn glared furiously at Anne.

Henry left the child where she lay and slowly approached the bed. His jaw was clenched so tight that as he passed me I heard his teeth grinding. Angry red blotches mottled his face. And briefly his hand brushed against the hilt of the dagger in his belt as if he longed to unsheathe it and smite Anne dead. Never before had I seen a man fighting so hard to suppress his rage.

"You promised me a son." He spoke these accusing words so softly that only those standing nearest the bed could hear. "The soothsayers promised me a son, 'a Tudor sun,' they said, 'that will shine over England in my image!'"

"It is not the prophecy that is mistaken, Sire, only the timing that is awry. A daughter this time, a son the next," Anne answered, but it was all bluster and show. I know, I saw the fear in her eyes.

Standing beside the bed, Henry breathed deeply. We all watched as that massive chest rose and fell.

"As you say." Henry exhaled long and slowly, then nodded resignedly. "A girl this time, a boy the next." He bent to brush a brisk kiss against Anne's cheek. "You must do better next time, sweetheart," he advised, his eyes boring deeply into hers to make sure she understood that he would not be so tolerant of another failure.

"Next time." Anne nodded, smiling with a confidence I knew she did not feel, before, still weak and wan from the travails of childbirth, she fell back against her pillows and pressed a hand to her brow, shielding her eyes as if she could no longer bear to look upon those who had borne witness to her failure.

"Next time . . ." Henry repeated before he turned his back on her and strode quickly from the room, with most of the court trailing after him.

Beside the table where the newborn Princess Elizabeth still lay, watched over by Mary Boleyn and the midwife, Thomas Boleyn and his brother-in-law Norfolk lingered.

"What a waste!" Norfolk growled, grimacing with distaste. "A shrieking cunt born of a shrieking cunt!"

"Aye," Thomas Boleyn agreed, glancing first at his newborn granddaughter then back at Anne, "what a waste!"

Together they hastened out after the King to condole with him and apologize profusely for Anne's failure, lest any of the blame touch them.

While King, court, and country unenthusiastically celebrated the birth of the new little princess, Anne remained in bed, stricken with an excruciating attack of "White Leg," that dreaded ailment that often strikes women after they have given birth, causing their limbs to swell to the point where one fears the skin will split. For nearly a month she kept to her bed, lying still and waiting to either recover or die as is every woman's lot, and weeping because Henry refused to let her suckle her own child.

I was there, standing by the bed in a pose of ready assistance, when her breasts were bound. I saw the tears raining down her face beneath Henry's stern, unrelenting stare as the midwife silently wound tight bands of linen around Anne's heavy, leaking breasts.

"You are the Queen, Madame, as you are so fond of reminding everyone, not some peasant woman squatting in a field to give suck to her child! For our son I engaged the finest wet nurse in England, but since we have no son . . ." He paused and glared meaningfully at Anne, letting his words sink in, reminding her yet again that the fault was hers entirely. "For our daughter she shall suffice."

It was only when she held Elizabeth that Anne seemed truly happy. Once I walked into her bedchamber with the aged Lady Wingfield and found my husband sitting on her bed with an arm draped around Anne's shoulders, smiling down at the cooing red-haired infant on her lap.

Once again, Anne was marveling over those tiny hands.

"Five fingers!" she breathed, counting them for what must have been the thousandth time, as if she needed to constantly reassure herself that her daughter had not inherited her deformity. "Five fingers, George!" Joy lit up her face. "Only five!"

"Yes"—George nodded indulgently— "she has five fingers now just as she did when last you counted them, only a moment ago, darling Nan. Look, she has our hands!" He extended one of his own graceful, long-fingered hands and compared it with Anne's and Elizabeth's. "Musician's hands—her fingers will be long and slender, just like ours. Aye, Nan, this little one is one of us!"

"Indeed she is. When she is old enough I think I shall appoint Smeaton to be her music master."

"A fine idea," George agreed.

"She has Henry's hair," Anne said, toying with the tufts of red, trying vainly to shape them into ringlets.

"But she has your face, and your eyes, and"—George chuckled as Elizabeth emitted a hearty cry and began to flail her fists about until the wet nurse came running—"methinks she has inherited both her parents' tempers!"

"I think so too. Heaven help her and anyone who dares cross her!" Anne laughed as she sadly relinquished her babe to another woman's breasts.

Rage bubbled and boiled inside me and a silent scream filled my lungs. How I hated her! And, at that moment, I hated my husband! Would the day ever come when George would sit upon my bed, with love overflowing from his eyes, and his face wearing a doting smile while our babe curled a fist around his finger? But we had no child, nor any real hope of having one. I considered myself fortunate if he came to my bed even once a month. No matter how hard I tried, I could not coax him to couple with me more often. Despite what the physician had told me, I had not shared this knowledge with George. I knew, if I did, he would cease to come to me at all. When he did come he did not bother to hide his boredom and distaste; he was more like a man who must submit to the tooth-puller than carnally know his wife. The look of love in my eyes and on my face only made things worse. When he mounted me our expressions were so different, and so distressing to us both, that I was glad when he finally lost all patience and roughly turned me away from him, grasped my hips and pulled to make me kneel on all fours upon the bed, then proceeded to take me as if we were a pair of dogs. And when he was finished, before I could even turn around to face him, he was gone, and the door leading to his chamber was already closing, and locking, behind him.

"Ah, Lady Wingfield," I said loudly, as one must since the poor old thing was as deaf as a post and nearly as dumb as one, "do you not hate to intrude upon a scene of such domestic bliss?"

"Then do not intrude," Anne said simply. "Go away."

"Yes, Jane, do," George echoed tersely. "Go away."

"Come, Lady Wingfield!" I shouted in her ear. "The Queen desires to be alone with my husband!"

Seizing the bewildered old beldame by the arm, I guided her back out even as I struggled to hold back the hot, angry tears. I will not let them see me cry, I kept repeating to myself, I will not let them see me cry. But someday I hope by God to make them cry.

And then *I* will laugh at *them!*

The entire court was awestruck by Anne's devotion to her daughter. It seemed there were not hours enough in the day for her to hold and admire Elizabeth. She wanted to have the baby beside her all the time; she wanted to bathe and dress her and change her soiled napkins, instead of entrusting such duties to the nursemaids. And while Elizabeth slept, she busied herself with examining the fabrics the London mercers sent, selecting vivid shades of green, orange, yellow, red, purple, and amber to fashion exquisite little gowns and caps, which Anne lovingly embroidered herself.

And when in December Elizabeth was, at Henry's command, sent away to Hatfield House to set up her own establishment as befits a royal princess, Anne wept an ocean of tears.

"Can she not stay until after the New Year?" she pleaded.

"No!" Henry replied, firm and unyielding.

"Just until after Christmas then?" Anne begged.

Again the answer was a curt and emphatic "No!" and Anne was advised to cease thinking so much about her daughter and turn her mind instead to getting a son.

"I fulfilled my end of the bargain," Henry reminded her darkly. "I married you and made you Queen, but you have failed to uphold yours! You promised me a son!"

In the end, on a cold, wintry day, with the wind pulling and whipping wildly at her purple and crimson skirts, sleeves, and long black hair, Anne stood in the courtyard and watched the litter bearing her baby away from her until it was completely out of sight.

I watched from a window above as George went out to her and lovingly draped a fur-lined velvet cloak about her shoulders and leaned down so that his chin rested against her shoulder and their cheeks touched.

When Elizabeth's litter was no longer even the tiniest speck on the horizon, Anne turned, threw her arms around George's neck, and wept.

I wept too, but not for Anne or Elizabeth. I cried for myself because no one else would, and because I knew there was naught that I could do to elicit such a display of tenderness and affection from my husband, the man I loved with all my soul and heart. Sometimes I thought I was mad to love a man so much when he was so callous and cruelly indifferent to me, but I could not help myself; I could no more stop myself from loving George Boleyn than I could stop myself from breathing.

❧ 18 ❧

It soon became apparent to everyone at court that the lady in the storm-tossed ship called *Love* was floundering. Like the little lady in the brooch Anne had given Henry as a New Year's gift to seal their bargain, she was in dire peril and all around bets were being laid on whether she would sink or swim. Henry's attentions were no longer centered solely upon Anne. His caresses had grown casual, and his visits to her bed less frequent. His eyes and thoughts often wandered, straying most often to a king's favorite hunting ground—the queen's ladies-in-waiting.

Yet luck was with her, and on Christmas Day Anne announced that she was again with child.

Henry was ecstatic. He swept her up in his arms and spun her round and round. "I knew you would not disappoint me, Anne!" he cried as he covered her face with kisses, then dropped to his knees and lavished yet more kisses upon her belly.

But she did disappoint him. A fortnight later, Anne awoke and found herself lying in blood. Perhaps it was too soon after the birth of Elizabeth, or else despair had delayed her courses, but Anne certainly was not pregnant.

She was terrified to tell the King, and with good reason.

From behind a tapestry I watched through a moth hole as his jaw tightened and twitched and his eyes narrowed to slits.

Anne tried desperately to explain and excuse her error. "I so wanted it to be true; perhaps I deceived myself, but I never meant to deceive you!"

"But you did, Anne, you did!" He pulled her close to him, his fingers digging deep into the soft flesh of her arm, as his eyes bored—as hard as marble and cold as ice—into hers, steady and unwavering, and devoid of sympathy or mercy. "Henceforth, be more careful in your calculations, sweetheart," he said, with a jovial veneer to mask the warning, and then he kissed her cheek and released her.

As soon as Anne's monthly blood had ceased to flow, he came back to her bed, out of duty rather than desire, and her womb soon quickened again.

Anne tried to think only of the child and turn a blind eye to Henry's amours. Fortunately for her, there were other things to distract her.

That spring two acts of Parliament were passed: the Acts of Succession and Supremacy. The first acknowledged all children born to Henry and Anne as the only legitimate heirs, and the second declared Henry the Supreme Head of the Church of England and officially denied the Pope any say in England's affairs. Now all the tithes and taxes the people had paid to the Catholic Church would pour into the royal treasury. And every man must swear to abide by these new laws or else bow his head to the headsman's axe.

England was thrown into a state of upheaval as men grappled with their consciences. To acknowledge Anne's offspring as the lawful heirs would mean bastardizing Princess Mary, the daughter of their beloved Queen Catherine. And by accepting Henry as Head of the Church of England they would be turning their backs on the Pope and putting their souls in peril. Many a man spent hours on his knees praying for the answer, or for God to give him the courage to stand up for his convictions even if it meant torture and death.

Meanwhile, slowly but surely, Cromwell stepped into Wolsey's place, and implemented a devious plan for the dissolution of the monasteries, to funnel their wealth directly into the royal coffers. Their treasures were confiscated, their sacred relics dismissed as frauds and cast out onto the dung heaps, and the monks and nuns who had provided succor for the sick, homeless, and dying were turned out to become beggars themselves, while the monasteries and their lands were given to Henry's favorites or auctioned off to the highest bidders.

Then the blood began to flow and all England rued the day Anne Boleyn had been born. In May an entire order of monks, still in their homespun habits, were dragged through London on hurdles to Tyburn to be hanged, drawn, and quartered, all because they refused to forsake the Pope and deny the validity of the King's first marriage.

When the Acts were proclaimed, Sir Thomas More resigned his post as Chancellor. Citing ill health, he withdrew from public life to live quietly with his family in Chelsea. But everyone knew it was really because "the most honest man in England" would not go against his conscience. Henry knew it too and, his fury blinding him to their years of friendship and the many pleasant hours they had passed together discussing astronomy, geometry, and philosophy, sent Thomas More to the Tower to reconsider.

A month later the kind-eyed scholar, devout Catholic, and devoted family man mounted the scaffold and proclaimed, "I die the King's good servant—but God's first!"

We were playing cards when the cannons boomed to tell us that Thomas More was no more.

"God's blood!" Henry roared, flinging down his cards and rising so abruptly that his chair crashed backwards onto the floor. His eyes shot lightning bolts of fury at Anne. "The most honest man in my kingdom is dead because of you! As God is my witness, if I had it all to do over again, I would not!" He reached out and overturned the table, sending cards, coins, and wine cups clattering to the floor.

Anne sat very still, calmly meeting his hot, accusing stare, as red wine from her overturned cup pooled in her lap, in the crevice between her thighs, before it seeped through her ash-colored satin skirt. A diamond-heavy hand rested protectively upon her belly, now swollen great with Henry's child. Then, slowly, bracing her hands against the arms of her chair, she stood up.

"Rather than condemn me, you should thank me for all that I have done for you. It was I who extricated you from a state of sin and made you the richest prince that ever was in England. Without me, you would never have reformed the Church and dissolved the monasteries to your own great profit and that of every Christian soul in England!"

Henry's shoulders heaved with fury and his hand shot out to grasp Anne's throat. How easily those strong, pink, sausage-fat fingers curled round that slim, swanlike neck, its bones as delicate as a bird's beneath the thin sallow skin. It would not require much pressure at all to snap it like a twig.

A gasp arose from Anne's gentlemen friends and all instinctively took a step closer to her, as if they would have dared defend her against their sovereign lord. Verily, I would have liked to have seen them try it, the foolish, presumptuous knaves! Though I admit, my heart jolted at the sight of George's hand upon the jeweled hilt of his sword.

But Anne was not afraid. Without flinching, she held Henry's gaze, as if she was daring him to do it. As he took a step closer, his own expanding belly brushed against hers, reminding him of the child within. Instantly, he released her throat and stepped back.

"I will say no more, Madame, for the sake of my unborn son, and neither should you." His fingers brushed briefly against her belly, as if it were a talisman, before he turned his back and briskly left the room.

A few days later Anne woke in the dead of night, screaming as if her stomach were being impaled with red-hot knives.

The midwife and Dr. Butts came, but there was nothing they could do.

Anne sat up in bed, rocking, keening, gritting her teeth, and hugging her knees, fighting with all her might to keep the eight months' child within. "It's too soon!" she screamed, her face a contorted mask of pain. "It's too soon! God help me!" But He did not. Across the room the gilded cradle glittered mockingly in the candle-light as, with a final scream of agony, Anne lost the fight and fell back against her pillows in defeat as her womb disgorged its bloody contents onto the white sheets.

The midwife silently swaddled the stillborn prince in a cloth and carried him away. I opened the door for her and, seeing her, King Henry ceased his anxious pacing and approached her.

The midwife trembled and kept her eyes averted.

"A boy?" he asked.

Fear gripped her throat and she could not speak.

"Was it a boy?" he repeated and, when still she did not answer, he grabbed the bundle and unwrapped it to reveal the bloody and blue-tinged corpse of a perfectly formed male infant.

Over the midwife's shoulder, Henry glared at Anne, weeping and rocking inconsolably on her bed. But not a word did he speak to her, either in anger or comfort. Instead he turned his back and walked away.

Anne gradually recovered her strength, but a deep melancholia enshrouded her. Henry was drifting further and further away from her, and she was powerless to pull him back.

George was the only one she would bare her heart to.

"Do you ever look back, George, and find the moment when everything went wrong, even though you know you cannot change it?"

"Don't look back, dearest. It will only eat at your heart," George counseled, coming to stand behind her, to embrace her, as she stood gazing out the window.

"Calais," she continued, as if she had not heard. "Once a woman surrenders herself to a man, even though that is what he wants her to do, he instantly loses all respect for her. Some men are just better at hiding the truth than others, and some do not even bother to try."

"Nan." He spoke her name so softly, so tenderly, as his hands massaged her shoulders. "Come now!" he cajoled, turning her around to face him. "Where is that bold, fighting spirit I know and love so well? I know the pain is great, but it will pass. Hold your head up high, put on your best jewels and your finest gown, and let the world see you as you truly are, my brave, fearless Nan, and go out and win him back! You know you can; you're so clever! And the next child will be a boy—a healthy, thriving boy!"

Listlessly, Anne shook her head. "It is no good, George; he is no good."

A quizzical frown furrowed George's brow. "Dearest"—he paused uncertainly—"what do you mean?"

"I mean it takes two to make a child, George, and more often than not when Henry comes to my bed he is unable to play his part."

"Nan! Listen to me, dearest. Never, if you value your life, breathe a word of this to anyone! Not another living soul; do you hear me, Anne?" His knuckles paled and shook as his fingers dug urgently into her shoulders. "It would be death to anyone who dared even hint . . ."

"I know it, George," she sighed. "It is always the woman who is at fault and never the man."

"It is a curious thing," I said from the corner where I had sat for so long, silent and forgotten, alone with my embroidery and dreams of vengeance, "that His Majesty encounters no difficulty in Madge Shelton's bed."

"Madge?" Anne's face blanched and she took a step back and dropped down onto the window seat. "Madge Shelton? My cousin betrays me with the King? No, I do not believe it!"

George flashed me a warning look, but this time I ignored him. This time I would speak!

"As you will." I shrugged and bent over my embroidery once again. "But I believe they tarry in the Lime Walk even now."

"Very well then, we shall see!" Anne rushed from the room with George hot on her heels, begging her to calm down and not let her temper get the best of her.

"Nan, wait!" he cried. "Let your temper cool before you confront him!"

But Anne Boleyn was beyond seeing reason; she was lost and stumbling blind in a fog of red fury.

With a satisfied smile, I cast my embroidery aside and followed them. This I had to see!

"Filthy-minded scandalmonger!" George hissed at me. "I'll wager you made the whole thing up!"

"No, husband!" I trilled, shaking my head so vigorously that my French hood was knocked askew. "I saw it all through the key-hole, and heard their lusty sighs and cries of passion! I watched him spread her thighs and heard him groan with rapture as his seed gushed out."

"Jane!" George gasped, appalled by my frankness. "Control yourself!"

"Stop!" Anne threw up her hands. "Don't tell me any more! I don't believe it. I cannot. Not Madge!"

"Well, there have been others," I offered. "Did you not know that a stable of pretty young girls is maintained at Farnham Castle for the King's pleasure? Agents scour London and the Continent for more beauties to add to the collection. And have you not heard William Webbe's complaint? Assuredly you must; it's common knowledge. He was out riding near Eltham Palace one Saturday, with his sweetheart sitting before him in the saddle, nestled lovingly against his chest, when lo and behold, who should appear but the King! Without a by-your-leave, he nudged his horse alongside and leaned over to sample the wares. He kissed her, right there in front of her betrothed, and then, liking it so well, he scooped her off Master Webbe's saddle and onto his own, and galloped off to the castle to ravish her at his leisure! It was hours before he sent her back, walking bandy-legged with her privy parts swollen and aching and a bloodstain on her petticoat!"

Now that I had begun, I could not stop myself. As Anne hurried towards the Lime Walk I kept right in step with her, taunting and needling her all the way.

"And whenever the mood strikes him he dons a workman's clothes and incognito to London he rides, to have his way with a tavern wench or a whore from the streets; best pray that he doesn't take the pox and pass it on to you, Anne, or any babes you bear will be born blind or simpletons!"

"That is enough!" George grabbed my arm and pulled me back so forcefully that the laces attaching my sleeve to my bodice snapped. "Say one word more, Jane, just one more," he warned, his hand reaching down to coil round the hilt of his dagger, "and I shall slice your tongue out and ensure silence everlasting!"

We were entering the Lime Walk now, and there, halfway down its length, shaded by a canopy of lime branches, stood the King and Madge Shelton, locked in a passionate embrace.

Anne flew at them like a madwoman, wrenching Madge from the King's arms, slapping, pummeling, and clawing her like a tigress, tearing the French hood from her head and twining her fingers in her cousin's luxuriant honey-blond hair to rip it out by its roots.

Henry was so astonished by this sudden vicious attack that he just stood there gaping while Madge Shelton burst into tears and sank to her knees in supplication, lifting her arms in a vain attempt to ward off Anne's ceaseless rain of blows.

"Nan! Leave off, Nan, leave off!" George seized her around the waist and pulled her away, Anne kicking at Madge until she was beyond reach.

"Sheath your claws, you hellcat!" Henry stepped forward and grabbed Anne's wrists, trying at the same time to keep a safe distance from her nails, which were already caked with Madge's blood. He grimaced and shouted an oath when she kicked his shin.

"Cousin, I swear, I intended no harm!" Madge Shelton wailed. "I thought better me than some rival who would work against you. Forgive me, please; I meant no harm!"

"Nan." George tightened his hold around her waist and shook her gently to get her attention. "Nan, there is merit in what she says."

"Let me go!" Anne tore her wrists away from Henry. "I know all about you now; I know what games you play! Jane has told me all!"

At the mention of my name, and the furious flash of Henry's eyes in my direction, I took a step back and stared down guiltily at the ground, wishing it would open up and swallow me.

"Aye"—Anne nodded vigorously—"I know all about your passel of whores at Farnham Castle, your trips to London in common clothes, and how you go about snatching women right out of the arms of their affianced husbands whenever they take your fancy and afterwards send them back as damaged goods too sore to walk! And now, I discover, you dally with my own cousin! How dare you, you lying whoreson, how do you dare?"

The breath caught in my throat. Surely she had gone too far now, to call the King of England a "lying whoreson" right to his face!

"You will shut your eyes and endure as your betters have done before you!" Henry roared. "I have the power to humble you as much as I have raised you! It is your misfortune that I no longer love you, but you must accept it!"

Anne snorted and her chin shot up, proud and defiant. "My misfortune, you say?" she sneered. "It is my misfortune that you no longer love me? Well, Sire, I never loved you! Though I told you I did so often I was afraid I would come to believe it myself. You're a coarse brute and I hate and despise you, and I'll hate and despise you until I die!" She shook off George's restraining hand. She could not stop herself; now that her tongue had been unloosed she would not bridle it. And on and on she went, as years of pent-up hatred poured out of her mouth. "I might have been happy had it not been for you and your minion Wolsey. I once knew the love of a good man, loyal, honest, and true; so gentle, he could not bear to squash a beetle or swat dead a fly. And never doubt for a moment that I would not rather have been Harry Percy's countess than Henry Tudor's queen! But no, you had to have me, and what Henry Tudor wants he shall have, and my father forced me into your arms. He said it was either you or the convent; I could take my pick, so I chose you. If I didn't have a mind of my own, I would have gone the way of my sister Mary; like a child's toy, amusing today, cast aside and forgotten tomorrow. But I held my ground; I didn't bend to your will, you bent to mine. And love me still or not, I am Queen of England and not your cast-off whore!"

"Dangerous words," Henry growled and took a step towards her. "You speak dangerous words, Madame. . . ."

"I speak the truth as I find it!" Anne screamed.

"Do you think the Crown is set so firmly upon your head it cannot be dislodged? Do you think your arse is so secure upon the throne you cannot be pushed off? Love and hate aside, Madame, we had a bargain! I kept my end; I married you and made you Queen, but you have failed to keep yours! You promised me a son, yet all you've given me is another worthless girl!"

"Oh no." Anne shook her head fiercely. "Elizabeth is not worthless, as time will show; there's not a meek or timid bone in her body! And if you want a legitimate son so badly, you would do well to come to my bed instead of cavorting with whores and risking the pox, and gushing your precious seed into that trollop's cunny"—she pointed at Madge—"when everyone knows she's lain with half the men at court. I suppose you mean to get a child off her just to prove you can. But what good will that do when it is a legitimate heir you need, not another bastard? Like it or not, Henry, you need me!"

"Aye"—Henry glowered as he walked past her—"and I like it not!"

I hurriedly stepped aside and curtsied, meekly bowing my head in his massive shadow, quivering as he stared down at me, not daring to look up again until I heard his footsteps receding down the graveled path.

When I returned to the palace, four guards were waiting to take me to the Tower of London. I protested; I demanded to be taken to the Queen—my sister-in-law, I pointedly reminded them—but they ignored me and laid hold of my arms. I screamed for my husband, but if he heard, he did not heed me. Nor did they accede to my demands that they tarry a moment for me to get my cloak, for I knew the Tower to be a dank, cold place, but even this most reasonable of requests they ignored.

For seven days and seven nights I sat shivering upon the floor, huddled forward, hugging my knees as the cold invaded my bones, to keep from leaning back against the stone wall lest the icy, oozing chill seep through my gown. Fleas bit my skin, making it itch maddeningly, and lice invaded my hair and crawled sickeningly across my scalp. Twice a day I was given hard bread and tepid water and I grew well accustomed to the sound of my own belly growling out in hunger, begging to be fed; yet all my complaints and reminders that I was sister-in-law to the Queen and a Vicountess, Lady Rochford, availed me naught. In a prison that had at various times housed the highest in the land, I was a woman of no importance. So I sat there, all alone in my cold, dark little cell, listening to the black beetles and inquisitive rats scuttling about, and dreaming of revenge. I plucked pieces of straw from my thin pallet and snapped them between my fingers and wished that I could do the same to Anne's neck. And George . . . He left me there, alone, no caring word, warm blanket, or woolen cloak did he send to me; he left me there to suffer in silence. As I snapped the straw between my fingers, my thoughts of him swung like a pendulum between love and hate.

I vowed I would make him pay!

✌ 19 ✌

That summer the King and Queen went on progress as usual. The tension between Henry and Anne increased with every day that passed. Everyone watched and waited with bated breaths for the inevitable break.

In September the royal cavalcade galloped into the courtyard of Wolf Hall, Sir John Seymour's modest manor in Wiltshire. The house itself was far too small to accommodate the royal retinue, and servants immediately began erecting tents on the sprawling pastureland that surrounded the house, shoving aside the woolly white sheep, while the courtiers stood idly about fanning themselves, mopping their brows, sipping cold wine, nibbling sugar biscuits, and complaining about the rusticity they must endure for six whole days.

Sir John Seymour, a portly, graying country gentleman with a balding pate, paunchy belly, and deferential but jovial manner, and his wife, the still lovely Lady Margery, came out into the courtyard to welcome the King and Queen. With them came three of their five children—their sons, Edward and Thomas, auburn-bearded and in their early thirties, one taut-lipped and the other smiling, and their eldest daughter Jane.

Jane. Jane Seymour. Well-a-dee, well-a-day, I thought; so once again I meet the only Jane who is plainer than me. I had known her briefly when she served as one of Queen Catherine's ladies, but when the Spanish Queen was sent into exile, away too went Jane Seymour, home to Wolf Hall to busy herself with the buttery and larder and other domestic pursuits. A bland and boring, whey-faced creature, at seven-and-twenty she was still unmarried and likely to stay that way. A brainless little ninny, she barely had sense enough to answer "yea" or "nay" whenever a question was put to her. King Henry barely allotted her a glance as she curtsied before him, her head bowed demurely in its gable hood so that her big, beaky nose pointed down at the ground. She was so meek she dared not even raise her little eyes of pallid, nearly colorless blue until he had passed her by. And the look Anne gave her was pitying and disdainful as her dark eyes took in the old-fashioned gable hood and the high-necked partlet, or yoke, of white lawn that modestly filled in the square-cut bodice of her plain gray gown. A dowdy little nobody who would live and die a spinster, worthy only of pity and contempt—that was everyone's assessment of Mistress Seymour. But on the morrow we would learn that appearances can be deceiving.

It was just another hunt. Men and their mounts and baying hounds crashing through the forest, with the ladies following, to please their husbands and lovers and, most of all, the King. The ladies were more concerned with whose riding habit was the most becoming and winced at the shrill clarion call of the hunting horn, hoping it would all be over soon. All except Jane Seymour. In the saddle she proved fearless, a true Diana, Goddess of the Hunt, equally the match of the most courageous and able man, charging ahead in determined, single-minded pursuit of the stag, taking every jump without qualm, heedless of the burrs, branches, and mud that deterred the other, more fastidious females.

Afterwards, when we were riding back to take our ease and enjoy a sumptuous picnic, something happened that caused Mistress Seymour's horse to take fright. Perhaps a serpent or some small furry animal crossed its path. Whatever the cause, suddenly the air was rife with frightened whinnies and snorts as the great bay hunter bucked and reared and kicked his hooves in the air. Jane Seymour dropped her riding crop and held on for dear life. They were beneath a tree, and the branches caught and tore away her gable hood; then her hair, plaited and coiled at the back of her head, also became ensnared. The pins pulled free, falling to the ground to be mashed into the earth beneath her horse's mad, crashing hooves, and the long braid unfurled and became tangled in the grasping branches.

It was King Henry himself who rode to her rescue, masterfully quieting the frightened horse and untangling her hair.

And what hair it was! Verily, we were all amazed to see the glory that Jane Seymour kept hidden beneath her hood. Lustrous, wavy, abundant masses of white-blond hair of such a hue that it is rarely seen except on a child no older than two. It was the kind of hair the moonlight gilded silver and the sun made sparkle with a radiant life of its own; white kissed with the barest hint of yellow. But what a waste! Such hair belonged on a temptress, a Snow Queen, not a plain, prim little spinster like Jane Seymour.

The King pulled the bedraggled Mistress Seymour, in her mud-splattered and tattered brown fustian riding habit, from her saddle and onto his. For a moment his bearded chin rested atop the disheveled glory of her wild, tangled tresses, and his lips planted such a brief, feather-light kiss there that the lady herself did not even feel it. It was so swift and light that only a few of us saw, and even then, most did not believe and thought their eyes deceived.

"She looks good on a horse," Anne observed tartly from atop her own mount, immaculate in her black velvet habit with a spray of black and white plumes swaying gracefully atop her hat. "What a pity for her that there are no horses in the King's bedchamber."

"Perhaps she will ride the King as well as she does a horse," I suggested.

"Shut up, Jane!" George and Anne snapped as one, swatting at me with their riding crops.

"He will sleep with her and give her some paltry trinket or a manor house, then marry her off to some obliging fool when he gets bored," Anne surmised.

Even I, at the time, thought the same.

There was dancing that night in the Great Barn, an immense thatched-roofed outbuilding so large it nearly dwarfed the house itself. The Seymour family held all their great celebrations there—weddings, feasts, and holiday revels.

Anne and her friends greeted this information with much mirth and mockery. Francis Weston quipped that they should attend the festivities clad as barefoot yokels in homespun garb, ragged, dirty, and threadbare.

All of them—Anne, George, Weston, Brereton, and Norris—made such a din laughing, jumping and spinning about, clapping their hands, shouting, and stomping their feet in a parody of high-spirited peasants kicking up their heels at a country dance, that the King himself came in to see what all the ruckus was about and sternly reprimanded them for their rudeness in making jests at their hosts' expense.

In truth, the Seymours had done an admirable job transforming their barn. Fine tapestries had been tacked up on all the walls, and garlands of lavender, rosemary, and other sweet-smelling herbs draped the rafters. Great lanterns, suspended from the roof beams, lit the scene. A new wooden floor, sturdy, flat, and polished until it shone, had been laid down especially for this occasion, and outside, to accommodate the overspill of dancers, a ring of glowing torches surrounded the yard, raked and swept clean of rocks, with any holes and ruts filled in so that it was firm and flat and fit for dancing feet.

A long trestle table had been pushed back against the far wall. Though the family's silver intermingled with much pewter—the Seymours being an old family, but of modest means—both the quantity and variety of fare was bountiful. There were trays heaped high with crayfish, mutton, venison, chicken, beef, fish, sausages, and meat pies; fritters, tarts made of custard and various fruits, nuts, and spices; great rounds of yellow cheese; loaves of bread, with earthenware tubs of fresh churned butter, honey, and several kinds of jam; and, in the center of it all, a gigantic spice cake made with red currants and nuts, frosted with frothy white cream that peaked like waves. To drink there were casks of beer, ale, cider, mead, claret, malmsey, and perry, the Seymours' famous pear wine made from fruit from their own orchard. There was no grandiose roasted peacock or swan re-dressed in its feathers, or boar's head with gilded tusks, nor were there any fantastically sculpted sugar or marchpane subtleties. "But," Sir John Seymour explained, "we thought Your Majesty might welcome a simple country repast as a change from the more sumptuous fare you are accustomed to at court," and he was rewarded with a broad smile and a hearty slap upon the back from Henry.

When Sir John informed him that all such things—the harvesting of honey from the hives, the making of butter, cheese, and preserves, and all that had to do with the provisioning and care of the household—were entrusted to his daughter Jane, Henry bade her sit beside him and asked her a multitude of questions, leaning forward, plainly enthralled, lavishly praising her domestic accomplishments, calling her the perfect chatelaine; a paragon of housewifely virtue.

Through it all, Jane Seymour blushed and kept her eyes turned down, staring at her hands, folded primly in her lap. She answered his questions in as few words as possible and in a voice so soft Henry had to lean forward to hear her.

Clearly rankled by her husband's neglect, Anne laughed, too long and too loud, flirted outrageously, and danced every dance, but not once did Henry look her way.

When we returned to court Jane Seymour came with us, as Anne's newest lady-in-waiting, appointed, per the King's command, as a reward to the Seymour family for their gracious hospitality.

❧ 20 ❧

Christmas found Anne desperately trying to remind Henry of the passion she had once aroused in him. Gowned in evergreen velvet with enormous emeralds about her neck and edging her French hood and low square-cut bodice, with Mark Smeaton—proudly sporting the new forest green velvet doublet she had given him—sitting, like a dog, at her feet, accompanying her on his lute, she raised her voice plaintively in song, her chin quivering with hurt pride, reproach, desperation, and unshed tears as she reprised Henry's ode to undying love—"The Holly."

"Green groweth the holly, so doth the ivy.
Though winter blasts blow never so high,
Green groweth the holly.

As the holly groweth green
And never changes hue,
So I am, and ever hath been,
Unto my lady true.

As the holly groweth green,
With ivy all alone

*When flowers cannot be seen
And greenwood leaves be gone.*

*Now unto my lady
Promise to her I make:
From all others only
To her I me betake.*

*Green groweth the holly, so doth the ivy.
Though winter blasts blow never so high,
Green groweth the holly."*

When she finished she arched an eyebrow at Henry. It was a question and a challenge all rolled into one, conveying more than words alone could ever say.

The courtiers stood about uncertainly and turned to look at Henry, waiting to take their cue from him before they risked applauding.

Slowly, the rubies on his deep red velvet and gold brocade doublet flashing blood red in the candlelight, Henry turned his back on Anne.

A few paces away stood Jane Seymour, eyes demurely downcast, staring at her clasped hands. She was beautifully garbed in a gown of icy blue satin adorned with white ribbon roses nestled amidst a trellis of silver embroidered foliage. The low, square bodice was filled in with a white lawn partlet delicately edged with blue and silver embroidery. Upon her head she wore a gable hood with a snood of matching ice blue satin to contain her hair, and a border of pearls to frame her face. The color did wonders for her eyes; their pale, practically colorless blue seemed to absorb the color of her gown, intensifying them to a startling glacial blue, like ice over a pure running river. Before our eyes she was blossoming like some rare, night-blooming flower.

Wordlessly, Henry approached her and held out his hand.

Mistress Seymour shyly looked up to meet the King's ardent

gaze as, after but a moment's trembling hesitancy, she laid her hand in his.

Henry's hand closed around her trembling fingers like a trap.

"The air in here stifles," he announced. "Mistress Seymour, will you accompany me into the garden, where the winter air is pure, crisp, and clean?"

Jane Seymour nodded and answered softly, solemnly, "Where Your Majesty leads I shall follow. Like Our Lord in Heaven, thou art my shepherd."

The crowd parted, the gentlemen kneeling and the ladies sinking into deep curtsies, their bright, jewel-hued skirts pooling gracefully around them, to let the King and his new ladylove pass. Only Anne remained standing in stunned and silent humiliation. George, as always, was beside her, and through it all, as Henry made his preference known, Weston, Norris, and Brereton had been edging nearer.

"Eternal and evergreen shall ever be my love for you," Anne said softly, scornfully, bitterly repeating the words Henry had spoken the night he dedicated his song to her. "What liars men are!" she seethed, tossing her head contemptuously.

"Not all men, darling Nan," George answered. His hands gently clasped her shoulders and he leaned in so that his forehead touched hers. And there they stood, brow to brow, leaning into each other, as close as two peas in a pod.

"Not I, dear lady!" Francis Weston exclaimed in mock indignation.

"Nor I!" Henry Norris asserted proudly.

"Nor I!" echoed loyal Will Brereton.

"Nor I," Mark Smeaton, still seated at her feet, whispered in a voice too soft for Anne to hear; but I read his devotion in the movement of his lips. Then, unnoticed by Anne, he gently lifted the hem of her gown and pressed it reverently to his lips. But there were others who did notice. I was one of them, and Cromwell was another.

Sensing my gaze upon him, Cromwell turned my way. His dark, hard, penetrating eyes met mine, and a shiver slithered down my spine as he favored me with the briefest of nods, acknowledging me and what we both had seen; the knowledge we now shared.

"Knowledge is power!" I could almost hear him speak the phrase that might as well have been his personal motto, it was so often upon his lips.

Forsaking the festive warmth of the Great Hall, where Anne was laughing now amidst the fawning attentions of the men she had just dubbed her "evergreen gallants," and calling for wine, to drink a toast "to the myth of undying love!" I stepped out into the garden and drew the sharp wintry air deep into my lungs.

The ground was covered with snow as thick and white as ermine; icicles glistened like sharp, silvery daggers in the moonlight, hanging from the trees and eaves; and frost twinkled on the bare branches like diamond dust on lace. And there, in the midst of it all, stood the King and Jane Seymour.

Jane shyly averted her eyes as Henry held both her hands in his. Tenderly, he leaned forward and pressed a chaste kiss onto her lips. Then, with a sudden lunge, he tore the gable hood from her head and down spilled her hair, silvered by the moonlight, to swing about her hips.

"Why must you hide such glory?" he demanded as he caught her hair up in handfuls and pressed the pale, silken strands against his lips.

"Though I am a maid still, I am not a child, Your Majesty, and at my age it is not meet for any man but a husband to look upon my hair," Mistress Seymour meekly explained, eyes once again averted as the royal mouth continued to ravish her hair with devouring kisses.

"Jane!" With what eager yearning he breathed her name. "Jane, my gentle, modest Jane!" It was like a prayer, he spoke her name so reverently.

He let her hair fall and his arms reached out to draw her into his embrace.

"Love," he pleaded, "let me hold you against my heart as I hold you within it!"

Quivering, Jane Seymour took a step back, bobbed a quick,

clumsy curtsy, then picked up her skirts and fled, like a frightened rabbit, back into the palace.

"Jane!" Again Henry Tudor sighed her name, head thrown back, eyes shut, savoring it on his tongue. "By your love I shall be redeemed!" He threw up his hands and, twirling and laughing joyously, began to dance in the snow beneath the light of the moon.

❧ 21 ❧

Like a great beehive, the court was abuzz with gossip about the duel—"The Night Crow" versus "The Dove"—and wagers were being laid fast and furious all around about who would triumph. I put my money on "The Dove." I was so confident that I pawned my pearls, my mother's legacy to me, and staked that and all the coins I could spare on Jane Seymour. Had they been mine, I would even have staked Grimston Manor, Beaulieu, and Rochford Hall, but, alas, the deeds were all in George's name.

Jane Seymour and the King were everywhere together—riding for pleasure or in pursuit of game, at the ponds feeding breadcrumbs to the swans, strolling in the physic garden discussing herbal curatives, exploring the twists and turns of the maze, praying in the chapel side by side, touring the palace kitchens, visiting a new litter of spotted hunting hounds or a newborn foal in the stables or the falcons in the mews, and picnicking beneath the trees when all was lush and green again. When Jane embroidered he was there, sitting at her feet, serenading her with love ballads on his lute, reading aloud from morally wholesome works, and handing her her embroidery silks. And when he had one of his frightful headaches—megrims the doctors called them—he would lay his head in her lap, like a little boy, and close his eyes, and let her massage his brow and temples and apply a soothing poultice of chamomile.

But when Henry sent her a purse of gold she refused it, falling upon her knees before the messenger and humbly entreating him to convey her deepest thanks to His Majesty, but she could not accept his gift; her honor was beyond price. When he sent her a brooch with his likeness ringed in diamonds she returned this also, imploring him not to send her jewels, but his likeness alone and unadorned instead; that would be of far greater worth to her than all the diamonds in Christendom.

The King was completely besotted with his "gentle Jane." He sent her a simple locket, oval-shaped and crafted of the purest gold, plain and unadorned as she requested, with his likeness inside. Upon receiving it, she pressed it to her lips and swore to wear it over her heart always. Countless times a day she was seen to open it and gaze lovingly down upon his features.

But did she truly love him, or was it all a calculated seduction masterminded by her clever brothers? Was she their puppet, or the mistress of her own mind? Was she playing him the way Anne Boleyn had? These questions I cannot answer. No one could ever divine what went on inside Mistress Seymour's mind. She kept her own counsel, and from the commencement of their courtship until the day we laid her in her coffin she remained an enigma.

While Jane Seymour and the King contented themselves with the simple pleasures, courting like a milkmaid and her swain, Anne threw herself into showing the world that she did not care; and, perhaps, in doing so she might also convince herself.

The "pastimes in the Queen's chamber" quickly became notorious for their frenzied gaiety, which often lasted until dawn's first light. Wild dancing, music, singing, flirtations, high-stakes gambling, drinking, feasting, ribald riddles, poetry, kissing games, bawdy banter, and brazen jests—and worse, some said—went on inside Anne's apartments.

Anne was living on the razor's edge and had become reckless in her despair, and her band of "evergreen gallants" were with her every step of the way.

To challenge Jane Seymour, with her quaint high-necked dresses of dove gray, delicate pink, pale blue, butter yellow, and mint green, Anne threw down the gauntlet and ordered a dozen magnificent jewel-encrusted and exquisitely embroidered gowns in black, blood red, emerald green, sunset orange, tawny, russet, carnation, sapphire, royal purple, silver, and gold, all with her signature sleeves, often trimmed with costly furs, and French hoods and slippers to match. The bodices were cut low to display the firm mounds of her high-trussed breasts—no modest white partlets for her! And ropes of large, lustrous, creamy pearls ringed her neck, usually with her favorite pendant, the one George had given her—a golden *B* from which three large teardrop pearls dangled—resting in the hollow of her throat. "*B* for Boleyn or Bitch?" a popular jest asked.

But Anne was now three years past thirty, and the constant fear and uncertainty had begun to show upon her face. She looked gaunt, haggard, and drawn, which caused her eyes to appear larger still—"The Goggle-Eyed Whore" indeed—and dark smudges appeared beneath them. There was a pinched look about her mouth and a subtle sagging of her cheeks. Fine lines appeared upon her brow and around her eyes and mouth. Though she had always been slender, she was losing weight at an alarming pace, and for the first time in her life she had to resort to a bum roll to pad her hips beneath her gowns. "That thin old woman," the Spanish Ambassador contemptuously called her. And her breasts were no longer quite as high and firm, or her belly as flat, as they had been before she became a mother, but her boiled leather stays trussed high the first and flattened the other.

To fight the ravages of time, she applied masks of egg whites to her face to tighten the skin, and cleansed it every morning and night with rosewater. Twice a month she bathed her entire body in a mixture of buttermilk and red wine. But she kept away from "Dead Fire"—quicksilver, or mercury—the stringent and agonizingly painful treatment that her grandmother, the Dowager Duchess, swore by. Aye, it burned away the wrinkles and lines but at what cost! It blackened the teeth and made them protrude from the gums like a mule's, fouled the breath, and left the skin scorched, red, and coarse, and sometimes permanently tinged jaundice yellow or bilious green, so that daily applications of lard were required to soothe it, and white lead face paint became a necessity to disguise the discoloration. Anne thought the cost was too high to pay and resorted to more moderate methods instead.

She plucked her brows into thin, graceful arches and lined them and her dark eyes dramatically with black kohl, painted her lips blood red, rouged her cheeks with cochineal, and scented her person and hair with rare perfumes brought at great expense from the Orient.

But not all the rouge, exotic perfumes, and fascinating gowns in the world could help her now. Only one thing could save her—a son—and for that she needed Henry.

❧ 22 ❧

Against all the odds, she did it. Even though it was just for one night, and had nothing to do with love, or even liking, she did it. For one last night, he was hers again. But did she have God or the Devil to thank for it?

How did she do it? She danced—a dance of desperation.

Upon Anne's orders a large round stage with a short flight of steps at the front was erected in the Great Hall. Tantalizingly veiled with a sheer, gauzy midnight blue curtain spangled with gold and silver stars, it piqued our curiosity, and as we supped we speculated about what we were about to see.

A strange, heady incense that made us feel pleasantly giddy and lightheaded, filled the air. And there was the most peculiar music, the likes of which we had never heard before; slow, undulating, throbbing, and sensual, some of us could not help ourselves and began to sway slowly in our seats. It was played by Moorish musicians—wherever had they come from?—with skin black as tar. Turbans swathed their heads and they were garbed in tunics and full, baggy, billowing trousers made of vivid, jewel-hued silks, and upon their feet they wore golden slippers with pointy toes that curled in upon themselves.

The curtains parted and we sat up straight and gasped. Granted, the Tudor court was a bawdy place, but this . . . it took our breaths away; we were spellbound and appalled, but not one of us, no matter how outraged, could look away or leave.

To the left of the stage, Francis Weston lolled indolently upon a golden throne, wearing a robe of royal purple with a circlet of gilded laurel leaves. A goblet was in his hand and he raised it often to his lips, and every time he lowered it a young woman, naked but for bands of cloth of gold about her breasts and hips, replenished it from a large golden flagon. And at his feet, his hair and the whole of his skin painted gold, naked but for ropes of pearls around his hips and a golden pouch to contain his genitals, knelt Mark Smeaton with his lute.

Francis Weston was portraying King Herod, the voice of Tom Wyatt informed us, startling us, as until then no one had noticed the poet, who was apparently to act as our narrator, lounging upon the steps, wearing a gold-bordered white tunic and sandals, and holding a small gilded harp.

Beside King Herod, perched haughtily upon a slightly smaller throne, was Madge Shelton as Queen Herodias, in regal purple robes and a jeweled coronet, being fanned with peacock feathers by her gilded and scantily clad slave—Henry Norris.

To the right of the stage, in a very short tunic and tall boots of shiny black leather, and a black half mask, stood Will Brereton, a long-handled axe clutched in one gloved hand and a length of silver chain in the other. The chain was attached to a collar, and that collar encircled the neck of the prisoner kneeling submissively at his feet—John the Baptist—George!

My blood began to race at the sight of him kneeling there, bare but for a light blue loincloth, with his skin not gilded, but rubbed with a glistening oil that contained just a hint of gold dust.

There was a movement at the back of the stage, and slowly, climbing a staircase, the twin of the one in front, a figure wrapped in cloth of silver appeared. By the shape it was plainly a woman, but she was wound so tightly in her all-concealing silver shroud she could only move in the tiniest, mincing steps. Her face was completely hidden in the shadows cast by the material draped over her head, which formed a makeshift hood.

When she reached center stage she began to slowly emerge from her cocoon.

First a graceful, long-fingered hand appeared, the nails gilded and every finger ringed with diamonds and pearls; then a bare arm, with bangles of gold about the slender wrist. She turned her back to us and flung both halves of the silver sheet open wide. She released it and it shimmered to the floor, revealing a second shroud, this one cloth of gold.

On all fours, Henry Norris crawled across the stage to retrieve the silver sheet, and several ladies sighed meltingly at the sight of his muscular gilded flanks revealed by the gold loincloth. As he reached out a hand, she suddenly spun round and a dainty bare foot with gilded toenails emerged, its ankle encircled by tiny tinkling gold bells. To stay his hand she stepped on it, but only lightly, and he instantly dropped flat, prostrating himself upon his belly, and ardently kissed her little foot. She jerked it away, and as she did so he caught hold of the golden shroud and yanked it off. Then, on hands and knees, dragging both silver and gold sheets, he scurried back to kneel beside Queen Herodias.

Now we saw her entire body, draped from head to toe in a night-black veil trimmed with tiny gold bells. She raised her arms, and as she spun around the hem billowed out and we saw beneath it several layers of colorful veils.

Then Salome began to dance. But it was no dance we knew, no courtly pavane, galliard, or lavolta. Sensuously she twirled and swayed, undulating her lissome body like a serpent, mesmerizing us with every movement as, one by one, she shed her veils—black, purple, sapphire, emerald, scarlet, yellow, saffron.

When the last veil fell, our eyes were wide as dinner plates and our mouths so agape that every tooth in our heads could be seen. A servant pouring wine into the Duke of Norfolk's goblet kept pouring even when it was full and overflowing onto Norfolk's lap. But Norfolk didn't even notice. Like everyone else, he could not tear his eyes away from the spectacle before us.

There she stood, arms upraised, black hair swaying and hanging straight to her knees, a golden idol demanding to be worshipped, a black and gold Circe, wearing a gown that poured over her body like molten gold, its sleeveless bodice cut low in a deep V, the point of which almost touched her waist. Her skirt was slit thigh-high in front and back and on both sides to reveal her bare legs.

There was the shrill, grating sound of a chair sliding, scraping back, and then King Henry was striding across the floor and bounding up the steps to confront Anne.

There they stood, face-to-face, staring at each other for a long, tense moment, during which no one dared blink or breathe.

Suddenly he stooped, grabbed hold of her, and slung her roughly over his shoulder.

"If you dare cavort like a whore before my court, then, by Heaven, I shall treat you like one!" he roared as he left the stage. Anne did not struggle or protest; instead she went limp and let him carry her away.

I did not hesitate. Pleading a sudden stomach upset, I scurried out and ran, with my skirts hitched up high above my knees, to Anne's bedchamber and leapt inside a cupboard with latticed doors I could peep through and have a direct view of the bed.

An instant later Henry kicked the door open, splintering wood and breaking hinges. He dumped Anne on the bed, and grasped her gown and tore it off her shoulders, all the way down to her waist, revealing that she had also gilded her nipples.

"Harlot's tricks!" he cried, pinching and twisting them savagely. Anne yelped in pain and Henry slapped her.

Swiftly, he ripped away the rest of the fragile cloth-of-gold gown, and in frayed and tattered tinsel ribbons it floated down onto the floor.

"Just like a whore!" he spat. "Not a stitch on underneath!"

"Please, my lord, not like this!" Anne cried.

"Shall I take you like the bitch you are? Would you like that?" Henry grasped her hips and turned her, positioning her on all fours. "Are you in heat, my bitch?" His meaty fingers dug into her cunny. Heedless of Anne's cries, he pulled her back against him and ground his loins hard against her buttocks. "That performance you gave tonight would certainly suggest you are! So I shall do what you want and mount you!" He ripped off his great bejeweled codpiece—a magnificent padded mass of gold embroidery and rubies—tearing the laces in his haste, and flung it onto the floor.

Gripping hard her hips, he plunged into her full force.

Anne screamed as if she were being torn asunder. Instantly he clapped a hand over her mouth to stifle her screams, and continued to thrust into her, stabbing hard and deep, ignoring the tears that poured over his fat pink fingers.

"Do you know what the people say of you, Madame?" he continued between grunts and thrusts. "They call you the Witch Queen! Methinks they are right—you must have bewitched me! How else could my eyes have been dazzled for so long when there is nothing about you to desire or love? You must have worked some spell upon me. You made me desire you and turn the world upside down to have you, to shed blood and imperil my immortal soul and kingdom, all for you!" He thrust savagely again and Anne tried to squirm free. "Hold still, damn you!" His fingers dug deep into her naked hips. "Born of love, lust, indifference, or hate, I must have a son! Do not think for a moment that this pleasures me any—you disgust me! You with your shrew's tongue and skinny stick of a body! You are more skeleton than flesh-and-blood woman, and what flesh there is of you sags!" He savagely twisted first one breast and then the other, followed by the slight slackness of her stomach. Anne grimaced with pain, and more tears squeezed out from between her tightly clenched eyelids as her body shook with silent sobs.

"Tell me, Nan, did you make a bargain with the Devil to get me? Was it worth it?"

Suddenly his florid red face, dripping with sweat, contorted, twisting until it resembled a leering devil mask, and a long, guttural sigh escaped him as he came, spewing his seed deep into her womb. He was still for a moment; then he withdrew, contemptuously releasing her, letting her fall facedown, sobbing, onto the bed.

He stood there towering over her, with his flaccid prick dangling like a worm on a hook, flanked by the limp, torn laces that had held his codpiece in place. Never before had I seen such intense hatred upon a human face. Then, without a word, he grabbed her long hair and wiped his cock off with it, scooped up his codpiece, and drew the folds of his red velvet surcoat modestly across his loins.

At the door he paused and tore off one of the gold medallions that decorated his doublet and threw it at her. "Here!" he spat contemptuously. "I always pay my whores!" Then he was gone, leaving the broken door sagging open wide so that any who cared to might witness what he left behind him.

A little while later, Anne, her face red and swollen, her lips puffed and bleeding from where she had bitten them against the pain, levered herself up slowly from the bed. She stood there, swaying beside it, with Henry's seed trickling down her legs and blood smearing her thighs; then, wincing with every step, she staggered across the room to her prie-dieu and dropped down onto her knees.

Hands clasped tightly, desperately, in prayer, she lifted her tearstained face to the crucifix and benevolent, sad-eyed statue of the Virgin, with her compassionate face and mantle of celestial blue.

"God help me! Holy Mother, help me! Please!" Fresh tears poured down her face, and her lips quivered uncontrollably. "Let my womb quicken and bring forth a son! Help me; my fate is in your hands."

They must have heard her. Incredibly, her prayers were answered.

❧ 23 ❧

On the seventh day of January 1536 Catherine of Aragon breathed her last. Before she expired she somehow found the strength to write one last time to the only man she had ever loved.

"Lastly, I vow that my eyes desire you above all things," she wrote, sheer willpower guiding her pen as agonizing pains stabbed her breast. She signed it "Catherine, Queen of England."

When the embalmers cut open her chest they found a hideous black growth hugging her heart in a deathly embrace.

When her death was announced at court Henry donned the brightest, gaudiest yellow he could find, arraying himself in it from cap to shoes, and ordered everyone else to do the same.

Anne was at his side in a gown of rich golden-yellow brocade encrusted with diamonds and edged with black lamb's wool, with a diamond-dusted veil of beautiful yellow lace draped, like a Span-ish mantilla, over her French hood. A triumphant smile graced her lips, and her right hand rested upon the mound of her little round belly that was just beginning to show.

Never before had she looked so beautiful. This time pregnancy seemed to agree with her. Gone were the dark-smudged hollows beneath her eyes, and her cheeks were no longer gaunt, but pleasantly fleshed out, and her skin was smooth and clear. She was radiant, glowing with health and vitality.

Their daughter, Princess Elizabeth, was with them and, like her parents and the court, clad in brilliant yellow. Laughing, Henry tore off her little gold-embroidered cap to show off her fiery Tudor-red hair and swung her up onto his shoulders and paraded her around the Great Hall.

"God be praised, the harridan is dead!" Henry cried again and again, all smiles and good cheer. "Now we are free from all threat of war!" With no aunt to avenge, the Emperor Charles now had no reason to invade.

Jane Seymour seemed like just another face in the crowd. Anne had done it again; she had bounced back from the very brink of failure. Seeing them walking side by side, fawning over their daughter, tousling her red hair and kissing her cheeks, they appeared the very image of a happy couple very much in love.

"Bravo, Anna Regina! I knew you could do it!" George smiled, his eyes full of love, as, garbed in sunny yellow satin, he doffed his yellow-plumed cap and knelt at her feet.

Anne reached down to caress his bearded chin. She smiled but did not speak. There was no need for words between them. There never was. The look in their eyes said it all.

But the appearance of love renewed was merely a façade, a charade, to keep Anne calm for the sake of the precious cargo she carried in her womb.

On the day of Catherine's funeral I was with Anne when she caught the King dandling Jane Seymour upon his knee, chuckling as he nuzzled her with his bristly red beard. She giggled as he chucked beneath her chin and a blush suffused her pasty cheeks.

Anne instantly flew into a rage.

Henry leapt up guiltily and Jane Seymour tumbled to the floor.

"Sweetheart, I'm sorry!" Henry exclaimed as he stooped to help her up.

"Aye, she acts the part of a whey-faced prude, and she certainly looks the part, I grant you," Anne said tartly, "but I see now she is nothing but another court whore masquerading as a lady!"

Henry drew himself up to his full height. "Mistress Seymour is a pure and virtuous lady!"

"Ah, yes, I heard that her virtue is beyond price; did she not start that rumor herself? Let me see now." Anne, the consummate actress, tapped her chin thoughtfully. "I seem to recall something about a purse of gold. She returned it to you, did she not, with the message that her virtue was beyond price? Yet the fine bay hunter and the services of the tailor who fashioned her new riding clothes she readily accepted." Anne arched her gracefully plucked black brows. "Are not the very linens that touch a woman's body more intimate than coins? And the horse itself, I'll wager, was worth more gold than was in the purse she rejected. And to wear a married man's portrait around her neck . . ." As she spoke, Anne reached out and took the locket in her hand. "That does not seem very pure and virtuous to me!" Her fist closed tightly around the golden oval and she twisted the chain and yanked viciously.

Before the delicate gold chain snapped, it bit into Jane Seymour's neck. What little color there was in her pale face drained away as blood began to trickle from the wound, and a bright red stain spread slowly across her high-necked white partlet. Her hand rose gingerly to feel the wound and came away bloodstained. She gasped, wobbled, and Henry caught her just as her knees gave way.

Anne looked on, serene and smiling, swinging the locket round and round by its broken chain.

"I will deal with you later!" Henry said ominously as he scooped up the swooning Mistress Seymour and carried her from the room, bellowing for a physician.

Smiling gleefully, I scurried after them, eager to ingratiate myself.

"Your Majesty, if you will take Mistress Seymour to her chamber, I shall bring Dr. Butts forthwith! Please let me help; I am a good friend to Mistress Seymour and it grieves me to see her injured, and by my own sister-in-law!" I pursed my lips disapprovingly, making where my allegiance lay plain as day.

Thus I was allowed by the very grateful and anxious monarch to remain at Jane Seymour's bedside and even to assist Dr. Butts when he arrived.

It was I who carefully snipped away the bloodstained partlet, frowning over the ruin of the dainty pink rosebud embroidery edging the collar. I saw the lust in Henry's eyes when I peeled it away and revealed the bare, round white mounds of her breasts above the mint green bodice.

I hovered helpfully at Dr. Butts's elbow, handing him what he required, as he cleansed the wound, applied a soothing salve, and bandaged it in clean linen, and, lastly, administered a small dose of poppy syrup to help her rest and numb the pain. And all the while King Henry paced back and forth at the foot of the bed, gnawing his knuckles and darting worried glances at his ladylove lying pained and pale as death upon the blue satin coverlet of her modest maiden's bed.

When Jane Seymour at last, in poppy-induced oblivion, slept, the doctor was dismissed, and Henry also waved me out, saying, "I will sit awhile with Mistress Seymour."

Curtsying, I withdrew, but only into the anteroom, where I knelt and pressed my eye against the keyhole.

Henry moved to sit on the bed beside her. He leaned over to caress her brow and face, letting his hand trail slowly down, gliding over her neck, carefully bypassing her injury, and down, over the exposed upper portions of her breasts, bared for the first time before the eyes of a man.

Jane Seymour moaned and her eyelids fluttered but did not open as he leaned forward and pressed a kiss, chaste at first but then more ardent, onto her pale pink lips. Her arms rose then, seemingly of their own accord, and went round his neck and her body arched up to meet his.

He was upon her in a trice, fat fingers fumbling to lift her skirts and unlace his codpiece.

Her legs parted and, like her arms, lifted to twine round him, and I saw her thighs, plump and pasty-white, above the pink ribbon garters and white stocking-tops. As her legs wrapped round him, one pink satin slipper fell to join his cast-off codpiece on the floor.

Covering her face and throat with kisses, he removed her gable hood and plucked the pins from her hair so that his hands could dive into the white-blond waves.

I started at the feel of a hand upon my shoulder and spun round to confront the grim, unsmiling countenance of Thomas Cromwell.

He waved me aside and, with a grimace, lowered his bulk to kneel before the keyhole. After a moment he stood up and gestured that I might resume my place. But he did not leave; instead he remained, standing, hovering behind me, the fur edging his black coat tickling my cheek, as he leaned forward and pressed his ear against the door.

Jane Seymour mewed like a frightened kitten when he entered her, and her arms and legs tightened around him as he thrust and grunted his way to satisfaction, sounding for all the world like a greedy pig at trough.

Afterwards, she rolled onto her side and drifted deeper into slumber while Henry washed himself and put his garments right, then sat down to wait for her to wake and realize that she had left maidenhood behind her.

Bleary-eyed and still a trifle dazed, she sat up, wincing at the unexpected pain between her legs. It was then that she noticed her raised and rumpled skirts and tousled hair spilling down about her shoulders. Her eyes widened as the truth dawned on her. Her mouth quivered and the tears began to fall like rain.

"Nay, sweeting, do not weep, do not despair. . . ." Henry implored.

"How can I not? When all that I held most dear—my virtue, my honor—is lost? My father, my brothers, the court, they shall all think me a wanton!"

"Nay, sweeting, all will be well. By my soul, I would not see you dishonored. I would sooner fall on my sword than cause you disgrace!" He leaned over and kissed her brow. "No one will think ill of you, and we shall keep what has passed between us a secret until you are able to take your place honorably at my side. . . ."

Outside the door Cromwell and I exchanged startled glances. Did he mean . . . Could he possibly mean . . . marriage?

"Ah, my little love, my little queen!" Henry sighed blissfully as he scooped up flowing handfuls of her hair and lifted them to his lips.

"Dear heart," he continued, "did you know that I am three years past forty? I have reached the age where a man's lust is not so quick to kindle as it was in youth. I want a sweet and docile wife, a quiet, pleasant, gentle, loving wife, not a she-devil, or a screaming, vengeful harpy; I want peace and no more turmoil, bloodshed, and arguments. I want you, my gentle Jane!" He took her hand and raised it reverently to his lips. With another sigh he heaved himself to his feet. "I must go now, dearest, before I am tempted to again despoil this treasure. O Queen of my heart, rest now and worry not; I promise you all will be well!" He stooped and kissed her fervently.

Jane Seymour merely sat there as dazed and bewildered as if she had just been struck by lightning.

Cromwell and I shared another astonished glance, then hastened away as Henry turned his steps towards the door.

Did I warn Anne? No! Of course not. I wanted to see her cast out, brought low, sunk into the very depths of disgrace and despair, mired so thick she could never claw her way back out, and I wanted that plain Jane Seymour to be the instrument of her destruction! What a comeuppance, what a humiliation it would be for that smoldering, black-haired temptress, with all her clever witchery and wiles, to be pushed aside to make room for pure and demure Jane Seymour, that paragon of domestic virtue!

❧ 24 ❧

Henry was now in full retreat from Anne. Even though her belly was swollen big with his child, he could not abide to be in the same room with her. Her laughter grated on his nerves. The sound of her voice made him scowl and wince. He often sought refuge in sport—the archery butts, tennis court, bowling green, or tiltyard. It was the latter he retreated to on the afternoon of the 29th of January 1536, leaving Anne alone with her ladies, talking, sewing, and listening to the devoted Smeaton strum his lute.

I needed a breath of fresh air so I excused myself—I knew I would not be missed—and went out to watch the joust.

Jane Seymour was there too, seated in Anne's place in the royal box.

Henry, armor-clad astride his great white warhorse, rode up to receive her favor, a kerchief exquisitely embroidered by her own hand with bluebells and buttercups. He pressed it to his lips before holding up his arm for her to tie it around.

Watching from nearby, his opponent, Sir Francis Weston, glowered with his single eye at the smitten King and simpering Mistress Seymour.

"By God and all his Saints, King or not, I shall best him!" he vowed hotly.

"Have a care what you say," Will Brereton warned. "Francis, it is the King you speak of!"

"I do not care if it is Lucifer himself!" Weston flared. "Go quickly to the palace, Will, and ask the Queen to send me her favor to wear. I will be her champion!"

And the King was made to wait, his horse pawing impatiently, while Weston's squire dallied, making certain all his master's equipment was in order, checking and rechecking every buckle and strap, until Brereton galloped back to bind a kerchief of scarlet silk, embroidered with Anne's haughty white falcon, around his upper arm.

Only then did King and knight take their places, position their lances, and let their visors clang down, poised to dig their spurs in and charge the moment Mistress Seymour gave the signal.

Never before have I seen a man more determined to win than Francis Weston. His lance struck the King's armored chest so forcefully it dented the breastplate. I watched in horror as the King flew backwards from his saddle and lay motionless in a cloud of billowing dust. The mighty warhorse reared, flailing its hooves high in the air, then slowly began to fall backwards until its full weight came crashing down upon the King.

There was much screaming from the people in the stands, and many ladies, including Jane Seymour, fainted.

"The King is dead! Lord save us, the King is dead!"

The squire who reached him first and wrenched off his helmet, followed fast by Dr. Butts, said nothing to contradict this. Suddenly the air was rife with panic, hysterical sobs and keening laments. People raced about in utter confusion, courtiers and commoners alike, tearing their hair and clothes, screaming, embracing, colliding with and tripping over one another, blind and witless in their despair.

Francis Weston's face went ashen and he swayed in his saddle, and had it not been for Will Brereton he would have fallen.

Bending over the King as several hands moved swiftly to divest him of his armor, Dr. Butts advised, "Best keep this from the Queen for now. . . ."

My eyes met the cunning dark weasel eyes of Anne's uncle, the

Duke of Norfolk. Each of us knew beyond a doubt what the other was thinking.

Norfolk hated his haughty niece. She had served her purpose, and now that her star had fallen, he—like her equally unscrupulous father—had no further use for her. To these two hard-hearted, ambitious men, being on the winning side was all that mattered.

Even then Thomas Boleyn and his wife were in the royal box with a vial of smelling salts, trying to revive and comfort Mistress Seymour, lamenting to her father and brothers that they had not themselves such a dutiful, obedient daughter and fine, stalwart sons.

"Do you mean it might cause her to miscarry?" I asked.

"Aye," Dr. Butts nodded as he rolled up his sleeves and gave his full attention to the King.

Our eyes met again and this time we didn't tarry. Norfolk and I were off and running, sprinting towards the palace. He lost his feathered cap and I lost both my slippers, but neither of us cared, as we jostled and elbowed and pushed and pulled each other. We both wanted to be the first to tell Anne this most distressing news.

"The hell you will!" We started at Francis Weston's outraged roar and looked back to see him running behind us, casting off the pieces of his armor left and right, with Will Brereton right behind him, dodging the falling armor. "I know your game, you viper-tongued bitch, and you, you loathsome reptile!" he shouted.

"The King is dead!" we screamed as we burst into Anne's chamber. Weston was right behind us; he grabbed my skirt just as we pushed through the door, and tried to pull me back out into the corridor, but I kept running and it tore right off, so that I stumbled and fell into the room wearing only my petticoats and bodice.

"He's dead!" I crowed. "The King is dead! What will happen to you now? Everyone hates you!"

"With no legitimate male heir, civil war is a certainty!" Norfolk chimed in as he caught his breath and smoothed down his hair and clothes.

Anne bolted up from her chair with a bloodcurdling scream.

"No! No, it cannot be! Whatever shall become of me?" Her eyes darted about desperately, and those watching her all pointedly stepped back and looked away, making a great show of tweak-ing sleeves, polishing rings, examining fingernails, or looking out the windows, studiously ignoring her. "The people hate me! They shall rise against me! Who will protect me? And my Elizabeth? My little girl! Who will fight for my daughter's rights? Who will safe-guard the throne until she is of an age to reign?"

Suddenly her eyes went very wide and she doubled over, gasp-ing, hugging her belly.

George arrived then. He pushed and elbowed his way through the crowd, shouting for them not to just stand there gawking, but to get the midwife and a doctor. He carefully gathered Anne up in his arms and carried her to her bed. Before he was even halfway there the sleeves of his cream silk doublet were soaked through with Anne's blood.

"You bitch!" Weston spat. "See what you've done! If you were a man, I would break every bone in your body and last of all your neck!"

With a mad, outraged scream, I flung myself at him. Soon, the three of us—myself, Weston, and Norfolk—were rolling on the floor, fighting tooth and nail, and shrieking curses and insults at each other while Brereton tried to pull us apart. The courtiers, ladies, and servants were torn between observing the bloody throes of the Queen's miscarriage and watching us roll on the floor, brawling like drunkards in a tavern.

The tangle of our bodies blocked the door, and a page in royal livery stumbled over us and cracked a tooth upon the floor before he staggered up and tried unsuccessfully to make himself heard above the din.

Both my sleeves were torn away, and I slapped Weston's face and accused him of trying to strip me naked to humiliate me.

"Nay, Madame, I would not offend people's eyes in such a way!" he retorted.

Nearly blind with rage, my hand groped for Norfolk's dagger.

"No!" Brereton screamed as I hurled myself at Weston, aiming directly at his remaining eye. Brereton's booted foot kicked the dag-ger from my grip, and when I rolled to retrieve it his foot came down upon my hand. As I tried to squirm free, Brereton tottered and al-most fell. As he sought to steady himself his weight pressed down fully upon my hand. There was a sharp snap like a dry twig as a small bone in the back of my hand splintered and I howled in agony, startling the room into abrupt silence.

Taking advantage of the sudden silence, the page boy—his cap lost, blond hair rumpled, hose and livery torn, his palms and knees scraped and bleeding from his fall—shouted in a reedy voice crackling between manhood and adolescence, "The King is not dead; merely stunned!"

With a shriek, I lunged myself at him and sank my teeth vi-ciously into his ankle.

Bleeding from both nostrils, Norfolk sat up and regarded me strangely. "Good Lord, woman, you really are mad!" he exclaimed, speaking the words that, by their expressions, seemed to be in everyone's mind.

Then all was forgotten as the midwife with her apprentice, a doctor with his assistant, and an apothecary surged in, all talking at once, shouting instructions that sent the servants scurrying, and Anne became the center of attention once again.

She lay screaming upon her blood-soaked bed, naked from the waist down, knees bent and thighs spread wide, as the midwife rolled up her sleeves and tried to stop the bleeding and save the King's unborn child.

George knelt on the bed, ignoring the midwife's orders to de-part. He leaned over Anne, grasping both her hands tight, willing her to stay in this world as her blood continued to pour out.

"Stay with me, Nan, stay here with me!" he pleaded and com-manded urgently, tightening his grip as her eyes started to roll up so that only the whites showed. "No! Stay, Nan, stay here with me!"

"Husband"—I touched his shoulder—"you should go; it is not proper for you to be . . ."

Before I could finish, his hand swung back and caught me full upon the mouth. Even before my mind had time to register what had just occurred, he had already turned his attention back to

Anne, coaxing and commanding her to fight for her life, while I reeled about, spots dancing before my eyes, blood pouring from my nose and lip.

My tongue probed gingerly at an incisor wobbling precariously in its socket.

"Right at the front, George—I shall lose a tooth right at the front! Oh! How could you?" I wailed as tears flooded my eyes, for there was no way to fix firm again a wiggly tooth.

But George did not care about me or my tooth; all he cared about was Anne.

Henry Norris soon brought word that the King had recovered his senses and Mistress Seymour was at his side, holding his hand.

"Jane!" That was Henry's first word, a beatific sigh, when he opened his befuddled blue eyes and saw her sitting there. And there she stayed, patient as a saint, bathing his bruised face, adjusting the bandages that swathed his head when he complained that they pinched, giving him a spoonful of honey to make the apothecary's medicine more palatable, and holding his hand when the pain in his leg reached a crescendo under the surgeon's nervous fingers and cruel instruments. Never for a moment did she leave his side, not even when the bone chips were removed, the blood spurted, and the vile, greedy black leeches were set down to suckle the seeping wound.

As Jane Seymour was firmly cementing her place in Henry's fickle heart, Anne was fighting her own body, determined to keep in what her womb was equally determined to spit out.

"Please, God, no!" she screamed to no avail. God had—like all sensible men—abandoned her.

With a shattering scream the midwife's apprentice fainted and all around stepped back from the bed, their hands rising to form the sign of the cross or the symbol to ward off witchcraft. Some ladies screamed and fell fainting to the floor, others hid their eyes and turned away, or fled the room, hysterical and babbling incoherently about monsters and demons.

It was a son, fortunately born dead, for it was a monster much malformed. It had two faces but one huge head, carpeted with wispy tufts of carroty hair, so large it had savagely ripped Anne's flesh during its egress. The little shoulders slanted sharply so that the right was higher than the left, and the spine was as crooked as the letter *S*, while all four limbs, though perfectly formed with the proper number of fingers and toes, were devoid of bones and as limp and dangly as a jellyfish. But between its tiny flaccid thighs a perfectly formed male organ was plainly visible. This was Henry's much-longed-for prince. Indeed, it even had Henry's blue eyes!

Seeing it, Anne went wild, shrieking like a madwoman, and had to be restrained lest she do herself further injury. Already she had lost so much blood it was a wonder that she still lived.

After taking a deep, steadying breath and crossing herself, the midwife bent again to her work.

"She'll not bear again, will she?" I whispered.

The midwife paused in the act of sewing up Anne's badly torn flesh with catgut thread and, after darting a furtive glance at her patient, now resting and subdued by a strong dose of poppy syrup, answered, "It is not likely. She must partake of red wine and red meat and raspberry tea to replenish her blood and strength, and allow herself half a year's respite from the marriage bed before she even thinks of trying again, but . . ." Her voice trailed off, and she shook her head.

But even as she spoke I could tell that she knew what we all knew—that, for Anne, time, and Henry's patience, had run out; she would not be given another chance.

Someone brought me a cloak and I sat upon the window seat, huddled in its folds, watching and waiting. Once, I dared venture across the room again to touch George's shoulder as he sat with his dark head bowed in despair.

"Go away, Jane," he said tonelessly. "Never speak to me again; henceforth, I shall share neither bed nor board with you. And do not ask why; you know why."

"Because I came to warn Anne that . . ."

"You did not come to warn, Jane, you came to gloat, to glory in her misfortune, to frighten her. Perhaps you even intended to cause this." He gestured angrily towards his sleeping sister, lying still and pale as death upon her bed. "Do not bother to deny it. I shall never forgive you or Norfolk for what you did today. I will have nothing more to do with either of you."

"But you saw that thing!" I protested. "It was a mercy it was born dead. Had it lived . . ."

George turned his face away from me, and no matter how hard I tried he would not look at or speak to me again.

Hours passed and, huddled on the window seat, I cried myself to sleep.

I was startled awake by the door crashing open. Limping and leaning heavily upon a crutch, with his head swaddled in bandages, King Henry came to stand at the foot of Anne's bed. His blue eyes blazed with hell-hot anger as he glared down at her; his chest heaved mightily, and his face was flushed and mottled scarlet. Had a painter been present and taken his likeness, then he would surely have called the finished portrait "Majestic Rage." Henry's hands curled into tight fists and shook hard, and I knew he was fighting the desire to kill Anne with his bare hands.

Ever so slowly, Anne turned her face from the wall. Her dark, deep-sunken eyes were dull and listless and her sallow skin looked as if it were made of yellow wax. She shakily levered herself up into a sitting position, wincing and whimpering at the pain, and George hastened to assist her, piling pillows behind her back and holding a cup of poppy syrup to her lips, urging her to take just a sip. I could see every bone in her hand—and her nails, once shiny as pearls, now dull, cracked and gnawed—when she raised it to brush her hair back from her face.

"My lord, I . . ." she started, then faltered as tears started to roll down her sunken, hollow cheeks. "I thought . . . they told me you were dead!"

"All the more reason to hold on to my son—England's heir!" Henry's voice boomed. "Why didn't you die instead of my boy?"

George took a step towards him, but Anne's hand shot out to stay him. When he looked down at her she shook her head and her eyes pleaded, "Stay silent; I need you!"

For a tense moment he wavered between attack and withdrawal; then he nodded and stepped back and sat down on the bed beside Anne, holding tight to her hand to give her the courage she needed.

"My lord . . ." Anne tried again. "Had it not been for the shock . . . I am certain . . . next time . . ."

"Next time?" Henry bristled. "By Heaven, Madame, there will not be a next time! You'll get no more boys by me!" He turned his back on her and limped from the room.

"Henry!" Anne wailed plaintively, reaching out entreatingly to him; but he ignored her, and she fell back against her pillows sobbing, "I have failed! God help me! I have failed!"

"As God is my witness, I would like to kill him for that, and all that he has done to you!" George cried, quaking with anger. "Oh, Nan!" he sighed, compassion overcoming his rage. He lay down on the bed beside her, and carefully, tenderly, gathered her in his arms. "Do not cry for him, Nan. He's not worth it; no man is!"

"Oh, George!" she sobbed. "I'm not crying for Henry Tudor— I'm crying for myself!"

I watched my husband lying on his sister's bed, holding her as he had never held me, until I could stand the sight no more; then I crept from the room.

No one had to tell me; I knew. The end was nigh. Already the winds of change were blowing and soon they would reach gale force.

❧ 25 ❧

For weeks Anne lay weak and weeping in her bed, staring at the walls and waiting for her body to heal.

Only Meg Lee, Madge Shelton, and her childhood nurse, old Mistress Orchard, dared attend her; all her other ladies flocked to Jane Seymour.

Even Mary Boleyn was gone, though not through any disloyalty. Anne banished her in a fit of jealous pique because she could not bear the sight of her own sister's happiness and pregnant belly.

Mary had at last found the happiness she so richly deserved, and the fact that her husband, William Stafford, was a nobody, a common soldier, without fortune, title, lands, or lofty name, and ten years younger than herself, mattered not a jot to her. They were head over heels in love and gloriously happy, but they had married in secret, without asking royal permission lest Anne and Henry forbid them, and did not reveal the truth until Mary's stomach began to swell with his child.

But Anne still had her "evergreen gallants" to console her.

Mark Smeaton came every day with doglike devotion to play his lute for her.

Weston, Brereton, Norris, and Wyatt visited too, often bringing delicacies like anise comfits, sugarplums, and marchpane to tempt her appetite. For hours they would sit with her and try to coax a smile, "the only prize worth winning," according to Weston.

George, of course, was always there. "My only constant," Anne called him. He practically lived in her rooms; heaven knows, he never came to mine, and visited his own only to bathe and change his clothes. Where he slept and whom he slept with I do not know. I tried to tell myself I was past caring, but every time I felt my tooth wobble my rage was born anew, and lust for vengeance consumed my soul and made my mouth water.

When she finally found the courage and the strength to step across her threshold, Anne saw for herself how greatly the tide had turned against her.

Nearly every woman had taken Jane Seymour as her personal model for dress, demeanor, and deportment. Except upon Anne's own head, there was not a French hood to be seen. Every woman stood with her hair hidden and her head boxed in by a gable hood, with her eyes downcast and her hands demurely clasped. Every bodice was filled in with a modest, white lawn partlet. Most of their jewels, except an occasional, unostentatious brooch or ring, had been put away. Their gowns, once a rainbow of bright colors, were now pale, pastel, dark, or drab.

Looking like a walking wraith, with her sallow skin almost transparent, her bones protruding, and her eyes feverishly bright, Anne stood out most conspicuously in her night black velvet gown and French hood spangled with diamond stars. And her black hair swung glossy and gypsy-free down her back, adorned with diamond stars.

Nervously, she toyed with the big golden *B* resting in the hollow of her throat, attached, as always, to her favorite pearls, as she gazed warily about like a frightened animal. She took a step closer to George and tightened her grip on his arm, shaking like an old woman stricken with palsy.

Everyone kept their distance. There were no curtsies or bows. Thomas Boleyn and the Duke of Norfolk pointedly turned their backs and engaged Cromwell in conversation. And Elizabeth Boleyn turned to Jane Seymour and complimented her for resurrecting modest and traditional English dress; it was so much nicer than those decadent French styles favored by her daughter.

All around her conversations quickly resumed and people made a great show of pretending to ignore Anne while surreptitiously watching to see what she would do. Would she break down in tears or fly into one of her famous rages?

"Cowards!" Francis Weston sniffed contemptuously as he elbowed his way through the crowd, followed by Will Brereton and Henry Norris.

"Aye." Brereton nodded, wrinkling his nose and exaggeratedly sniffing his gilt pomander ball. "Not all the perfumes of Araby could disguise this great stink of cowardice!"

"Mark well, we at least have the courage to be true, and the rest of you be damned!" Norris added boldly.

"Most Gracious Majesty, pray forgive us; we were detained." Weston jangled his velvet purse and explained, "A dice game."

Thus they became marked men. Now was the moment of truth when the fools from the wise men would be parted. Crafty, devious Cromwell was watching, and he would not forget. And, if perchance he did, I would be there to remind him.

One of the diamond stars fell from Anne's hair.

"My star has fallen," she quipped as all four men bent to retrieve it. "Should I take that as an omen, I wonder?"

"Of course not!" they scoffed.

Anne smiled, grateful but unconvinced. "They do say that the brightest stars burn out the fastest!"

George ignored me entirely now; we never spoke at all. When we met he looked through me as though I were a woman fashioned of glass. He would not even speak to me at table. If there was anything he absolutely must say it was conveyed to me via a servant. I must have poured my heart out in a hundred letters, yet all of them were returned to me by the bearer I sent them with, their seals intact. He would not hear me or even read my words. I tried countless times to throw myself in his path, weeping and begging for mercy, begging him to hear me out; but every time he blindly passed me by, leaving me feeling like a ghost or phantom desperately, but futilely, trying to convey some message to the living, but doomed to failure. Our marriage was over and there was nothing I could do about it. I knew I must accept and resign myself to the facts, yet I could not. I had to keep trying every waking hour to break the barrier he had erected between us. George was my world; he meant everything to me, and without him my life was a worthless, pallid, living death.

In April I discovered that he had found a new diversion—Anne's pet musician, Mark Smeaton.

"I told him to take off his clothes and get into bed, and he did!" I overheard George boasting to his friends over their wine cups. "Afterwards, I told him to put on his clothes and get out, and he did!"

But Smeaton—poor simple, lovestruck Smeaton—longed for more. Like so many others, he made the mistake of letting George Boleyn touch his heart. He had yet to learn that charm, the appearance of interest, shared laughter, and carnal lust combined do not equal sincerity. For George, lovers were for the moment's pleasure, and once the moment had passed, they meant nothing to him. Smeaton thought George was his friend; that was his first mistake. Thinking that what they did in bed actually meant something was his second.

Once, seated nearby with my embroidery, I watched them together. George got up from the window seat and started to leave, but Smeaton, womanlike and clinging, begged him to stay. He had that look in his eyes I knew so well, the look of a woman who watches, hurt, angered, and bewildered, as the man she loves leaves her bed and begins pulling on his clothes with cold, silent efficiency, ready to leave now that he has been sated, while she is, like a plaything, put back upon the shelf and forgotten.

Impatiently, George shook off Smeaton's hand.

"I'll go my way, and you go yours and leave me be!" he snapped as he had so many times before, at so many others, turning his back and casually dismissing yet another lover without a qualm, care, or remorse.

Part of me wanted to set aside my sewing and go to Smeaton, touch his hand, and tell him "I understand," but no, my hard heart said, let him suffer like all the rest!

Across the room, Anne was laughing with Norris and Weston, the three of them darting surreptitious glances at Madge Shelton, sitting nearby, bent over her embroidery.

"Why do you not just marry her and have done with it?" Anne inquired of Norris, who had been betrothed for years to the flighty Madge, with no hope of leading her to the altar anytime soon.

Norris shrugged. "Methinks I shall tarry awhile," he said, though everyone knew it was Madge herself who tarried; she enjoyed her free and easy ways too much to think seriously of settling down with just one man.

"Perhaps you look for dead men's shoes?" Anne batted her lashes coyly. "If any misfortune befell His Majesty you would look to have me!"

A hush fell as the folly of her words sunk in.

Norris, his round baby face draining of color and his blue eyes wide with alarm, shook his head vehemently. "May my head be struck off if ever I thought such a thing! It is treason, Madame! Have a care what you say, even in jest!"

Treason! I pulled my embroidery thread so taut it snapped. It was dangerous banter they were indulging in, and I resolved to commit every word of it to memory.

Then Weston came rushing to the rescue, as always was his wont. "If you tarry too much longer, I shall try for the fair Madge myself!"

Whereupon Norris reminded him that he was married and the father of a newborn son, and thus should not be dallying with the Queen's ladies. Besides, though no one said it, everyone knew Weston had sampled Madge's charms already.

"Aye"—Weston grinned cheekily—"but it is not Madge I come here to see. There is one here whom I love far more than Mistress Shelton or my lady wife."

"Oh?" Anne arched her brows. "And who might that be?"

"It is yourself," Weston answered.

"Flatterer!" Anne tapped him playfully with her fan. "I have had enough of court gallantry for today; I shall go and discover what ails Master Smeaton—he looks so melancholy."

As Anne approached, Smeaton fell to his knees and bowed his head low in a futile attempt to hide his tears.

"Mark?" She reached out and gently tilted his chin up. "Why so downcast?"

Across the room, George flung an arm about Weston's shoulder and threw back his head, laughing at some jest. Seeing this, Smeaton's lovelorn eyes blazed with jealousy.

Anne saw it too, but she misunderstood.

"Mark." She turned his face back to her and said gently, as if she were speaking to a child, "You must not look to have me speak to you as I do to them, for they are gentlemen born, and you are not."

"Oh, no, Madame, a look will suffice!" Smeaton gazed up at her with worshipful eyes, boldly raising his fingertips to brush briefly against the too slender wrist of the hand that still lingered upon his chin.

Anger flashed in Anne's dark eyes and she snatched her hand away. "Do not presume upon my kindness, Master Smeaton!"

In an indignant swirl of purple satin skirts she spun round and returned to her friends, leaving poor, lowborn Smeaton behind to wallow in misery, hopelessly in love with not one but two Boleyns, and with no hope of possessing either.

❧ 26 ❧

On the final day of April 1536 Anne sought respite from her sorrows with her daughter in the gardens of Greenwich. Only Meg Lee and I attended her, sitting on benches on opposite sides of the garden, she with a book of scriptures and I with my embroidery.

Dressed all in black satin, Anne stood out starkly against the colorful blossoms and greenery flourishing all around her.

Laughing, she knelt with her arms outstretched and Elizabeth, face puckered with concentration, red curls the color of autumn leaves spilling from beneath her gold-embroidered orange cap, gathered up the stiff, rustling folds of her gown, and toddled determinedly into her mother's arms.

Anne embraced her and swung her up onto her hip.

"Soon you will be too big for Mama to lift!" she cried as she spun around, laughing, with her gypsy hair swinging free.

She paused suddenly and looked up at the King, standing frowning down at them from his window above. The smile on her lips faltered and she shivered a little and hugged Elizabeth closer.

Elizabeth reached out to grasp the golden *B* at Anne's throat.

"Look there!" Anne pointed up at Henry. "Wave to Papa!" she cajoled, smiling encouragingly and settling Elizabeth more comfortably upon her hip. "Go on, wave to Papa!" she urged as Elizabeth, showing herself to be a true Tudor, refused to wave and instead scowled up at her father as she tightened her grip upon her mother and matched Henry Tudor stare for insolent stare. Indeed, it would not have surprised me if the little minx had stuck out her tongue at him.

But Henry's lips did not even twitch towards a smile. He turned his back on them and left the window.

Anne's face fell and her eyes shut tight as she willed herself not to weep.

"Papa gone!" Elizabeth piped up. "He did not wave at me, so I did not wave at him!" There was a slight, sulky tremor in her voice as if she were about to cry.

"Weep not, my daughter," Anne said, resting her cheek against the top of Elizabeth's head. "If you remember only one thing I have taught you, remember this: No man is worth crying over! Guard your heart, Elizabeth, guard it as if it were your greatest treasure; keep it under lock and key, and be wary of who you let near it, lest you be betrayed. Let no man be your master; be mistress of your own fate instead. Never surrender!"

"Never!" Elizabeth echoed, throwing back her head and shaking her lion's mane of red-gold curls.

I shivered at the proud conviction in her imperious little voice. I had no doubt that the precocious wench would remember every word, but how much, I wondered, did she understand?

Footsteps crunched upon the gravel and we all turned to see George approaching. Like Anne, he was dramatically clad in black satin, with the ruffled collar and cuffs of his white shirt encrusted with blackwork embroidery.

"Did you see?" Anne asked.

"Yes." George nodded, smiling broadly and taking Elizabeth into his arms when she smiled and reached out for her "Uncle George."

"It is over, George. He really has turned his back on me. His heart is set on Jane Seymour, and now, I fear, I shall go the way of Catherine."

"You needn't," George replied. "What was Catherine's mistake?"

"Her stubbornness and pride!" Anne answered promptly. "She was so determined to hold on, even when she knew all he wanted to do was push her away. I always said she should have taken the best terms he offered and left with her head held high."

"Then why do you not take your own advice? If you must leave, Anne, do not go like a whipped dog with its tail tucked between its legs, but with your head held high like the queen you are! But do not wait for him to offer; make your own terms. Be reasonable and calm. Take him by surprise, for he shall be expecting tears and tempest. Surprise him; tell him you want to part as friends."

"I shall retain my title of marquess, and I must have a sizable income; it shall cost him dearly to be rid of me, and I shall not go to a nunnery or some cold, crumbling castle in the marshlands. . . ."

"France," George interjected. "We shall go to France. We shall have a chateau and live in grand style and keep a court of our own, filled with the most amusing people!"

We! How that *We* stabbed at my heart! It stole the breath from me! I could not believe my ears. George intended to leave me, to run away to France with his disgraced sister and her bastard brat. He was going to leave me! No, oh no, this could not be!

"Yes!" Anne breathed excitedly. "Oh, George, do you mean . . . you will go with me, follow me into exile?"

"I would follow you anywhere!" George took a step closer and leaned his forehead against hers. "I do not care how far away, or if I have to brave fire, ice, savage winds, churning seas, or desert sands to get there; where you go I will go. Do you think I could live without my soul?"

"No, for no more could I, George. We are like one soul separated into two bodies—one male, one female."

"Like two sides of a coin," George said. "Gemini! Twin souls, though not twins by birth."

It tore my heart out to see them standing thus, embracing with their foreheads touching, with Elizabeth nestled between them, posing the only barrier between their bodies, as if they were proud parents and she their very own child. The rage came surging up with such force I feared it would kill me. I could not breathe properly or even see clearly for the starry mist drifting before my eyes.

Then, as so often happens, reality intruded upon their charming little idyll. "But Elizabeth . . ." Anne glanced down worriedly at her daughter. "George, I cannot let her be declared a bastard!"

"No, that must not be," George agreed. "She must retain her rights and keep her place in the succession; after any male heirs born of the King's next marriage, of course."

"George!" Anne pulled away from him and stamped her foot. "That whey-faced prude, that Seymour bitch! May she be barren or the whelping kill her! I would rather see her brats strangled at birth than take the place of my Elizabeth!"

"Anne, stop raging at me; you know better; you know me better than that! That is merely what you tell Henry, to placate him; be amicable and agreeable. Now, calm yourself and think; review the situation: two wives, two acknowledged mistresses, and all the tumbles on the side, and how many sons does he have? Bessie Blount's boy is puny and consumptive—he'll not see twenty, I wager. Already they say he coughs up blood. As for our sister Mary's boy . . . well, none can say for certain whether he is the King's or Will Carey's son. So what makes you think Jane Seymour will fare any better than you or Catherine? She is but five years younger than you, so she has not extreme youth upon her side. Let things be for now, Anne. I promise you Elizabeth shall not be forgotten. But get the best terms you can now, while there is still time. Let Henry feel he is being generous, and plot strategy later when the time is right. He'll not live forever, and may not be capable of siring more children; and if, when he perishes, he has no legitimate male heir . . ."

"There is always Elizabeth, healthy and vibrant and so like him! And around her, I think—despise me though they do—many shall rally! Look at that red hair, George, and that mutinous scowl, and see the way she grips so possessively. She is a Tudor through and through—none could ever doubt it!"

I jumped at the sudden and unexpected touch of a hand upon my shoulder and spun round to find Thomas Cromwell standing behind me.

"Forgive me for startling you, my lady, but I find it very sad that you must watch from afar rather than be yourself at the heart of such a loving family."

His voice was as silky soft and knowing as the hiss of the serpent who tempted Eve in the Garden of Eden must have been. "Look at them," he hissed as, without asking permission, he settled his bulk beside me on the bench.

Anne and George were now walking away with Elizabeth toddling hand in hand between them, and Anne was prattling about how clever her redheaded brat was, how she already knew her letters and had started her first embroidery stitches.

"Look at them," Cromwell hissed insinuatingly in my ear. "Did one not know otherwise, one would think they were lovers."

I started at his words—had I not said, had I not thought, the same thing myself?

"They are as close as lovers; would you not say so, Lady Rochford?"

My head whipped round to boldly meet his dark, emotionless gaze.

"They *are* lovers!" I exclaimed, the blood sizzling in my veins.

There it was; the lie was upon my lips, but in my heart I believed it. And so the die was cast, even though it was loaded with malice.

"They are lovers!" I repeated. "None ever existed more devoted than they are!" Thus I reiterated my words with greater firmness and conviction, when I should have taken them back. But I did not. I chose to let them stand. At the time, it felt so good and so right. It was high time that someone understood and condoled with how I felt, even if it was that loathsome, treacherous creature Cromwell. Sometimes, anyone is better than no one.

Cromwell heaved his heavy body up and held out an ink-stained hand to me.

I sat there and stared up at that loathsome creature, that oily, poisonous toad of a man, who was entirely the King's creature. None was more devious or devoid of feeling than Thomas Cromwell, and there was not a lawyer anywhere who was more ruthless, unscrupulous, or cunning. Oil glistened from every pore on his fat, inscrutable face, bull neck, and on every strand of his thick, chin-length dark hair. Oh yes, he was an ugly, oozing creature, and I hated him, but he gave me exactly what I needed, and for that I shall be forever grateful.

The next thing I knew we were in his bedchamber. As he deftly peeled each garment from me, pausing to kiss the curve of a shoulder, the crook of an elbow, or the uneven bump on the back of my hand where the little bone had broken and failed to properly mend, showering me with such pleasant little attentions that no man had ever before given me, he condoled with me, and consoled me, layering my soul with the balm of sympathy.

Anne, he said, should be shut away in a nunnery. Not some light, fashionable order where she could keep lapdogs and lovers and buy herself the rank of abbess, but a strict order with a rigorous routine of fasting, prayer, and silence; where the nuns wore coarse habits, with hair shirts to mortify their flesh underneath, and were shaven bald beneath their wimples.

"Oh, yes!" I sighed meltingly. "Yes! She should be locked away from the world of men!" But what I really meant was that she should be locked away from George. Then he would be all mine and, in time, he would forget, and then he would turn to me, and I would be there waiting for him with my arms open wide and my heart gushing with love for him.

As he laid bare my body, I in turn laid bare my heart, pouring into that cunning weasel's ear all my bitterness, hate, jealousy, and spite. The only detail I omitted was George's occasional forays into sodomy, as the punishment for that was a fiery death chained to the stake, but all else I told him. Every act of intimacy and affection I had witnessed between him and Anne I recounted; and, calling forth all my hatred and resentment of his friends, I named names, four of them to be precise—Francis Weston, Henry Norris, William Brereton, and his melancholy little plaything, Mark Smeaton.

When Cromwell lowered me onto the bed and I spread my legs wide to welcome him, I betrayed my husband with my body as well as with my words. Which was the greater sin I leave for others to decide.

❧ 27 ❧

After that it all happened very quickly.

"So what happens now?" I asked as Cromwell, fully dressed again in his heavy black garments and gold chain of office, stood behind me, lacing me back into my boiled leather stays.

"I go to my house in London. I have a dinner engagement with a very important guest," he said as he left me, without a kiss or farewell, coolly ordering his valet to fetch a maid to help me finish dressing while I stood shivering in my petticoats over what I had just done. I couldn't take it back; I couldn't undo it, even if I wanted to. The truth was, I didn't want to. Despite my twinge of nerves and foreboding, my conscience was clear; I felt no qualms about what I had just done because I knew deep down in my heart that all I had said was true. Their love was incestuous—it might have been chaste, but it was incest and unseemly and unnatural and a sin, and it was up to me to quash it out since no one else would do it, and now . . . now I had Cromwell on my side, a man known for getting things done! As for the other men—Weston, Norris, Brereton, and Smeaton—they were fools, weak fools, and they deserved to be punished. They also had come between me and my husband, and they all loved Anne Boleyn.

* * *

When I entered the Great Hall that night, everyone was speculating about Cromwell's "very important guest." It was none other than Mark Smeaton. Cromwell had no love for music, so why would he invite a lowly musician to sit at table with him like an equal?

The court was rife with rumors, as word trickled out that Smeaton had been bound to his chair at the dinner table. A cord with strategically placed knots had been tied around his skull and twisted ever tighter by the insertion of a stick, while Cromwell calmly questioned him and enjoyed a dinner of roast chicken followed by three large helpings of custard.

The knots bit deep, and Smeaton's skin—as fair and delicate as a female's—split, and the pressure upon his eyeballs was unendurable. He moaned and screamed and wept in agony, until, driven nearly mad by the pain and fear, the poor boy named names—three to be precise: Francis Weston, Henry Norris, and William Brereton.

The next morning King Henry left abruptly after the first joust of the May Day tournament. He ordered Norris, still panting and dripping with sweat, to doff his armor and ride with him to London.

Norris never returned to court. His loyal valet rode back, weeping and near collapse, and told us that his master was now a prisoner in the Tower of London.

All the way to London, Henry had pleaded, berated, cajoled, and threatened, promising Norris his freedom, forgiveness, and riches galore if he would only confess that he had committed adultery with Anne, and thus help Henry rid himself of "that she-devil" so he would be free to marry Jane Seymour without any protracted legal battle.

"Never!" was Norris's answer. "I will not lie and besmirch her honor or mine!"

A chivalrous man to the last, he even offered to act as the Queen's champion and defend her honor in armed combat against the King himself or the proxy of his choice.

All Henry's attempts at bribery and coercion failed, and he ordered the guards to take Norris to the Tower.

"Perhaps a brief stay there will change your mind!"

"Even if I stayed a thousand years it would not change my mind!" Norris shouted to his sovereign's back. Then, shaking off the guards, he walked, bold and proud, into the Tower of London with his head held high.

Seized by terror, I ran to warn George, but someone had gotten there before me—his father.

Sir Thomas Boleyn, though always a coldhearted, calculating man, was also an eminently practical one, who never let sentiment blind him. I prayed fervently that he would be able to persuade George to do the right thing. After all, if her own father could so easily abandon Anne and turn his back on her without the slightest twinge of remorse or shame, why could her brother not do the same?

"This is no time for sentiment, you fool! Abandon her publicly, and do it now, while you still have the chance. Save yourself! Leave her; go to Hever, Beaulieu, Grimston, Rochford Hall, wherever you will, as long as you go, and stay away—from the court and from her!"

"She is my sister!" George exclaimed.

"And you are my son, my only son," said Thomas Boleyn, "and I would save you if I could. This is your last chance, George, your only chance; for the love of Christ, boy, see reason and seize it!"

"Devil take you and your precious reason!" George shouted. "You go! Go on; scurry away like the coward you are. Go back to Hever or to Hell for all I care! But I will not follow you. I will not forsake her as long as there is breath within my body. I will stand by Anne until the last drop of blood is wrung from my body!"

"Then you are doomed. Good-bye, George," Thomas Boleyn said curtly, nodding briefly to me as he went out. He was a man who knew when to cut his losses.

"George!" I rushed in and flung myself at his feet. "Please! Listen to your father! They are all deserting her. Resist her, George—

just this once, resist! If you don't, in the end it will kill you! I know it will, I know!"

"Woman, cease this detestable blabbering. We are talking about my sister! Yes, they are all abandoning her; even our own father and mother turn tail and run, but, by Heaven, I will not!"

He started for the door and I flung myself down and caught hold of his ankle.

"You are going to her?"

"Of course I am going to her! Do you think anything in this world could keep me from it? She needs me."

"I need you too!" I sobbed. "Oh, George, please! Don't go!"

"Let go of me, Jane." He shook free of me and walked quickly out the door.

Weeping wildly, I scampered after him on my hands and knees, lunging and grasping at his ankles, so that he had to pause every few steps to shake me off before I lunged and grabbed again.

"Don't leave me, George!" I sobbed. "Without your love I am nothing!"

"Then you are nothing," he retorted without pause.

At the top of the stairs he called to the guards, "Restrain my wife; she is distraught!"

While I struggled and screamed in their arms, my husband ran down the stairs and out of my life.

He never reached her. Anne was already taken.

Her uncle, the Duke of Norfolk, personally conveyed her to the Tower. The people of London thronged both banks of the Thames, spitting down onto the barge and jeering "The Goggle-Eyed Whore" on her way.

Through it all, Anne said not a word. Not even when it began to rain.

"See, even the heavens weep for your shame!" Norfolk shook his head in disgust.

But Anne merely sat there, staring straight ahead, as if she were blind and deaf to all around her.

Master Kingston, the Lieutenant of the Tower, was there to meet her when the barge docked at Traitor's Gate.

"Master Kingston, shall I die without justice?" she asked plaintively.

"The poorest subject of the King hath justice, Madame," he answered.

At that, Anne threw back her head and laughed like one deranged, until she slumped breathlessly against the damp-oozing stone wall, hugging herself, as tears poured down her face. She knew better than anyone what kind of justice she could expect from the King.

George was taken at Whitehall, fighting to reach the King and protest Anne's arrest. He very nearly succeeded. He made it all the way to the privy chamber door before he was caught and dragged away to join the other prisoners in the Tower.

Weston and Brereton were taken the next day. To make plain their disdain for the charges laid against them, they did not allow being arrested to disrupt their dice game; they simply scooped up their dice and coins and took them with them in the barge. They played all the way to Traitor's Gate.

Thomas Wyatt was the last to be arrested, but it was merely a ploy to ensure his silence. Cromwell had all the evidence he needed, and Henry had no intention of harming so fine a poet. But no one must be allowed to go free who would dare speak out in Anne's defense, especially not a man with Wyatt's gift for words. Ironically, of the men accused, Wyatt was the only one who was truly guilty of carnality with Anne; he was the one who had taken her virginity, and I don't think he ever stopped loving her.

❧ 28 ❧

On the 12th of May 1536, before a crowd of two thousand people, lowborn and high, crammed shoulder to shoulder in Tower Hall, Francis Weston, William Brereton, Henry Norris, and Mark Smeaton stood trial for committing adultery with the Queen and conspiring to kill the King.

I was there before dawn, and even then the crowd was so thick I had to fight my way through. Fortunately I did not have to fight for my seat; Cromwell had sent one of his servants to hold a place for me.

Anne was not allowed to attend. Cromwell thought it was better to keep her confused and ignorant, and thus, hopefully, dull the knife-edge of her wit. When it was her turn to stand trial, he wanted a broken, terrified woman who would cower and weep before her judges.

Weston, Brereton, and Norris entered Tower Hall as confident and calm as if they were attending just another court function—some banquet or entertainment, nothing to be solemn or upset about.

All three of them were dressed elegantly. Brereton wore jet-beaded mulberry satin, Norris fawn silk accented with deep brown velvet, and Weston dazzled every eye in a gaudy green doublet encrusted with emeralds, pearls, and gold embroidery.

Weston's delicate young wife and aged mother were seated in the row behind me, and as he passed Weston paused to smile down at them and lovingly caress his wife's tearstained cheek and squeeze his mother's wizened hand. These two women had offered the King a fortune of 100,000 crowns to save their beloved rogue, but Henry had refused them. Why accept, when if Weston were condemned, all his goods—his money, property, and lands—would be forfeit to the Crown?

The lowly born Smeaton came last. He could not walk; he had to be carried in. Upon arriving at the Tower after his torturous dinner with Cromwell, he had been racked for four hours, leaving his body broken and crippled, before they moved on to other tortures. Both of his eyes were swollen purple and black to such an extent he could scarcely open them, and his mouth was puffy and distorted, with both lips scabbed over. But his hands—his beautiful musician's hands!—were a mangled mess of purple, black, and red flesh, every finger broken, and all the nails torn out. Master Smeaton would make no more music, and for this he wept copious tears, sobbing piteously again and again "my music, my music!" as he held up his ruined hands.

The three gentlemen took their places, standing tall and defiant before their judges, while Smeaton's broken body was draped over the back of a chair, since he could not stand unaided.

The evidence against them was a litany of the absurd, and all about me the crowd exchanged incredulous glances. Anne had given money and gifts to all of them. And with Weston, Brereton, and Norris she had danced, laughed, and played cards. "Well, what of it?" The people shrugged. Were they not all firm friends of years and years? And she was Queen of England and entitled to dispense gifts to those she favored. Why make such a to-do and pother over a few coins and trinkets, jests, and dancing? Each of the gentlemen had at one time or another worn her favor while competing in the joust, or dedicated poetry or songs to her. Again the people asked, "What of it?" They were gallant gentlemen of the court and such things were expected of them. As for Smeaton being summoned to her chamber to play his lute and sing, well,

"What of it?" He was a court musician; was that not what he was paid to do? Yet all of this, Cromwell claimed, constituted proof of adultery. The people shook their heads, clucked their tongues, and rolled their eyes.

Dates were cited, but they were easily disputed and discredited. The accused were either not at the same place on the date in question or else Anne was confined to bed recovering from a pregnancy and thus in no condition to dally with a lover. As for the plot to kill the King, that was even more absurd. Weston had ridden against him in the joust and unhorsed him, causing His Majesty grievous bodily injury and his life to be, for a time, despaired of. Hearing this, eyebrows shot high and people shook their heads, utterly dumbfounded. King, knight, or commoner, any man who competed in the tiltyard risked injury and death. How could this possibly be construed as a murder plot? Then there was that damning remark about Norris looking for "dead men's shoes." Unwise, yes, but in what context had it been said? Might it not have been an ill-advised jest? But to Cromwell the context was irrelevant; the fact that it had been said was enough for him.

Like starving dogs, these three clever gentlemen fell upon the evidence, tearing it to shreds. Indignant and contemptuous, haughty and witty, they swaggered about, made jests, and laughed in Cromwell's face.

Only Mark Smeaton, always the obedient servant, obliged by falling down and washing the floor with his tears as he repeatedly insisted, "I am guilty and deserve death!"

Aye, Smeaton was guilty of fornicating with a Boleyn, but it was not Anne. Her he had only worshipped and adored, but with my husband George he had committed sodomy, a crime and a sin that led to the stake and eternal damnation. Perhaps he saw his mangled hands as God's just punishment?

"May God have mercy on you and forgive your lies," Francis Weston said as he stared down at the sniveling Smeaton.

"Can you not see they have broken his mind as well as his body?" Norris cried. "A man in such a state would admit to anything!"

"Poor gentle songbird, would you not rather the truth be your last song instead of Cromwell's infernal lies?" Brereton shook his head and sighed pityingly.

Aye, it was a grand performance. And with these three gentlemen the crowd fell completely in love. But none of that mattered. The trial was a farce that had nothing to do with justice, only the will and whim of the King.

"The evidence is such that it can stand on its own!" Cromwell declared when Brereton challenged him.

"Liar!" Brereton shouted, his voice ringing in the rafters. "It is a house of cards so fragile no man dare approach too near or breathe upon it lest it topple!"

"Even with only one eye I can see that it will not stand up to scrutiny!" Weston exclaimed.

The jury did not even retire from their bench. All four men were condemned to die a traitor's death, the most ghastly and painful imaginable—they would be taken to Tyburn and hung, drawn, and quartered.

"Weep not for us, but for the absence of justice from England!" Weston advised the crowd as they were led back to their cell in the Beauchamp Tower.

❧ 29 ❧

hree days later it was George's turn, and Anne's. As peers of
T the realm, they were required to face a jury of twenty-six
peers, including Anne's old love, Harry Percy, the Earl of Northumberland.

My father, Lord Morley, also sat upon the jury. He hated to be a
part of "this mockery of justice," as he called it, but he knew that
the King's will must be done.

Thomas Boleyn wanted to be there too. Hoping to ingratiate
himself with the King, he had openly reviled his children and said
it would be his pleasure to sit in judgment on this pair of incestuous traitors it had been his loins' misfortune to sire, but Cromwell
decided to excuse him lest it reflect poorly upon the Crown that
the father of the accused had been allowed to sit upon the jury.

Apparently it was not considered in poor taste to have the uncle
of the accused preside over the trial, and Norfolk happily obliged
by acting as Lord High Steward.

May 15 dawned a beautiful day. The sky was a clear, cloudless
blue and the weather pleasantly warm, but inside Tower Hall it
was sweltering. Once again, two thousand people of all classes
were crammed together, even sitting on each other's laps, and lin-
ing the walls; and more waited outside. The odors of unwashed
bodies and sweat were so oppressive that perfume and pomander

balls were not just a nicety but a necessity, though in the end they did little good. Several women fainted from the heat and stink.

Anne was led in first. Every head turned in her direction; people stood, craning their necks and on tiptoes, trying to get a glimpse of her. She was infinitely calm and regal, which surprised many, given all the talk of mad, hysterical laughter, wild, uncontrollable weeping, and alternating bouts of desperately rising hope and deep, plunging despair. She wore a gown of black velvet, open in front to reveal a kirtle of lustrous copper satin. Large, creamy pearls alternating with beads of amber and gold, edged the low, square-cut bodice. Her long, hanging sleeves were trimmed with deep fur cuffs of the softest brown sable, with a reddish sheen that hung bell-like over her hands. Pearls also edged her black French hood; and about her neck, so slender and long and easy to sever, she wore her favorite pearl necklace with the distinctive gold *B* with three dangling teardrop pearls.

Then George was brought in, and though their guards tried to keep them apart, they found each other. George swept her up in a fervent embrace, and Anne wound her arms tightly around his neck and buried her face against his shoulder. Then Master Kingston intervened, and George was led to the platform where he must face his judges, and Anne to a chair nearby.

How my heart ached at the sight of him! Its beating was so fast and furious I thought I would die. Thank God, they had not tortured him. He was all in somber black relieved only by the immaculate white ruffles at his throat and wrists, and his black hair and beard were immaculately combed and trimmed.

Then the trial began. How ably he defended himself! He made me blush and feel stupid and ashamed at the absurdity of the evidence, much of which I had supplied and Cromwell had twisted to make his case.

George was accused of always being in his sister's company, often entirely alone with her in her private rooms. He had even been seen to lean down and kiss her as she lay abed.

"Can a brother and sister not speak privately without being suspected of incest?" George interjected. "My sister is not just my sister, she is also my dearest friend; our understanding is perfect and complete, and we have always taken great delight in each other's company."

"The Queen," Cromwell intoned gravely, "incited her own natural brother to violate her, alluring him with her tongue in his mouth, and his tongue in hers, and also with gifts, base conversations, and other infamous acts; whereby he, despising the commandments of God, and all human laws, violated and carnally knew his own natural sister."

"That is a foul lie!" George exclaimed hotly.

"Silence! It is not your turn to speak!" Norfolk said sharply, then nodded to Cromwell and bade him continue.

Together with their friends, Cromwell alleged, George and Anne had ridiculed the King; making fun of his clothes, his great puffed and padded shoulders and enormous codpieces, saying two men could fit inside one of Henry's doublets. And they disparaged his poetry and songs, deeming their own compositions superior.

Cromwell claimed to have evidence that the so-called "Princess" Elizabeth was in fact George Boleyn's daughter.

When she knew for certain she was pregnant, Anne had sent the joyous news by letter to her "beloved brother."

"Was that natural behavior?" Cromwell asked insinuatingly.

After the child was born, he continued, George had been seen sitting most familiarly beside the Queen upon her bed, expressing great admiration for the child, and was heard by two witnesses— one of them his own wife, and the other the late, but much esteemed Lady Wingfield—to declare, "This little one is one of us!" Old Lady Wingfield had testified to this on her deathbed, asserted Cromwell, "and that, my lords, is not a place one wants to be with a lie upon one's lips!"

George folded his arms across his chest and cocked his head. "How very inconsiderate of Lady Wingfield to die when we have need of her! Is there a necromancer present so we might have this evidence direct, instead of as hearsay?"

The whole room erupted in laughter and Norfolk leapt to his feet, shouting for silence.

George, Cromwell continued, had even been heard to threaten the King's life, saying he would like to kill Henry for all that he had done to Anne. To this statement his wife could attest, having been in the room at the time it was said.

"Oh, let us have it plain!" cried George. "The principal instigator of these accusations is my own wife; is that not so, Master Cromwell?"

"Who better to supply such evidence than that much aggrieved and greatly wronged woman who has suffered long and much for love of you?" Cromwell countered.

"Aye, I daresay she considers herself such," George agreed. "My wife is a volatile, vindictive shrew, whose jealous fancies often surpass the bounds of reason. Can we not have some witnesses to her character? It would only be fair, since upon the word of this one woman you are prepared to believe this great evil of me!"

"There is no need to besmirch the reputation of Lady Rochford," Cromwell said pointedly. "She is not the one on trial."

"If there were any real justice here, she would be—for perjury!" George exclaimed. "As for her love for me, you can see how well she loves me, to bring such a false, foul, and malicious charge against me and to blacken my name and that of my sister!"

All about me people were turning in their seats and murmuring to each other. Bets were being laid ten to one that George would go free; some were so confident they staked all that they possessed upon it. The evidence against him was laughable, paltry, insane!

I knew the truth—he loved her more than any. She was the most important person in the world to him, but hearing it spoken aloud it sounded completely absurd; the wild, convoluted ravings of a jealous wife toting up years of accumulated grievances. Even I began to believe that my husband would be acquitted, and that while Anne was banished to a nun's bleak convent cell, I might have one more chance. I was willing to forgive all, if only he would love me and come back to me.

Was it not suspiciously convenient that Lady Wingfield had died? those about me were saying. And those of the court who had known her were quick to inform the others that she had been in her dotage and her mind often wandered haphazardly in the past, and confused people and events. She even sometimes failed to recognize members of her own family. Thus, could anything she said of the Queen and her brother really be deemed credible? And in her later years, she had also been quite deaf; so anything she claimed to have heard was questionable.

And why should the Queen not inform her brother of her pregnancy? As for his remark about the little Princess being "one of us," could that not be in reference to some shared family resemblance? Again a remark was being bruited out of context, so how could anyone rightly judge it?

Anne and George had always been devoted to one another, others from the court asserted, and of their affinity Lady Rochford had always been insanely jealous. One woman reported she had seen me standing at the foot of a staircase, screaming at George, accusing him of being in love with his sister. "I have no liking for the Queen," she said, "but I cannot deny the facts, and what I have myself heard and seen." And others had similar tales to tell of quarrels between us that they had overheard or witnessed. Another told of seeing me bite a page boy when he contradicted the rumor that the King was dead of his jousting injury. They said I had always been in the thick of things, trying to make trouble for the Queen, wishing her ill, and gloating at her every misfortune.

Deeply embarrassed, I drew the hood of my cloak down lower and slumped down farther in my seat, hoping and praying that no one would recognize me. It all sounded so silly now; if lives had not been at stake it would have been a comedy!

"Enough!" Norfolk, followed by a clerk bearing a single candlestick upon a pewter tray, approached George and handed him a small folded square of paper. "Due to the sensitive nature of this question, it will not be spoken aloud lest it cause His Majesty undue embarrassment and distress. Read it and merely answer yea or nay, then burn it in the flame of this candle and we will be done."

As George's long, slim fingers unfolded the paper, a smile spread slowly across his face and a defiant, devil-may-care sparkle lit up his eyes.

Anne sat forward in her chair, gripping tight its arms, pleading with him with her eyes; she knew exactly what he meant to do, because she would have done it herself had their positions been reversed. Their eyes met. They both knew her life was forfeit. It was impossible for the court to rule in her favor when four of her supposed paramours had already been condemned. And though George still stood a chance, it all came down to this moment, to this vital piece of paper in his hand.

George turned and stared out boldly into the crowd, and, I swear, he looked straight at me and smiled. Then he began to speak and the world came crashing round my feet.

"Did the Queen say that she was unlikely to conceive because the King lacked potency and vigor when he came to her bed?"

George had just thrown his life away! With that one bold, rash, suicidal gesture he had shattered all hope of his acquittal and ruined numerous gamblers.

"Nay, my lord," he said, smiling brightly as he followed Norfolk's instructions and burned the paper, "those were not her exact words. And I would not want to answer in a manner likely to prejudice any issue that may result from the King's next marriage."

The babble of voices filled the courtroom; everyone was talking at once. Now they knew what this was all about—Henry had his eye on a third wife, most likely Mistress Seymour. And to marry her, he must first be rid of Anne, but he wanted no more messy divorces; no, to kill her was the easiest, quickest, and surest way. To let her live could lead to all manner of trouble, especially about the rights of the little Princess Elizabeth. With Anne dead, he could put an end to all that and simply bastardize their daughter.

By reading that paper aloud, George had done much more than humiliate Henry by informing the public that the King's masculine powers were waning; he had transformed "The Goggle-Eyed Whore" into a heroine. He had also signed his own death warrant.

It all happened very quickly after that. There was no recess; the jury was polled right where they sat. The verdict was guilty; not one man dared dissent. George was condemned to suffer the same fate as Anne's other lovers: to be hanged, drawn, and quartered. As Norfolk read out the verdict in a flat, toneless voice he was hissed and booed loudly by the crowd.

I had to lean forward, my stays creaking in protest, and put my head between my knees to keep from fainting. George had made his choice, public and plain. He had chosen her over me. He had declared to the world that he would rather die a traitor's death with Anne than live with me.

"Guards, you may remove the prisoner," Norfolk directed from his seat beneath the gold-fringed canopy of state. No remorse shadowed his voice or his features.

As George descended from the platform, Anne leapt up and ran to him. A guard made a move to intercept her, but with a single look she froze him.

"Oh, George, why?" she asked tearfully. "Why? You could have saved yourself!"

George flashed her his most winning smile. "You know why— because I cannot imagine my life without you in it!" He enfolded her in his arms and held her long and close against his heart as she clung to him and wept. When they stepped apart, still holding hands and standing at arm's length, gazing at one another with such loving tenderness, he began to speak, quoting scriptures solemnly, and, recognizing the verse, Anne joined him.

"Entreat me not to leave thee, or to return from following after thee, for whither thou goest, I will go."

Tears streamed down Anne's face and he cupped it between his hands and pressed a lingering kiss onto her brow.

Then the guards were upon them, pulling them apart. Anne caught George's face between her hands and kissed his brow just as he had hers; then he was led away, back to the cell he shared with the other condemned men in the Beauchamp Tower.

Anne shook off her guards and stared defiantly out into the crowd. "I do love my brother!" she said proudly. "Shame on anyone who tries to sully that love with lewd and evil imaginings!"

Every eye was upon her as she mounted the platform. She moved with such elegance, black velvet skirts whispering against the steps as they trailed behind her, hanging sleeves with their deep fur cuffs swaying gracefully. As she reached the top, a shaft of sunlight poured in through the high arched window and she was bathed in golden light. Anne knew all about appearances, and she paused there, just for a moment, artfully posed, her right hand rising to pluck at the golden *B* resting in the hollow of her throat.

For the first time in her brief reign, willing cries of "God save the Queen!" reached Anne's ears. The woman they had once reviled, damned, and cursed had become a martyr to wronged wives, and every woman whose husband or sweetheart had ever strayed was firmly on her side. Now, when it was too late to matter, the people of London had fallen in love with Anne Boleyn. But at least she could die knowing that in the court of public opinion she had won.

Seated upon the bench with the other peers, Harry Percy gasped aloud. His face drained of color and he pressed a hand against his heart, complaining to those around him of a sharp pain, and begging to be excused.

"Sit down, man, it will all be over soon!" Charles Brandon, Duke of Suffolk, barked, grabbing hold of Percy's red velvet robe and pulling him back down onto the bench.

The picture Cromwell painted of Anne was all evil black and harlot scarlet. He depicted her as a rampant adulteress. She was, he insisted, a woman unable to curtail her carnal lusts and impulses, a woman who went after what she wanted, seducing and beguiling the men she desired, brazenly touching and kissing them to stir their lust, and showering them with gifts and money afterwards to ensure their silence. She shamelessly made use of the condemned men, including her own brother, as her personal stable of studs, in a vain attempt to conceive a male child and deceive her husband into believing that it was his legitimate heir. A tale was told, supposedly straight from the lips of the dying Lady Wingfield, about Mark Smeaton being concealed inside a cupboard in the Queen's bedchamber and brought out whenever Anne called for "something sweet."

"There never lived a greater whore than Anne Boleyn!" Lady Wingfield was reputed to have said upon her deathbed.

Again, as in the previous trials, dates were cited, all of which Anne vehemently contested, many occurring when she was great with child or recovering from a birthing or miscarriage.

Imperiously, she demanded that the midwives, doctors, and nurses be summoned to testify that she was incapable of intercourse upon these dates.

"Do you think I was so lust-mad that I would couple with a lover upon bloody sheets while suffering the agony of white leg mere days after my daughter was born?" she demanded.

In the audience old Mistress Orchard, Anne's childhood nurse, who had been present throughout all her pregnancies, stood up and begged to be allowed to speak. "I am an experienced nurse, my lords, and I can tell you it is not possible, no woman would . . ."

Norfolk ordered her to sit down and be silent or else she would be evicted from the court. Such testimony, he said, was unnecessary; the jurors had enough facts to render a decision.

Impulsively, Anne spun round and threw her arms wide, as if she would embrace the crowd. "I appeal to every woman here who has ever borne a child or helped birth one!"

Almost every woman in Tower Hall jumped up and shook her fist or shouted abuse at Norfolk and Cromwell, all of them speaking at once, creating an unholy din. They knew Anne was telling the truth and that justice was turning a blind eye, and now, thanks to George Boleyn, they knew why.

"Sit down!" Norfolk bellowed. "If another person speaks without my permission I shall clear the court! Silence! I will have silence!"

Grudgingly the women fell silent and resumed their seats, but by the looks they gave him I could not help but think, woe to Norfolk if ever he encountered them alone in the street. Oh, how they hated him!

"I now call upon my fellow judges to render the verdict. As for myself," Norfolk announced, "the evidence is clear; I find the prisoner, beyond a doubt, guilty on all counts."

One by one the twenty-six peers were polled and each man raised his voice to echo Norfolk and pronounce Anne "Guilty!"

When Percy's turn came he sat there trembling and ashen-faced, his mouth gaping open and closed. His jaw quivered so he was unable to speak.

Suffolk elbowed him sharply. "Go on, man, say it and have done! You know what you have to do; now do it!"

"I can't! I can't!" Percy sobbed, doubling over and clutching his belly, being gnawed from within by the cancer that would soon kill him.

"My Lord of Northumberland," Norfolk said sternly, "may we have your verdict, please?"

"G-G-Guilty!" He stammered the one word they expected of him, for he had not the courage to say otherwise, and then he fell in a dead faint onto the floor.

Norfolk glared at him with marked distaste—never could he stomach a weakling—then proceeded to pass sentence on his niece.

"Because you have offended the King's Grace and committed treason against his person, the law of the realm is this: that you deserve death and you shall be burnt or beheaded at the King's Pleasure."

Anne's eyes closed briefly, then opened again and gazed heavenward as she clasped her hands and raised them. "O Lord, O My Creator, Thou knowest whether I have deserved this death!"

All about me people were crying, women were wailing and fainting, and men were shaking their heads and grumbling in protest at this parody of justice.

But Anne was not done. She had more to say and, breathing deep to steady herself, she turned once more to face her judges.

"Gentlemen, I think you know well that the reason why you have condemned me is something other than the evidence presented here today. . . ."

In the crowd there were murmurs about "another marriage" and "Jane Seymour."

"My only sin against the King has been my jealousy and lack of humility. But you must follow not your own conscience, but the King's. I have prepared myself to die, and regret only that my brother and other innocent men must lose their lives because of me. I would most willingly suffer many deaths to save them, but, since it is the King's Pleasure, I shall accompany them into death, content in the knowledge that I shall dwell with them forevermore in endless peace and joy at the foot of the throne of Our Lord." With that she turned and swept gracefully down the steps.

Percy was then being carried out upon a door that had been

hastily unhinged to serve as a makeshift stretcher. Anne paused to allow him and his bearers to pass, and his hand shot out and grasped her sleeve.

Summoning what little of his strength remained, Percy raised his head and croaked one plaintive word: "F-F-For-g-g-give!"

It was then that Harry Percy was granted his moment of grace. Anne took his hand in both of hers and squeezed it reassuringly. "Willingly!" she declared. "Most willingly!"

Percy fell back gratefully, smiling wanly. "Th-Thank you!" he whispered fervently as his eyes shut and he drifted from consciousness once again.

Head held high, with no sign of hysteria or tears, Anne left the courtroom. As she passed, people sank to their knees, weeping openly, men doffed their caps, and hands reached out to touch her skirts.

"Good people"—Anne paused in their midst—"with all my heart I thank you and humbly beseech you to pray for me and the men who are unjustly condemned to die with me."

When she was gone the crowd quickly dispersed, with much grumbling and lamenting. Had the King heard them, his heart would have trembled at the hatred and disgust. "A tyrant no better than Nero!" I heard a young scholar call him.

I waited until they were nearly all gone before I left my seat. In the last row Mary Boleyn sat weeping and hugging her great belly. Her husband, Will Stafford, sat beside her with his arm draped round her shoulders, speaking in soft, soothing words.

"Uncle Norfolk would not let me speak!" she sobbed. "I begged him, but he would not let me. He said I must think of my children and—for their sake—I agreed. I kept silent and now they are condemned! Oh, Nan! Oh, George!"

"Darling, nothing you could have said would have made any difference," Will Stafford gently insisted. "It was not justice that was done here today, but the King's justice, and those are two very different things!"

When she saw me, Mary struggled to her feet and lumbered towards me. With great alarm I noticed the trail of blood she left behind her, dripping from beneath her skirts.

"Jane!" she gasped. "Why? Oh, how could you do such a terrible thing? You must go to Cromwell, or Norfolk, the King himself if you can." She grimaced and doubled over gasping, grasping her belly. "You must!"

"Darling . . ." Will Stafford put his arms around her and tried to lead her away. "Come, there is nothing you can do here. We must get you home if we can, and summon the midwife."

Mary dropped down, squatting and grimacing, clenching her teeth, as blood seeped through her skirts in an ever expanding stain.

I looked away; I could not bear to see the blame in her beseeching blue eyes.

"Jane, please, tell them you lied! You must explain; tell them why! Please, Jane, this goes beyond right and wrong—it is life and death! Do not let my brother and sister perish because of your lies! Recant now, while there is still time. Do you really want to live with this on your conscience? And when you die, you must face God. . . ."

I stepped back, evading the hand she stretched out to me. "I will summon help!" I said as I fled Tower Hall, running as fast as my feet could carry me. I did not stop running until I reached my barge.

But, to my everlasting shame, I did not summon help. I left Mary to miscarry a stillborn child and nearly die herself in the same courtroom where her brother and sister had been condemned.

ॐ 30 ॐ

I ran straight to Cromwell's rooms, tearing off my cloak and pushing past his startled manservant, rushing straight into the bedchamber. Though I was shivering mightily, as if I had just come in
from a snowstorm instead of a warm May day, beneath my clothes
my body was slick with sweat and I struggled to be rid of them. I
could not unlace myself and ordered Cromwell's man to do it for
me, ignoring his modest protests and offers to send for a maid.
When he did not act fast enough, I seized the dagger from his belt
and, angling it clumsily behind my back, sliced through the laces
of my gown and stays. Gratefully, I shrugged out of my burgundy
damask gown, petticoats, and leather stays. I left them where they
fell and, kicking off my shoes and tearing off my gable hood, I
crawled into Cromwell's bed wearing only my shift and stockings.

I had just pulled the covers up over my head when my stomach
churned and I almost tumbled out of bed as I groped frantically
beneath it for the chamberpot. I retched into it, shuddering at the
taste of the bitter bile.

Gasping and wretched, I fell back limply against the pillows and
stared up at the canopy as my head reeled and spots danced before
my eyes. My mouth tasted vile, but I had not the strength to raise
my head and call for a drink. When I could no longer stand the sight
of the dancing dots, I shut my eyes and rolled over onto my side,

drawing up and hugging my knees. It was then I noticed a soreness about my breasts. Gingerly, I touched them, but my courses were due any day, so I thought no more about it. Instead, I thought of all the hours that I had spent here in this bed betraying my husband. Almost every night since I had opened my heart to Cromwell had been spent here. If my pleas for clemency failed, I would be responsible for his death and I could not bear that. Weeping, I let myself drift into an uneasy, guilt-racked slumber.

I awoke some hours later when Cromwell came in.

"You may get up and dress now, Lady Rochford," he said coldly as he went straight to his desk.

"But . . ." Confused and sick, I sat up.

"You can go now, Lady Rochford; our business is concluded," he said as he dipped a quill into the ink.

"It is not!" I flung back the covers and leapt out of bed. "My husband has been condemned to die!"

"Do not ask me to save him. I cannot. While your husband may or may not be guilty of incest—the truth is immaterial—he is without question the Queen's most loyal supporter, and as such he cannot be allowed to live."

"But if Anne were to die?" I knelt in my shift at his feet like the most wretched and pathetic supplicant.

"He would openly proclaim the King her murderer and transfer his loyalty to her daughter, the Princess Elizabeth, and we cannot have that," Cromwell said brusquely, brushing my hand off his knee.

"But you said Anne would be sent to a convent!"

"No, Lady Rochford. I said she *should* be sent to a convent. Recollect, I promised nothing. . . ."

"And nothing is what I get!" I sobbed bitterly.

"Was not your conscience eased when you made your confession to me?" Cromwell asked silkily.

"Yes, but . . ." I shook my head distractedly. "Nothing has gone as I expected! I care nothing for the other men—let them die!— but George . . . I love him! And he is to die the most horrible death imaginable!"

"Perhaps the King will be merciful and commute his sentence to a simple beheading," Cromwell suggested.

"Will he?" I asked hopefully.

Cromwell shrugged. "I do not know, Lady Rochford. I merely do as the King commands me."

"You monster!" I struck at him with my fists. "Have you no conscience? Have you no heart? I don't know how you sleep at night!" Cromwell caught my wrists and thrust me away. "I do not know how I shall sleep at night!"

"If you will consult an apothecary, Lady Rochford, I think you will find that there are many fine sleeping potions. I am confident you can find one that will suit your needs. Now if you will excuse me, I have work to do." He called his valet and ordered him to summon a maid to help me dress.

"It is over between us, isn't it?" I asked.

Cromwell nodded as he picked up his pen and bent over his work again. "You have served your purpose and are of no further use to me."

"That is truly all I was to you?" I asked.

Again Cromwell nodded. "It was the simplest way to get the information I required. You longed for affection and to unburden yourself, and I needed a foundation to build my case upon. His Majesty thought at first to use witchcraft as the means for her destruction. There is the matter of the deformed child, and her sixth finger, and the people have long believed that she bewitched His Majesty, by some spell or other dark, supernatural means. But I am a man firmly entrenched in this world, and I find adultery much more tangible than superstition; and His Majesty chose to be guided by my counsel. He knew I would not fail him."

"But you have failed me!" I cried.

Cromwell put down his pen and looked at me. "How so, Lady Rochford? I never spoke of love or an enduring affair, nor did I make you any promises."

"You said revenge would be sweet! But it isn't! It isn't sweet at all! I shall have to live with what I've done for the rest of my life. You lied, Cromwell, you lied!"

"No, Lady Rochford, pray recollect I said: I think you will find that after all you have endured, revenge will be sweet. You disagree? Well then"—he shrugged—"I was mistaken, as is everyone from time to time. No one is infallible."

He spoke the truth and I could not dispute it; instead I bowed my head and, with shoulders sagging, went to put on my clothes. When at last I put on my cloak to hide my severed laces, I lingered at the door for a moment, but he did not even look up to bid me good-bye. At that moment the only person I hated more than Anne Boleyn and Thomas Cromwell was myself.

It would be Anne who would do for George what I could not. Like me, she would have moved heaven and earth to save him. Swallowing her pride, she wrote to Henry, begging, "If ever the name of Anne Boleyn has been pleasing to your ears, let only myself bear the burden of Your Majesty's displeasure."

It worked, and Henry decided to be merciful. When Cranmer appeared at the Tower to hear Anne's last confession, he also came to bargain. If Anne would sign a document annulling her marriage, thus declaring her only child a bastard, Henry would commute the sentences of all five men, including the lowborn Smeaton, to beheading; and the axe, he promised, would be newly sharpened instead of blunted from prior use. As for Anne herself, an expert headsman would come from France to take her head off swiftly with a sword, instead of the more cumbersome axe. As a testament to the great love he had once borne her, Henry was prepared to grant her the easiest and swiftest death of all, but only if she would sign—otherwise, she would be burned on Tower Green and the men dragged through the streets of London to Tyburn, to be hung, cut down while they still lived, and disemboweled and hacked to pieces. The last thing they would see would be their own entrails being thrown into the fire. Only Anne had the power to save them.

So she did it. With tears in her eyes, Anne signed away her daughter's birthright, annulled her marriage, and declared herself a whore who had never truly been Henry's wife. The grounds cited were Henry's liaison with Mary Boleyn, which placed Henry and Anne within the forbidden degree of affinity, and made any marriage between them unlawful without a special dispensation; and a supposed precontract with Harry Percy which, in the law's eyes, was just as binding as an actual marriage.

"Fancy that," Anne chuckled wryly as she read the document. "Harry Percy and I have been married all these years and neither of us knew it!"

"Make no mistake, Cranmer," she said afterwards while the ink was drying, "I do this only for them, to spare George and our friends the greater torment. But I am not the fool Henry Tudor thinks I am. If I refused to sign he would merely create a new law whereby he could have his way. I only pray that someday Elizabeth will understand and forgive me."

As Cranmer prepared to go—I heard later from the ladies who attended her—she inquired after Henry and was told that he distracted himself with hunting, feasting, and masques, and all manners of merrymaking from the moment he arose until he laid his head upon the pillow at night.

"To quiet a guilty conscience perhaps?" Anne wondered. "He is no fool, my husband, and I am sure he realizes that if I have never been his wife, as the document I have just signed so attests, then I cannot be guilty of adultery—for without marriage there can be no adultery—so to kill me now would be outright murder. I am sure he realizes that, my clever husband." She spoke with biting sarcasm, and then she smiled, clucked her tongue, and shook her head. "Whatever has become of that conscience that used to disturb him so, and gnaw upon his mind like a dog does upon a bone? Has he found a way to rid himself of that too?" She then gave way to a bout of hysterical laughter of such intensity that the timid Cranmer crossed himself and quickly fled.

❧ 31 ❧

May 17, 1536—that was the day George died.

I stood at the foot of the scaffold, shivering in my widow's weeds. My stomach churned and twice I had to duck beneath the structure to vomit. My request for a last meeting with George had been denied. He did not want to see me, but I was determined to see him.

Norfolk and Cromwell were also there, with the Duke of Suffolk, as the King's official witnesses, but I ignored them all and they ignored me.

In the hope of deterring a large crowd, Anne's paramours were scheduled to die just after dawn, but, for once, Cromwell's strategy had failed. The people of London had taken these men to heart. To them, they were heroes sentenced to die unjustly, and they were determined to see them off properly with many tears shed and prayers said.

In the Bell Tower, from behind a grate, Thomas Wyatt wept as he looked down upon the sorrowful scene.

Above him, upon the parapets—where the ravens, the black birds of misfortune, perched boldly—stood Anne, surrounded by guards and her female attendants. Meg Lee and Mistress Orchard were weeping volubly, imploring Anne to return inside. But Anne was determined to stay.

"I will not forsake them at the end, as they never forsook me," she said.

She also had been denied a last meeting with George; it was Henry's way of punishing them because George had read that paper aloud.

George was led out first. He wore somber and unadorned black velvet with the collar of his pure white shirt unlaced and open wide to bare his neck. Behind him, Norris and Brereton followed, similarly clad in stark black and white with their necks exposed. Next came Francis Weston, and the crowd gasped in astonishment, then began to applaud as he smiled and waved back at them.

Flamboyant to the last, Weston was clad from head to toe in startling, vivid scarlet, spangled with ruby brilliants like the drops of his blood that would so soon be spilled. Unlike the others, he wore a wide-brimmed red hat with a jaunty plume, gloves, and a velvet cloak.

"Aye"—he nodded to the crowd—"I am dressed for travel, for what is death but the greatest journey?"

Weston's age-bent mother broke from the crowd and tried to force her way to him, but was held back by the guards. "My lamb, led to the slaughter!" she sobbed, stretching out her arms to him.

"Nay, Mother, be not so dramatic; you'll steal my scene!" he chided fondly, winking and blowing her a kiss.

Last of all came poor Mark Smeaton, his broken body slung limply between two guards, with his mangled hands draped over their shoulders, and his bare, broken toes, sticking through his ruined black hose, dragging in the dirt. His clothes, the same black-bordered gray silk doublet he had worn to his ill-fated dinner with Cromwell, hung from him in filthy blood-, urine-, and shit-stained tatters.

"Wyatt!" Suddenly Brereton spun round and shouted up at Wyatt's window in the Bell Tower. "Weep not for us, man, but write! Write!" he repeated urgently. "Make us immortal; let us live forever in a poem! Only you can do it for us!"

As George neared the scaffold, I thrust myself into his path. He made to step around me, but I would not let him. I started to speak, but he stopped me.

"I will not hear you, Jane."

"George . . . Please! I am so sorry! I did not know . . . I did not mean . . ."

George folded his arms across his chest, arched an eyebrow skeptically, and stared straight at me witheringly.

I quailed beneath his scorn and lowered my eyes in shame, and quickly stepped aside. Though there was much I wanted to say, I knew there was nothing I could say that would justify what I had done, and no apology, no matter how heartfelt, could make things right. My husband was about to die and the fault was mine in part.

"I . . ." Tears rolled down my face, and my lips trembled as he started to mount the scaffold.

But I could not leave things as they were. I ran after him and caught his sleeve.

"I love you, George!" I cried plaintively. I had to say it one last time!

George pulled free of me and continued up the thirteen steps.

"Have courage, George!" I called after him.

George paused at the top of the steps, then turned to stare down at me.

"No, Jane, you have courage, for you have far greater need of it than I do! You have to go on living, while I have only to die. And someday, Jane, you too will die, and then you will have to answer to God for what you have done. He—in this case, she—who sows the whirlwind must expect to reap the storm. Good-bye, Jane."

He turned his back on me, squared his shoulders, and went to meet his fate.

As he removed his black velvet doublet he paused and stood for a long moment, squinting and staring up at the faraway figure atop the Bell Tower. He raised his hand and she did the same, and they stood for a long moment looking at each other as if they could bridge the distance and touch palms. At last he turned away and paid the executioner his fee.

"I forgive you for what you are about to do," he said as he pressed the gold coin into the big calloused hand.

Moving to stand beside the block, George turned to address the crowd.

"I am come hither to die and not to preach a sermon. Trust in God and not in the flatteries of the court and the vanities of the world. Had I done so, I think I would still be alive as you are now. Good people, I entreat you all to pray for me, and now I submit to the law that has condemned me." He knelt before the wooden block. Once more, he turned to face the crowd. "I do love my sister!" he said proudly, defiantly; then, almost as an afterthought, he added, insolent and grudgingly, just before he laid his head down, "God save the King!"

I moved alongside the scaffold. I wanted to be close to him in his final moments. I hoped in vain that he would look at me, or speak to me, one last time.

I could not bear to watch as the axe came down, and squeezed my eyes shut tight. With a horrendous thud it fell, cutting through skin and bone, making such a sickening sound; and I felt the warm wetness of George's blood splash onto my face.

So perished my husband, the love of my life, the man who was everything to me. Now he would never love me or come back to me. I had failed at the only thing that had ever really mattered to me— my husband had never loved me, and when his life ended so did all hope for me.

As the executioner bent to retrieve the head I moved away. I could not bear to see it held aloft by its hair while the executioner intoned the customary words: "So perish all the King's enemies!" No one cheered this gruesome sight; the people watched it all in stony silence.

Atop the Bell Tower I saw Anne crumple. Her attendants rushed to bend over her. After a few moments they raised her to her feet and tried to lead her away. But she would not go; instead she braced herself against the parapet and forced herself to watch the rest.

Norris died next. Bravely mounting the scaffold after George's corpse had been removed, he stood for a moment, pale and gulping, staring down at the blood-sodden straw. Then, courage triumphing over fear, he turned to address the crowd.

"I know the Queen to be innocent of the charges laid against her, and I would rather die a thousand deaths than speak falsely and ruin an innocent person. God save the King. I hope you will all pray for him, and for me as well."

He removed a ring from his finger and pressed it into the executioner's palm, then knelt, grimacing at the feel of my husband's tepid blood seeping through his hose, and laid his head upon the block.

With a whoosh and a thud the axe descended and the chivalrous Henry Norris was gone.

The executioner picked up the head, held it aloft, and spoke the traditional words; then the corpse was removed, stripped, and dumped unceremoniously into a crude wooden coffin to await entombment beneath the floor of the Tower's chapel—St. Peter ad Vincula.

Again there was no applause. The people respected these men too much to celebrate their deaths.

Will Brereton boldly climbed the scaffold steps and went straight to the executioner, paid him in gold, and forgave him, then moved quickly to kneel before the block.

"Have you nothing to say?" the Duke of Norfolk asked incredulously. It was a rare thing indeed for a condemned man to forgo his final speech.

Brereton paused thoughtfully. "Good people, judge ye best whether I deserve this!" he said simply, and laid his head down.

Again the axe fell and another head was held aloft.

With typical dash and daring, Francis Weston came next. A young woman in the crowd tossed a single red rose to him and he caught it deftly, held it to his nose, and blissfully inhaled its perfume. At the top of the steps he casually removed his gloves, then doffed his wide-brimmed scarlet hat and sent it flying, spinning out over the crowd. Hundreds of hands reached for it, fighting for this most precious of souvenirs.

With a flourish, he swung the red velvet cloak from around his shoulders and fastidiously spread it over the bloody straw so he need not soil the knees of his fine red silk hose when he knelt.

Watching him, the executioner frowned; the clothing of the dead were his perquisite, and when the nobility died he often made a nice profit.

Noting his expression, Weston exclaimed, "Oh, cheer up, man, there's plenty left for you! Look at all these rubies!" He indicated his gem-spangled doublet. "A sensible fellow like you can live well for years on these, unlike me; if I were to go on living they'd be lost in a dice game within an hour!" With a winning smile, he plucked from his ear a dangling ruby drop as big as a walnut and tucked it into the executioner's hand.

"Now, friend, do quickly what you have to do! But hold a moment, if you will; I must speak to these fine people who have come to see me die!"

With arms spread wide as if to embrace them, he turned to face his enthralled audience. Smiling, he placed a hand upon his heart and bowed low as they sighed in adoration.

"Verily, my heart breaks that I must take my leave of you all, but I must rejoin my friends who have so bravely gone before me. I had thought to live in abomination twenty or thirty years yet, and then in my old age to make amends; I never thought I would come to this." With a grand sweep of his hand he indicated the block. "And so, good people, I bid you all a fond farewell and entreat you all to pray for me! God save the Queen!" He turned and waved up at Anne. "And the King too!" he added tartly.

With another bow he spun gracefully around, dropped to his knees, and laid his head upon the block. So died the flamboyant Francis Weston.

When the executioner held his head high by its unruly red locks, his young wife let loose a bloodcurdling scream and fell down in a dead faint.

Lastly, Mark Smeaton was carried up the scaffold steps.

"Masters all," he sobbed, "please pray for me—I deserve this death!"

He had no coin with which to pay the executioner, and for this he sobbed an apology; his ruined clothes would have to suffice, as he had nothing of value.

His eyes so swollen he could hardly see, he groped blindly for the block and laid his head down.

The axe fell with an angry thud and the executioner snatched up the head and shouted, "So perish all the King's enemies!" before he let it fall contemptuously into the blood-soaked straw, leaving it for his assistants to deal with.

Smeaton died last because he was the only one to proclaim his guilt, and Cromwell hoped this would stick in people's minds. But it did not; the people saw Smeaton as a lowly coward, equally deserving of pity and contempt. It might make a good story—the Queen and her lute player—but everyone knew it was not true.

Afterwards, I walked around the scaffold to stand beside the five coffins. I knelt beside George's and eased off the lid. I would see him, I would kiss him one last time!

Gently, tenderly, as if it were a baby, I lifted his severed head and cradled it against my breast. I stared down into the dull, death-glazed brown eyes, then bowed my head and pressed a long, deep kiss onto the half-parted lips. My tears fell like rain onto his handsome face and I stroked his black beard and smoothed his hair. It was matted with blood, and my hand came away red-stained and sticky.

I felt such a strange, drowsy, almost dizzy bewilderment, as if I were wandering lost in some terrible dream—a nightmare from which I would wake any moment, screaming.

I heard a man clear his throat and looked up to see Master Kingston standing before me, and beside him his stern-faced wife, staring down at me with hard eyes. As the jailor's wife she had much experience in dealing with deranged females and, alarmed by my behavior, her husband had summoned her.

I did not realize then that I had been kneeling there, crooning to and rocking my husband's head, for half an hour.

Gently, I laid George's head in my lap and held out my blood-stained hands to show the Kingstons.

"George's blood is on my hands!"

Lady Kingston nodded grimly. "Yes, it is."

Her sad-eyed husband, who had seen so much of death, torture, and madness, also agreed.

Master Kingston beckoned a servant and bade him "see to my Lord Rochford's remains," and my beloved's head was lifted from my lap even as I protested and reached out my hands for it.

The Kingstons grabbed my arms and pulled me to my feet. But

I fought them off. I must kiss George one last time! I ran back to clasp his head against my breast again, and caress that beautiful, beloved honey skin, now tinged with the gray of death, and press my lips to his.

I screamed and wept when it was wrenched roughly away from me. The Kingstons began to drag me firmly away, back to my barge, even as I dug my heels into the dirt and screamed my beloved's name.

As the oars dipped into the dirty, stinking river water, I sat there staring down at my bloodstained hands and knew they could never truly be washed clean. Every time I looked at my hands I would see it there, and so would many others whenever they looked at me. No woman would ever embrace such a treacherous female as a friend, fearing I would one day use her secrets and confidences against her. And no man would ever again take me to wife, for fear that I might someday bear false witness against him and send him to the block.

Cromwell had lied again; I would not be regarded as a heroine by everyone who hated Anne Boleyn. Even her enemies would revile my treachery.

At some point I began to scream—I cannot recall if it was while I was still upon the river or back inside the palace. I only know I started, but for the life of me, I cannot remember when I stopped.

❧ 32 ❧

By the morning of May 19 I had recovered my wits enough to attend Anne's execution. Indeed, nothing in this world could keep me from being right there beside the scaffold to watch her die.

When she stepped out of the Tower and raised her face to the sun for the last time, she was wearing a long, ermine-trimmed white satin robe that flowed out gracefully behind her. With each step a blood red satin skirt peeped through its folds. And coiled like a sleek black snake speared with diamond-tipped pins, her hair was pinned high to bare the nape of her neck.

As she made her way to Tower Green, escorted by her female attendants, guards, and Master Kingston, she showed no sign of fear or sorrow. Her eyes were clear, dry, and bright, and her steps never faltered.

There was no more of the morbid jesting she had so freely indulged in during her stay in the Tower. "Queen Anne Sans-Tête, Queen Anne Lackhead, history shall call me!" she had quipped, her wild laughter sending shivers down the spines of all who heard it. "Decapitation shall be my fate, because Henry's love turned to hate!" Of the French executioner imported especially for her, she had said, "I have heard tell the executioner is very good, and I have a little neck!" And as she was carefully choosing her clothes, she remarked, "While I select a gown to die in, Jane Seymour is trying on her wedding gown! Out with the old, in with the new!" Leaning in the window, breathing in the night air for the last time, she gave an exaggerated sniff. "Master Kingston, is that a whiff of bridal cake I smell borne upon the breeze?" But there was none of that now. She was calm and ready to meet her fate.

At the foot of the scaffold she hesitated. Master Kingston held out his hand to help her up the steps. But it was not fear that stayed her.

"Master Kingston." She spoke loud and clear, because she wanted everyone to hear. "Please commend me to His Majesty, and tell him that he has ever been constant in advancing me; from a private gentlewoman he made me a marquess, from a marquess he made me a queen, and now that he has no greater honor to bestow upon me, he gives my innocence the crown of martyrdom."

Then she gathered up her skirts and ascended the thirteen steps.

Aye, I hated her, it's true—and I still do—but she was undoubtedly the bravest person I have ever known.

At the top of the steps she unclasped her robe and let it fall backwards into the arms of Meg Lee, and I saw then that over her blood red satin kirtle she wore a plain, unadorned gown of black damask with a deep, square bodice cut so low the curves of her shoulders showed.

Head held high, as imperious as the queen she still believed herself to be, she went to meet the executioner. He was a tall man, dressed all in black and wearing a half mask.

Gallantly, the French executioner knelt and kissed her hand and they spoke softly for a few moments in French. Her voice was lilting and cheerful, and her dark eyes flashed with a beguiling sparkle. She reached up behind her neck and unclasped her favorite necklace—the pearls with the golden *B*—and pressed it into his hand. Then, with apparent regret, he began to instruct her.

After she had made her parting speech, she was to kneel just there—at the center of the scaffold—and look straight ahead. Unlike with English executions—so clumsy, so messy, with the big, cumbersome axe—there was no need for a block.

"Good Christian people," Anne began to speak. "I am come hither to die according to the law, and therefore I will speak nothing against it and accuse no man. I pray God to save the King and send him long to reign over you, for a kinder or more merciful prince there was never, and he was ever a good and gentle sovereign lord to me. . . ."

Oh! If she had run at Henry screaming obscenities and attacked him tooth and nail and driven her knee into the royal codpiece, Anne could not have made her meaning plainer! It was all there in her manner and voice. Her sardonic tone and the way she arched her brows and cocked her head spoke volumes. It was brilliant! No one could fault her words, but they were like pellets of poison rolled in honey and sugar. The phrasing was unerringly correct—it sounded just like a proper leave-taking—but the way she said it . . . If Henry had been there he would have run up onto the scaffold and throttled her, or seized the great two-handed sword and beheaded her himself!

"I submit to death with good will, asking pardon of all the world, and yield myself humbly to the will of the King. And if any person will meddle with my cause, I require them to judge best. Thus, I take my leave of the world, and heartily desire you all to pray for me."

With swift grace, she turned and sank to her knees, taking a moment to arrange the drape of her skirts more becomingly, and fold her hands placidly in her lap, letting the deep, hanging cuffs of her famous sleeves fall over them.

Meg Lee tottered towards her, nearly blind with tears, clutching a white linen cloth—a blindfold. But Anne waved it away and stared straight ahead; she would face death as boldly as she had faced life.

"To Jesus, I commend my soul!" she cried.

A swift slash of silver steel ended Anne's life. So died the only woman who had ever made a fool of Henry Tudor, challenged and denied him.

At that very moment the Tower cannons boomed to let Henry know that he was now free to marry Jane Seymour.

A good Catholic, the French executioner crossed himself and murmured a prayer, then reluctantly bent to do his duty. In heavily accented English he spoke the traditional words as he held her head high. "So perish all the King's enemies!"

Suddenly the air was rife with screams, and dozens of women

fell fainting to the ground, some of whom were injured and trampled by those who fled in terror.

Anne's lips and eyes were moving still, opening and closing. When at last they stopped, eyes frozen wide in an accusing stare, she was looking right at me.

True to her words, Anne had left Henry's life with her head held high, but by a French executioner's hand, and not her own damnable pride.

Very gently, the French executioner lowered her head and laid it in the straw, and with a tender brush of his hand that was almost a caress, he closed her dark eyes. His face showing pale below his mask, he stumbled down the steps and called for wine. His manservant came running with a leather wineskin and, brushing aside the pewter cup, the executioner raised it to his lips and gulped it down. When he turned round and saw that his assistant was stripping the corpse, he shouted angrily, "Her shift, leave the good lady her shift and some dignity!" Her clothes were his perquisite, so his orders were obeyed.

Meg Lee and Mistress Orchard came to wrap her body in a length of black cloth. It was only then that they discovered that no coffin had been provided, and an old battered arrow chest was hastily brought out to fill the need.

I watched mutely as Anne's makeshift coffin was lowered down into the vault beneath the floor of St. Peter ad Vincula to rest atop George's coffin, beside their dearest friends and the lowborn, love-struck musician.

"Now they are at rest," Meg Lee said.

"Who?" I asked blankly, my mind again wandering lost, confused, and dizzy, in a strange, swirling mist.

"Anne and George—your husband," she added, seeing my blank, bewildered stare and the way I crinkled my brow quizzically at the mention of his name.

"No!" I shook my befuddled head adamantly, as I stared down into the dark and dusty vault.

They were both gone now, the person I had loved most and the person I had hated most, and I had helped kill them both.

"He is not my husband; he was never really mine."

Part Two

Jane Seymour
Anna of Cleves

1536–1540

❧ 33 ❧

Ten days after Anne died, I watched the King marry Jane Seymour in the chapel at Whitehall. Both wore radiant white satin, though the more superstitious members of the court whispered that it was not meet to marry in diamonds and pearls as they symbolized tears and sorrow.

"This time I marry for love!" King Henry crowed, jubilant and smiling, conveniently forgetting his grand, all-consuming passion for Anne Boleyn, and not once throughout the ceremony did his eyes leave his beloved's face.

Framed by shining, abundant waves of white-blond hair, crowned by a chaplet of pearls and white roses, Jane Seymour's face wore an expression of breathless awe, as if she could not quite believe this was truly happening and expected at any moment to awaken from a dream.

I watched the sunlight streaming in through the stained glass window bathe her in an eerie blue light and, in spite of the warmth of the day, I shivered. She looked like a woman drowning in blue, the way her pale face, hair, and gown absorbed the color. My mind would hark back to this day eighteen months later when I watched her die, with her face and lips tinged blue, gasping for air.

Afterwards, Henry showered his beloved in pearls, pouring a

basket filled with large, lustrous white pearls over her head, and draping long ropes of them about her neck and waist.

"Pearls for my pearl!" he cried, laughing as she spun slowly around in happy bewilderment, pearls dripping from her hair and the folds of her gown to scatter upon the floor with a sound like raindrops on a tile roof.

Jane Seymour made her debut as Queen that night. She entered the Great Hall wearing a gown of rust-red velvet, with a gold fish-net pattern embroidered on the wide cuffs of her hanging sleeves, and a gold and black gable hood hiding her hair. Pearls, double-stranded and interspersed with ruby-centered gold roses, bordered her hood, edged the modest square neckline of her gown, and encircled her throat and waist. In the hollow of her throat rested a pendant of gold acanthus leaves set with an oval-shaped ruby and a square emerald, with an enormous pearl dangling like a milky teardrop beneath.

Personally, I thought the gown a poor choice. Anne Boleyn could wear red, but when she did, she dominated the color; not so her bland, pasty-faced successor.

Servile, demure, meek, subdued, and placid as a sheep, Queen Jane took as her motto "Bound to Serve and Obey."

I was there, also bound to serve and obey, walking behind her, the black sheep, snubbed and shunned by most of the court. But as long as I lived and England had a queen, Cromwell, on behalf of his grateful master, promised there would always be a place for me as one of her ladies-in-waiting.

Jane Seymour took Anne Boleyn's place on May 30, and on May 31, I went mad. That morning I stopped making excuses, tallied up the facts, and admitted that I was carrying the Devil's child.

I had tried to ignore it. I had tried to deny it. I blamed my grief over George's death for drying up my courses; and, after all these years of marriage and what the learned physician had said, my womb had remained stubbornly barren. But I could not run away from the truth forever; I had to confront it. The Devil, not God, had heard my prayers and decided to give me a child—but not my husband's child.

Vainly, I tried to rid myself of Cromwell's creature, but it would not die. I downed in a single gulp the vile, stinking black-green concoction I bought from a toothless old hag in a dark London alley. But all it gained me was bilious green skin and loud, sulfurous farts and belches. The Devil's imp remained lodged firmly in my womb, resting and biding his time, waiting to be born. I rolled upon my bed, writhing and gripping my belly, until the whole room was rife with the aroma of rotten eggs. My frightened maid fled, gagging at the stench; then I staggered weakly to the window and flung it open wide. Leaning queasily upon the sill, I gulped in mouthfuls of fresh air and then I vomited.

Next I sat in a tub of water just as hot as I could bear, rivulets of sweat dripping down my face as my skin turned first bright pink then boiled-crayfish red, hoping to scald it out. When this also failed I hired a rough cart and had myself driven about for hours, being jostled and jounced over the worst rutted and rock-strewn roads the driver could find, trying to jar Satan's spawn from my womb. When I dragged myself, weary and aching—with every tooth feeling like it had been jarred loose—up the palace stairs, I turned impulsively, spread my arms wide, and flung myself down. When I picked myself up again I felt a mocking flutter in my belly, as if it were laughing at me and saying, "I am still here! You cannot get rid of me!"

In desperation I tried to claw it out. Standing in my room with my nails blood-caked and deep, stinging scratches furrowing my belly and oozing bright red blood, my maid caught me squatting and preparing to insert a long knitting needle.

I was given an elixir of poppy to render me docile and taken from court by my father for a "much-needed rest" in the country.

I remember little of my confinement except it was passed under watchful eyes, restraints, and in a state of almost perpetual sleep that ended with urgent commands to "Push!" and intense searing, tearing pain, like a great zigzag of lightning shocking me back to my senses, before I fell briefly back into oblivion again.

I nearly screamed the house down when I discovered that creature had been given George's name. They thought it would please me! Everyone thought that George was the father. Everyone knew how much I had always wanted a child, so they were all struck dumb with amazement when I rejected it. No one could understand why I couldn't bear the sight of my baby. When they tried to place the loathsome thing in my arms, I shoved it away and turned my face to the wall. When it cried, I ordered them to take it away before I silenced it forever by bashing its head against the wall.

Satan's imp was hastily farmed out; sent to live with strangers. My father would see to its care and education, and I was back at court by Christmastime.

Once again I felt life had made a mockery of me. Perhaps God, I thought, has a sense of humor and I am one of His favorite jokes. When I die and step through the pearly gates of Heaven, I fully expect to find Him doubled over and howling with glee, laughing at me.

When I tried to sleep I would hear George and Anne laughing. I would clap my hands over my ears, but it had no effect; I could not shut it out no matter how hard I tried.

The court I returned to was a very different place from the one I had known.

Now that they were gone, we realized how much the flamboyant Francis Weston, stalwart Will Brereton, and chivalrous Henry Norris had been a part of our lives, and how much their lively wit and escapades had made us laugh. And George and Anne . . . together or apart, they could light up a room; they were both absolute magic! Perhaps it was black magic, but it was magic just the same. Now they were all gone, dead; candles snuffed out much too soon. Though it was all the King and Cromwell's doing, the finger of blame was also pointed at me, and I would spend the rest of my life waiting for an absolution that would never come. They called me "The Red Widow" and said my black widow's weeds made a mockery of George's memory, and that I should have worn red to match the blood on my hands and the ineradicable scarlet stain that was like the mark of Cain on my soul.

I watched as Anne's initials, crest, and motto were scraped off the walls or painted over, and the stitches unpicked from the banners, canopies, and coverlets, and replaced with Jane Seymour's. Her portraits were taken down off the walls to be either burned or consigned to dusty attics, as every trace of her must be removed. Henry wanted no reminders.

It was as if Anne and her "evergreen gallants" had never even existed. No one dared speak their names, and their surviving kin all crept away like thieves in the night, retreating into seclusion and silent disgrace. Both Anne's parents would be dead within two years; first the elegant and patrician Lady Elizabeth in 1538, followed by ambitious, ruthless Thomas Boleyn a year later. It was as if neither could survive the embarrassment. Keeping their heads was not enough; it was not their son and daughter they mourned, but the loss of the King's favor. It was as if all the light had gone out of their lives and they had been condemned to perpetual darkness; without Henry VIII to illuminate their lives, it was just not worth going on.

Even Elizabeth, Anne's greatest failure, the princess who should have been a prince, was bastardized and banished to Hatfield. It angered the King to see Anne's dark, defiant eyes staring back at him from out of their daughter's face.

Only Thomas Wyatt, who had emerged from the Tower a bitter and disillusioned man, dared break the silence. Out of Will Brereton's request was born the poem "Circa Regna Tonat (Thunder Rolls Around the Throne)." It was George's warning to beware of the vanities of the world and the flatteries of the court, set to verse as only Wyatt, who lived to tell the tale, could render.

> *Who list his wealth and ease retain,*
> *Himself let him unknown contain.*
> *Press not too fast in at that gate*
> *Where the return stands by disdain.*
> *For sure, circa Regna tonat.*

> *The high mountains are blasted oft*
> *When the low valley is mild and soft.*

Fortune with Health stands at debate.
The fall is grievous from aloft.
And sure, circa Regna tonat.

These bloody days have broken my heart.
My lust and youth did then depart,
And blind desire of estate.
Who hastes to climb seeks to revert:
Of truth, circa Regna tonat.

The Bell Tower showed me such a sight
That in my head sticks day and night:
There did I learn out of a grate,
For all favor, glory, or might,
That yet, circa Regna tonat.

By proof, I say, there did I learn:
Wit helpeth not defense too yearn,
Of innocence to plead or prate.
Bear low, therefore, give God the stern.
For sure, circa Regna tonat.

There were other verses circulating secretly, I soon found out. They were only spoken about in whispers and recited in deepest secrecy lest the King find out.

On the last night of his life, George had taken up his lute and pen to compose one final song. He asked Master Kingston to deliver his lute and writings to Anne after he was gone, so that she might finish what he began. And she did. Brother and sister collaborated one last time on one last song.

Oh death, rock me asleep
Bring on my quiet rest
Let pass my very guiltless ghost
Out of my careful breast.

Ring out the doleful knell,
Let its sounds my death tell;
For I must die,
There is no remedy,
For now I die!

My pains who can express
Alas! They are so strong!
My sorrow will not suffer strength
My life for to prolong
Alone in prison strange!

I wail my destiny
Woe worth this cruel hap, that I
Should taste this misery.

Farewell my pleasures past,
Welcome my present pain
I feel my torments so increase
That life cannot remain.

Sound now the passing bell,
Rung is my doleful knell,
For its sound my death doth tell,
Death doth draw nigh
Sound the knell dolefully,
For now I die!

Even as George was writing these verses, Anne had the same idea herself; it was always thus with them. It was as if they could read each other's mind even when they were apart. This poem was hers alone.

Defiled is my name, full sore
Through cruel spite and false report,

That I may say forevermore
Farewell to joy, adieu comfort,
For wrongfully you judge of me;
Unto my fame a mortal wound,
Say what ye list, it may not be,
You seek for what shall not be found.

In death, poetry, and legend they had all found immortality. And I would be remembered alongside them, my name a byword for jealousy, treachery, betrayal, and lies. I found my immortality in infamy; I had unjustly become one of the villains in Anne Boleyn's tale, my true innocence blotted out and obscured by bloodstains.

In October 1537, Jane Seymour, "the entirely beloved," died giving Henry his heart's desire.

For three days and nights she labored and screamed her throat raw on soiled, sweat-soaked, bloody sheets. The heaving of her great belly and the straining ache of her privy parts wore her strength down to a shadow.

In desperation the midwife pressed a handkerchief filled with black pepper against her nose, hoping that a bout of violent sneezing would dislodge the infant from her womb.

The doctors huddled together fearfully, debating whether to cut her open in an attempt to save the child. Which was more important—the child or the mother? Which would the King prefer to save? Surely it would be the child; the King could always get another wife! Was one not just as good as another?

On her bed of pain, Jane Seymour heard them and silent tears coursed down her face. Did she perhaps then think of Catherine of Aragon and Anne Boleyn, the once beloved and then discarded queens, who had come and gone before her?

But before they could resort to the knife, it all ended happily in the wee hours of October 12, when the Queen was delivered of "a goodly fair boy."

As Henry cradled the precious bundle in his arms and cooed, "At last, my boy, my precious boy!" we hastily combed Jane's tangled, sweat-matted hair, propped her torn, limp, exhausted body up against a mountain of pillows, and draped an ermine-edged crimson velvet mantle about her shoulders.

When Henry bent to place a kiss upon her cheek and prattled on about her giving him "a Duke of York, a fine brother for our Edward, next year!" Jane Seymour smiled wanly. No one noticed that her life was slowly slipping away. They were too busy drinking toasts to the newborn prince and congratulating the King.

Jane Seymour had triumphed where her two predecessors had failed, and when she was laid in her coffin two weeks later, she was also enshrined in Henry's heart as the perfect wife, the paragon to which no other could compare, the only one who never disappointed him.

I was one of nine-and-twenty ladies—one for each year of Jane Seymour's life—who walked in solemn procession behind her coffin, escorting her to her tomb, carrying a lighted white taper clasped in my hands, clad in somber black with the plain white linen headdress that symbolized death in childbed.

In the years that followed George's death, I lived, yet I did not live. I woke up each morning and went to bed each night, ate my meals, said my prayers, dressed, and sewed, and served the queen if there was one, but my life lacked meaning and purpose. Without love I was nothing. I was six years past thirty and foresaw for myself a bleak and empty future. Alone in my bed at night I would think of George and weep because I would never feel his touch again. Nor was there any realistic hope that I would ever find someone else to love me; not now, not after what I had done. No man, whether he was in the market for a wife or a casual dalliance, would touch me; I was stained with blood.

I saved some of George's clothes and sometimes I would take them out and spread them on the bed. I would lie there in a welter of shirts, hose, breeches, doublets, cloaks, gloves, and hats, and gather them against my breast, bury my face in them and inhale deeply, hoping to catch his scent. I would rub my cheek against the fabric and remember the day he wore this, and this . . . the cherry red, black, evergreen, peacock blue, butter yellow, russet, tawny, orange fiery as a sunset; I had only to close my eyes and my memory would conjure up a vision of him, tall, handsome, and proud.

At night he appeared like a ghost in my dreams. I would see him, walking away from me, in the stark black and white clothes he had worn the day he died. I would follow him from his cell in the Tower all the way out to the scaffold, calling to him, begging, entreating him to "Come back to me and forgive everything!" Yet no matter how much I pleaded, how loud I cried, or how fast I ran, I could never close the distance between us; I could never catch up with him. He always evaded my touch and he would not turn and look at me, nor did he speak to me. Upon the scaffold, where the block should have been, she—Anne Boleyn—awaited him in black velvet, sable, and pearls. I watched in horror as George went to her and enfolded her in a passionate embrace and kissed her as a lover would. It was then that I always woke up screaming.

No one would ever believe how much I loved him. I would have sold my soul to the Devil to get him back, but neither God nor the Devil would heed my prayers. My penance was clear—I would be forever condemned and despised as the madly jealous and vengeful wife who had lied and sent her husband to the block.

Only I did not lie. I did not! He loved her more than anything or anyone. His love for her was unnatural, more than merely a brother's affection for his favorite sister, and so was hers for him! To one another they were entirely devoted. But everyone was blind to the truth. I did not kill George; he killed himself. When he read that paper aloud he had knowingly and deliberately committed suicide. He could have saved himself, but he chose not to. He wanted to be with Anne; he knew she was going to die and he chose to follow her. It was his decision to die. I did not kill him; he chose to die. I wanted him to live! I wanted him to love me and come back to me! Why could no one see that? Why did no one believe me?

Then, in 1540, "The Flanders Mare" trotted into Henry's life and I resumed my duties as a lady-in-waiting.

Anna of Cleves was four-and-twenty, German, Protestant, and eager to please but utterly incapable of doing so. She was singularly lacking in all the graces. She could not dance, play an instrument, recite poetry, carry a tune, roll the dice, or deal a hand of cards, and had been reared to believe that all such things were the Devil's vices. Her mother and governesses had diligently taught her that needlework, housewifery, and prayer were the only suitable occupations for a noblewoman.

Henry married her only to cement Cromwell's Protestant alliance; now that Catholic France and Spain were friends again, England needed an ally to tip the balance of power back in her favor.

Henry liked Holbein's portrait of her well enough to wed her, but not enough to bed her once he saw her in the flesh. Then he wrinkled up his nose and pronounced decisively, "I like her not!"

Aye, she was a rank, vile thing, with her guttural broken English that sounded like a hog grunting greedily at trough, and she possessed a marked aversion to bathing. Her dowdy German gowns, with their round skirts without trains, fussily gathered sleeves, and overly ornate bodices, hid a plump, slack-breasted, sagging bellied body that—to be perfectly blunt—stank.

Several times a day we scrubbed her down with vinegar and lemon juice and doused her with perfume. Once, in exasperation, I grabbed a pair of sewing scissors and snipped away the thick, matted clumps of stinking hair from her armpits. Several times a day I brought her cups of hot clove water to gargle with and kept a box of mint comfits always close at hand, but even then her breath always stank of beer and onions.

Her Dutch caps, with their sheer gauze wings, golden fringe, and great Orient pearls, were the only pretty thing about her, but beneath them her waist-length hair, as yellow as cheese, was so greasy and slick it was a trial to make the pins stick. I loathed to touch it and afterwards could not wash my hands fast enough.

And she was stupid beyond measure! As a lady of the bedchamber, I had noticed there had never been the telltale virgin's stain on the bedclothes, and His Majesty's distaste was quite apparent, and indeed it could not be faulted. So I undertook one day to question her about it, making my manner and voice most concerned and solicitous as I expressed the hope that she would soon give Prince Edward a little brother.

"I think Your Grace is a maid still," I said knowingly.

"Nein." She shook her head vigorously and I nearly gagged at the stench of her. "How can das be so? Vhen de King he comes to mein bed he kisses me und he biddeth me 'gut night, sveetheart,' und in de morning he kisses me again und he biddeth me 'gut morning, sveetheart,' und vhen he take his leave of me he biddeth me 'farevell, darling.' Is das nicht enough?"

I almost laughed in her face.

"Madame," I said, endeavoring to compose myself and keep my features and tone serene when it was all I could do not to burst out laughing. "There must be more—a great deal more—or it will be a very long time before we have a Duke of York."

"Nein." The dimwit shook her head. "I know no more. I am content und I receive as much of His Majesty's attention as I vish."

Six months later we were all greatly relieved when she amicably agreed to a divorce and to let Henry adopt her as his sister to preserve diplomatic relations, and trotted out of his life as placidly as a mare being turned out to pasture to make way for wife number five—Katherine Howard.

Part Three

Katherine

1540–1542

❧ 34 ❧

Katherine Howard danced into my bleak, gray life like a beacon of brightest sunshine. Her bubbling laughter and bright smile contained all the warmth my cold heart craved. Ten years had come and gone since I had seen her last. And, though she was but fifteen, the shy little bud I had met on the Dowager Duchess's lawn had already burst into full bloom and become a lush and sultry rose.

I remember the day she arrived to take up her duties as a lady-in-waiting to Anna of Cleves. It was a sweltering summer's day that turned us all into leaden-footed laggards, weighed down by our court finery. But for the first time since George died, I felt alive. Already I loved her, that little angel whose memory I had for so long treasured. I would watch over her at court, I vowed, and keep her safe from harm and guide her; she would be the daughter I had always wanted but never had. Perhaps this was God's gift to me, and in Katherine Howard I would find redemption and a kind of love—a far better love—that I had never known before—the sacred and pure love of a mother and her child.

She wore a gown of angelic white satin with the low, square bodice modestly filled in with a partlet of white lawn fashioned with a collar that opened in the shape of a V, pointing down to her pert little breasts, trussed high by her stays. As she stepped daintily from the Duke of Norfolk's barge, she raised her skirts and petticoats much too high, giving us all a glimpse of shapely legs sheathed in white stockings held up by white ribbon garters tied in pretty bows just below her knees and, even more startling, a flash of the creamy skin of a pair of plump thighs. Some even swore they caught a glimpse of the auburn curls between.

As she set her satin-shod feet down upon firm ground, the chin strap that held her white satin French hood in place snapped. As she reached up to grab hold of it before it tumbled into the Thames, her hand knocked awry the thick bun of auburn hair pinned loosely at the nape of her neck.

She pouted her lips—as red and ripe as cherries—in a little moue of annoyance and shook her head vigorously, like a wet dog, and sent the pins flying every which way, so that a mass of unruly auburn curls tumbled all the way down to her tightly-laced waist. And we were all enraptured. There was something about her that drew every eye—male and female—in her direction and made the day seem brighter and hotter still.

Looking from a window above, King Henry leaned hard upon the windowsill, grimacing as he put too much weight on his bad leg, swathed in stinking, pus-sodden bandages. At first sight little Katherine Howard lit a raging fire in the old King's loins and made his mouth water.

Down below, the Duke of Norfolk was frowning and about to step forward to chastise his niece for her unladylike behavior when the sunlight, flashing on the emeralds and diamonds that encrusted the King's great puffed sleeves as he leaned on the windowsill, caught Norfolk's eye. At the King's look of spellbound longing, the scolding words died upon his lips.

The wheels of Norfolk's mind began to turn, calculating and assessing, weighing the risks and odds. Two of his nieces had caught the King's eye before. Mary Boleyn had a brief moment of glory as Henry's mistress before she was cast aside like a toy that no longer holds interest. And Anne had soared to the highest heights before she came crashing down like Icarus burned by the sun. So what could little Katherine Howard do? That was the question.

❧ 35 ❧

The Duke of Norfolk summoned me to Lambeth, where the Dowager Duchess and her household were currently in residence.

I was delegated to play the role of chaperone, to keep silent and blend into the scenery, and, most important of all, be Norfolk's eyes and ears. I was to sit unobtrusively upon a garden bench in my respectable widow's weeds with my embroidery.

"My brother-in-law Boleyn told me how it was done," Norfolk explained. "A garden of roses and a green gown. If it worked once, it will work again; it is a myth that lightning never strikes twice. The King is smitten already, and Katherine—thank Heaven!—is not the willful, tart-tongued shrew Anne was. Katherine is pretty and pliant, as a woman should be. We can control her!"

And there she was, waiting in the rose garden, docile and demure in spring green silk, innocent and unspoiled, with her hair unbound as best becomes a virgin.

Grimacing at the pain in his leg, and leaning heavily on his cane, King Henry slowly descended the stone steps into the rose garden, assisted by his favorite Gentleman of the Privy Chamber, Thomas Culpepper.

The robust, golden Tudor King lived now only in the vain

palace of Henry's mind and others' fond memories. Now on the threshold of fifty, Henry's youth, health, and beauty were long gone.

Beneath the many layers of bandages, wound round and round his leg like the linen wrappings on a dead Egyptian king, a fetid ulcer lurked, and leaked foul, putrid, yellow pus. The old tiltyard injury had never truly healed despite the physicians' repeated lancings, leechings, and applications of a costly ointment made from ground Orient pearls, and he could no longer walk without a cane. Now that he could no longer take regular exercise and indulge in sports or dance, his bulk had grown so great that he often had to be carried about in a specially constructed chair, borne by several stout-backed, strong-shouldered men; his great bed had to be reinforced so that it would not collapse beneath his weight; and a winch was utilized to lift him into the air and lower him down onto his horse's back.

He tried to disguise his ever-expanding size by favoring doublets with great padded shoulders and ornate, puffed, and slashed sleeves, worn with creaking corsets underneath. Indeed, I had it on good authority that three goodly sized men could fit into one of Henry's doublets.

And to his face, Father Time had not been kind. It was fat and florid, with great pouches of pink fat that threatened to obscure the squinty blue eyes that now required spectacles with rock-crystal lenses from Venice, great quivering jowls, a nose bulbous and red with broken veins, and a cruel little pink rosebud of a mouth that seemed to always be pursed in a petulant pout. A jaunty, jeweled, feathered cap concealed his bald pate and the fringe of sandy gray that ringed it like a monk's tonsure. And his beard had also grown sparse and lost its youthful ruddy hue.

All these things combined had robbed him of his good humor and left a cantankerous, tyrannical ogre in its place.

"Steady on, Your Grace," Thomas Culpepper said, jovial and encouraging as, grunting and red-faced, the old King staggered and clutched at Culpepper for support.

Thomas Culpepper—now there was a man to delight the eye

and make a woman's heart flutter! Just looking at him made my knees wobble as if the bones in my legs had turned to jelly.

He was a young rake in his middle twenties, tall and handsome, with tawny hair and hazel eyes, who bore himself with a confident swagger. He was also a heartbreaker; kind in the getting, cruel in the quitting. And the broken hearts, letters, and barrels of tears that were afterwards shed by the ladies he seduced were the trophies he prized most and loved to boast of. Culpepper loved no one but himself. To him, honor was the stuff of sermons and something the minstrels sang of, not a principle to live by. He was no poet or wit, like George and his friends had been, just a handsome rascal who delighted in living on the knife's edge of danger; risk was the most powerful aphrodisiac to Thomas Culpepper. He was the kind of man who liked to duck beneath the bed, inside a cupboard, or out a window an instant before the lady's husband walked in.

Recently the court had been rife with the tale of his rape of a park-keeper's wife. While out hunting with his friends, Culpepper had spied this rustic beauty in a woodland glen and determined to have his way with her there and then. When she refused him, he had his companions hold her down. A woodsman heard her screams and came running to her rescue, only to have Culpepper plunge a dagger into his heart. For this crime, he was sentenced to hang, but Henry hated to lose such a jolly companion, and none but Culpepper, he claimed, could minister so tenderly to his bad leg; so he pardoned him, dismissing it all as just a youthful escapade.

Breathing heavily and dripping with sweat, Henry stood for a long moment leaning upon Culpepper, while his beady eyes, lost in a morass of florid pink fat, squinted into the distance at Katherine. And, like a lovesick young swain, he laid a hand over his heart and sighed deep and long.

It was then, from my unobtrusive perch upon a garden bench, that I noticed something—Katherine was not looking at the King. Oh no, Katherine Howard had eyes only for Thomas Culpepper!

The tip of her pink tongue darted out to lick her cherry lips, and her breasts began to heave beneath the tightly laced bodice of her green gown. Verily, I felt as if I could actually hear the blood racing hot and fast within her veins, and feel the heat and wetness blossoming in the secret pink flower between her thighs, so palpable was her lust.

And Thomas Culpepper, hungry like a wolf, was also licking his lips and staring back at her with the bold, appraising eye of a practiced seducer.

Katherine looked ready to flop on her back and spread her legs for Master Culpepper. And I knew I must do something quick, since she had not the wit to save herself; so, clearing my throat loudly, I rose and curtsied deeply, and bid His Majesty welcome to the rose garden of Lambeth.

The spell broken, Katherine started, then followed my lead, sinking hastily into a deep curtsy, modestly averting her eyes to the petal-carpeted ground.

Beaming his delight, Henry lumbered towards her with Culpepper's help, and raised her to her feet.

"What a beauty you are!" he exclaimed as he tilted her chin up and leaned forward to scrutinize her face at close range.

To her credit, Katherine did not flinch at his charnel breath, not even when he planted a wet, smacking kiss on her forehead. She met his gaze with the wide-eyed innocence of a child naïve and newly emerged from the nursery.

"Come, walk with me, Katherine; show me the garden!" Henry cried, his face wreathed in smiles.

And so, with Henry supported between the two young people, Katherine on his right and Culpepper on his left—leaning backward to dart coy, flirtatious glances at each other around the oblivious King's great bulk—they proceeded along the garden path.

As I watched them go, I felt foreboding settle in my stomach like a stone. I knew no good could ever come of this. The King would forever stand between these two would-be lovers, always fancying, and being led to believe, that it was he who played the role of lover, when in truth Katherine and Culpepper had already cast him as the cuckold.

When Culpepper and Katherine lowered the winded and weary King onto a bench, their hands met behind his back. Their fingers entwined and clasped briefly before they broke apart. Culpepper then withdrew to stand at a discreet distance, and the courtship began.

Henry plucked a pink rose from the bush behind him and presented it to Katherine.

"Mistress Katherine, do you know why you are fairer than this rose?"

Katherine paused in the act of raising it to her nose and shook her head so that her auburn curls bounced.

Henry sat for a long moment staring at her, his breath coming shaky and deep. He reminded me of a dog that stares longingly at a leg of mutton upon the banquet table, but dares not pounce on it.

"Because you have no thorns." Henry reached out a trembling hand to caress her cheek.

In spite of herself, Katherine shuddered, shut her eyes, and leaned into his touch.

"You are my Rose Without a Thorn!" Henry declared.

His sweaty hand slid down her throat, following its curve, until his palm lay flat, with one fingertip just touching the rise of her breast.

"A neck as fair as this has no need of jewels, but you shall have some nonetheless," he promised as he leaned in to press a long, wet, drooling kiss onto her throat. Katherine arched her neck and moaned.

"Culpepper!" Henry abruptly pulled away from her. "Your arm, lad; get me on my feet!" With their help, he lumbered up, the knee of his bad leg buckling, so that Katherine cried out in alarm and clutched tightly at his arm when he almost fell.

"Mistress Katherine," he said with solemn formality as he raised her hand to his lips, "I trust we shall meet again soon."

"I hope so, Your Grace," Katherine answered with a curtsy.

Once the King's back was turned, Katherine sat down on the bench, leaning back on her palms, with an expectant look upon her face. When Thomas Culpepper looked back, as she seemed to know he would, she spread her thighs beneath her green silk skirts and laid the pink rose the King had given her in her lap, so that its head pointed to her feminine parts.

Thomas Culpepper nodded. He got the message.

A slow, sensual smile spread across her lips and Katherine nodded, licking her lips like a cat that has just enjoyed a forbidden dish of cream, satisfied that it was only a matter of time.

❧ 36 ❧

Henry VIII and Katherine Howard were married discreetly at Oatlands Palace on the 28th of July 1540, the same day that Henry's creature Cromwell laid his head upon the block.

It was his fate to also, like his many victims, learn how fickle is the favor of kings. When Anna of Cleves's person failed to deliver the promise conveyed by Holbein's portrait, Cromwell's days were numbered. And Henry's lust for Katherine Howard proved to be the last nail in his coffin.

Henry must have her whatever the cost, and ordered Cromwell to rid him of "The Flanders Mare." When Cromwell dithered about the German Protestant alliance and how time and better acquaintance might render the Lady from Cleves more pleasing, he found himself being dragged from the Council Chamber, while Norfolk and the rest drummed their fists upon the table and chanted, "Traitor, Traitor, Traitor!"

"Most Gracious Prince, I cry for mercy, mercy, mercy!" he wrote from his cell in the Tower. But Henry's silence was his answer. And Cromwell went the way of all the others who had disappointed Henry Tudor.

Cloaked and masked, I went to watch him die. I still thought he was wrong; revenge was not sweet. How could he ever think that it would be so? The cost of vengeance, I had found, was far too dear, and there was no turning back the hands of time.

The headsman was a novice, a boy of sixteen, and this his first execution. He bungled it badly and it took repeated blows of the heavy axe to take off Cromwell's head.

I shut my eyes and winced at every blow, the thud of the axe descending, Cromwell's dying screams as the axe cut through flesh, bone, and gristle to the scarred and much-used wooden block; and remembered his hands and lips upon me, like snakes crawling over my naked skin, and his loathsome prick burrowing inside me to do what my husband never could and sow a seed that would take root and flourish. Yes, Cromwell gave me what no man ever could and I hated him for it. Not only did he give me false hope, he gave me a child; but it was a child that I could not love or even suffer the sight of. His willing ear drank in all my grievances and years of pent-up jealousy, spite, and sorrow, but he lied—I had not become a heroine to everyone who hated Anne Boleyn— instead the tide had turned, and Anne had become the heroine and I the villainess wielding the blood-stained sword of vengeance. I had lost what I was trying desperately to save—my husband. Thanks to Thomas Cromwell, I would always be remembered as "The Red Widow," with my husband's blood forever on my hands; and whenever people heard my name they would instantly think of lies, the jealousy of embittered wives, and treachery.

Yes, I had a lot to thank Thomas Cromwell for—that is what I thought of as I stood beside the scaffold and watched him die.

"The King has never had a wife who made him spend so much on dresses and jewels as she does, and every day it is some new fancy or caprice," was the Spanish Ambassador's apt assessment of Henry's fifth queen.

Kat was a glutton for ornaments and finery, and she saw them as her just reward.

Not since Anne Boleyn had Henry been so smitten; he could not keep his hands from her, and his eyes followed her everywhere. When they sat at table, he would reach out a greasy paw to fondle her, roving over her bosom and leaving behind shimmering smears of grease and gravy stains. But Katherine stoically endured and said not a word, while her mind kept a tally, later to be converted to jewels and gowns, of every disgusting touch, each slurping, slobbery kiss from those fat lips, and each time she must take between her hands the flaccid worm of his manhood that hid behind the gargantuan mockery of his gigantic jewel-encrusted codpiece and try to coax it to the necessary firmness and guide it between her thighs.

The mercers of London would bring their finest silks, satins, velvets, brocades, and damasks, and, laughing and carefree as a child, Kat would dance, skip, and prance round the room in her bare feet, wearing nothing but her shift, holding a long length of silk above her head and letting it billow out behind her as she ran from one end of the room to the other. Then she would twirl round and round and wrap herself in its shimmering folds until she fell down laughing, dizzy, and breathless, ignoring the disapproving frowns of the merchants and her attendants. It was all very undignified behavior for a Queen, as I constantly had to remind her.

Norfolk ordered me to keep close and become her confidante. Together we were captain and first mate of the good ship *Katherine* and we must try to steer her in the right direction, else she run aground upon the sharp, perilous rocks and founder. As long as she stayed afloat so would our fortunes. And I tried—just as if she were my own daughter—to guide her, and teach her what was dignified and proper. I had, after all, been a lady-in-waiting to the four previous queens, but everything I said to her seemed to go in one ear and right out the other.

Every night as I helped her prepare for bed, I would brush her hair and dispense the wisdom I had learned from each of the previous queens, but Katherine merely hummed and played with the ribbons and accoutrements on her dressing table or prattled on about fashions or asked me to repeat any titillating gossip I had heard that day.

I realize now that she never really did love me. Katherine Howard was not a gift from God; she was not my redemption, after all, but my damnation. Sometimes I even think that Satan himself sent her as a gift for me. Her innocence was false. She was not a lamb of God, and, we are all too apt to forget, none quotes scripture quite so well as does the Devil.

❧ 37 ❧

On New Year's Day 1541, Anna of Cleves came bearing gifts as Henry's honorably adopted sister.

We were all dumbstruck at the sight of her. The dowdy, malodorous German dullard was completely transformed into an elegant and gracious lady!

All for Anna of Cleves was now golden, and her face, rosy-cheeked and round, was glowing with happiness instead of slick with oil emanating from her pores. An elegant green velvet cap, as flat and round as a pancake, ornamented with gold and pearls and white ostrich plumes, sat jauntily upon her head, crowning a mass of shining yellow curls that were like spun gold; and, at the nape of her neck, held in place with diamond-tipped pins, her long hair had been tightly braided and coiled into a bun. She wore a sumptuous emerald green velvet gown, its long trailing sleeves gathered with golden bands above her elbows and slashed so that puffs of her cloth-of-gold under-sleeves showed through, and its long, full, round skirt was slashed in front to reveal a gleaming kirtle of pleated cloth of gold. Large emeralds sparkled at her ears and around her neck and on her fingers. A fan of ostrich plumes and a little gold and green enameled comfit box dangling from a jeweled chain at her waist completed the ensemble.

She was clean and immaculate; her breath, body, and hair smelt

of perfume and spices instead of ale and onions, sweat, and unwashed armpits.

Graciously, she sank into a curtsy at the foot of the dais where
Henry and Katherine sat enthroned and thanked them for receiving her. She now spoke English tolerably well, with an accent, of
course, but most charmingly.

Henry sat forward, his jaw agape. When he embraced her as his
"dear sister," his pudgy hands lingered a trifle too long upon her
waist, as did the lips he pressed against her discreetly rouged cheek.

When he released her, Katherine also embraced her, kissing her
heartily upon each cheek, impulsively declaring, "Now you are my
sister too!"

This time I noted it was the lips and hands of Anna of Cleves
that lingered to prolong the embrace. When they drew apart I saw
her arch one finely plucked, kohl-lined brow and the nearly imper-
ceptible nod Katherine gave in answer.

Then the Lady of Cleves called her servants to bring in her
New Year's gifts for the royal couple—a matched pair of snow-
white horses caparisoned in mauve and purple velvet with silver
trimmings, and two lapdogs, droopy-eared spaniels with cream and
chestnut coats and big, soulful brown eyes. Katherine took them
onto her lap, cuddling and cooing to them, until the King called a
lackey to take them to the royal kennel.

The King and Queen were so delighted with their gifts that
they invited the Lady of Cleves to dine with them, and so the two
women—the current queen and the former one—sat at the banquet table in the Great Hall with King Henry between them.

Afterwards, when the musicians played, but Henry's bad leg
prevented him from dancing, Anna stayed, dutiful and seemingly
content, by his side while Katherine hurried off to find a partner,
for it was one of Henry's chief delights to watch her dance.

The ladies and gentlemen of the court exchanged knowing
glances when Katherine went straight to Thomas Culpepper and
imperiously held out her hand.

They were a beautiful couple: Culpepper in a honey and gold
brocade doublet, and Katherine in pure white satin with a kirtle of
white brocade adorned with daisies, their petals made of looped

white silk ribbon, with golden discs for their sunny yellow centers, and a veil of white French lace trimmed with pearls cascading over her auburn curls down to her hips. When they danced, lust hung hot and heavy in the air, like a canopy after a rainstorm, heavy with the weight of water, that threatened to burst and drench everyone beneath. The air seemed to sizzle between them, and any who dared step too near risked being scorched by their lust. I know, for did they not burn and blind me?

When the candles burned low and the sleepy crowd began to creep away to their beds, until only the weary musicians and the royal couple's attendants remained, slumping exhaustedly against the walls, Katherine and Culpepper were still dancing; the only couple now, gliding gracefully across the floor, palms pressed together or fingers intimately entwined, staring deep into each other's eyes, breaking their entranced glance only when the dance required them to turn or step apart.

In his chair the corpulent King nodded and dozed after too many cups of wine and too much rich fare, his plumed cap slipping down over his eyes. In slumber his body lost all dignity and restraint and he snored, belched, drooled, and broke wind often, so that beside him the Lady of Cleves frowned, wrinkled her nose, and rapidly fluttered her fan.

At last Culpepper fell laughing to his knees. "No more, no more! Your Majesty, have mercy upon me, I implore!"

"No!" Katherine pouted, grasping his hand and trying to pull him back up. "You cannot be weary! Rise, Tom; I want to dance!"

"We've been dancing all night!" With a groan Culpepper flopped down flat upon the floor and let his weary limbs sprawl. "One pavane more and I shall perish!"

"Sister." With a rustling of skirts, Anna of Cleves left the table. "I vill dance mit you."

Katherine clapped her hands and whooped delightedly. She spun round and round, giggling giddily, and would have crashed into Anna of Cleves and knocked them both down if the German lady had not caught and steadied her in a warm embrace.

For a long moment the two women clung, until Kat pulled away and ordered the musicians to "Play!"

"Away!" Katherine kicked playfully at Culpepper's rump as, making a great show of his fatigue, he crawled away on his hands and knees to sit leaning against the wall. "I shall dance now with my sister! I trust she will not disappoint me!"

Through several stately measures, and just as many lively ones, the two women glided and cavorted, and something more . . . they danced like a man and woman. There was something between them; they behaved like . . . lovers. And no, I was not mistaken or the victim of lewd fantasies. I had been at court for many years, serving all of Henry's queens, and I knew very well that women often danced together, to learn and practice their dance steps and to amuse themselves when no male partners were present, but this . . . this was something entirely different. I was not the only one to notice it.

Thomas Culpepper caught my eye and, jerking his head towards Kat and Anna, arched an eyebrow inquiringly.

I shrugged and shook my head and spread my hands. There was no explanation I could offer him; I did not understand it myself.

With a great snort and a bout of gruff coughing, the King started awake. Seeing the two women dancing a boisterous jig, spinning about, hitching up their skirts, showing their garters, and kicking up their heels, he began to applaud. He threw back his head and roared with laughter, until his face turned scarlet as a strawberry and he began to cough so that Culpepper had to rush to pound his back.

Spinning round wildly hand in hand at arm's length, heads thrown back, they finished and fell laughing onto the floor. They giggled and kicked their feet in the air, their skirts falling back immodestly around their hips, showing the King—and everyone else facing them—quite a bit more than was proper, until Henry urged them to desist, saying he was too old and drunk to be tempted by such a pleasing show.

With Culpepper's help, Henry levered himself painfully to his feet and called for more wine to drink a toast to Kat and Anna. Then, with a great belch, he ordered his gentlemen to help him to bed.

Yawning and stretching, Katherine's weary ladies approached, but Kat airily dismissed them.

"You may retire; Lady Rochford shall see me to bed," she said, then spun back around to speak with Anna—but she had already slipped away.

Though the room was now deep in shadows and only the musicians remained, packing up their instruments, Katherine tarried, idly traversing the floor from one end to the other. Even when the musicians' footsteps had faded away and the embers were dying upon the hearth, still Katherine lingered.

"Go!" She spun round to where I stood, yawning in the shadows, impatiently waiting for her. "Await me in my chamber!" She stamped her foot imperiously and made a shooing motion with her hand.

I confess her curtness and imperious manner hurt me. I knew she was Queen and entitled to put on regal airs, but in my heart of hearts I still saw her as that little angel on the lawn at Lambeth, and I found it hard at times to reconcile the little girl with the woman she had become.

"Very well, Your Grace." I curtsied and, making no attempt to conceal my irritation, strode briskly out the door.

I passed Culpepper in the corridor. He was returning to the Great Hall. I waited until he went inside, then I crept back to the doorway and stealthily slipped inside, letting the shadows and my black gown hide me.

There they stood, in the flickering light of the guttering candles, locked in a passionate embrace. Katherine's arms wrapped tight around his neck, and their lips pressed close, while one of Culpepper's hands cupped her breast. No shyness or awkwardness impeded their embrace; they knew what they were doing and, in that moment, I knew by the way their lips and bodies fitted together that this was no spontaneous first embrace—they had done this before.

My stomach lurched, and I knew that ahead of us all disaster loomed. Then came such a sad, sinking feeling that I was almost overwhelmed by it, the intensity of my disillusionment and sorrow. Katherine Howard was no longer that little angel whose memory I had kept alive in my heart all these years. Every time she misbehaved I made excuses for her, putting it all down to boisterousness, youth, girlish high spirits, and a wayward childhood spent without a mother's love and guidance. But I was only deceiving myself. Katherine didn't want a mother's love or guidance; she didn't want me except to have me wait on her and do her bidding. All Kat wanted was to have her own way. No matter how much I wanted to pretend that she was my own daughter, Katherine never had and never would think of me as a substitute mother; all she saw in me was just another lady-in-waiting. And, once again, it was my fate to mean less than nothing to someone I loved.

Breathlessly they broke apart.

"Why did you not do this when you were still a maid?" Culpepper demanded, his voice husky with desire.

Katherine took a step forward until the tips of her breasts, restrained by the tight, taut satin of her bodice, grazed his chest.

"You can be certain of one thing, Tom Culpepper—if I tarried still in the Maids' Chamber I would try you!"

She let her hand trail slowly down his chest to cup his bulging codpiece. "And perhaps I will not let my fortuitous change in circumstances stop me; some things are just too good to pass up!" And with these words she turned away and headed for the door.

After she had gone, I withdrew quickly and, taking the longer route, ran as if my heels had sprouted wings, to reach Katherine's quarters before her.

Winded as a horse that had just won a race, I burst into Katherine's bedchamber and nearly fell into the lap of Anna of Cleves.

Almost upon my heels, Katherine came in, humming and prancing prettily. Oh, that giddy girl, she was so unmindful of the dignity that a queen should possess! Always at such times I wanted to take her by the shoulders and shake her. But Henry loved her so; to him she was like a breath of fresh air, his perfect "Rose Without a Thorn," and any flaws others assigned to her he dismissed as jealousy and malice.

With a rustling of skirts, Anna rose. In her hand was a glass jar filled with golden honey that glimmered like liquid amber in the firelight.

"From mein own hives," she explained as she removed the lid. Her eyes fixed unwaveringly upon Katherine's face, she dipped a finger into its sticky depths.

"Taste!"

I watched in amazement as Katherine sucked long and hard, almost greedily, upon Anna's finger.

"Ah, *Liebchen!*" Anna sighed ecstatically.

Then they were in a fever to undress. Katherine turned so that Anna could unlace her. Beneath her breath, Anna cursed in her native German as her hasty and impatient fingers fumbled with the laces; then she turned to offer her own back. Kat swore volubly, colorfully as a drunken sailor, as she struggled with the laces.

"Shall I leave you?" I asked hopefully, averting my eyes and blushing hotly; this was something I had no desire to witness. It shook me to my depths; I could not believe it was happening.

Was there no end to Katherine's folly? Tonight she was acting like a bawd and flaunting it proudly. Everyone was already whispering about the way she singled out Master Culpepper every time there was dancing, and there was talk about certain looks that passed between them. And tonight I had seen for myself; this was beyond mere court gallantry and flirtation. This was not like Anne Boleyn and her "evergreen gallants." This was serious; this was treason.

"Go sit by the fire, Jane," Katherine answered, ignoring my unease. "We shall need you afterwards." Then she dismissed me from her thoughts and forgot all about me. Nothing mattered to Katherine but the fulfillment of her own whims.

In a rush, their garments fell—headdresses, over- and under-sleeves, bodices, overskirts, kirtles, stays, petticoats, and shifts.

Balancing first upon one foot and then upon the other, just like a stork, Anna kicked off her shoes, untied her garters, and took off her stockings, then knelt at Kat's feet to remove hers. She sucked each of Kat's little pink toes while Kat quivered and moaned and reached out to brace herself against the bedpost lest she fall over.

I staggered over to the fireside chair, still warm from the Lady of Cleves's plump, dimpled posterior, my knees shaking, and my eyes fit to pop. My face was flaming hot and so red that I feared I would at any moment be struck down by apoplexy.

Giggling and naked as newborns, the "Rose Without a Thorn" and "The Flanders Mare" clambered into Katherine's big green and gold brocade and satin bed and drew the bed curtains shut. A moment later Kat leaned out and grabbed the jar of honey from the table beside the bed.

I took up Katherine's abandoned embroidery and tried to ignore the noises emanating from behind the bed curtains—the cries, sighs, muffled laughter, and the sound of the great cupid-carved headboard knocking gently against the wall.

The warm glow of a candle flame peeped from between the swaying curtains and I whispered a quick prayer. "Please, God, do not let them set the bedding alight!"

A little time later Katherine's bare arm emerged, fumbling to set the jar of honey back on the table. It fell and went rolling across the floor and Kat, laughing still, pulled back the bed curtains and hopped out to retrieve it. I gasped at the sight of her, and this time I truly feared my eyeballs would burst like grapes trod underfoot. A glaze of golden honey oozed down her chest, stomach, and legs, and matted the auburn curls between her thighs; and a single drop, like an amber tear, dripped from one stiff rosy nipple.

"Oh, Jane, if you could see your face!" Kat cried, clapping her hands and doubling over in laughter, before she turned and leapt back into the bed.

"Lick me clean!" she commanded, and flopped flat onto her back with her legs spread wide. Then, mercifully, Anna of Cleves took pity on me and whisked the curtains shut.

At dawn's first light they staggered out of bed, yawning, sticky from head to toe, hair a tangled, matted mess, reeking of honey, sex, and sweat.

Katherine imperiously demanded a bath.

"I have done what Henry could never do!" she crowed triumphantly. "I have ridden The Flanders Mare!"

"Ja, Liebchen." Anna embraced her and nuzzled her neck. "Und it vas de greatest ride of mein life!"

The two royal ladies withdrew back behind the bed curtains while the tub was carried in and three weary, bleary-eyed scullery maids staggered upstairs toting pails of steaming water.

At Katherine's command, I knelt beside the tub and soaped and rinsed their hair. They closed their eyes and lounged, limp and lazy, in the hot water strewn with dried lavender, chamomile, and rose petals, sighing as a curtain of steam billowed up around them and flushed pink their skin.

"Are you happy, Anna?" Katherine asked.

"Ja, Liebchen!" came the reply, as an eager hand reached out to playfully pluck at Katherine's nipples.

"No, I don't mean like that," Katherine said as she extended a foot beneath the soapy water to tease with her toes between Anna's thighs. "I mean, are you happy now that you are no longer Queen? I was afraid you would hate me for taking your place."

"Nein, Liebchen, I could never hate you!" Anna exclaimed as she lifted Kat's foot and pressed it to her lips. "Your cousin Anne Boleyn, she vonce took as her motto 'de most happy,' but, *nein,* it vas not her, but I who am de most happy. Vhen mein brudder say I must make dis marriage mit Heinrich, dat it is gut for Cleves und for me, I make a study of de vives who came before me because I make up my mind not to go deir vay. Catrin of Aragon, she so stubborn, she vas left to vaste avay in a drafty old castle, de prisoner of her own pride because she try to hold onto vhat she haf no hope of keeping und haf alreddy lost. Anne Boleyn, she know vat Heinrich cannot haf he go mad to get, but vat he alreddy haf he despises, und she also know dat a mistress is like a rag a man uses to vipe his arse mit. But eidder vay—vife or mistress—he own her; she his to do mit as he please, und vhen his fancy turned to anodder, dis time he discover it easier to kill her radder dan go through vhat he did mit Catrin to divorce her. Und poor Jane Seymour, everyvon so busy celebrate de son dey forget about de mudder, und she take de childbed fever. So me, I set out to displease Heinrich; I vant him to be unhappy mit me; I study how best to displease him, und

I do it. I play de fool und mein Deutche maid, she help me to make mein body und mein breath to stink und mein hair un-vashed und greasy. I von de game, even dough Heinrich never know ve play von, und he still not know. I agree to everyding he ask; I not fight or dig in mein heels; I smile und nod und say '*Ja*, Heinrich!' und now I am his sister und he haf made me rich. I haf dree manor houses und he gif me £4,000 a year, so I keep gut table und haf many guests to gossip mit und play de cards mit und dance; und I vear new dresses every day, und I haf diamonds, a pet parrot, many fine horses, und mein own musicians to play for me vhenever I vish. I haf all dat I desire. Heinrich haf given me de greatest gift of all—he haf made mè a voman of independent means; no more can mein brudder tell me vhat to do, say to me go here, marry dere; *nein*, vhen he divorce me Heinrich gif me mein freedom, und dat is de greatest gift of all! So you see, *Liebchen*, I am de most fortunate vife of all, und de most happy!"

Katherine nodded mutely, and I think in that moment she did see. Anna of Cleves had held up a mirror and shown her the truth, and how aptly the motto she had chosen fit. Katherine had "no other will but his." She was Henry's to use and command—his chattel, his servant, his concubine, prisoner, and slave all rolled into one under the name of "wife." And, like poor dead Jane Seymour, she was "bound to serve and obey" until the day death parted them.

Sorrow clouded her eyes and Katherine sank lower into the tub until soapsuds clung to her chin in a foamy white beard.

Vain, empty-headed little fool that she was, even Katherine knew which of the two of them had gotten the better bargain.

❧ 38 ❧

In February the ulcer upon the King's leg became clogged, and the resulting infection caused his face to turn black. Both his fever and his temper soared. Melancholy overwhelmed him, and for a fortnight he withdrew into the seclusion of his bedchamber, seeing no one but his doctors, apothecaries, chaplain, body servants, and those who were essential to the running of the realm. The doors were barred to everyone else, including the Queen.

Though she went every day with a basket of treats to tempt his appetite, Katherine was always turned away. Henry could not bear for his "Rose Without a Thorn" to see him this way—ugly, rotting, and decrepit in his sickbed, so different from the proud, golden, majestic monarch of his portraits.

No doubt many times as he lay upon his great bed, wallowing in pain and self-pity, after the physicians had left with their leeches and lancets, he would stare in sullen, envious silence at the handsome and lusty young Master Culpepper as he bent over the stinking, swollen leg supported by a mound of pillows, to gently apply the costly ointment made from pulverized pearls and wrap it in fresh bandages, the pristine snow-white strips slowly turning an ugly yellow as the pus seeped out.

As he bent to his task, Culpepper's touch was so tender and careful, but what did such kindness matter when it was given by one whose body was still firm, muscular, and trim, all hard manly slenderness, from the tips of his perfectly formed toes to the top of that full head of tawny hair? No balding pate hid under that jaunty plumed cap dear Katherine had given him as a reward for the great care and devotion he bestowed night and day upon her royal husband. No ulcer, stubbornly refusing to mend, festered upon Culpepper's firm thigh, and no noxious yellow pus seeped out to stain his silk hose. And at table Culpepper could eat and drink his fill, confident and secure in the knowledge that he could ride, fence, wrestle, dance, and make love, to keep the fat at bay.

The legs of mutton, strong wine, and marchpane and sugar confections brought comfort to one who was no longer young and could no longer move as sleek and surefooted as a cat, but they also added fat like a lady's layered petticoats to Henry's already substantial torso. He had always been a big man; now he was a dangerously obese one, a mountain of flesh, with a temper like a volcano.

Meanwhile, a giddy girl, drunk with power, held sway over the court. While everyone else went about hush-lipped and on tiptoes trying not to disturb the King, slumbering like a sick lion in his den, Katherine skipped, pranced, and ran about, always smiling, with laughter or a song on her lips. She shocked the servants when, flush-faced, with her French hood askew and her hems torn and muddy, she skipped into the kitchen and asked for bread and honey after a game of hide-and-seek in the hedge maze.

She danced with the court gallants every night, indulged her love of finery every day, and often played with the royal children.

She had wheedled Henry to have Anne's daughter brought from Hatfield, and lavished gifts and kindness upon the solemn-faced little girl, who, with her fiery locks and temper, was so much like her father it was a shame she was not a boy. Yet there was no mistaking she was also Anne Boleyn's daughter. Just like her mother, Elizabeth would not be cowed or cower before Henry, even though she was just a slip of a girl. Not quite seven years old, she matched him stare for stare and gave him answer for answer, often mirroring Henry's favorite pose as she did so, standing with her hands on her hips and her feet planted firmly apart. Even if he had the power to strike off her head, as he pointedly reminded her he did, she was not afraid of him, and she told him so to his face. Once I even saw the little tyrant throw a leg of mutton at the big tyrant, and staring out of her angry face I saw Anne Boleyn's eyes.

After his temper cooled, Henry would always laugh and exclaim, "By the Holy Cross, Bess, you should have been a boy! Oh, what a King you would have made! Aye, it is a pity, but no wench could ever rule England." Then he would sigh and shake his head resignedly.

But Elizabeth would always stamp her foot and retort, "This wench can and will!"

But Henry just laughed until tears ran down his face.

As for Henry's much-vaunted boy, the prince he prized above all else, Edward was a pale, cold, emotionally sterile boy. From birth he had been insulated in a pristine, flawlessly clean nursery, where anything that touched him was washed three times a day with strong soap and vinegar. Thrice daily his rooms were swept, the costly carpets beaten, and the floors and walls scrubbed until the serving maids' arms and backs ached as if they had been racked, and they staggered away, stoop-backed. The laundresses broke their backs, and their hands cracked and turned red as boiled crayfish zealously tending his clothing, linens, and bedding. Doctors visited him daily and scrutinized each movement of bladder and bowels, and his brow was felt hourly for any hint of fever. A food taster tested each meal before Edward was allowed even one bite. And even when he misbehaved, as all boys will, Barnaby, his whipping boy, endured Edward's punishment by proxy. The day Prince Edward was set down in the garden to play and ingested a grasshopper, such a panic ensued, with all his attendants rushing about like chickens in a barnyard frightened by a fox. The negligent nursemaid was given a strong tongue-lashing and dismissed, and Prince Edward was dosed with purgatives by the royal physician until his insides were as clean as his rooms.

Katherine's tender heart was greatly moved by the plight of these two motherless children, and she did her best to befriend them. She bought a set of gaily painted carved wooden animals from a peddler in London, much like the old battered set she had shared with her brothers and sisters when she was a child, and got down on her hands and knees and made the animals move and mimicked their sounds, baaing like a goat or sheep, clucking like a hen, whinnying like a horse, and mooing like a cow. But Edward and Elizabeth just sat and stared. They did not know what to think of this new stepmother. Their lives had been spent amidst large retinues of governesses, tutors, nursemaids, and assorted servants, none of whom ever dared to play with them like normal children, and instead filled their heads with Latin verbs, Greek translations, history, and royal protocol.

Despite their youth, Henry's two youngest children had more wisdom in their heads than Katherine did. As much as I loved her, I must admit, she was stupid beyond measure. How else can I explain her folly? Is youth really sufficient excuse for such rash conduct? Even with her cousin Anne Boleyn's fate illuminating the treacheries of the royal court like a lighthouse does a dark harbor, Kat refused to heed the warnings or be guided by those who knew better.

❧ 39 ❧

One day while the King was still secluded in his sickroom, Kat stood primping before the big silver mirror that had once belonged to Anne Boleyn.

Except for the jewels Henry had given her she was completely naked. Jeweled clasps shimmered in the auburn curls cascading down her back. Necklaces of pearls and precious gems encircled her neck. From elbow to wrist, her arms were covered with bracelets. She wound ropes of pearls around her ankles, and rings sparkled on every finger. Those that had belonged to Jane Seymour were too large and had not yet been cut down to size, so Katherine put them on her toes.

Laughing, she took up a diaphanous sea green scarf and wrapped it around her waist, ordering me to tie it in a bow in back and "make it pretty!" And onto this she pinned every brooch she owned, including the one Henry had given her as a New Year's gift—a great crowded cluster of diamonds, rubies, and pearls.

I shook my head disapprovingly at her play, but I said nothing; I knew she would not listen.

"Here is the dress you wanted," I said, standing before her with it draped over my outstretched arms, hoping she would take the hint and decide it was time to get dressed. It was Kat's favorite— the tawny velvet gown with the sable-trimmed sleeves and sea green and gold brocade kirtle and under-sleeves that she had worn when Holbein painted her portrait.

"Take it away!" Kat commanded, never taking her eyes away from her reflection. "I have decided not to wear it! I shall receive him as God made me, wearing only the jewels the King gave me."

"But you cannot!" I gasped.

Slowly, Kat turned to regard me, her eyes hard and bright as emeralds.

"You forget yourself, Jane," she said coldly. "I am Queen and can do as I like. Besides"—she shrugged, turning back to her mirror—"like this I am more beautiful than in any gown. Many have told me so, and so many people could not be mistaken! Look, Jane." Her hands rose to cup her breasts and, holding them like an offering, she turned to face me. "Are they not as round and rosy as apples ready to be plucked?" Her thumbs rubbed her nipples and before my eyes they puckered and hardened, changing from a pallid pink to a warm rosy coral.

Embarrassed, I looked away, but Kat saw my blush and burst out laughing.

"Don't be such a prude, Jane!" she said sulkily, pouting her lips as she flounced over to the bed and sat down.

"I don't know what your grandmother was about, allowing you to grow up so brazen and wayward!" I exclaimed.

"My grandmother didn't care a fig for me!" Kat cried hotly, tossing her hair and drawing up her knees, hugging them tightly to her chest. Her chin quivered and suddenly she was just like a little child in need of comfort. My anger melted and I went to sit beside her and put my arm around her.

"Dear heart," I said gently, "I am sure you are mistaken; the Dowager Duchess is a gruff old thing but . . ."

"I am not mistaken!" Kat pulled away from me. Then she began to speak, launching into a sad and salacious chronicle. At last I began to understand what had happened to my angel.

She told me about the Maids' Chamber, the long room at the top of the house where, in two rows of curtained beds, six to each side of the room, the Dowager Duchess's ladies slept, two to a bed. Every night at the stroke of midnight their lovers would sneak in, bearing gifts and the makings of a feast—fruits, meats, wine, sweets, bread, and cakes—and they would make merry until three or four in the morning.

Kat was five years old when she was first brought to live with her grandmother and put to sleep in the Maids' Chamber. The women seemed at first disgruntled, Kat recalled, complaining that now that there was a child in their midst everything would be ruined. Then Alice Restwold, who was to be Kat's bedmate, took matters into her own capable hands.

"She was so kind!" Kat sighed. "She called me 'poppet' and 'dear heart.' She gave me a cup of warm milk that made me very sleepy, then she stripped off my clothes, put them in the trunk at the foot of the bed, and tucked me under the covers, all nice and warm. I was shy and asked for my shift, but she said, 'Now, now, poppet, you are going to sleep, so what need have you for clothes?' And she sat beside me, stroking my hair and crooning a lullaby until I fell asleep."

A few hours later, Kat awoke and, peeping through the old faded green damask bed curtains, beheld a scene like nothing she had ever seen before.

On every bed couples lounged in various states of undress; some were even completely unclad. Some were enjoying picnics— the sight and smell of the food made Kat's little belly rumble— while others embraced and lay back with their bodies and limbs entwined. And there was much puffing, grunting, groaning, and sighing as naked male buttocks pumped between splayed feminine thighs.

Alice Restwold, who could not lie abed with her lover now that she must share with Kat, sat on the trunk at the foot of the bed directly opposite upon which Joan Bulmer was groaning beneath the weight of her lover. Completely naked, Alice spread her thighs and grabbed the head of the man kneeling before her and thrust his face between her legs, clutching tight at his hair as she threw back her head, whimpering and moaning. And on another bed, Eleanor and Margery lay giggling as they played with each other's cunnies while their lovers looked on, frantically tugging and rubbing at their exposed organs before they suddenly leapt onto the bed and took possession of their respective sweethearts. Side by side, shoulder to shoulder, they coupled, and then changed partners.

Suddenly Alice's eyes, half-closed in ecstasy, snapped wide and she clapped a hand over her mouth to stifle a scream. Up she bolted and, wrenching apart the bed curtains, dragged Kat out, naked before them all, to denounce her as a spy.

Head hung in shame, with tears rolling down her plump baby cheeks, Kat stood forlorn and trembling, futilely trying to hide her nakedness as they all clustered around, every mouth unsmiling, eyes glaring angrily, accusingly.

But once again, the always reliable Alice had a plan. Sitting down on the trunk that held Kat's clothes, she took the little girl onto her lap and explained the need for secrecy, and what a "harsh-hearted old dragon" the Dowager was. She wanted everyone else to be as dried up, crusty, and miserable as she was, and would rather her maids lived as nuns instead of the lusty young things they were. She was jealous of their youth and beauty and the men who were drawn to them. And now that Kat was one of them, she must help them; she must keep their secret, and never breathe a word about what she had seen to anyone, or else they would all be punished, including the "Little Kat who tattled."

"Alice made me swear an oath," Kat remembered. "They all took turns telling all the horrible things that would happen to me if I betrayed them—my head would be shaven bald and blistered with hot mustard plasters, and my cunny would be sewn shut tight, the goats would lick the soles of my feet until I went mad, and my tongue split in two so that it would be forked like a devious lying serpent's, and all sorts of terrible things." She shuddered at the memory.

"But it all sounded so thrilling!" Kat sighed, shifting her position and letting one leg dangle off the bed while she continued to hug the other knee. And there was such a wistful, faraway look in her eyes, it was as if she actually longed to be back in that den of debauchery.

"And I wanted desperately to fit in," she continued, "to be liked; and they were trusting me, depending on me—a little girl of five—to keep this great big secret and keep them safe! I felt so important for the first time in my life, and it made my little heart puff and swell with pride. I gave my word; I swore on anything and everything they liked that their secret was safe with me. After that they were all smiles and welcomed me with glad hearts and open arms. And from that night on, I was no longer a spy peeping through the bed curtains, I was one of them. And it was all kisses and caresses. They taught me about my body and its secret places, and I learned to show and touch myself without shame and to invite others to pet and play with me. And I learned what amusing toys men carry about concealed inside their codpieces! Oh, I was a bold, mischievous little thing! I became their pet, their Little Kat, and everyone loved me! I went from lap to lap, and they gave me sips of wine, and fed me strawberries and cherries, and morsels of meat, and gave me kisses, and stroked me until I purred like a kitten. All my shyness fled, and I would walk about unclad and watch the lovers' play. I would crawl into bed with them and worm my way between their bodies to claim my share of the kisses and caresses. And I fell asleep in a different bed every night. But no one ever dared tamper with my maidenhead. I was a Howard girl and the Dowager's granddaughter, and that presumption might lead to the scaffold. But we feasted and made merry and played all sorts of naughty little games! Oh, what jolly times we had, Jane!" she exclaimed with undisguised longing.

I pursed my lips and said not a word. It made my heart ache to think of that innocent child thrust into a world she was far too young to understand. Those wanton maids had turned my angel into a slut to save themselves; they had made her a partner in their debauchery, so she could never claim innocence if they were found out. And yet, when she spoke, though the words were bawdy as a whore's, her face was as innocent and beatific as the most devout novice on the verge of taking her vows, or a virginal saint tragically destined to die young, sweet, and pure.

"And Grandmother never knew, at least not for years and years," Kat continued. "The girls in the Maids' Chamber were all of good families, sent to be trained for places at court or to make good marriages; and as long as we attended faithfully to our music and dancing lessons, never missed Mass, embroidered beautifully, and acted as ladies-in-waiting to my grandmother and helped her bathe and dress, we were left to our own devices, and that suited us all quite well."

"Then along came Henry Manox," Kat sighed. "Grandmother chose him to be my music master when I was thirteen. His hair was black as a raven's wing and his eyes were blue like the sky. He towered over me, and my knees went weak as water the moment I saw him. I wanted to tear off my clothes and lie down at his feet and shout 'I am yours!' But he wanted only one thing—my maidenhead. That pious, sour-faced prude Mary Lascelles—she was new to the Maids' Chamber and always trying to spoil our fun, preaching at us to repent our sinful ways—told me he had been boasting that he meant to have me even if I was a Howard girl. But I was in love and refused to listen. And one summer's day when we were hiding in the cool darkness of the chapel so that he might suck my little nipples and play with my cunny, I rashly promised it to him, even though it would be painful to me, as long as he promised faithfully that he would be good to me thereafter. And he did; with hand on heart, he gave his word. Then Grandmother came in and caught us together, and me with my skirt up and my bodice down. She dismissed Manox and dragged me back to the house and all the way upstairs to her bedchamber. She tore the dress off my back and walloped me with her cane until my body was all over bruises. And she threatened to beat me longer and harder still if she found me to be with child. I lay huddled at her feet, sobbing that it was not so, as I was a virgin still. 'Hmmp, I shall see for myself!' she said, and sat down in her chair and pulled me backwards across her lap, so that I was lying with my feet flat on the floor and my head hanging down so all my blood rushed to it. She spit on her finger and thrust it inside of me. And oh, how it hurt! I screamed, but she was satisfied that I was intact and ordered me to stay that way until my wedding night. Then she shoved me off her lap and ordered me from her sight.

"After Manox, I died a little inside. Though my hymen had not been breached, something inside me was broken, and I decided I would never let anyone touch my heart again; the pain was far too great."

I could hear the remembered hurt in Kat's words, and when she paused for a moment to swallow deep, I saw tears glimmering in her eyes.

"Then along came Francis Derham. His hair was brown and his eyes were too. And he was the most alive and exciting person I had ever known, but he was also the most patient, kind, and gentle. I felt so safe with him! And I could talk to him; I could tell him anything without fear that it would change his love for me. And when he laughed at me, he was not laughing at me, he was laughing with me, because he loved me, and I made him happy. He said that I was his heart's delight. When he held me, he said that everything he had ever wanted was right here in his arms! He was a gentleman by birth, but from an impoverished branch of the family, and he often undertook commissions for my grandmother and Uncle Norfolk. The first time he looked at me I felt like a hive of bees was buzzing in my belly, and my heart came alive again. It was like a slate from which Henry Manox had been wiped clean. He was everything I had ever dreamed of, except rich. And he loved me; he really, really loved me! He brought me presents: a cap of pale pink satin embroidered with gold and sea green lovers' knots, and green silk to make a gown to match my eyes, and a heart's ease—a pansy—made of silk by an old blind woman with very skillful hands, who made silk flowers for all the grand ladies at court. Her services were much in demand, but Francis persuaded her, busy as she was, to make a flower for him to give me as a New Year's gift. I have it still. He begged me to be his bride, and though I knew that as a Howard girl I was too lofty a match for the likes of him, my heart could not resist. And in secret we did handfast, though afterwards, because I knew I had been rash, I would always pretend that our calling each other 'husband' and 'wife' was only a jest. And in his arms I left maidenhood behind, and for many nights afterwards—more than a hundred!—we lay together as husband and wife. And no other couple was as happy as we."

At this most dangerous of revelations the breath left my body and my head began to spin. Stars and spots danced before my eyes even when I shut them. I did not want to hear this; I did not want to know this. I did not want her to be like this. I wanted her to be an angel again, sweet and pure, not a girl as savvy in the ways of the flesh as a tart who walked the London streets. Foolish, foolish girl! Did she not understand? If this Derham fellow was still alive, then Kat's marriage to the King was bigamous and invalid. She was precontracted to Francis Derham, that was clear. They had hand-fasted, and by English law that constituted a marriage. God save us all if the truth ever came out! By being Kat's confidante, I now realized, I was playing a most dangerous game. And if the truth ever came out, in the eyes of the law I would be as guilty as she for keeping her secrets. Henry would never have married this girl if he had known what she really was; he thought she was innocent and pure, his "Rose Without a Thorn"! He had no idea how many men—and women too, apparently—had dallied in this garden before him! And I hoped—for all our sakes—that he never found out.

"But Fortune's smiles are fleeting," Kat sighed, still lost in her memories and oblivious to my distress, "and Henry Manox would have his vengeance. It was torture to him to know that another had succeeded where he had failed. He left an unsigned letter on Grandmother's pew in the chapel, suggesting that she visit the Maids' Chamber after midnight. Grandmother caught me with my arms and legs wrapped tight around Francis. We were naked and his manhood was inside me, where it had been so many times before. Grandmother raised her cane and brought it down hard on Francis's backside, and he snatched up his clothes and fled while she vented her rage on me. She beat me bruised and bloody. She had Uncle Norfolk dismiss Francis from his service, and she herself would see no more of him—I think she secretly fancied him; she has always been immoderately fond of handsome young men—and with no means or prospects he decided to go adventuring in Ireland. He is a pirate upon the high seas now. We parted bitterly; it hurt me much to know that he would forsake me, though he did assure me he was 'like to die of grief.' But my pride was hurt, and I held my head up high, determined that he would not see me cry, and told him, 'You may do as you like, Francis Derham; you go your way and I shall go mine!' And for many a night afterwards I cried myself to sleep. I tore up every letter he sent me, then I begged Alice and Joan to put the pieces back together and read them to me, as I did not know my letters well enough to do it myself. But I never answered them; I was too proud, and my heart felt as if it had been pierced through with a sword, it hurt so much. And I did not want to hear his excuses or invite more pain into my life."

My heart went out to her. I reached out and drew her close and kissed her brow. "You really loved him, didn't you, poppet?"

Kat answered with a limp, halfhearted shrug and the voice of a jaded, melancholy whore who has seen too much. I marveled yet again, as I had done so often of late, that she was only fifteen.

"There's no such thing as love, Jane; it's just a dream we all aspire to, and the stuff of songs and stories that fuel our hopes and longings. Aye, there is passion, but passion is not love, Jane, though we like to delude ourselves into thinking it is. But it dies quick; it is a flame that flares high, blazes bright, and soon dies, and all we are left with are the cold ashes of memory."

Sometime she seemed so wise, and yet she was such a fool.

"Well, at least you did not conceive a child from all that passion," I said. "That at least is something to be thankful for."

"Of course I did not!" Kat exclaimed, as if I had just said the most ludicrous thing she had ever heard. "I know how to meddle with a man without making a child! In the Maids' Chamber we had many such tricks—sponges soaked with vinegar or the juice of lemons, pessaries of beeswax, and special teas brewed with rue and pennyroyal. And do you know about the Gloves of Venus, Jane? They are sold discreetly beneath the counters of the glovemakers' shops in London, and one must ask for them in a whisper and by name. They are sheaths made of animal gut, which a man fits like a glove over his member to keep his seed from going where it should not. But I preferred to have Francis's sword sheathed inside me. Ah!" She heaved a great sigh and flung herself back onto the bed, lying with her arms stretched overhead and her legs spread wide, while her eyes shut in what must have been a most blissful memory indeed.

"One night when we lay naked upon my bed, he produced a pessary of beeswax and bade me—oh, so lovingly—to bend and spread wide my knees, and he inserted it inside me so gently that I cried out to the others to come gather round and 'see what good care my husband takes of me!' They watched us make love—all except that prude Mary Lascelles—and I was glad; I wanted them to see! Not a one of them except Mary Lascelles had not seen, fondled, and caressed me. They were like my family; they loved me, and I know every last one of them was glad to see me so happy, even though they could not help but envy me.

"After a time, my pride gave way and I begged Grandmother and Uncle Norfolk to bring Francis back to me; he was my husband, and I belonged body and soul to him. But Uncle Norfolk slapped my face and said that never again was I to speak of this 'game of marriage,' that it had all been 'pretend,' but even so I was never to allude to it or else he would crush me like a beetle beneath his boot. None of it had ever happened, he insisted; it was all a dream, a foolish, girlish fancy, and I was a maiden still, and a Howard girl; my good name was everything, and he had other plans for me. And then he spoke of the court. When Cousin Anne died, I wept because I thought my dream of being a lady at court had died with her. Then Uncle Norfolk resurrected my hopes and promised that a far better match than Francis Derham awaited me. He said I must be a good girl and patiently bide my time, and Fortune would soon smile on me. And he was right.

"Now here I am at court." She waved a hand to indicate her luxurious surroundings. "Queen of England, yes, but also an old man's fancy. But at least I have Tom." She wallowed on the bed and sighed gratefully and hugged herself at the thought of Tom Culpepper. "And he is mine, and I am his. . . ."

"No! No! No!" I protested, pounding my fists upon the bed and shaking my head. "You are the King's, Kat. You belong to him, not to Thomas Culpepper! Please, have a care what you do. This is serious business, Kat!"

"I shall not go the way of my cousin Anne Boleyn, if that is what you are afraid of," she said with a confident toss of her curls. "Anne died because Henry's love died, but that will not happen to me! Henry loves me more than he has ever loved anyone. I am his "Rose Without a Thorn'; that is what he calls me!"

"A rose without thorns is easier to pluck," I snapped, "and you have been plucked aplenty, my girl!"

I shut my eyes and suppressed the urge to scream. I had to sit on my hands to keep from slapping her and shaking her. She was so young, so confident that everything would always go her way; she could not even contemplate a future when the King's eye might wander to someone new. If she disappointed him in childbed, with a daughter, stillbirths, or miscarriages, or failed to conceive at all, her days, like Anne Boleyn's, would be numbered.

"Men say many things, Kat." I tried again to make her see. "You must know yourself. . . ."

"Are you presuming to call the King a liar, Jane?" There was ice in her eyes and voice. "Are you disputing the truth that everyone can see? Henry loves me! He loves me!"

"Kat, you are a fool if you truly think the King's love will save you if you and Culpepper are found out!"

"But we shall not be found out if you help us. Oh, say you will, Jane. Please!" she grasped my hands and pleaded. "Think for a moment what I must endure, what being loved by the King truly means!"

Then she began to describe her nights in the King's bed, and her words painted such a grotesque picture in my head that pity soundly defeated my better judgment.

She told me all about the tiny pellet filled with fish blood she surreptitiously inserted inside her cunny as she squatted over the piss pot before she climbed into the great royal bed on their wedding night to become Henry's "virgin bride." How proud Henry had been of that red rose-petal stain marring the white sheets the next morning!

And all the subsequent encounters where Kat must scale and straddle that great mountain of decaying old flesh. Henry could not mount her; his bulk would crush her to a pulp. Stark naked, with her thighs straining like a wishbone about to snap, Kat would sit astride him, smiling and playful as a kitten, leaning forward to rub her pink-tipped breasts against his chest or maneuver her hot little cunny back and forth over his manhood, trying to persuade it to rise and come inside. Sometimes his member roused, only to droop at the crucial moment, or else he would spew just before he entered her. On nights when his member remained stubbornly flaccid, he would draw Kat forward to sit astride his face while he licked and slurped the pink petals of his "Rose Without a Thorn." Kat would brace her hands against the headboard and in silence weep with shame and something more disturbing . . . the slow, deep sensual stirrings sparked by that old man's fat pink slug of a tongue slithering around her privy parts.

"I know what you are thinking, Jane. He is old and I am young, not yet sixteen, but it is not so uncommon for people to live to a great age nowadays; many live into their sixth or seventh decade. By the time Henry dies I might be old myself. Or I might die first, like Jane Seymour, in childbed. I know Henry loves me, Jane, but . . . We all want some kind of love, but sometimes what we are given is not enough. I'm young, Jane, and I want to live and have fun while I'm alive, and make every moment count! And I need love like a flower needs sunlight and water to thrive!"

Tears filled my eyes, I was so moved by her plight—this pretty, vivacious young thing bound to serve and obey in Henry's bed, because, as Kat's own motto so rightly said, she had "no other will but his." And I knew, despite all the dangers, I would help her, for I knew all too well what it was like to live without love.

"But you must be careful," I insisted. "If Culpepper gets you with child . . ."

"Then I shall earn Henry's eternal gratitude by giving him a strong, lusty boy brimming with health and vigor, not like that pallid, pasty-faced little thing he got off Jane Seymour. And everyone will be happy—I shall have Tom, Tom shall have me, and Henry shall have a son!"

Before I could say more there was a knock upon the door.

"Open it!" Kat nudged me, shooing me towards the door as she sprang up and rushed back to her mirror, to pinch her cheeks to give them color and wipe the lingering traces of tears from her eyes.

Tom Culpepper, resplendent in russet velvet and white silk, hovered uncertainly on the threshold, eyes wide and mouth agape at the sight of Kat wearing only the King's jewels. He made to take a step forward, then hesitated and took a step back instead.

"Come in, Master Culpepper, come in!" Kat cried, impatiently tossing her curls. "Don't dawdle on my doorstep! Come in and tell me how my husband fares!"

When he still hung back, no doubt debating the risks of dallying with the Queen, Kat ran to him and pulled him inside, positioning him so that he stood with his knees backed against the bed.

"Now, Master Culpepper," she said, nuzzling her naked body against his chest, "how fares my husband today?"

Culpepper opened his mouth to answer, but before he could, Kat asked another question. "And how fares you?" And with these words she shoved him hard so that he toppled backwards onto the bed.

Laughing delightedly, Kat clambered up on top of him and began tearing at his clothes, tugging impatiently at the fastenings, like a greedy child unwrapping a present, while Culpepper implored her to have a care; he could not be seen to arrive immaculate and then depart in disarray with his clothes in shreds.

"Mark me," I said clearly as I pulled the door shut behind me, "this will all be found out one day!"

But they ignored me. No warning, no matter how grave, could stem the tide of their passion.

❧ 40 ❧

That summer the King decided to go on progress to the northern provinces to quell the spirit of rebellion that was flourishing there, and to show the people their beautiful new queen. It was a massive undertaking, traveling thousands strong, with guards, servants, doctors, apothecaries, priests, the Privy Council, and most of the court and their families and servants; with horses, carriages and litters, luggage carts, and tents to house the overflow from the manors and castles where the royal party would stay, since no town had inns or lodgings enough to accommodate them all.

At each stop along the route—Lincoln, Pontefract, York, and Hull—Kat had me ferret out all the back stairs and doors that were so vital to her clandestine romance.

Several times we were almost caught.

Once a watchman came upon a door left unlocked and promptly fastened it. This door led to a staircase and, at the top, another door through which Culpepper could gain entry to Kat's bedchamber. Finding it locked, Culpepper had to crouch down in the shadows and pick it while his manservant nervously stood guard.

Another time some ladies dawdling in the courtyard saw Kat leaning from a window favoring Culpepper with such fond and loving glances, which he returned with equal ardor, that only a fool would have doubted that there was something between them.

Next they were nearly caught coupling in the Queen's privy closet.

Sometimes Kat came to my bedchamber to rendezvous with Culpepper. After the King had gone to bed—early, as was now his wont—she would tell her ladies that she was going to visit me. In my bed she would linger for long ecstatic hours, coupling blissfully with Culpepper, while I sat sentinel by the fire, trying to block my ears to the sounds of their lovemaking. And her ladies would be left to wait until two, three, or four in the morning, dozing in their chairs and wondering what the Queen was about, paying such lengthy visits to Lady Rochford and at such late hours.

Another night, when Kat was entertaining Culpepper in her own bed, the King came unexpectedly to the door, having impulsively decided to spend the night with his wife. To his great astonishment, he found her door locked and bolted. How frantically we scurried about! Culpepper grabbed his clothes and dashed naked out the back door, and Kat splashed water and perfume all about, scrubbed vigorously between her thighs, and pulled on a prim white nightgown and cap of the modest style made popular by Jane Seymour, while I stammered excuses, and fumbled, intentionally clumsy, with the lock and bolt.

At Pontefract, Kat's past came back, like a ghost, to haunt her when Francis Derham swaggered back into her life.

By this time, I should mention, many old "friends" had already come to join Kat's household; Alice and Anthony Restwold, Joan Bulmer, Kate Tilney, Margery Bennet, and Roger Damporte, to name but a few. Since Kat had been proclaimed Queen, all had come calling with a litany of woes—an unhappy marriage, sickness, dire need, sorrow sharp as nails—and something more . . . veiled hints and insinuating remarks about the past—all those "jolly times" in the Maids' Chamber. It was doubtful that the King would be amused if he heard the tales Kat's old friends could tell.

Now came Francis Derham, fresh from the road in dusty brown leather and creamy linen.

With a grandiose flourish, he swept off his white-plumed cap and bowed low before he sent it sailing across the room and kicked the door shut behind him. In three strides, he crossed the room and took Katherine in his arms.

"Let go of me!" she cried, struggling weakly, and most unconvincingly.

"How now, Madame, what's this?" he cried jovially, smiling broadly to display a mouth full of fine white teeth. "Is a man not entitled to kiss his wife when he returns from a long journey?"

"Don't call me that! Not even in jest! I am not your wife, and never was," Kat cried, her eyes darting about frantically, fearfully, as if the walls might suddenly have grown ears—as indeed they might, for any royal court, even one on progress, is full of spies.

"But you are, Kat." Derham smiled, reaching for her again.

Katherine ran across the room and ducked behind a heavy chair, using its back as a shield and bracing herself against the wall.

"Touch me not! Say what you want and then be gone, and trouble me no more!"

Derham's lips spread in a devilish smile as he strode across the room to kneel upon the chair's seat so they were face to face.

"You know what I want, Kat," he said softly, as he reached up to toy with a tendril of hair that had escaped from her French hood. "To have my Little Kat sit on my lap again. Would you not like that, Kitten? Would you not like me to reach beneath your skirts while you sit curled contentedly on my lap, and stroke your Little Kitten until you purr?"

"No!" Kat cried, clamping her hands over her ears. "No! Do not say such things! I will not hear you!"

"But you have, Kitten; you have and you do. And more than that"—he nodded knowingly—"you want it, and you want me, as much, perhaps more, than you ever did before."

"I do not! I cannot! Oh, why do you not go away and leave me be?" She stamped her feet and sobbed.

As she whisked a hand across her face to wipe the tears away, her fingers brushed against one of the heavy gold and ruby eardrops that pulled so cruelly at her little ears. They were magnificent, weighty things; they strained her earlobes until the tender flesh was swollen and bright pink, but the rubies sparkling darkly against her pale skin like drops of warm blood were so becoming that Kat would gladly suffer the pain to wear them. Now, with trembling fingers, she began to remove them, struggling with the cumbersome clasps.

"Here!" She flung them in Francis Derham's face.

"Nay, poppet." He shook his head and put them back in her hand, curling her dainty little fingers tight around them. "I don't want your pretties, or money either; I want only to be near you. To watch you, my darling wife, and know that you are watching me, even though you pretend not to, and to know that you want me, deny it though you will, as much as I want you; and that between your thighs your Little Kitten is hot and dripping wet with lust for me."

Kat closed her eyes and sagged weakly against the wall.

That was when Derham seized his chance. He reached round the chair, grabbed her wrist, and pulled her around to sit upon his lap. He kissed her hard, bruising the trembling lips that were as red as ripe cherries, just like her crushed velvet gown.

Kat burst into tears and buried her face against his shoulder and let Derham hold her.

When her tears at last subsided, Kat pulled away from him and got shakily to her feet.

"If I appoint you my private secretary, will you be content with that?" she asked.

"Aye, as long as His Majesty lives I shall be, but upon his demise, I shall reclaim what is rightfully mine," he said, then went to retrieve his plumed cap. "Well then, wife," he said, coming back to stand before her, smiling devilishly with hands upon hips, and booted feet planted wide apart, "kiss your husband and I shall take my leave of you!"

"No!" Kat said stubbornly, and turned away.

"Kiss me!" Derham insisted, grabbing her wrist and pulling her back into his arms. There was a rustle of velvet and satin as he gathered up Kat's full skirts and reached between her thighs.

Kat pulled away so suddenly that she stumbled and fell sprawling on the floor in a pose that a man could easily interpret as an invitation.

Laughing, Derham displayed his fingers, glistening wet with the juices of feminine lust. Slowly, he licked them, one by one, his eyes never leaving Kat's tearstained face. Then he bowed deeply, set his cap jauntily upon his head, and headed for the door.

"Francis!" Kat, leaning on her elbows with her legs asprawl, called after him. "If you ever try to use the past against me, I swear you shall suffer for it!"

Her voice sounded so childish, petulant, and tremulous as she made this threat, it carried no more weight than a feather.

"I'm sure I will, Kitten." Derham chuckled as he pulled open the door. "I'm sure I will, just as you are suffering now!"

As soon as he was gone, Kat leapt up and flung her arms around my neck. As she soaked my shoulder with her tears I could feel her little heart banging against the cage of her breast, and even though I wanted to scream, "You stupid, stupid girl!" and slap and shake her for taking that dangerous man with his damning secrets back into her life, I could not do it. I could not raise my voice or my hand against her. I could only hug her close and try to console this little girl who, imperfect though she was, was still, no matter what she had done, the daughter of my heart. Why was it always my destiny to love those who did not love me?

That night, as the summer rain tapped gently upon the red tile roof, Kat and Tom Culpepper sat naked and cross-legged upon her bed, ravenously devouring savory meat pies and licking their greasy fingers.

I sat by the fire trying to ignore what was happening on the bed. Kat would not let me leave the room when they were together like this. I sometimes wondered if she derived some sort of cruel pleasure from making me stay, making me watch as she flaunted her beautiful young body and reveled in her lover's touch, all the while knowing that no man had ever loved or lusted after me the way they did her. For me, Katherine was a constant reminder that the worst punishment of all is to long for love but never receive it.

When Kat took another bite and the warm juices trickled down her chin into the cleft between her breasts, Culpepper leaned forward to lick them up.

Suddenly the door opened and we were all too stunned to move or speak; instead we froze exactly as we were.

Fortunately, it was not the King; it was Francis Derham instead, come to visit the woman he considered his wife, bearing a bottle of wine and a basket of strawberries for old time's sake.

"Well, Madame," he frowned and said coldly, "I see you are faithful to neither of your husbands!" And he turned on his heel and kicked the door shut behind him.

Culpepper turned inquisitively to Kat, but she just lay down in the center of the bed, drew her knees up to her stomach, curled up in a ball, and said not a word.

He prodded her for an explanation, but when she continued to lie there mute and unresponsive, he stood up and began to put on his clothes.

"Very well then, Kat, when you decide who you want, be so good as to let me know," he snapped, and slammed out the door, reckless in his anger.

"Oh my darling, my poor, poor darling!" I cried as I ran over and lay down on the bed beside her, curling my body around hers, and hugging her close.

But Kat just lay there in silence, sucking her thumb.

❧ 41 ❧

As you may well have guessed by now, as I am writing this account from my prison cell in the dark heart of the Tower of London, the whole sordid truth came out, as it always will.

Mary Lascelles, the "pious, sour-faced prude" who had frowned so upon the lusty late-night antics in the Maids' Chamber, told all to her equally pious brother. He insisted it was her duty as a good Christian woman to confide what she knew to the proper authorities and arranged for her to have a private audience with Archbishop Cranmer.

Ironically, on that very day Henry was kneeling at the altar in the royal chapel, where the entire court had assembled for a special Mass of thanksgiving in honor of "that jewel of womanhood," Queen Katherine.

Sitting serenely in white satin and pearls, Katherine listened to the King singing her praises with her eyes demurely downcast and hands folded modestly in her lap. Nothing about her betrayed the truth that she was a wanton adulteress about to be found out. She looked the very picture of wifely perfection that Henry's words painted her to be.

That afternoon when Cranmer's feeble courage at last sufficiently asserted itself for him to seek audience with the King,

Henry refused to believe it. He dismissed these allegations as slander, base and false, a jealous, vindictive slur upon his wife's good name. But, ever cautious, he ordered Kat to be confined to her apartments until an investigation could clear her name. He commanded Cranmer to see to it at once, so that his darling would not languish too long in secluded anguish. Henry vowed he would see her persecutors brought to justice, and then all England would see what happens to those who dared to cast aspersions upon his most beloved wife's good name.

"Is she not my 'Rose Without a Thorn'?" he demanded time and again of Cranmer, as if he were seeking reassurance.

Cranmer cowered like a whipped dog before his royal master and said meekly, "I hope so, Sire, I certainly hope so," before he bowed his way out and ran to find Norfolk.

Meanwhile, in her apartments, Kat, seemingly without a care in the world, was making merry. The musicians were playing and she was dancing with her ladies.

Like a flock of colorful birds in their bright, beautiful gowns, they swirled and spun about, skirts billowing and rustling, swishing and swaying, laughing and chattering as they changed partners and linked hands.

Abruptly the music died as Cranmer, grim and solemn-faced in his scarlet vestments, swept in with the Duke of Norfolk, hatchet-faced in a humor black as a storm cloud beside him, and four guards following after.

The musicians hastily set aside their instruments and knelt, and the ladies curtsied deep. Only Katherine was left standing, like a white candle surrounded by a wreath of colorful flowers.

"It is no more the time to dance," Cranmer dolefully announced.

"Lady Rochford, you will remain," said Norfolk. "All others await me in the adjoining chamber."

Mystified, they filed out. When the door closed behind them, Norfolk purposefully approached Katherine, his face, like his heart, hard as granite.

"Tut, tut, you little slut!" he said, clicking his tongue and shaking his head. Then his hand shot out and dealt her a stinging slap.

"Was ever a man more accursed in his nieces than I? Your cousin Anne Boleyn did not drag me down with her and neither will you! The King is in the chapel now, weeping, bewailing his misfortune, and I shall go and condole with him. I shall crawl to him on my hands and knees and beg his forgiveness and tell him that you should be burned alive for the infamous harlot that you are! And it would please me immensely to light the flames myself!"

Around me the room began to waver and spin. My knees began to buckle and quake and I had to grab hold of the mantel to keep from falling.

I saw the color drain from Katherine's face until, except for the smarting red mark Norfolk's slap had left on her cheek, she was pale as sepulchral marble. Then she began to scream, great, long, keening wails. Cranmer winced and Norfolk scowled and ordered her to cease. But Kat, standing there white as her dress, stared past them blindly, as if terror had robbed her of her sight, uttering scream after piteous scream.

Though my limbs felt weak as water and starry darkness was fast encroaching upon my sight, I shoved myself away from the mantel and lurched unsteadily towards her.

"Now is your chance, Kat!" I cried as my knees gave way and I crumpled to the floor. "Run to Henry, Kat! It is your only hope! Run!"

Somehow, my words broke through the wall of terror surrounding her and, gathering up her skirts, she ran, darting this way and that to evade the guards. When Cranmer moved to block the door she lowered her head and plowed into him, butting his soft stomach like a goat.

Down the corridor she ran, screaming Henry's name at the top of her lungs. Behind her came the guards, in heavy-booted pursuit. Kat flung herself full force against the chapel door, hammering it with her fists until they bled.

Inside the chapel Henry sat alone in his pew, head bowed, as tears dripped down his quivering pink jowls. Muted by the heavy wooden door, Kat heard him command the musicians to play and the choir to sing. "Louder!" he bellowed at them. "Louder!"

Kat slumped tearfully against the door, pounding it halfheartedly with the flat of her palm, pleading with him to hear her. But he would not; with the music and singing he had made himself purposefully deaf and drowned out her screams.

Kat was doomed. As she slid to the floor, weeping, the guards caught up with her. They grabbed her wrists and pulled her up and began to lead her back to her rooms, where she was to remain for the time being, under guard.

"Let me go! I am the Queen! Unhand me now, you brutes! I am the Queen!" she cried, childlike and petulant, as she tried to break free. They had to drag her, kicking and screaming, back down the corridor. In the tussle her French hood fell off and her auburn curls came tumbling down. Her gown was torn, and as she dug in her heels she lost both of her little white satin slippers. They were left lying there in the corridor, midway between Katherine's rooms and the royal chapel, in mute testimony to her mad and futile dash for mercy.

"When the King learns how you have treated me he will have you boiled in hot oil for laying hands on me!" she threatened.

"Let me go! I am the Queen! I am the Queen!" Kat sobbed piteously, as they thrust her back inside and she fell weeping on the floor beside me.

The door slammed shut and there was the rattle of halberds as the guards took up their posts, barring any from entering or exiting without permission.

In the next room, Cranmer and Norfolk were already addressing Kat's attendants, apprising them of the allegations that the Queen was guilty of light and immoral living. Any who had relevant knowledge were urged to come forward; failure to do so would be deemed concealment and considered treason.

When Norfolk came out, Kat grabbed hold of his ankle. "Uncle, please! Help me!"

"Let go of me, you slut!" he spat, kicking free of her.

Kat next grasped Cranmer's robe. "Mercy!" she implored. "I am but a young and foolish girl, my lord!"

"I know you are"—Cranmer paused to look down at her, grave but kind—"and I shall remind the King." Then he too was gone.

"Lady Rochford!" Norfolk paused imperiously at the door. "Come!" he commanded, as if I were a dog.

Kat struggled up onto her knees, slipping on her satin skirts, tearing them at the waist, and falling down and banging her chin upon the floor, before she finally regained her feet. She flung herself into my arms and buried her face against my shoulder.

"If any word of Culpepper comes out I will deny it," she whispered, "and I beg you to do the same!"

Before I could answer, a guard took hold of my arm.

Kat fell weeping to the floor again.

As I was led away, she caught hold of my black skirt.

"Promise me, Jane!" she pleaded tearfully. "Promise me!"

I could not, so I did not, and instead pulled my skirt free and let myself follow wherever they would lead me.

More than three months would pass before I would see Kat again.

I was taken to the Tower of London and lodged in the Beauchamp Tower, in the same cell where George had spent his final days. I found this comforting; it made it easier to pretend that he was still with me. My whole body tingled and shook with the sense of his presence. The fear left me and I felt alive again. I made a tour of the cell, letting my fingers roam over the walls, caressing the cold stone, for surely his hands had touched it sometime, somewhere. I was like one in a trance, until my fingertips sank into a rough indentation. My fingers explored further and found it was not some pit or flaw in the stone, but some kind of carving.

I banged upon my cell door and screamed for Master Kingston. When he came, I implored him to please shine his lantern's light upon that wall and let me see.

"Oh, that," he said as he obliged me. "Anne Boleyn's falcon. Your husband carved that while he was . . . waiting."

And there it was, as Master Kingston said, Anne's falcon emblem carved into the wall, the crude, hasty work of a man who knew he had little time. But, as I peered closer, I noticed certain discrepancies. This version of Anne's falcon wore no crown and did not clutch a scepter, like Anne herself, it had been stripped of royal regalia.

Lovingly, because George had carved it, I traced it with my fingertips, just to touch where he had touched.

"He thought of her to the last," Master Kingston remembered, as he stood beside me gazing at the falcon.

I nodded as tears filled my eyes, and swallowed hard to force down the lump rising in my throat. "He loved her more than life itself," I said, my voice a choked and bitter whisper.

"Indeed," Master Kingston acquiesced, eyeing me carefully, no doubt fearing I would at any moment fly into a frenzy. "Their devotion to one another was quite remarkable."

Soon afterwards I was taken from my cell to be questioned by Norfolk and Cranmer.

For the second time in my life, I betrayed someone I loved.

The moment the door was opened before me I rushed in and threw myself at Norfolk's feet.

"Do not let her misdeeds tarnish me! I am innocent; I swear it!"

Norfolk stared down at me coldly. "You were never innocent, Lady Rochford!"

"I am!" I insisted. "I did only what the Queen bade me, though I did warn and plead with her constantly to desist. I am the King's loyal servant! I wanted to tell him, I swear, but he loved her so, and I could not bear to break his heart!"

Suddenly I heard laughter, her laughter—I recognized it at once. Then she was there, plain as day—Anne Boleyn in her black velvet and pearls. This was no misty, diaphanous phantom; she was real and solid as a flesh and blood woman! But only I could see her, though when she moved to stand behind Cranmer's chair and laid a hand on his shoulder, he shivered mightily and ordered another log to be thrown upon the fire.

"Loyal?" Anne's voice dripped with disbelief. "You? I doubt you even know the meaning of the word!"

"Shut up! Shut up! Shut up!" I screamed, clamping my hands tight over my ears, stamping my feet, and circling wildly.

Cranmer cleared his throat nervously. "Lady Rochford, are you quite well?"

"I am loyal, I am!" I cried.

"No, Jane, you are as cowardly as they come," Anne insisted. "You are not only a coward but a turntail; you will say anything to save yourself. Did you learn nothing from George and me?" She sighed and shook her head sadly, answering her own question. "Neither you nor my little cousin Katherine has profited from our example. George knows how to be true, Jane, but not you, not you."

I screamed and lunged forward, staring hard at her from across the table that separated us.

"True to you, you mean! George loved you best, he always did! That is why he never loved me. You stole the love that belonged to me! Was he not my husband? Was I not his wife? His love was rightfully mine. But you came between us. How dare you? How do you dare come here now to torment and distract me when I must justify myself before these men? I must convince them of my innocence! Kat is guilty, but I am not! She is guilty, just like you were! But at least she did not take George away from me; she only hurt an old man's vanity and puffed-up pride! What a little harlot she is, always naked, always strutting about touching herself, playing with her breasts and cunny, making me stay in the room while she frolicked in bed with Culpepper, just to taunt me and remind me that no one has ever wanted me the way they want her, and never will! Even Culpepper taunted me! Once when I fell asleep by the fire he woke me by pinching my nipple, tweaking it hard through my gown. When I leapt awake he laughed at me and asked how long it had been since a man had touched me, and when I blushed he laughed and said there was no need for me to thank him! Even when I was young I never had even a hint of the beauty God gave that little harlot, nor did you either. But you had other talents! You cast a spell to make men believe you were beautiful, to make them fall at your feet and swear their undying love and devotion to you, and only the purity of Jane Seymour, God rest her sweet soul, could break the spell!"

Breathlessly I sagged, weak and panting, against the chair I gripped.

Norfolk and Cranmer just stared, the first utterly unruffled, and the other nibbling his lower lip and growing more anxious by the moment. And the ghost of Anne Boleyn threw back her head and laughed long and heartily.

"You'd do well to say no more, Jane," Anne advised me. "You have shocked poor Cranmer with all this bawdy talk."

Furiously, I flung myself across the table, overturning inkwells and scattering papers and quills.

"I will kill you!" I screamed so loud my throat felt as if it were being raked raw.

Cranmer leapt up, his chair crashing to the floor, and ran out, shouting for the guards and Master Kingston.

Norfolk just stepped back and continued to regard me coolly. The man really did have ice water instead of blood in his veins.

"Poor Jane!" Anne laughed. "You cannot kill me. Have you forgotten? I am already dead!" To remind me, she reached up and lifted off her head.

As they led me away, I hung my head and wept.

"It is all because of that foolish, wanton girl that I have come to this!"

"No, Jane." Anne, her head now seamlessly back in place, looking as if it had never been cut off, appeared walking beside me. "Justice has brought you to this place."

With a piercing scream I broke free and ran blindly along the dark corridors, screaming, begging them to let me out, to send me to another prison, anywhere where the ghost of Anne Boleyn could not reach me.

But, of course, they ignored me, and back into my cell they thrust me.

I stood at the door, listening to the clank and screech of the old heavy bolts and locks, and the footsteps of Master Kingston ringing against the flagstones, the keys rattling on his belt as he walked away.

When I turned around she was right there behind me. I stumbled in midstep and fell right through the phantom shade of Anne Boleyn. Instantly I felt as if a thousand knives, sharper than the sharpest blades and colder than the coldest ice, were stabbing into every part of me.

With my skin turning blue and my body shivering uncontrollably, colder than I have ever been, I fell screaming to the floor. Try as I might, I could not still the spastic twitching and jerking of my limbs. I lay there writhing and convulsing helplessly, like one in the throes of a fit, and there was nothing I could do but wait for it to stop or for someone to heed my screams.

I heard raised voices and running feet followed by the rattling of keys and locks. Then, mercifully, Master Kingston flung wide the door.

With my lips, blue as indigo, and my teeth chattering so hard I felt their edges chip, I smiled my gratitude as my body stilled, and before my eyes everything went black.

With painful cuppings and blisterings, douches alternately scalding hot and icy cold, and powerfully strong purges intended to make me puke and shit out my demons, they tried to restore my sanity, but only succeeded in pushing it further away.

They twisted my nipples with hot pinchers, and wrapped my body in cold, wet sheets, and placed me deep in the dark, dank bowels of the Tower where no one could hear my screams. They put leeches on my breasts and between my legs, letting them suckle until their shiny black bodies grew fat on my nether lips, then they plucked them off and sprinkled my wounds with salt.

But still the ghost of Anne Boleyn did not depart; instead, more phantoms came to join her. Francis Weston, Henry Norris, William Brereton, and George—my beloved, darling George! Round and round they circled me, cool and detached, bearing witness to my suffering. "He who sows the whirlwind must expect to reap the storm," they reminded me.

As I lay there wretched and wracked with pain, shivering, naked, and degraded, I heard Master Kingston conferring with the King's chief physician, Dr. Wendy, who had replaced old Dr. Butts.

"His Majesty desires her recovery chiefly so that he may have her executed as an example and a warning to others," Dr. Wendy explained.

When I did not recover my wits fast enough to suit them, Henry simply created a new law allowing for the execution of deranged persons found guilty of treason. This was how he repaid the debt of gratitude he owed me. I had helped rid him of that she-devil! How could he forget so easily?

❧ 42 ❧

Cranmer and Norfolk interrogated me several times. Sometimes I babbled nonsense, irritating and irrelevant; other times I shrieked hysterically or tossed about, wild with delirium. And in between there were moments when the veil of insanity was torn away and I told them everything. I told them all of Kat's secrets—every confidence entrusted to me I shamelessly betrayed.

But judge me not too harshly. By this point in my wretched tale we have all shown our true colors; we have all tried to save ourselves at the expense of friends, lovers, and kin; we have all denied culpability and pointed the finger of blame elsewhere. And any collusion that ever existed between Kat, Culpepper, and me has been lost in the shuffle.

When she was questioned, Kat groveled for mercy and wept, trying to justify herself with her youth and wayward upbringing. Her grandmother, the Dowager Duchess of Norfolk, failed to give the vulnerable young girl entrusted to her care the proper guidance, and for this, she, not Katherine, should be held accountable.

Francis Derham was a handsome rogue and a winsome devil—everyone, including the man himself, agreed upon that—but to save her life Kat could not stick to a single story. At first, she claimed there was never anything between them. Then she cried and called Derham a monster who forced his way into her innocent bed, ravaged her, and stole her virginity. Next she admitted that on more than one hundred nights they lay together as man and wife. Yet—stupid, stupid girl—even when Cranmer took pity on her and patiently and repeatedly explained that if she confessed that there had been a precontract, or any sort of informal marriage ceremony, between herself and Derham then, in the law's eyes, this was tantamount to an actual, legally binding marriage, and thus for treasonous adultery she could not be condemned, as it would mean that she was never lawfully the King's wife, Kat still insisted that their calling each other "husband" and "wife" was just a game.

And when the question of Culpepper arose, Kat leveled the finger of blame at me. Yes, at me! "Lady Rochford," she said, "was the principal occasion of the folly!"

Poor Master Culpepper, she claimed, was struck by Cupid's dart at the sight of her; and I, insisting that he was pining away and dying of love for her, pestered and plagued her night and day, until, out of the goodness of her heart, Kat agreed to meet with him. But there was no truth to the rumors; they were never more than just good friends who flirted and bantered a bit in gallant, courtly fashion.

But to hear Master Culpepper tell the tale, it was something else entirely. The Queen, he claimed, relentlessly pursued him. She showered him with gifts—jeweled brooches, rings, gold chains, velvet caps, and even a fine chair. And when they searched his rooms, a letter was found wherein Kat declared, "It makes my heart die to think that I cannot always be with you," and signed herself, "Yours as long as life endures, Katherine."

Ah, yes, I remember well that damning letter! It was my hand that guided hers, slow and laboriously; the only letter Kat had ever in her short life written.

But in the end, being but a man with the usual healthy lusts and appetites, Culpepper confessed that with the greatest reluctance he gave in and met alone with Katherine. Though by God and all his saints he swore nothing of a carnal nature ever passed between them. Though they were both of a mind to, a suitable opportunity never presented itself. And all they ever did when they were alone together was talk.

And I, I was merely a lady-in-waiting acting upon the orders of my Queen, though I did often warn her that there would be dire consequences if her naughty deeds ever were found out. And upon the question of carnal intercourse, I merely said that, considering everything that I had seen pass between Culpepper and the Queen, I was certain that they had been intimately familiar. Perhaps I said more in even greater detail when I was distraught and mad, but if I did that was not my fault. I was the only truly blameless person involved in all this!

Henry Manox too was found and questioned. Naturally, he maintained his innocence throughout, claiming he never did more than grope beneath Kat's petticoats. "For the corruption of her morals I blame Francis Derham!" he zealously announced. And, guilty of nothing more than playing with a maiden's cunny, he was set free with a warning not to be so presumptuous in the future, lest that girl also someday become Queen of England.

Francis Derham, his handsome body needlessly ruined by the rack, admitted freely to the past as he had always done. He said they were lovers first, and then man and wife, but he swore that except in the matter of employment he never presumed upon their past relationship once Kat and the King were wed. Culpepper, he claimed, had succeeded him in the Queen's affections. When asked why he did not inform the King of Kat's unchaste past, he said that he was in Ireland when they married. Furthermore, how was he to know what Kat had and had not told the King? "When I was her husband she told me everything!"

Handsome Roger Damporte, Derham's best friend, who had also known Kat since those wild nights in the Maids' Chamber, confirmed Derham's story even after he had been racked and had every tooth and nail torn out.

All Kat's old friends from the Maids' Chamber were rounded up and questioned, and all the naughty deeds and doings of the past came out. All of them have been shamed, pointed the finger of blame at Katherine and her lovers, and absolved themselves completely. "She was not my daughter, niece, or sister," every last one of them insisted. "She was not my responsibility!"

Are we not all a sorry lot?

But now it is too late to unwind the tangled threads of truth and lies. Derham and Culpepper are two months' dead, both their beautiful bodies ruined by the rack. They were carted off to Tyburn on the 10th of December.

Derham, for unknowingly passing his used goods off on King Henry, suffered the full horror of being hanged, disemboweled, and quartered. While he still lived the organ that had dallied so intimately and often between Kat's thighs was hacked off and cast into the fire before his eyes.

But at the last moment, fond memories of Culpepper's tender ministrations to his bad leg, persuaded Henry to be merciful and commute his sentence to a simple beheading.

Even now, Derham's rotting limbs are on display in the four corners of London, with his torso in the center. But his head rots gray and sightless, being nibbled by the ravens, alongside Culpepper's, high on Tower Bridge so that all whose barges pass beneath can look up and see what fate awaits any man who dares to cuckold a king.

❧ 43 ❧

It is the 10th of February 1542 and I am now to leave this cell and go to the Queen's Lodgings, the rooms that Anne Boleyn occupied before both her coronation and execution. There I shall await Katherine. We will be together until the end, which Master Kingston says will come very soon.

We have both been condemned to die by Act of Attainder. There was no trial for us—Henry had learned his lesson with Anne Boleyn—so this time the public were not treated to any titillating and embarrassing revelations; instead the evidence was presented quietly and discreetly before Parliament, and they then rendered the expected verdict—guilty.

When Kat arrived we eyed each other warily, both of us fully aware of our inconstancy, our betrayals, lies, and treachery. Then, with a heartrending cry, she flung herself into my arms and I hugged her tight and forgave her everything, for the moment at least.

That was two days ago.

She weeps constantly and tries vainly to convince herself—and me—that our lives will be spared. Every time she hears footsteps her face lights up and she runs to the door, in happy expectation of a messenger come bearing a reprieve to restore her to her former glory. She bites her nails, twists and twirls her hair, and fidgets with her skirts and sleeves, endlessly complaining that they have taken away all her jewels and finery, leaving her with only four plain gowns, two of them black and the other two brown.

"I tell you he will not kill me, Jane! He loves me more than any! Am I not his 'Rose Without a Thorn'?"

"No, poppet," I tell her truthfully, "that was but an illusion. You deceived him, and Henry also deceived himself."

But Kat does not want to hear the truth; stubbornly she persists, as if I had never even spoken.

"I tell you he will not kill me! He loves me more than any. You will see. Hark! Footsteps! See? A messenger comes!" And again she runs to the door, waits, and when no one comes her face falls and hope dies, only to spring to life again next time there are footsteps in the corridor.

In the many hours I have had to think since I entered the Tower, I have often pondered this question: Does love ever truly make anyone happy?

Catherine of Aragon loved Henry steadfast and true for more than twenty years, only to be thrown out and discarded in the end. Henry threw all her love and devotion away with less regard than a London housewife displays when she throws the contents of her chamber pot out the window into the street below. Catherine died, longing for Henry to the last, vowing that above all things her eyes desired him most, while Henry donned gaudy yellow to celebrate her demise.

Anne Boleyn—my nemesis, my enemy—fascinated and captivated the King for seven years. He changed the world to wed and bed her, only to kill her in the end when his grand, soul-devouring passion burned out and hate flared up to take its place.

Jane Seymour was the third woman to wear Henry's ring, but did he truly love her, or only as a man loves an antidote to a deadly poison? She died before the truth could ever take off its mask and show its face.

Kat claimed not to believe in love. I think she played it as a game, and was herself in turn played by the men who were her partners in it—Manox, Derham, Culpepper, and the unwitting Henry. She was a shallow, giddy, beautiful butterfly, not destined to live a great span. In truth, I have never been able to imagine Katherine old.

And I, with all my heart, body, and soul, loved George Boleyn. I loved him so much that there were moments when I actually hated him because I loved him so much.

And George . . . George never loved anyone as he loved Anne. They were each the love of each other's life. Anne never loved another man the way she loved her brother. He read that accursed paper aloud because it was the surest path to the scaffold. "I cannot imagine my life without you in it"—with my own ears I heard him tell her why he had thrown away his life. He gave his life for Anne, and I know she would have done the same for him.

I ask again: Does love ever truly make anyone happy? Look back; there is not one happy story in the lot! There is passion, yes, and pomp and pageantry, but every story ends with blood and tears. Only Henry endures; only he will go on and mayhap love again, if he even truly knows what love is. Who will be wife number six, I wonder, and will her story also end in blood and tears? I will not be here to see; my days as a lady-in-waiting are almost done. Now I wait only for the headsman's axe that will end my life.

It is the night of the twelfth now, and tomorrow, Master Kingston says, we shall die.

Kat has made a most unusual request. She wants the block brought here so she can practice kneeling and laying her head upon it gracefully.

"I want to make a good death, like my cousin Anne," she says.

Master Kingston is of a mind to humor her, and while we await its delivery she hums and paces, and dithers about which of her equally plain black gowns she should wear for her rendezvous with Death.

When the block is brought in, she stares down at it for a very long time; then her body starts to quake and tears spring to her eyes.

"I die the wife of a King, but I would rather die the wife of Culpepper!" she wails, before falling to her knees and bathing the wooden block with her tears.

Dispassionately, I watch her back heave and her shoulders shake. But by it all I am strangely unmoved.

She is like a thief who is not the least bit sorry that she stole, only that she was caught and must endure the punishment. And I daresay Culpepper went to his death feeling exactly the same way.

It is Katherine's fault that we are here, in spite of the spirits' taunting, whispering from the shadows and stone walls about Justice and Divine Retribution. "He who sows the whirlwind must expect to reap the storm." But I have sown no whirlwind! The fault is not mine! The truth is inescapable; it is Katherine's fault that we are both condemned to die. But if I must point the finger of blame then I must go back further, to a time before Katherine was even born, to the one who began it all, the one upon whose shoulders all the blame belongs.

If it had not been for Anne, I am certain George would have loved me. Had it not been for Anne, surely I would have had a daughter of my own to love, and would not have had to pretend that that wanton little harlot Kat was mine and, out of love for her, go along with her folly. Had it not been for Anne, George would not have gone to the block. And oh, what pride he would have taken in having such a loving, devoted, dutiful wife! But there was an Anne, and she ruined my life; because of her my marriage was over before it had even begun. She destroyed me, so I do not regret having helped destroy her. Even though tomorrow I must die, and Cranmer urges me to clear my conscience so that I may die shriven of all my sins, of that I will never repent! Vengeance was mine and I did repay!

Kat is sleeping now, with her head cradled upon the block—a hard, morbid pillow—spent from grief and hope that is now as dead as Henry's love for her.

But I shall not sleep. I shall pass this, my last night, in wakefulness. George is with me now. And I have so much to tell him. I want him to know that even though he is now nothing more than a headless, heartless phantom that comes out of my prison walls to torment me, he still fills my world.

I bid him come and sit by me and let me tell him of a dream I have; it is my most precious dream, the hope I cherish more than any. He refuses. But I shall tell him just the same. And soon there will be time aplenty, a whole eternity, for us to sit side by side, hand in hand, as we never did in life.

For many years I have had this dream. I dream that when I stand humbly before God's throne, He will summon George to stand beside me. And then He will forgive us both, for everything; all our foibles, flaws, mistakes, imperfections, tiny and great, and errors of judgment. Together in Heaven's bliss we shall forevermore dwell in everlasting love and finally be husband and wife as we were meant to be, but never were in life; while Anne Boleyn roasts in the fiery pit of Hell, being turned slowly on a spit for all eternity by a fire-belching, sulfur-farting demon, and the Devil looks on, laughing to behold his concubine's fate. It is a dream I have that I hope with all my heart will come true when my soul from this life takes flight.

But what shall I say when I stand upon the scaffold before the people who have come to watch me die? That is what most worries and perplexes me. George will not help me. I shall not crib my dying speech from him, he says, nor will that bitch Anne deign to help me either, though both of them know I have not their wit for words. I shall have to do it all myself.

Shall I say what they expect of me? Shall I say this, George? Shall I say:

"God has permitted me to suffer this shameful doom as punishment for having contributed to my husband's death when I falsely accused him of loving in an incestuous manner his sister, Queen Anne Boleyn. And for this I deserve to die. But I am guilty of no other crime!"

Do you like that, George? No, of course I do not mean it! Except that I am guilty of no crime, every word of it is a lie! But shall I say it just for you, George? You see, my beloved, how great my love is for you? I am willing to die with a lie upon my lips. I will clear your name and besmirch my own, all for love of you!

I hope I shall die well. I am trying very hard to compose myself. If only George and Anne would stop laughing at me! They think it so amusing that having falsely accused one wife of adultery, Henry now has one who is guilty indeed, and that I, having helped send them to their deaths with my false and malicious testimony, am now condemned to suffer the same fate. Divine Retribution! Justice! He who sows the whirlwind must expect to reap the storm! I wish they would shut up! I cannot compose myself with them laughing and making such cruel sport of me! Oh, how their laughter rings! It is a wonder no one else can hear it! But when I ask, all shrink back from me with a strange and wary look in their eyes. I would try to deafen myself with a needle or a hairpin, but the vigilant Lady Kingston has taken all such things away from me. When I eat I must sip and slurp my soup like a peasant, and my meat arrives already cut, as if I were a babe. They will not allow me even a spoon! Even when I write, someone must be present to make sure I attempt no mischief, like drinking the ink or trying to puncture my eardrums with a quill. Yes, I am tempted to attempt this last; even though the tip is blunt, it might still do the deed and give me a blessed reprieve from the cacophony of the damned. I cannot bear their laughing at me! Will they never cease?

POSTSCRIPT

February 13, 1542

At seven o'clock on that frigid February morning, Katherine Howard, almost too weak to speak or stand, was led to the scaffold, begging for her life to the last. For Henry's fifth queen there was no French executioner, only an English headsman and his axe. She made a brief speech in which she begged the King's forgiveness and admitted that she deserved death. Then she knelt and laid her head upon the block.

Lady Jane Rochford was executed immediately after Katherine. Those who witnessed the event were of the opinion that she was "quite mad." On her way to the scaffold she carried on a frenzied, one-sided conversation with phantoms that only she could hear and see. Before she knelt in the straw, still wet with Katherine's blood, she gave the speech quoted in these pages.

The remains of Katherine Howard and Lady Jane Rochford were entombed beneath the chapel of St. Peter ad Vincula near those of Anne and George Boleyn and the friends who died with them.

THE
BOLEYN
WIFE

Brandy Purdy

ABOUT THIS GUIDE

The suggested questions are included to
enhance your group's reading of Brandy Purdy's
The Boleyn Wife.

DISCUSSION QUESTIONS

1. Discuss the roles guilt, jealousy, and vengeance play in the novel. How do these feelings affect and motivate Jane and influence the outcome of the story?

2. Discuss the relationship between Anne and George. Is incest a valid suspicion, or is this all in Jane's mind? Jane blames Anne because George does not love her, and she is convinced Anne ruined her marriage—is this true?

3. Discuss Catherine of Aragon and the stance she takes regarding her marriage to Henry VIII. She could have made things a lot easier for herself by giving in, but she chose to stand her ground. Do you admire her for this, or not? Do you think she did the right thing?

4. Discuss the song "The Holly" and the way it is used in the novel. It is sung twice, first by Henry and later by Anne. How does the meaning, the message conveyed by the song, change between the two performances?

5. Discuss Jane's relationship with Cromwell. Each uses the other; does each of them get what they are expecting from the relationship, or does it turn out to be more than they bargained for?

6. Discuss Mark Smeaton. Why does he admit to being guilty? Does torture alone induce his confession?

7. Discuss the impact the executions of George and Anne Boleyn have on Jane's life.

8. Discuss Jane Seymour. Did she really love Henry, or was her

every move calculated, either by herself or her family? Was she playing Anne Boleyn's game?

9. Discuss the role of childbirth in the novel. So much depends on it; it is a matter of life, death, and also, for queens and noble-women, of providing a male heir. Both Catherine of Aragon and Anne Boleyn lose Henry's favor when they fail to give him a son. Jane Seymour dies after giving birth to a son. Jane Boleyn has strong maternal yearnings; discuss how her dream of motherhood becomes a nightmare and how this influences her behavior.

10. Discuss Anna of Cleves's role in the novel. What do you think of her ruse to make herself unattractive to Henry?

11. Discuss Katherine Howard and the role sexuality plays in her life and how it influences the decisions she makes. Katherine's sexual experiences at such an early age often seem shocking to modern readers; discuss how our modern beliefs about childhood and child abuse differ from those of the Tudor era, when women were often married and mothers by the age of sixteen.

12. Discuss the role ghosts play in the novel. Are the ghosts Jane sees real, or are they delusions of her mind? Is Jane really insane?

13. Which of the five wives of Henry VIII who appear in this novel was the happiest one? The luckiest one? The unluckiest one? Discuss the five women and how they were alike and how they differed from one another.

14. Discuss the enduring fascination with Anne Boleyn. Of all of Henry's wives, she is the one most written and talked about. Why? What is it about Anne Boleyn that still captivates us more than four hundred years after her death?

15. Jane has long been vilified as the woman whose testimony helped send Anne and George Boleyn to their deaths, and who later aided and abetted Katherine Howard's adultery. After reading her story, in her own words, do you think she has been judged harshly or justly? Has your opinion altered? Are you more, or less, sympathetic towards her?